The Graves of Whitechapel

CLAIRE EVANS

sphere

SPHERE

First published in Great Britain in 2020 by Sphere
This paperback edition published by Sphere in 2021

1 3 5 7 9 10 8 6 4 2

A CIP catalogue record for this book
is available from the British Library.

ISBN 978-0-7515-7530-9

Typeset in Garamond 3 by M Rules
Printed and bound in Great Britain by Clays Ltd, Elcograf S.p.A.

Papers used by Sphere are from well-managed forests
and other responsible sources.

Sphere
An imprint of
Little, Brown Book Group
Carmelite House
50 Victoria Embankment
London EC4Y 0DZ

An Hachette UK Company
www.hachette.co.uk

www.littlebrown.co.uk

ire Evans divides her time between writing and her job Chief Operating Officer at Two Brothers Pictures Ltd, the vision production company behind *Fleabag*, *Liar* and *Baptiste*. She lives in London with her partner.

Also by Claire Evans

The Fourteenth Letter

For Karlos

CHAPTER ONE

February 1882

He'd walked here so many times before, the flagstones must have borne the imprint of his boots. Not so long ago the boots had been brand new, the russet leather emitting a rich sigh and the shiny studs on his soles a pleasing clank as they connected with the pitted Newgate stone – sounds which said, *I am but visiting, I do not belong here.*

The warden grabbed at his bound hands and pulled him forwards. A pointless gesture of power, for Cage had kept up with him, step for step. Cage remembered him from previous occasions, thin and tall, with a long face. Mcquarry? McEnnerey? He'd never bothered to learn their names.

They came to a stop, and another guard rolled a ring of keys from his belt. The keys were unnecessarily large it seemed to Cage, made for similarly sized locks that had a dual purpose – to keep you in of course, but also to remind you at all times that they were there, and so were you.

A riveted door yawned open. Had he been to this cell before, he wondered, and to visit which client? He pushed the thought away. He had no need for ironic reflection now, and no audience to share it with.

His hands were unbound, and instructions given. The water tank – not to be blocked by any means or you'd be cleaning it yourself. The basin, same thing. He rubbed at his wrists and sat down on the hard bunk. The guards carried on talking, but he wasn't listening.

Mac-something leaned down. 'How're you going to get yourself out of this one, eh?'

Cage smiled, but not at the man. Instead, he grinned down at his boots, scuffed and grimy, the only honest thing in this room.

Realising there was no sport to be had, the men left. The bolts were slammed across, top and bottom, the sound like an axe splitting wood. Finally Cage was alone. He closed his eyes and sagged backwards against the wall, letting go of it all – the lies and the excuses. The fight, too – that was gone now, and what was left was something bold and new: it felt like peace.

How was he going to get himself out of this one, the man had asked. He wasn't, that was the point. Cage Lackmann, the Poet of Whitechapel, lawyer of this parish, was guilty as sin.

He looked around him then. The glistening brick walls, the slash of grey sky high up in the wall. He was finally home. He'd known it would call to him, one day. All of his life, he had known.

CHAPTER TWO

Two weeks earlier

'Your honour, I call Mrs Winnifred Latham as our next witness.'

All eyes turned to the side door of the panelled room, the second largest courtroom at the Old Bailey. The public gallery behind the jury was packed, but Cage deliberately avoided scanning their faces. This particular judge, Henry Jacobs, disliked any barrister who played to the gallery. Besides, there were faces there Cage himself did not want to see right now.

Beyond the door, a steady tap could be heard, as Winnifred Latham made her slow progress from the relative comfort of the witness room. Each tap, theatrical and measured, increased the expectation of jury and gallery alike.

Her head appeared first, peering around the edge of the door, adorned by a widow's black lace cap. Beneath it, her wrinkled eyes asked the question, am I in the right place? At the sight of her, Judge Jacobs leaned down from his forbidding perch and summoned her with a kindly finger. With less patience, he urged a nearby clerk to get to his feet and help the octogenarian up the steps to the witness box. With a nod of thanks, she gripped the ledge before her, the struggle to stand upright despite the stoop in her back evident in her furrowed brow.

'Perhaps, madam, you would care to sit?' asked Jacobs.

'Thank you, sir, but I would rather stand and show my respect to this court.'

Her voice was light, floating like a feather around the room, and a slight whistle could be heard with each 's'. She read the witness vow at a solemn pace, each word new and earnest on her lips as her hand pushed down firmly on the King James Bible.

Now it was Cage's turn. 'Mrs Latham, thank you for attending the trial today.'

She acknowledged his thanks with a gracious nod before Cage continued, 'Perhaps you would recount for us, in your own words, the events of the evening of the twenty-third of November last year, from your unique perspective.'

The woman opened her mouth to speak but the prosecuting counsel was already on his feet. 'Objection, your honour. It is for the jury to judge whether this lady's perspective is unique or not.'

Jacobs waved the objection away impatiently. 'Please, Mr Whitaker, I would rather not keep Mrs Latham on her feet for longer than is strictly necessary. Perhaps you might save your objections until the end?'

The crowd tittered as Whitaker hastily sat down. Cage turned back to the witness stand. 'Do go on, Mrs Latham.'

The woman gathered herself once more. 'I remember it well, sir, for it was my birthday. My eighty-first.' She turned to the judge. 'I am precisely as old as this century is, sir, although not as fast paced these days.'

A smile threatened Jacobs's lips, but Cage frowned at his witness. This judge would be indulgent only to a point.

The woman continued. 'As was my custom, I had taken myself to the Belford Tea Rooms on Lisson Lane to mark the occasion. I spend my birthdays alone these days, since my dear William passed fifteen years ago. But they knew me there, and always made a fuss. They even made a small iced cake especially for me. You see, they always remembered the date. Sadly, they have since closed; I shall have to find somewhere else this year.' She smiled at the memory, before returning to her purpose. 'I left the tea rooms at a quarter to five. It was a pleasant evening, and I resolved to walk home past the park. It was unusually balmy, I recall, and my hip had not been tormenting me that day. The new gaslights they have installed on Victoria Road afford a lovely view of the duck pond, and I wanted to see them one last time before they left for the winter. You see, at my age, you never know . . .'

She cleared her throat and continued. 'Just as I turned into Victoria Road, I could see a commotion up ahead. A man was standing on the steps of one of the grand houses overlooking the park. He was shouting at another man, who was running at full pelt towards me along the street. I stepped back to remove myself from his path. He was carrying a silver tureen in his arms and had a large canvas bag slung over his shoulder. As he ran past, the bag clattered into me and caught my hat. The man stopped to untangle himself and to pick up a few items that had fallen to the ground. After a brief apology, he bolted away, leaving me quite breathless.'

As if reliving the trauma, Mrs Latham clutched a palm to her chest.

Judge Jacobs intervened. 'Are you able to continue, madam?'

She nodded bravely. 'I am almost at the end of my story, sir. Well, after that, as I'm sure you will understand, I felt a strong desire to return to my boarding house as soon as I could. So, I abandoned my plans to see the ducks and turned back, taking the shortest route home. I have to say, it knocked the stuffing from me for several weeks. I took to my bed for a short time and found it hard to leave the house for a while. When I finally returned to the park, the ducks were gone.' She smiled sadly.

Cage approached her. 'Thank you, Mrs Latham. I am sorry you had to relive those moments for us. May I ask you, though, to describe the man you saw that night?'

She nodded. 'He was tall; the bag on his shoulder was head height to me. His cap also fell off in the collision and his hair was dark, his complexion swarthy. When he bent to retrieve the items that had fallen, I noticed a tattoo on his hand, an anchor, I believe. Just here.' She pointed to the back of her left hand.

Cage turned to the dock, and the red-headed prisoner seated there. His hands were clasped together on the ledge, revealing not a single tattoo.

'Tell me, Mrs Latham, is this the man you saw that night?'

The old woman looked across to the man in the dock. The courtroom was silent as she scrutinised him.

'Most definitely not, sir. He looks nothing like the man I saw that night.'

The gallery breathed out and the chatter began immediately. The judge called for order once more.

Cage turned to the prosecutor. 'Your witness, Mr Whitaker.'

The prosecutor rose, a smile on his face even though he was shaking his head. 'Good morning, Mrs Latham. Perhaps you would begin by telling me how exactly you came to be here today?'

The woman looked back and forth from the prosecutor to the judge. 'I'm not sure I understand the question.'

'Then let me help you. How did it come to pass that the defending counsel stumbled upon your testimony? How did he even know of your existence when the police did not?'

'Ah, you see, I take *The Times* every day, sir. When I read of this man's arrest for a robbery in Victoria Road on the twenty-third of November of last year, I knew immediately that this must be the very same man who had clattered into me. That is when I came forward.'

'To the defending counsel, madam? Not to the police?'

She looked bewildered. 'Of course! The paper had also said Cage Lackmann was defending the man who was charged. Like many, I had followed the Pickering case closely, sir, so that meant only one thing to me. The police must clearly have the wrong man!'

Cheers broke out around the room, although Cage knew there would be one man in the gallery whose frown could have frozen the Thames at the mere mention of Pickering. Cage tried to look humble, but inside he was grinning from ear to ear. Whitaker had walked into that one with boots on, as he always did.

A red-faced Whitaker waited for the courtroom to fall quiet once more. 'Mrs Latham. The victim of this burglary, whom you say you saw standing on the steps of his house as this other man ran towards you, has sworn that he saw no other person in the street that evening. What say you to that?'

She shrugged. 'Sir, I am an old woman of limited means. I have worn the black for fifteen years. That I am invisible to most people is no surprise to me.'

Even Judge Jacobs smiled at this.

Whitaker's head dropped, but he carried on regardless, the sarcasm of defeat biting through his words. 'And finally, Mrs Latham, you expect us not to find it a coincidence that the Belford Tea Rooms have closed down so recently that no one there can corroborate the time you left or whether you were even there?' He continued before she could answer. 'And I presume that it is also a coincidence that you have recently moved to a new boarding house in these last few days since the owner of your previous home has conveniently sold up and moved to the Americas without leaving a forwarding address? That, in fact, no one, it seems, could prove you existed even a week ago?'

Cage's eyes were locked on the jury, and he saw two of its members shrink at Whitaker's line of questioning. This was going very well indeed.

He turned back to the old woman. When she spoke, her voice had acquired a strength that hadn't been there before. 'There is no coincidence here, sir. You see, no one will mourn my passing. Those I have loved are in the ground. You say I do not exist because others cannot offer their testimony to prove it. Then who is standing here before you, sir? I am real. I am here, sir, and I have a voice. If my loneliness is a crime, tell me, who is guilty? Me or you?'

The judge could do nothing to stop the applause that broke out. Even Whitaker sarcastically joined in with a slow handclap. 'No more questions, your honour.'

Winnifred Latham was dismissed, and tapped her way out of the courtroom, her head held high even as she leant on the arm of the stenographer who had leapt to his feet to help her.

Cage looked down at his notes, ready for his closing argument. With luck, they'd be done by lunchtime. Whitaker was already addressing the stony-faced jurors, going through the motions now. Cage looked back to the dock, risking a look at his client. Dub looked smug, leaning back on his stool, cock of the walk once more. Cage stared hard until Dub caught his eye. He immediately rocked forward and took up the agreed pose – hands clasped earnestly, as if in prayer, eyes wide and pleading his innocence.

Finally, Whitaker sat down. He rubbed at his whiskers and stared straight ahead, already disengaged, his mind clearly beginning to focus on the next case he needed to prepare for. You win some, you lose some: they both knew it. And Whitaker was clever: he saw the war, not the battle.

Cage stood up and approached the jury. His eyes cast down to the floor, he placed one hand on his hip, revealing the exquisite cut of his waistcoat that so emphasised his form. He caught his black curls at the back of his neck, beneath his barrister's wig, a gesture of distraction that would indicate the depth of thought currently being expended on his closing argument. The words had been carefully rehearsed for days now, but the jury didn't need to know that.

He opened, as he always did, with the bare facts of the case. A household has been burgled. A man is seen running away from said house, a silver tureen in his hands and a bag of swag over his shoulder. A shameful crime indeed, and his sympathies unquestionably lay with the householder who had lost such treasured possessions.

A loud cough from the gallery greeted this last statement, but Cage continued. 'Let us consider the evidence against my client, Mr Dubois. The prosecution's case rests solely on two things alone: one man's identification of Mr Dubois as the perpetrator of this crime, and Mr Dubois's unfortunate history as a convicted felon. Yet those two things are connected. For my client's previous conviction – a theft committed when he was yet a young man, with all the heedless stupidity of his age – was the very reason that the police in this case brought him face to face with the victim of this crime in an identity parade. Now, if you will, I would like to ask you all to look at my client, to really look, and imagine seeing him for the first time. What, would you say, is the most striking thing about him?'

All members of the jury turned to look at Dub, who thankfully had maintained his solemn pose in the dock.

'Surely, gentlemen, it is his red hair? And yet, in the householder's first statement, no mention of red hair was even made! The witness claimed under questioning that it was too dark to see the colour of the villain's hair that fateful evening, even under the street lamps. My contention is therefore very simple. If it was too dark to see the colour of his hair, the most distinguishable feature about my client, then obviously it must have been too dark to see him at all? And yet, in his understandable desire to see restitution for this crime, our householder picked out Mr Dubois from a parade of five others. It is not the first time my client has been victimised in this way. In the last year alone, he has been called to attend seven such occurrences. Seven! Surely it was only a matter of time before he was erroneously singled out?'

A few members of the jury imperceptibly nodded their heads as the question hung in the air. But Cage knew the real reason his client was sitting there today, when he had not the other six times: Dub's employer, Obediah Pincott, couldn't bribe or intimidate everybody.

'Mrs Latham came here of her own accord, to prevent this miscarriage of justice. A noble act, from a noble woman. If I had half her courage I would be a braver man than I am.' He pursed his lips to stop himself saying more, pausing until the emotion passed.

He looked up again and spread his hands wide. 'Mrs Latham talked about my reputation as a champion of the falsely accused, but I do not ask you to rely on that, but on the evidence, or rather the complete lack thereof. You saw with your own eyes today how eager Mr Whitaker is to victimise the innocent. When you look at my client, I ask you to see not just Mr Dubois, but Mrs Latham also, for are they not, in this, one and the same?'

Dub immediately stopped rubbing his pudgy red-veined nose and met the gaze of the jury.

Cage stepped closer, his hands resting on the warm wood of the box that enclosed the twelve men. 'You know, my mother once said to me that a lie can travel halfway around the world while the truth is still putting on its shoes. I don't care about my reputation, and I don't care about the trappings that reputation buys me. I don't ask you to find Mr Dubois innocent. I ask instead for something bigger than that . . .' He looked each man in the eye, one by one. 'I ask you to find the truth.'

It took just forty minutes for the jury to reach their verdict of not guilty. Cage pulled his trial wig from his head and strode through the halls of the Old Bailey, eager to make his escape. He had one appointment to keep, then he'd be free for the rest of the day. A bottle of good claret and his pick of the best whores in Whitechapel awaited him.

He could see Whitaker up ahead near the left doors, huddled close with Detective Jack Cross. Cross was berating the barrister in hushed tones, his meaty hand on the man's thin shoulder, fingers digging in. Cross hadn't seen Cage yet, and Cage wanted to keep it that way. He cast his eyes down and marched on.

'Excuse me, sir.'

Cage ignored the call from behind. It was always hard to leave the court after a win like this without being accosted by some tale of woe. He didn't have time for it today.

A hand appeared on his arm. 'Excuse me. May I speak with you, sir?'

He turned to see a soberly dressed young woman at his side, clutching a file of papers to her chest. He kept up the pace as he spoke. 'Certainly, but I am in a rush, as you can see, so you will need to be brief.'

The woman trotted at his side. 'It's about my husband, sir. He has been most wrongly accused of forgery, sir. His trial date has been set for next week. He was to be represented by Mr Manners, but we have no faith in him, sir.'

Stuart Manners was a senior barrister at Lincoln's Inn. Old school. Lazy.

'I'm sure he will do an excellent job for you, madam.'

'We are not so convinced, sir.'

'Did your solicitor recommend you approach me, madam?'

She paused for a moment. 'Not exactly, sir.'

Cage smiled – no surprise in that. 'Then I cannot help you. As a barrister, I can only be retained by a solicitor, I'm afraid.'

'Then we would be willing to change solicitors too, sir. We are willing to do anything. He is innocent, and we can prove it, sir.'

Cage stopped walking and turned to face her. She was pretty, beneath her dowdy hat and determined expression. There was also something vaguely familiar about her.

'Very well. Come and see me at my chambers tomorrow.

Here's my card.' He fished through his briefcase, but the pocket where he stored his business cards was empty – he had forgotten to refill from the box at home. Instead he took a single piece of his expensive letterhead from a crumpled sheaf within and handed it over.

Her face lit up in a rather delightful way. 'Thank you, sir. I shall.'

He bid her good day and charged down the steps of the Old Bailey, not wanting to be late for his meeting on Blackfriars Bridge. As he rounded the massive bail dock, he could see Dub, still backslapping with his cronies only yards from the courthouse.

Cage crossed the road, flipping up the collar of his mohair coat against the January wind that slapped him from all directions. Head down, he marched along the pavement, aware now of a coach that had slowed its pace in the road behind him. He didn't look back, but drove on, not stopping until he had turned into Ludgate Hill, away from prying eyes.

He came to a halt as the coach pulled up alongside him, black and sleek but without adornment, like a hearse. The two black horses snorted and stamped their hooves and he could feel their warm breath before it froze in clouds about their heads. The driver stared straight ahead, as blinkered as the beasts whose reins he gripped tightly.

Cage approached the window of the carriage and looked up at Obediah Pincott, his Slavic profile and shaved head etched clearly against the watery sky beyond.

Pincott looked down at him. 'Lackmann.'

'Morning, Obediah.'

The Russian greatcoat Pincott wore was buttoned up, the collar reaching over his ears. His head swivelled within. 'A successful day.' Each syllable was pronounced slowly in a thick Ukrainian accent.

'Indeed. But it's the last time. You know that, don't you? That idiot's days are numbered. He won't be so lucky next time.'

Pincott's deep-set, lashless eyes blinked slowly. 'My decision. Not yours.' The man was economical with words, as if they cost him something.

'Of course, Obediah. I was merely advising. He should lie low, for now at least.'

Pincott nodded, advice taken.

Cage felt emboldened. 'Payment in lieu would be most appreciated. January is a heavy month for expenses.'

'Wine and whores. They cost more in winter?'

Cage reddened, despite the cold. 'I have fees to pay. The Law Society—'

'I have cash-flow problem.'

Pincott rapped the side of the coach sharply, like a gunshot, and the coach moved out into the traffic. Cage cursed himself for asking the question. It made him feel cheap. Most conversations with Obediah Pincott did.

He turned towards Farringdon Street, and his meeting on Blackfriars. He thrust his hands into his pockets as he began the long walk across the river. The air was ice against his skin and his eyes began to water.

Honor Dossett was waiting for him in the centre of the bridge. She was motionless, her back straight in her red velvet coat as she stared down at the river below, her profile carved against the grey sky. A horn blasted from a barge and a cloud of steam billowed up around her. It was his entrance, but Honor was always the star of the show.

He was almost upon her before she turned and smiled at him. He bent and kissed her porcelain cheek. So smooth.

'Shall we walk?'

He picked up the small valise at her feet and she put her arm through his as they made for the south bank of the river.

'We'll have to be quick. I have to be at the Pavilion for dress rehearsal by three, and Granger is panicking.'

'Nothing new in that.'

'I do believe he has found a new level of hysteria for this one, if you can believe that to be possible. His eyebrows are falling out I think, quite bizarre, but you mustn't mention it tomorrow.'

'I might not—'

'Don't finish that sentence.' Her voice was steel in the wind. 'You'll be there.'

There was nothing else to be said. Of course he would be there – what was he thinking? Obediah Pincott. Honor Dossett. Freedom belonged to his clients alone.

She changed the subject. 'You won the case?'

'Naturally.'

'Was Cross very . . . cross?'

'Spitting.'

She cuddled up closer. Cage appreciated the warmth. It brought back memories. Some of them good.

Honor must have read his mind. She took his hand from his pocket and rubbed it between hers, her woollen gloves rasping across his skin. His hand had been warmer in his pocket, but he didn't complain.

'Obediah must have been pleased.'

'Not so pleased as to pay me promptly.'

She frowned. 'You've paid him back ten times over. He should treat you with more respect. '

'Don't worry. I have your fee.' They stopped walking and moved apart. He put down her case and dug into the inner pocket of his coat. She watched him with unblinking eyes, not making even a desultory effort to suggest payment could wait, despite his own lack of funds. He didn't expect her to.

He handed over a banknote. She took it and unclasped her bag, folding the note neatly inside. She closed the bag again, a hungry mouth snapping shut.

They recommenced their walk. 'And do I get a thank you?'

He smiled. It was the applause that had always mattered the most to her. 'Thank you. The ducks were a particularly nice touch.'

'I thought so.'

'Did anyone follow you?'

'A young boy. All the way to the boarding house. He is probably still waiting for Winnifred Latham to come back down those stairs. So is the landlord, no doubt. He didn't make her pay in advance.' She looked down at the case in his hand. 'Poor Winnifred. I liked her.'

'Maybe you can be her again. In time.'

Her mouth turned grim. He knew where this was going. 'I am always her, Cage. For twenty years. A longer sentence than hers. I'm just not as invisible, nor as sympathetic, and definitely not as gracious.' For a moment, he could see a whisper of Winnifred Latham ghost across her perfect features.

They had reached the other side and he passed the case to her. 'Well then.'

She stopped and turned towards him, raised one glove to his cheek. 'So handsome. The Poet of Whitechapel.'

His heart turned over at her words as he bent to kiss her cheek once more. 'Goodbye, Mother.'

CHAPTER THREE

The girl was kissing his neck. He could feel her dry lips against his skin, her hair, too, tickling his shoulders as she bent over him. He seemed to remember it was brown, possibly with a reddish glow, although that might have been the lamplight. He feigned sleep for a moment longer. He was comfortable, face down in the pillow like this.

Her fingers were playing with his hair now, starting to tug gently, a plea for attention.

'Hello, you.' She rasped in his ear.

He mumbled incoherently, hoping she'd let him sleep on. But her hand slid down his back, across his buttocks, warm and agile. She pushed her fingers beneath him and he instinctively turned.

'That's nice.'

'Nice? You had better words than that last night, you dirty bastard.'

His eyes snapped open. So, it was morning already. Three bottles of wine stood empty on the dresser. Three of his best. He only remembered opening two.

Her head was moving down his body, planting kisses on his belly. He met her eyes, smiling up at him, full of lust and promise. He must have paid her well already. He pulled her face to his. 'Why don't you be a sweet thing and stoke the fire?'

Her hands slid down once more. 'I've already done that, love.'

He grabbed her hands in his. 'No, really. It's cold. I need to get up.'

Her face changed then, desire replaced seamlessly with a friendly professionalism. She slapped him on the shoulder and launched herself off the bed. 'You're right, it's blinking freezing.' She approached a neat pile of clothes on the nearby chair. Cage watched her dress quickly while she chatted away. 'God, I'm spitting feathers. How can you drink that stuff? You have any tea?'

He nodded towards the stove.

'Right. Let's get this thing going.' She bent down and opened the burner, before shovelling some coal wastefully within. 'Shouldn't take long, it's still warm. How come you don't have a maid, anyways? Rich lawyer like you.'

Just how much had he given her?

She stood up and surveyed the room. He saw it through her eyes. It was large, at least, covering the whole top floor, and comfortably furnished, but it was only one room. He gave her the stock line. 'I'm not as well paid as you might think. Most of my work is pro bono.' Why was he justifying himself to her?

'Pro what?'

'Free.'

An unfamiliar word for a whore. 'Oh.'

He wanted to be alone, but she started on the tea, clearly unwilling to leave until she was fully prepared for the cold world beyond. Staying warm under the covers, he watched her busy herself. She was pretty, and young.

'What's your name?'

'Forgotten already? Mind you, you barely used it last night. You preferred other names.' Her eyes said she didn't mind. 'Agnes.' She patted her hair. Brown, definitely brown. 'Not the prettiest name, but I kept it anyways. It's not the name that counts, is it?'

'I suppose not.'

She touched the pot on the stove, as if she might warm it with her hands. 'Almost there.'

He smiled back. She was a nice girl. The familiar guilt enveloped him as she sat back down on the end of the bed.

'Cage Lackmann,' she said. 'Where does that name come from?'

There was no harm in talking, at least. 'It's short for Micajah. It's Jewish.'

'You're Jewish?'

'No. My father was. Apparently.' Cage sat up and leant back on the pillows, daring to expose his shoulders. The stove was beginning to do its job. 'My mother gave me his last name. Said it might be useful one day, if something ever happened to me. Said the Jews look after their own.'

The girl nodded her approval. It was the kind of strategy that would make sense to her. Was Honor like this girl once? Before Cage had ruined her life?

'Why do they call you the Poet of Whitechapel?'

He felt defenceless, naked beneath the covers as this girl interrogated him. She was just making conversation. Two colleagues passing the time of day.

He needed a piss. 'Perhaps you might pass me my breeches?'

'I think they're still in the bed.' She stood up and lifted the covers to help him look. 'Found them!'

She handed the bundle across. He felt curiously bashful

about his nakedness. His hesitation was obvious, and she turned her back to check the tea's progress as he pulled his trousers over his slim hips and retrieved his shirt from the floor. He grabbed the chamber pot from beneath the bed and relieved himself, while she hummed softly by the stove. It was all strangely domestic.

The girl wasn't to be distracted, though. 'Is it because of your speeches? In the courtroom? Never heard you myself but they say you get pretty fancy sometimes.'

'No. I had a poem published. Once. A long time ago.'

'Ooh, can you recite it to me?'

He could. Every word. 'I barely remember it now.'

'Ah, go on, let me hear it . . . Jesus Christ!' The girl almost dropped the teapot as a thunderous knocking commenced downstairs, the floor jumping at the violence of the pounding on Cage's front door.

Cage ran to the window and looked down. Detective Inspector Jack Cross was slamming the edge of his fist into the door. Behind him, three constables stood to attention. This was nothing good. Cage shook his head, trying to clear it.

Cross shouted up from the street. 'Open up, Lackmann!'

Cage lunged for his boots and pulled them on.

'Here.'

The girl held out his jacket and he grabbed it with both hands. 'Thank you.'

'I should go. Is there a back way?'

'Yes. Left at the bottom of the stairs, through the scullery. Not right.'

She pulled on her coat, no doubt used to making a hasty exit without explanations. 'Goodbye, Cage Lackmann.' A quick smile, and then she was gone.

He looked at the pot, now bubbling on the stove. For an absurd moment, he missed her. The banging downstairs continued, relentless. He tucked his shirt into his trousers, and as he looked down he saw the wine stain in the centre of his chest, pink and grubby, like yesterday's blood. He ripped it over his shoulders and flung open the third drawer of the dresser. A wine bottle toppled to the floor.

'We're coming in!' Cross shouted up.

What the hell was going on? Cage rooted around for a clean shirt. Nothing. He should have picked up his laundry days ago. He pulled on the discarded shirt, flung on his jacket and ran to the stairs, taking them two at a time. He turned into his office and ran for the door, pulling it open before the policeman could break it down.

Detective Jack Cross filled the doorway, silhouetted against the icy sun. Cage wrapped his arms about his chest as he shivered. 'What is the meaning of this?' The words sounded false even to him. The high dudgeon of a respectable man, his privacy grossly invaded.

The detective ignored his question and crossed the threshold. The constables that followed behind him seemed agitated, ready for something. This was bad. 'Right, lads. You know what you're looking for, so go and look.'

The three men immediately sprang into action. Two of them left the room to explore the rest of the house while the third remained in the office, opening drawers and cabinets and rifling through the contents.

Cage ran a hand through his hair. 'You have a warrant?'

Cross snapped a piece of paper in Cage's face before flinging himself into the chair behind the desk. 'Light the fire, Lackmann. It's freezing in here. We may be some time.'

The questions crowded in, but Cage knelt by the fire, aware that it was a submissive pose to strike before the dominating form of Jack Cross. Cage didn't pretend to fight those kinds of battles, not with men like Cross, who could snap his neck like a chicken's if he wanted to. And Jack Cross had always wanted to.

Cage took his time with the fire, making a show of it, of how composed he was, despite the stamp of boots from overhead as the search continued. Cross remained silent, too, looking pleased with himself, even though he clearly had a secret he was burning to share. Cage didn't like other people's secrets any more than his own. He stood up. Cross wasn't going to spill until Cage showed an interest.

'So, want to tell me what you're looking for? Maybe I can help.'

'It's all there.' Cross nodded towards the warrant on Cage's desk. He wasn't going to make this easy.

Cage picked up the paper and pulled a chair towards the fire, bumping into the constable as he did so. 'My apologies.' Ridiculous, in his own house, for God's sake.

Cross ordered the man to search the small scullery at the back, leaving the two of them alone as Cage read through the warrant documentation, a licence to search the Whitechapel chambers of one Micajah Lackmann. Everything was in order, although the purpose of the search was stated merely as 'Missing Person'. Cage frowned when he saw the judge's signature: Henry Jacobs. After yesterday's win, Jacobs would not have been easily persuaded to sign this, not without just cause. Cage read the warrant once more, slowly this time, hoping a more original question would occur to him than the glaringly obvious, but it didn't.

'So, who's missing?'

'Moses Pickering.'

Cage nodded, although he had no idea why. He turned back to the fire. It was beginning to take, but he grabbed the poker from its hook and prodded the smouldering pile anyway. 'I haven't seen Moses Pickering for five years.'

'I thought you'd say that.'

'You don't believe me.'

'Actually,' said Cross, leaning forward across the desk, as if he owned the place, 'I think that's entirely possible.'

'Then why are you here, Jack?' Cage looked around at the open drawers, papers dropped carelessly to the floor. 'Did you imagine I had him neatly filed away under P?'

When Cross smiled, his mouth turned downwards. It reminded Cage just how much this man hated him. In the silence, the hate was all there was.

Cage stooped to collect some of the papers from the floor. 'Why are you looking for Pickering?' He shuffled the documents into some kind of order, pretending to look at them. 'A missing person is beneath you, surely.'

Cross produced a slim envelope from somewhere within his thick wool coat and slapped it on the desk. He was enjoying laying this trail of breadcrumbs and leading Cage by the nose. Cage picked up the envelope and felt within, pulling out a half dozen or so of what must have been freshly printed photographs, the chemicals still emitting a thick odour.

Cage looked at the first one, a stark image of a small attic bedroom. He could make out a wooden floor, a stool on its side and an unmade single bed, sheets and pillows piled on top. A small leaded window cast a grid of light across the scene; the rest was in shadow. 'What is this?' he asked, bored of the policeman's games now. He wanted that pot of tea, then more wine maybe.

Cross shrugged. 'A crime scene.'

Cage asked, genuinely curious, 'You are using photographers now?'

'Obviously. The twentieth century is on its way, Lackmann. Even at Scotland Yard.'

Cage turned to the second photograph. The camera had been moved a yard or so to the right, and now Cage could see a lower leg protruding from the far side of the bed, the foot twisted at an awkward angle. It meant only one thing. Cage stared at the photograph for some time, arranging his thoughts.

'There's more to see, Lackmann. Don't spare yourself.'

Cage needed to sit down. He returned to the fire and looked at the next photograph in the pile. A body laid out on the floor, a sheet twisted loosely around it, an abundance of fair hair obscuring the head from the camera's position at the base of the bed. In the next photograph, the hair had been gently pulled back, revealing a delicate nose and a darkly painted mouth beneath. The camera had moved in close for this shot, leaving its tripod behind. The image was alarmingly detailed. Cage could see the open pores on the girl's skin, and the ends of her hair beginning to fray. A part of Cage's brain marvelled at the technology. But the other part of his brain had snagged on something in this picture of a dead young woman. Something wasn't right. When he realised what it was, he turned quickly to the last photograph, and the truth caught in his lungs.

Before him was a vulgar close-up of the face he had glimpsed in the previous image. The blond hair lay off to one side, replaced by short black tufts. The dark lashes, lined with kohl, cast butterfly shadows on the white skin beneath, and around the mouth, with its perfectly painted Cupid's bow, was an unmistakable rash of barely-there stubble.

Now he understood why Cross was here, and why Jacobs had signed that warrant.

He shuffled the photographs back into the envelope. 'You think Pickering did this?'

Cross actually laughed. 'Of course not. Why would I connect two dead fifteen-year-old boys, found five years apart, painted like whores, wearing identical wigs and strangled to death in their own beds? What a ridiculous notion, Lackmann.'

'Pickering was found innocent.'

Cross was in his face immediately. 'Then why has the weaselly bastard disappeared, eh?'

Cage had no answer. Cross backed off, turning towards the inner hallway as he yelled up the stairs, 'Anything, lads?'

A disembodied voice yelled back. 'Nothing, sir.'

Cross rapped on the bannister. 'Right, let's be off.'

Cage moved to one side as the constables crowded back into the room and followed Cross to the door. He found himself not wanting the detective to leave. He needed more information than this. 'Wait! You didn't really think to find him here?'

Cross turned and walked slowly back towards him. The nasty smile was back. Cage had the feeling he was about to hear what Cross had really come here to say. The rest had just been theatre. 'Course not. You're no fool, Lackmann. Arrogant? Yes. Fool? No. I just wanted to see your face when you realised what this is going to do to your career. Cage Lackmann, defender of the innocent, Whitechapel hero.' Cross's finger jabbed into Cage's chest. 'I hope you enjoy the papers tomorrow. Pickering is going to look guilty as sin. So, what does that make you? A fucking liar, that's what. And what use are you going to be to your boss now? What's the point of having a lying toerag for a lawyer if every judge and jury knows he's a lying toerag?' The finger jabbed once more. 'Defender of the innocent? You're a whore, Lackmann. Obediah Pincott's worthless little whore. Maybe Pickering should dress you up as one and squeeze the life out of you. I'd take those photographs myself, and piss all over them.'

The detective's eyes gleamed with retribution. Cage suspected he'd waited five years to serve up that speech, to have good reason to. And why not, he thought, as he watched Cross slam the door behind him with as much force as he'd beaten entry in the first place, because every word had been true.

If Moses Pickering was guilty, Cage Lackmann's future looked grim indeed.

CHAPTER FOUR

But Moses Pickering wasn't guilty. Cage didn't believe that for a second.

After Cross had left, he skipped the tea and chose a good claret instead, although stocks were low. He'd worry about that another time. Right now, he had to think this through.

Obediah Pincott had bought Cage's soul a long time ago. Cage remembered their first meeting only vaguely – at the time it had carried no import. Pincott was just another patron of the theatre troupe that Cage's mother belonged to. Although patron was too strong a word for it. It was hardly the man's interest in the arts that had brought him to the make-shift music hall in Whitechapel they occupied at that time. There was an angle of some kind, a play to be had – but not that kind of play. The only thing Cage could really remember was the man's chest, naked beneath the Russian greatcoat he wore, as it carried a life-size tattoo of the man's own face, each angle and shadow perfectly captured, the eyes as blank as those above. The thirteen-year-old Cage had briefly been fascinated by that tattoo, which bent and twisted as the man leant forward to pour the champagne Honor so loved. Pincott and Cage's mother had talked long into the night, but the boy had thought nothing of it, and had left them murmuring in the lamplight of the rear courtyard, sitting on two upturned chests amidst a chaos of random props. Cage had turned in for the night, crawling into his tiny cot after a long day of humping scenery and cleaning vomit from the stalls.

It was days later before his mother broached the subject. 'There is an opportunity,' she had said. Mr Pincott was willing to fund his education, both school and university.

The young Cage was bemused. 'But I want to be a writer.'

His mother had sniffed. Cage knew the gesture well, as if, with one intake of breath, Honor Dossett could eliminate all that disagreed with her about the world. And it worked a treat, always. Somehow, that sniff made everything hers. As the plan unfolded, Cage could feel something slipping away, floating on the wash of guilt he always felt where his mother was concerned. Because he owed her, more than even Honor herself knew.

So, he was to be a lawyer. Bought and paid for up front and owned in perpetuity. His nascent talent on the stage had not gone unnoticed. The courtroom was Pincott's stage, and Cage was his player. Only on the margins, to keep up appearances, could Cage take on other work. Up front, he had asked Pincott what kind of clients he could secure in this context, just so he was clear. The Ukrainian had shrugged his reply, as if it were obvious: 'The innocent ones.' It made sense, obviously: in defending the endless, guilty line of Pincott's henchmen and cronies, a balance would be required, to counteract the stench.

Moses Pickering did not obviously fit that description. When Cage met him, he was already on remand at Newgate, and a charge of murder levelled in the kind of spectacular detail that the newspapers delighted in. The fifteen-year-old son of the wealthy, if eccentric, Crewler family, with whom Pickering had lodged, was found dressed like a whore, raped and strangled. Cage Lackmann would not have touched the case with a barge pole, if it hadn't been for *her*. For Emma Kenward.

The name floated through his brain, a whisper that drowned out all else. She was a ghost to him now – he wasn't even sure he could really recall her face, not in detail – but she could drag her chains just as stridently as she had five years ago. He looked down at his desk and reached for the top drawer, knowing what he was going to do and hating himself for it.

First there was the photograph, buried beneath a pile of other papers. He tugged it from the drawer and placed it in front of him. It was her, but it wasn't her. He closed his eyes, tried to remember the essence of her, a shy smile as he touched her arm, a distracted frown as she dressed herself hurriedly, or a moment of surprise as she came upon him unexpectedly. Anything but this dead-eyed smudge of grey shadows in front of him. Not a lie so much as a horrible absence of truth.

He reached into the drawer once more and pulled out the pamphlet. It was slim, but expertly printed on thick paper, the title written in extravagant script: *Poetica Veridica*. Edited and published by Justin Kenward, illustrated by Moses Pickering. Cage turned the pages, flipping past Justin's tedious introduction, where he espoused the merits of each and every poem he had selected for publication that quarter, implicitly praising his own good taste more than anything else. Cage paused on page nine, which was marked with two overlapping circles made by the base of his own claret glass on separate occasions. He only ever looked at it with a drink in his hand.

The Sacrifice
By Cage Lackmann

Love, the sovereign virtue, Love divine
Triumphs o'er all, ceaseless, and sublime.
Time itself will bend the knee,
Even Death, conquered for eternity
And silenced by the clamorous choir,
For Love sings as you burn upon its pyre.
Unrivalled, unstinting and undefeated,
Love conquers all, ruthless and conceited.
But what I feel is greater still,
And drives me with a greater will.
Not love, for I know not its name
It shuns our knowing, denies our frame.
I hear its voice above your roaring fire.
Silent, yet louder than venal desire.
I know what it asks of me, and so
I defy this love.
I let you go.

He'd read and reread those words so many times that they meant nothing to him anymore. The poem was just another story, with a dark and bleeding heart. What would it be, he wondered, to read them for the first time? To let the words tumble upon you all over again, fresh and new. Maybe he should have asked Emma.

There was no illustration to accompany the poem. He'd always thought that somehow endearing: how the newly freed Moses Pickering had chosen to honour the man who saved him from the gallows by *not* illustrating his poem, as if his work might have denigrated, rather than enhanced, Cage's own contribution. But that was Pickering to a tee.

Murder was a crime borne of many things: hubris, desire, hate, envy . . . the list went on. But humility was not one of them. That was why Cage Lackmann knew in his bones that Moses Pickering was innocent. He simply lacked the arrogance to take a life that wasn't his.

Cage glanced up at the wall by his desk. Hanging next to his barrister's certificate was the small Rubens drawing Pickering had given him following his acquittal and release. At first, Cage had refused it.

'It is too extravagant!' Although Lord knows he had needed the funds.

But Pickering had shaken his head, insisting that the freedom Cage had won for him should cost him something. The four Rubens he owned were his most treasured possessions, and to give one away was the price Pickering chose to put on a man's life.

The drawing had hung there ever since: a lion's paw, soft in repose, its power stilled in that moment. Often Cage had challenged himself to sell it when funds were low, but the thought would pass quickly. It was a man's life, after all.

Another knock on the door interrupted his thoughts. It was too soft, too hesitant to be Cross returned to taunt him. It was a woman's knock.

Quickly, he straightened the room as best he could, collecting the documents strewn across the floor into a rough pile beneath his desk and stashing his wine in a filing cabinet. He pulled his jacket tighter to cover the stain on his shirt before opening the door.

For a moment, he couldn't place her: apricot skin, and a

tentative smile on her lips, a smile that faded as she responded to his blank look. 'Apologies, sir. You gave me your details yesterday?'

The woman who had harassed him at the court. 'Of course. Please, come in.'

He stepped back to let her pass, shutting the door against the cold.

'Please, take a seat, Mrs . . . ?'

'Smythson. Hazel Smythson. My husband's name is Francis.'

She perched in the chair by the fire, opposite the desk, and began to remove her hat, then caught herself. 'May I?' She rose to her feet and began to remove her coat also. 'It's wonderful warm in here, sir. I think I would boil in my own skin if I keep this on while we talk.'

He hadn't yet decided if this conversation would last long enough to warrant her removing either but, evidently, she had made the decision for him. He took the items, noting they were extremely well made despite their plainness, and hung them carefully on the coat rack.

'So, Mrs Smythson.' Cage sat in his chair and pulled himself towards the desk, his legs bumping into the pile of papers crudely stacked beneath. 'Before we discuss any aspects of the case, there are a few matters we will need to clarify up front. I like to be honest about these things. Firstly, as I have already made plain, I can only offer my services as a barrister via a solicitor retained by you. There are a small number of such gentlemen I work with on a regular basis, almost exclusively.' There was only one, to be exact, and he was no gentleman. 'The one I recommend you retain if you wish me to represent your husband in court is Mr Clifford Chester. He is very experienced, and as dedicated as I to the pursuit of justice.' Not to mention wine and whores.

She nodded earnestly so Cage continued. 'Secondly, I have to raise the issue of fees. I do much work pro bono, as you can see.' He waved an arm around the small room before leaning forward and meeting her earnest gaze. 'However, the time I am able to allocate to that side of my work is limited and much in demand. If I take your case –' here he paused, allowing the word 'if' to cause two delicate lines to appear between her brows '– I shall have to charge my full rate.'

'Absolutely, Mr Lackmann, payment is not a problem.'

He sat back in his chair, her relaxed approach to the subject unexpected. 'Three guineas, Mrs Smythson. Three guineas an hour.'

She nodded once more, taking the number in her stride.

'Plus expenses,' he said.

'Very well.'

He examined her, and the sense of familiarity returned.

'Have we met before, Mrs Smythson?'

She frowned. 'I don't believe so.' Then she leant forward. 'He's innocent, sir.'

It's what they all said. Some held more conviction than others, but they all said it, nonetheless. Cage smiled and nodded. As if he agreed. As if he even cared that much.

'I can't believe he might be imprisoned for something he didn't do. Surely that can't happen, sir? God won't let that happen?'

They always said that too, as if he were on personal terms with the Lord himself, knew the deity's mind and inclinations. In a way, he did. If Cage Lackmann was sure of anything in this life, it was that God cared even less than he did.

'The case is complex, Mr Lackmann, but it can be argued, and won, I believe, by a man as eloquent as you.'

The power of words: scratched and feeble on their own, yet when marshalled together into an army they could break hearts and bones, tear down citadels. Stories were his business. They paid the rent, put food on the table – just. From time to time, they also saved lives, or prolonged them, at least. An added benefit that he told himself made everything worthwhile.

Cage took his notebook from his briefcase, the spine snapping with an expectation he struggled to feel himself. He filled his pen with ink and held it above the page.

'Tell me everything.'

CHAPTER FIVE

After Hazel Smythson had left, Cage leant back in his chair, the ancient horsehair within scratching as he did so.

Her story had been succinct, the pertinent details clearly communicated. She had stumbled only once, requesting some water before continuing; it had taken him an age to find a clean glass in the scullery.

There was a mountain of evidence against her husband, of course, and very little in defence of him, beyond his wife's gritty commitment. She'd make an excellent witness, and others could be found, or with the help of Honor and her friends, manufactured. He'd arranged to introduce her to Clifford Chester the following day at the Old Bailey, and sort the formalities, as they would both be in court for a brief bail hearing for yet another of Pincott's more careless thugs.

He glanced outside. The light was fading early – maybe it would snow tonight. Watching a new production at the Pavilion was the very last way he wanted to spend the evening, but the tide of Honor's assumption was impossible to resist, even in those rare moments when he felt the strength to try.

He took his coat from the back of the door and strode out

into the cold. He took the short cut to the laundry a few streets away, not in the mood to greet any casual acquaintances, and passed through the choppy terraces of the drying lines, icy sheets puffing at his face with ghostly aggression. The rear door stood wide open, but the steamy heat within still hit like a wall, making him cough.

He found Mrs Castan at the mangle, feeding sopping garments into the machine as her fleshy forearm rotated the wheel with a force more appropriate for grinding mincemeat.

'Mrs Castan!' Cage beamed a smile.

She looked up, but her expression remained flat as her hands maintained their pace.

'I have come for my laundry.'

She gave a brisk nod of her head at this statement of the obvious, stopped her labours and moved towards the front of her shop. Moments later, she lumbered towards him, not, as expected, with a sack of clean shirts, but with a wood-bound ledger in one hand and nub of pencil in the other. Cage could feel his smile slide to the floor.

'Six weeks on account, Mr Lackmann.'

'Is it really? I apologise, I have been much distracted by my recent case.' He fumbled some change from his pocket, without an idea of how much was actually there. 'Please, take what you need.'

She put her ledger down and with agonising slowness picked the coins from his outstretched hand. She chose the largest ones first, placing them in piles of denomination on the table to her side. She took so long, his hand began to ache, until finally, all the coins were gone.

She looked at her ledger once more and made a note. 'That leaves two weeks owing.'

'Very well,' he breezed, 'I shall send the balance tomorrow. My shirts, if you please?'

She looked at him with her rheumy eyes and held his gaze for a moment, before nodding her head once again and waddling away. When she returned, he grabbed the bag from her hands and fled back the way he had come, his pace brisk as if he had somewhere of great importance to be.

It was dark again by the time he returned home. He filled a large pot with water in the scullery and took it upstairs to heat on the stove, finishing the last of the wine while he waited for it to heat. He thought of Agnes that morning, her surprise that he had no maid to wait on him, to keep the stove warm, the tea on the boil and to fill a bath whenever he so wished. Cage had always prioritised other things: fine wine, the leather sofa he now sprawled upon. Pincott didn't pay enough for him to have all these things, never had. Maybe a girl like Agnes could be persuaded to come to an arrangement? Warm his bed and his stove alike.

He didn't like where his thoughts were going. Cross had got under his skin, made him feel vulnerable. Cage washed himself with vigour when the water was barely lukewarm, and dressed quickly. He pulled his strongbox out from beneath the bed and opened it with the key hidden beneath the bedpost. Two notes were left. Without questioning the waste involved, he grabbed the smaller-value one and folded it into his waistcoat pocket. In front of the mirror, he ran his hands through his hair and arranged his cravat. He paused, evaluating what he saw. His fresh shirt glowed a snowy white, the skin of his neck was warm and vibrant in contrast and his dark curls glistened in the lamplight. Fuck them all, he thought.

*

When Cage arrived at the New Royal Pavilion Theatre, the last of the crowds were filing through the narrow, plain frontage on the Whitechapel Road. The lights that marked the spartan entrance though were blinding in their excess. People came from all over the city to see the performances here: maybe they needed the shining beacon to guide them with the promise of grandeur that awaited, lest their commitment waver as they journeyed through the shabby, dangerous streets of the borough in order to get here.

Cage joined the stragglers as they meandered towards the auditorium through a long passage richly decorated with gilt and flowers. The brightness continued; the crystal gasoliers that hung above his head were making him itch with heat, and he paused to remove his coat. A programme seller approached him, and he dutifully purchased a copy, trying not to think about the funds he had already expended on the ludicrously priced bottle of champagne he carried with him.

In the grand entrance lobby, he checked his things then hurried through to find his seat and join the thousands waiting for curtain up. The crowd was raucous with excitement, although their enthusiasm left Cage cold. He glanced around the cavernous space: Honor's company had only performed here a handful of times over the years, and it was by far the biggest venue that had welcomed them. It probably involved some nefarious deal struck by Granger, the small-time impresario Honor had worked with for most of Cage's life. The theatre was an aberration in the usual itinerary of suburban halls where they plied their trade.

Cage glanced down at his programme. *Isaac Granger presents Mr. Hazlewood's adaptation of Lady Audley's Secret, a cautionary tale of a woman's depravity. Lady Audley by Mrs. Dossett.* Cage's mother was too old for the role, in her fifties now, but she wore her years lightly – on the outside, at least.

Cage could detect movement behind the bucolic backdrop of Italian lakes and mountains. The lights began to fade, and the chatter dimmed. A single violin, its pure note swirling outwards, snuffed the remaining hum until all fell quiet and dark.

Stagecraft. He knew all about that.

After the performance, he found his way backstage. The usher guarding the door took an age to find his name on the list, for it was long, although Cage could see that only a handful of names were crossed out. No doubt the rest were agents and theatre managers, optimistically invited but predictably absent.

In the corridor that led to the dressing rooms, he heard Granger before he saw him, his voice rumbling towards Cage like fire in a tunnel.

'Glasses, everyone!' Three quick claps, his signature gesture, accompanied the request. 'We need more glasses!'

When Cage turned into the room, he was immediately assaulted. 'Darling boy!' The hug was all consuming. Granger still wore his costume – an ancient frock coat, the green velvet worn to mud on his shoulder. Dust and the earthy aroma of ancient sweat caused Cage to sneeze. Granger immediately pushed him to arm's length, hands gripping Cage's biceps painfully. 'Good God, are you ill?'

Granger's brow furrowed, and the thick coat of make-up crackled across his forehead like shattered ice. Briefly, Cage thought of the dead boy in the photographs, then thrust the image away.

'I'm fine.' He held up the champagne, and Granger seized it from him immediately.

The room was long, and lined with mirrors illuminated with bright lamps. The party was in full flow; all the usual faces smiled in acknowledgement as he pushed his way through. Honor was perched elegantly on the arm of an old sofa, a glass of champagne in one hand, a man younger than Cage in the other.

'Mother.' Cage bent to kiss her presented cheek.

'You came! You remember Freddie, don't you?'

Oh yes, he remembered Freddie Southgate. The man offered his hand with his usual *I'm sleeping with your mother* smirk. Cage took it. 'Congratulations,' he said flatly. Honor's latest beau had played her nephew on stage, the hero that eventually sees her exposed and brought to madness. It had been a limp performance, but the crowd had enjoyed his blond good looks and one-note delivery of moral condemnation.

Honor stood up. 'Freddie, be a dear, fetch my son here a glass of something nice.'

The man peeled away and Honor pulled Cage back down to the sofa, huddling together. 'So, was I very marvellous?'

'Always.' And it was true. 'Where do you go after this?'

'Richmond. Then Epsom. Blackheath in a month or so. All the best places.'

He smiled. 'Still, a week here must pay well?'

'Not a bean,' she whispered, her voice hard. 'Granger calls it our showcase, to shore up bookings for the coming year. It's nothing more than a grand indulgence.'

'You could say no.'

She laughed then and patted his hand. 'I've learned thousands of lines in my life. "No" isn't one of them.'

Honor continued to chat through their coming itinerary,

the few places she was looking forward to visiting again, and the long list of those she wasn't. Cage looked back across the room, to where Southgate was flirting with a dark-skinned girl with a halo of black curls that bounced prettily about her head. There was no sign he was taking his mission of fetching Cage a drink seriously.

'You really like him?' He couldn't help asking the question but refused to look at Honor as she replied. Cage felt the familiar tightening in his gut as the clouds gathered. He'd heard the words a million times, knew the pain of them, but every once in a while he needed to hear them again, to know they were still there.

'No, Cage, I don't really like him. But he is here, and he is warm, and he is alive. And that will do. That is better than nothing, because sometimes, just occasionally, I will wake in the middle of the night and not think of Charlie, not see his face in my mind, not have the name Charles Edgar Moore on my lips. Just sometimes.'

Charles Edgar Moore. Charlie. His mother's great love. He had entered their lives when Cage was only five. A stonemason by trade, handsome and kind. Perhaps the kindest. But nothing good in this world is made to last. The man was dead by Cage's ninth birthday.

Honor gripped his hand. 'It's this Thursday.'

He nodded. Every year, on the anniversary of Charlie's death, they visited his grave, a release for Honor, salt in the wound for Cage.

Cage took Honor's hand and pressed it to his lips. 'I should go. I have to be in court early.'

She rose from their seat before he could. Exits and entrances were always hers. She cupped his cheek. 'Thank you for coming.'

Then she glided away to join Granger and the compensation that was Freddie Southgate.

Back on the streets, Cage was grateful for the cold wind that had got up, despite the putrid Whitechapel tang it carried. It was late, and the thud of his own boots was his only company for most of the walk home. He wondered about calling in to the brothel where Agnes plied her trade, but funds were low. He'd asked Hazel Smythson to bring a sizeable retainer with her the following day. By tomorrow night, he should have replenished his wine stock, paid that old hag Mrs Castan and his other creditors, and have his pick of London's whores to see him through to sunrise once more. Maybe he would even put some aside and find new quarters, somewhere with an indoor privy, even.

Arriving at his house, he fumbled with his keys, but something caught his eye – a movement within, the drapes at his window rippling gently. He thrust the key into the lock and threw the front door back on its hinges. The door to the scullery was half open, and beyond that the door to the yard flapped in the wind.

'I say, who's there?' His voice sounded firm and strong.

Cage crept forward silently, approaching the scullery, his breathing growing harder as the shock settled like fresh snow. Was someone really here?

He reached towards the scullery door, his fingers touching the rough wood. Slowly, he began to push, the squeak of the door hinges like nails on a blackboard.

Suddenly a gust of wind slammed the door shut in his face. Cage leapt back with a cry. He heard the door to the yard slam with similar force, but it was several moments before he could gather himself to check for an intruder. Returning to the fireplace he grabbed the poker and charged through into the scullery. He flung open the door to the yard with a bravado he did not feel, the poker raised like a club above his head.

But no one was there. The yard was empty and still, but for the privy door that shuddered in the wind. Perhaps that was all it was: the wind. He brushed a snowflake from his cheek, and returned to the house.

Agnes would have left the door unlocked after her hasty departure that morning. He had been too distracted after Cross's visit to relock it. Cage lit the lamp on his desk. The Rubens drawing was still in its place. He ran upstairs to check his other possessions, but his already diminished wine rack and what remained of his funds were untouched. Just the wind, then. Cage Lackmann, scared of his own shadow.

He grabbed a fresh bottle and glass and returned to his office. Before he sat down, he lit all the lamps and laid a huge fire, one that would burn well into the night – he knew sleep would not come. He poured a glass of dark red liquid and sank into his chair, staring at the mounds of paperwork he would have to sort through come tomorrow.

He reached out to the nearest pile, idly leafing through. It was only then that he saw it: a photograph, tucked in among the random papers.

The image was immediately recognisable: he had seen it earlier that day – the painted mouth, the kohl-lined lids, smooth and peaceful in death. But the word, scratched in angry block letters on the back of the print, was new.

MURDERER.

CHAPTER SIX

Sleep did come, a precious few hours. He dreamt of the Cupid's bow mouth, the image bleeding into colour and growing animate, shaping a scream that remained silent however hard he strained to hear. Then he could see the face, too, only it wasn't the boy's face, crusted in sickly white: it was Emma's.

He jolted awake, knocking the dregs of his claret glass across his desk. He grabbed at the photograph, as if it were a precious thing, and tucked it inside his inner pocket, snug against his pounding heart.

He was late. There would be no time to change. The fire was still burning when he left the house, a risk that seemed meaningless in that moment. He found a cab easily enough, despite the snow that was beginning to fall in earnest. One of the windows refused to shut properly and the carriage was cold. His hand rested on his chest, atop the photograph. Had someone really broken into his house last night and left it there? Or had it been Cross, or one of his men? It was one of their images, after all. Did Cross really hate him that much?

At the Old Bailey, he took the grand steps two at a time: his normal practice, even when time was on his side. It created the right impression, a man with people to see and places to go, a man with choices.

The foyer bustled with its usual activity as he reached for the door, but he was sure he detected a hush as he entered, a stillness that hadn't been there moments before. He was familiar with the paranoia that came from a lack of sleep and dismissed it immediately. This was his building; he belonged here. He marched forwards in the direction of the prep room where he was due to meet Chester.

But people were looking, weren't they? Or rather, he realised, they were looking *away*. He slowed his pace, and deliberately attempted to catch the eye of one of the court officials he saw on a regular basis. But the clerk had just that moment started an intense conversation with a colleague, his eyes fixed and unblinking, his peripheral vision deliberately closed down.

'I say, old chap, might I have a word?'

Cage turned to see Finian Worthing, the chief court reporter for *The Times*, lurching towards him. Overdue for retirement, Worthing had walked with a stick ever since an accident had befallen him the previous summer.

'Finian, I'm surprised to see you here. It usually takes a high-profile case to prise you out of the Old Bell, particularly on a day like this.' It sounded more waspish than Cage had intended. He liked Worthing. But his nerves were like needles today.

'Indeed. Indeed. That's why I'm here.'

Cage was aware that people were paying attention to them, and he knew what was coming. The journalist had a rolled-up copy of his own paper tucked under his arm.

'May I?'

Worthing nodded and handed the paper over. 'Front page.'

It was worse than Cage had expected. The headline read

simply, 'Pickering Murder Repeated. Pickering Missing.' His eyes swam across the rest of the article, not really taking it in, although he noted that Pickering had not been seen since the day the new murder had taken place – information provided by Justin Kenward, Pickering's employer.

Cage tried not to think of the image that seemed to tingle against his chest. Or was it that single angry word that burned?

'You knew, I suppose?' said Finian.

Careful. Worthing was a gentleman, but also a journalist.

'I spoke yesterday to the authorities who are conducting enquiries into Pickering's whereabouts. Sadly, I have not seen or heard of Pickering in five years.' This last part was said quite loudly, as if Worthing were a little deaf.

The journalist dropped his voice and moved in closer, signalling the sharing of a confidence. 'It must have been a shock to hear the news. Another murder, the same circumstances, a similar victim. Such a specific crime, such a specific *predilection*, one might say.'

'All murders are shocking, Finian.'

'I'm not sure you really think that.'

It had been a stupid thing to say. Most murders were routine, humdrum affairs: sad at best.

Cage rolled the newspaper once more. 'May I keep this?'

Finian ignored the question. 'So, do you think him guilty, Cage? I have to ask.'

'There is no answer that wouldn't damn me, one way or another.'

'No comment, then.'

'Including that one. Good day, Finian.'

With a forced smile, he turned on his heel, the rolled-up paper still in his hand. He was glad to find the main prep room relatively unoccupied, and one of the aproned hosts actually in attendance, a rare sight indeed. He ordered some coffee, then checked in briefly at the duty registrar's office. His was the third case up, which gave him a good half hour to gather himself. Hazel Smythson was then due to meet him and Chester in the foyer at eleven.

He found a desk beneath the windows, his back to the room. He opened his briefcase and spread his papers untidily around, to create the impression of diligent preparation, but a bail hearing for a first-time offender was rarely a taxing endeavour. The accused was barely nineteen, a cousin of one of Pincott's main lieutenants, and with a cherubic face to boot. For a charge of common assault, he doubted the prosecutor would even fight the contention of bail.

The coffee arrived, hot and strong. With cup in hand, he read the Pickering article, slowly this time. Worthing had deployed his usual poetic metaphors to hint at the facts: the young boy had been dressed in a *deliberate* style, and had been *raped* of his life, and so on. All to ensure that the words elicited no more than an 'Oh my!' from his dainty, middle-class readership. Those who wanted to know more would have to snatch furtive glances at the *Globe* or the *Evening News* over the shoulders of other commuters on their journey home. What it boiled down to, though, was clear. Five years ago, fifteen-year-old Nathaniel Crewler had been found by a servant, strangled in his own bed. The boy had been dressed in women's clothes and wore a wig of blond hair, his face made up theatrically. And now, the same thing had happened all over again. A different boy, but the same crime.

Cage smelled Chester's approach before he was within five yards of him. He turned around. 'Good morning.'

'Not for you, it isn't.' Chester grabbed a chair and planted it close, before wedging his large behind into the seat. His excess flesh flopped around the arms as he wiped a film of sweat from his milky forehead with a wrinkled, grey handkerchief.

'You've read the paper, I take it,' said Cage.

'No.' Chester patted his greasy locks into place. 'But Pincott has.'

The news was to be expected. 'He wants to see me?'

Chester leant back in his chair and gave him a dead-eyed stare. Of course Pincott wanted to see him.

'I'll go after we've finished here. I've found a new client, a lucrative one, Hazel Smythson. She is to meet us here at eleven. A forgery case, easily won, I think. I could brief you now – we have time.'

Chester shrugged and smiled, revealing crooked teeth. 'You ever heard of Nero, Lackmann?'

'The emperor?'

'Fiddled while Rome burned.'

'Rome isn't burning.'

Chester reached for the newspaper on the desk, rolled it once more and smacked it against Cage's chest. 'Yes, it is.'

The solicitor struggled to his feet. 'I'll see you in there. No theatrics, if you please.'

It was advice he would have heeded anyway. At the appointed time, Cage kept his head down as he moved through the narrow corridor to the courtroom. The bail judge today was thankfully inexperienced, brought in from the Berkshire assizes to cope with the backlog that always built across the winter months, the number of thefts and arrests being inexplicably proportionate to the risk of starvation and death by freezing.

Their case was dispensed with quickly and bail was granted.

Cage stood with Chester in the foyer as their young charge was released into the cold. At the last moment, Cage called him back and gave the lad his gloves.

'Hoping for salvation today, are we?' said Chester.

Cage ignored him and cast around for a suitable spot in which to wait for Hazel Smythson. The stares and whispers continued, and he wished he were anywhere but here. He even thought he could hear it, the single word, repeated over and over, slyly and quietly by so many that it rolled around the walls and built to a scratching hiss meant for his ears alone: *Pickering, Pickering, Pickering.*

His gaze caught on a young boy, walking steadfastly towards him, carrying something in his hands. For a wild moment, Cage thought it might be another photograph, another word to go with *murderer.*

'Are you Cage Lackmann?' the boy asked.

Cage stared down at him, an absurd desire to say no on his lips.

The boy took his silence for assent and thrust a note towards him. 'This is for you.'

Cage took it and the boy sprinted to the doors, his mission completed.

Cage's hands were shaking as he opened the envelope. The note inside was short and to the point. Hazel Smythson wasn't coming.

Cage handed the letter to Chester.

'Ah. Salvation isn't yours today, it would seem.'

Cage could have punched him in the face.

'Never mind.' Chester snapped on his own gloves. 'Time to meet your maker, I think.'

CHAPTER SEVEN

It was snowing by the time Cage reached the lanes of Whitechapel, although the weather seemed to have no impact on the crowds and clutter that crammed the tiny streets. The snow turned to slush as soon as it landed, no match for the pervasive muck of the borough that deterred any attempt to blanket over its true nature. The street prostitutes remained proudly bare shouldered, their withered arms shivering as they grasped and shouted their demands. As he turned into Dodd's Lane, the crooked buildings kinked towards each other, forcing the snow here to fall only in the centre of the road, a thin white line of mostly undisturbed purity as the citizens kept to either side, protected by the overhanging roofs. Up ahead, he could see a group of children rolling balls from the fresh snow, their feet bound tightly with sacking, now sodden black and frozen solid, a pointless parental gesture.

Cage bent down and rolled his own snowball, compacting the ice in his frozen hands. He aimed at the largest boy and flung his missile overarm. The snow exploded on the boy's shoulder, to squeals of delight from his friends. The group ran towards him, ready to launch, but he ducked into the Pestle and Mortar pharmacy just in time. He turned to see their disappointed faces through the grimy window. Maybe they'd wait for him. Maybe they wouldn't.

'He's expecting you.' The pharmacist's head barely reached above the counter he stood behind.

Cage walked towards him. 'No need for a password today, then?'

The little man's smile held a note of genuine sympathy. Cage wished it hadn't.

The dwarf held aside the grubby curtain that led through to the back of the shop, and Cage passed into the darkness beyond. He felt around the rear wall for the familiar catch, released it, and pushed open the door to Pincott's hidden compound.

It looked different in the snow, like some bucolic Alpine scene, which was ridiculous in itself. The large yard around which the compound lay was normally home to abundant activity: dray horses dragging carts laden with goods of a dubious nature, men huddled in small groups, eyeing the others with mistrust, the occasional dog fight to make them forget their own battles. Today the yard was empty, carpeted in white, and the ramshackle buildings that lined the perimeter were locked up tight against the cold. A chimney in the far corner belched black against the silver sky, and Cage headed in that direction, his boots squeaking through the virgin snow.

He shoved against the door of Pincott's quarters, but it refused to budge. He raised his hand to knock, just as the door was yanked open from the inside. For a comic moment, he stood there, his fist about to biff Dub on the nose. The red-headed Scot ignored the opportunity for banter and shouted over his shoulder, 'The lawyer's here.'

Not Cage, not Mr Lackmann. Just *the lawyer*.

Cage smiled at Dub as he entered. 'Enjoying your freedom, Mr Dubois?'

Dub grunted, conversation never his strong point.

The room was barely above freezing, despite the flames in the grate. Daylight lacerated the wooden-slatted walls – the fire didn't stand a chance against the flimsy structure. Despite the cold, Pincott sat at a table far from the fireplace, his long limbs spilling out of the chair and his greatcoat open, revealing the twin skull in all its glory on his pale, hairless chest. Cage would have been hard pressed to say which version of his boss looked least amused.

Pincott's death stare followed Cage as he crossed the room and took a chair at the table: it was usually piled with money but today it was empty. Maybe Pincott had been telling the truth about his cash-flow problem.

Cage spoke first. 'The Pickering situation: it's most unfortunate for all of us, and has taken me completely by surprise, I have to admit. Cross came to see me yesterday and—'

'Yesterday?'

Shit. He should have prepared.

'Yes, apologies Obediah, I should have alerted you, but I was convinced that Pickering would turn up, I didn't anticipate—'

'No. You didn't.'

Cage let the words hang in the air. The silence grew uncomfortable, for him at least, but what was the point in saying anything more? It wasn't his silence to break.

Eventually, Pincott spoke. 'What did I tell you? All those years ago?'

'The innocent ones.'

'Yes. The innocent ones. Just them.'

'I think he still is, Obediah. Whatever it looks like, whatever has happened here, it's not Pickering. I'm not sure what else I can say?'

Pincott leant forward, the light slicking across his black pupils as he held Cage's gaze. 'You could say: do not worry, Obediah, I will find Pickering, I will prove him innocent again, I will sort this out and all will be as it was.'

Cage ran his hands through his hair, ice catching against his fingers. 'The police are searching for him; they have the resources. If they find him . . .' Cage held up both hands in a placating gesture, '*when* they find him, I shall sort this mess out, make no mistake. And we're still assuming that the real culprit isn't found in the meantime, even if Pickering eludes them. Cross will be exploring all avenues.' Cross would be doing no such thing, of course, but Cage was comfortable with the lie – it was his own pleading tone that made him feel sick.

But Pincott was shaking his head, slowly from side to side, as if the gesture caused him pain. 'I do not own Cross. I own you.' Pincott's finger jabbed into Cage's chest, right where the photograph of the dead boy lay, as if he could tattoo the word *Murderer* across Cage's heart.

How the hell was he supposed to find Pickering, if the resources of Scotland Yard could not? There was something else, too, something deeper he had to avoid, whatever the price. He'd promised himself to stay away, never to see her again, except in his dreams.

'What if I can't, Obediah? What if I can't find him?'

Pincott leant back in his chair. 'Then find another story. You like stories, don't you, Poet of Whitechapel?'

'And what if there is no other story? Just two dead boys and a missing man? Just so I'm clear?' Like holding a gun to his own head, but he would know it all.

'Then find another job. Right now, you are no use to me.'

And there it was, the bottom line. Pincott cocked his head to one side, and Cage shivered despite himself at the reptilian scrutiny.

'Do you remember the question I asked you at our first meeting?' continued Pincott.

Cage shook his head. He had been a child, and Pincott nothing to him, this man who bought a life with banknotes, judiciously counted out as if the scales of such a transaction could be balanced to precision.

'I asked you, what you want to be, when you grew up. You know what you said?'

Cage shrugged. 'A writer, no doubt?'

'No, is not what you said. The word you said was – happy. You wanted to be happy.'

Pincott laughed then, and Dub joined in: Cage had forgotten he was even there. As the laughter subsided, he saw his opportunity.

'We were all children once, I suppose,' he said, although the image of Obediah Pincott as a child refused to come to mind. 'I will try my best to do as you ask, Obediah, and with a fair wind, I hope we can resolve this quickly. Might I trouble you for this month's retainer? There will be expenses in searching for—'

Pincott's hand slapped hard across his face, the palm open, a woman's slap but with a man's strength. Cage spluttered, pressing his fingers to his cheek, shock and pain roiling into soupy humiliation: the kind of slap an angry parent gives a child, judged to hurt in all the right places.

Pincott rose from the chair, unwinding his limbs, and stood before him. With one hand he tipped Cage's face to his, forcing him to meet those eyes. 'Find Pickering. Prove him innocent or point the finger elsewhere. No more retainer. No more clients.' As if it needed saying twice.

Pincott let go of him and moved away. Cage got to his feet, ignoring the desire to raise his hand once more to his burning cheek. His eyes were watering now, God damn them.

He walked towards the door. 'I shall keep you informed, obviously.'

'Cage,' Pincott called, his voice even.

Cage half turned, his hand on the door latch and his eyes steadfastly focussed on the filthy sawdust strewn across the floor.

'The Kenwards. They will be the key.'

Cage nodded. They always had been.

CHAPTER EIGHT

'Hello, love. Come to see me? Or someone else?'

Cage smiled up at her and leant back in his chair. 'Just escaping the cold. Beyond that, I had no plan.'

'That's a no, then.' Agnes pulled a chair out and sat at the tiny table, knocking his wine as she did so. 'Oops, sorry. Shall I fetch you another?'

'Yes. And another, and then another.'

'Ah!' She put her head in her hands. 'Trouble?'

'Could say that.'

She nodded her young head, trained to empathise even when she didn't understand. It was beguiling, though, and maybe she did understand? Trouble – it all boiled down to that word, however you looked at it.

'So.' She sat back. 'You're drowning your sorrows.'

'Nope, I'm afraid my sorrows have recently learned to swim.'

'What, then?'

He swirled the last of his wine around his glass – his fifth tasted no better than the first. 'I am finding my courage. I believe I might have misplaced it somewhere.'

She giggled like a co-conspirator, a genuine sound. Right at that moment, she was the only friend he had.

'Something to do with that copper? The one with the loud knock and the bad temper?'

Why not share the joke? 'His name is Jack Cross.'

'Go on!'

Her shawl had dropped slightly from her shoulders, revealing the swell that lay beneath. He remembered the comfort it had given a few days earlier, a lifetime ago. He looked around him. The small shabby saloon was a front only, a token attempt to mask the building's real pleasures. He was the only one there.

'There's cheaper places to drink, you know.'

'I know. I don't want to waste your time.'

'You want to talk? That's fine. Only it costs the same.'

He looked at her hard. Why did her youth bother him so much? 'Don't you hate what you do?' he asked.

Her eyes fell, the question unexpected. 'I don't know what you want me to say.'

He stood up and threw some coins on the table, enough for the wine alone. 'Neither do I.'

Cage turned the corner into Elgin Gardens, escaping the biting wind of Ladbroke Grove. His feet felt numb, reluctant to take him there, maybe. It had been almost five years since he'd last walked this street. It had been late summer, and the lavender to the front of the Kenwards' house had been in vivid bloom, casting its scent with abandon as it burst across the boundary wall. It had been the last thing he had said to her – *the scent is strong tonight* – but she had said nothing in return, her eyes shining with recrimination. Now the plants were stripped bare of all perfume and colour, revealing the angry stubs of hardy twigs that lay beneath.

He stopped at the front gate. The house had been freshly

painted, the flat, white stucco contrasting with the lustrous black door. The eager geometry of the patterned tiles that led up the grand steps was also new. His mood darkened to see Justin investing such care in his home. Was his wife also a beneficiary of such attention?

The servant who answered the door was another new addition – a stout young woman in a smart maid's uniform, the starch in her apron snapping briskly as she turned to let him in. Cage introduced himself and was asked to wait. Left alone, he looked around for further signs of change, but saw none. The hallway was disturbingly familiar, even the arrangement of dried flowers on the centre table was the same. His eyes were drawn towards the stairs, the faded, oriental carpet that ran the full length to the half landing above, where the stained-glass window cast a halo of deceptive yellow light. He remembered the warmth of that very light, on his neck, as he had fallen to his knees and pushed her skirts aside, his hands sliding up her pale thighs.

'Cage Lackmann. It's been too long.'

Justin Kenward strode towards him, hand outstretched. Cage wasn't sure what he had expected, realising only in that moment that he had put no thought to what Justin might have learned in the intervening years. Not the truth, obviously.

'It has indeed, Justin. Although I am sorry for the circumstances of our meeting.'

Justin's handshake was vigorous. 'As am I.'

Justin led them into the front parlour, and the sense of familiarity intensified.

'Please.' Justin gestured towards the Chesterfield, but Cage chose one of the chairs by the window. Anything but that sofa, with the paisley throw that had once warmed them now lying innocently across its arm.

Justin was keen to get down to business, which suited Cage. 'Cross has been to see you, I suppose?'

'Jack never misses an opportunity to torment.'

Kenward smiled. 'You did for him that day. On the stand.'

Cage remembered it well – the detective's face growing redder by the moment, as Cage dissected and then enlarged every tiny error or omission of the investigation into the Crewler boy's murder and the subsequent blind persecution of the gentle, fastidious Moses Pickering. In truth, the prosecution had nothing. Character and circumstance was all. Moses had been on the premises the night the boy had died, but then so had others: his elder brother and countless servants. But Pickering's unmanly presence had seen him singled out for attention: an *unusual man*, to use the prosecution's words, with *repugnant tastes*. Moses's timidity under questioning had been interpreted as guilt. Whatever his predilections, Cage doubted the faint-hearted Pickering had ever acted on them, and no evidence was ever produced to that effect. But the aspersion had been enough to see him charged.

'Where is Moses? Why has he run?' Cage asked.

Justin's smile fell. Without it, Cage could see he had aged, although the boyish roundness of his amiable face was still there. He ran his hands through his hair, the blond tufts springing up as he did so. 'I have no idea. I last saw him in this very room. We were discussing the upcoming edition. Moses had finished most of the illustrations, and there was just one more to deliver. We talked the poem through – quite compelling in its bleakness, how it used the metaphor of a graveyard for lost hopes and dreams – but Moses was unsure whether the illustration should also take such a literal approach. My own view was—'

'When was this?' Cage had no time for the man's literary pretension.

'Monday. Moses left at about five. Cross says the boy was killed that night.'

'What else did Cross tell you?'

'Not much. He returned yesterday. He seems convinced the crime is identical to the Crewler boy. We had an altercation, I suppose. I suggested he should spend at least some of his time and resources investigating who the real culprit might be, and not jump down this rabbit hole of assuming Moses is guilty all over again. That agitated him.'

'I did the same.'

Justin shook his head. 'The thing is, Cage, it seems I was the last person to see Moses. He didn't return to his apartments, his landlady didn't see him. He just disappeared that night, took nothing with him. I had thought he had taken off in fright the moment he heard of the circumstances of this boy's death, that somehow he found out before the police could come for him – you know his temperament as well as I. But the timeline doesn't work, Cage. He was missing before anyone found the boy's body.'

'Are you saying you think he did it?'

'No!' Kenward ruffled his hair once more. 'I don't know. I don't know what to think.'

'What did Cross want?'

'Pardon?'

'When he came back to see you yesterday.'

'I'm not sure, really. He ran through the timings again. Spoke to Emma, too, although she was out that last day Moses was here.' Just hearing the name on his lips made it hard to breathe. Kenward continued. 'Other than that it was general chatter about the publication, contributors and such. Oh, and he looked through some of Moses's sketches and preparatory drawings, took a few with him, although I don't see the relevance.'

Neither did Cage. What's more, Detective Jack Cross didn't do general chatter about anything.

'What do you know about the boy who died?'

Justin shook his head. 'Nothing. I didn't think to ask.'

'Do you have any idea where Pickering might have gone?'

The blond man shrugged. 'There's an aunt, Kent I believe, I don't know where. I told Cross the same thing. Moses always carried his pocket book with him – sketches, names, his whole life was in there. Maybe there are letters from his aunt at his apartment—' He broke off and snapped his fingers. 'The Crewlers will have the address, I think. They sent his things there when he was in prison. The first time.' A haunted expression settled on his face. Cage wasn't the only collateral damage here. *Poetica Veridica* was Justin's life.

'I'll need his current address. I want to meet this landlady for myself.'

Kenward looked up at him, a raised eyebrow reanimating his features. 'Why are you doing this? Getting involved again?'

'You know me. Champion of the innocent.' And slave to the guilty, who hold the leash as tight as they dare. A mongrel would have more dignity.

The door to the parlour pushed open, and suddenly she was there, standing before him, the reprieve he had hoped for denied him at the last.

He rose to his feet – less out of politeness than an instinct to run.

Her hair was as dark as ever, no trace of grey, and her skin as white. He stared as she moved towards him, couldn't stop himself, thirsty eyes drinking in the reality after all this time. The tiny mole just in front of her ear, marking the hollow of her cheekbone. How had he forgotten that, when other truths plagued him so relentlessly?

She held out her hand. For a bizarre moment, he didn't know what to do with it. In the end, he grazed her cold fingers with his – a limp, peculiar gesture.

'Mr Lackmann.'

'It's a pleasure to see you again, Mrs Kenward.'

Last names. Surely that would have jarred? But Justin Kenward seemed oblivious. The man stood up and brushed the creases from his trousers. 'Right, let me get that address for you. I shan't be a moment.' He shambled out of the room, leaving the two of them alone.

Her gaze hadn't left his, but her face was composed, so unlike the last time he had stood this close to her. He noticed a few fine lines around her mouth, maybe because her lips were pressed so firmly together, as if to stop something spilling out.

'How are you?' His voice sounded high and strange.

She blinked then. 'The same.'

What did that mean? Still in love and desperate to be saved from her marriage? Or so angry at his failure to do so that she had clawed his face?

She walked past him to the window, turning her back. 'So, another boy. Must be bad for business.'

No champion of the innocent charade here. 'Yes. It is.'

'You want to find him first.'

He said nothing.

Her back was straight, and the neck of her blouse was high.

The tips of her ears were pink, as if all the warmth in her had flooded there, flinching from the ice.

'You don't write poetry any more. Not for us, anyway. Not for me.'

'Emma . . .' His hand reached out as if it had a mind of its own, encircling her arm. The silk of her gown was slippery, hard to grasp. He tightened his grip and pulled her around to face him.

She was smiling, and the shock of that smile made him drop his hand, for there was nothing but misery in it.

She stepped closer, her eyes shining as she tipped her head to his. He could feel her breath against his skin as she whispered, 'You did this.'

He raised his hand once more, cupped her chin, his thumb bruising across her mouth as if he could wipe that smile away. 'I loved you,' he said.

Her laugh was deep throated and genuine. 'So what?'

Footsteps in the hallway pulled them apart. Justin Kenward re-entered the room and thrust a piece of paper towards Cage. 'Here you go. Good luck to you. I hope you find him.'

'Thank you for your time. I'll keep you informed.' Cage was at the door now, and the temptation to keep going without turning around was hard to resist, but Justin had more to say.

'Forgive me.' The man cleared his throat. 'Looking for Moses may be time consuming. If a retainer is required, I'd be happy to oblige.'

Cage bit down on the word *yes* before he could say it. Emma's face was in shadow now, the daylight streaming past her like a river flowing around a rock.

Justin filled the silence. 'I hope I haven't offended.'

'Not at all, but that won't be necessary.' Like cutting his own leg off.

Cage nodded professionally at them both, then closed the door behind him.

Out on the street, he walked swiftly, not caring which direction he took. Her words came back, the rasp of *you did this.* Almost as powerful as the word on the back of the photograph – *Murderer* – the word he was trying so hard not to think of, and the writer of that word even more so.

Sometimes words did not need marshalling together to tear down citadels, they could do it all on their own: no poetry – and no poet – required. The only thing a single word needed to wield that kind of power was to be true. For in his time, Cage Lackmann had murdered so much more than love.

CHAPTER NINE

Night had almost come by the time he reached Kilburn, the grey sky breathing gently to black. Moses Pickering lived in a former coaching inn on the main thoroughfare. The solitary building stood before him now, the windows dark. On either side the land had been flattened to make way for the relentless march of new housing that was spreading north as each new track of iron railway was hammered into the ground. As Cage crossed the road, he could see the ancient sills crumbling and the daubed walls sinking downwards, sliding back into the earth. Whoever was holding out here against the tide of progress was wasting their time, for the building itself had given up the fight long ago.

It was a strange place for Moses to have moved to, after the grandeur of the Crewler house, his previous abode. At the time of Nathaniel's death five years ago, Moses had been spending most of his wages renting the neat but tiny gatehouse that guarded the entrance to the Crewler estate. What was left over was scrimped into a small but effective purse dedicated to the purchase of art, illustrations mostly. Cage couldn't imagine Pickering in the sad and dismal place that stood before him now.

Cage ducked beneath the crooked arch that hid the front door, a hulking black thing that seemed held together by varnish alone. He thumped the heavy iron knocker against its plate, and heard the whisper of crumbling plaster above him.

The slam of a heavy bolt on the other side of the door brought on another avalanche of decay. Then the door opened, and a lantern was thrust in his face, temporarily blinding him.

'Can I help you?' The 'h' was pronounced with effort, indicating it normally went unused.

Cage dusted shards of plaster from his hair as his eyes adjusted to the sharp light, the smell of paraffin wafting with each swing of the lamp. The woman was tiny. Even with her arm held high the lamp barely reached his face.

'Certainly. I am working with the investigation and we have a few more questions regarding Mr Pickering.'

The light continued to waver in the silence.

'I apologise for bothering you again, Mrs . . . ? I'm afraid Detective Cross neglected to pass on your name.'

The mention of Cross unlocked her tongue. 'I told the inspector everything I knew. Which is to say, not very much. I know very little. Other than what I read in the papers.'

Cage changed tack. 'Even so, this is an important matter and I shan't take up much of your time. And I need to see Pickering's apartments. Now, if you please.'

The lamp moved backwards and he followed her over the threshold into the dark panelled hall.

'Mrs Chappelhow,' she said. 'Bessie Chappelhow.'

'You have a fine establishment here.'

The deflection worked. Her back straightened and, ignoring the omission of his name, she embarked on what was clearly a well-trodden path. 'My great, great grandfather built this place, the year the mad king came to the throne. Named it after him he did, the George Inn. A fine place it was. The Prince Regent even stayed here once when his carriage was rutted out on the turnpike, claimed he ate the best duck alamode he had ever tasted, under this very roof. But times change, don't they?' She reached for the large set of keys that dangled from a chain that swamped her waist and thumbed through them. 'They built the New Inn down the pass nigh on thirty years ago, just as my husband and I, god rest his soul, inherited the George. No one came here any more, history has no value in these modern times. But we soldiered on, turned it into a boarding house, made ends meet, we did. Now they want to tear us down.' She unsnapped one of the keys before turning towards the stairs. 'You coming or not?'

He followed her as she trudged upwards, her feet doing a better job than his at avoiding the loose boards.

'Three years now, I've told them no. They can burn this building with me in it if they wish, but I ain't leaving first. Watch out for the rotten step.'

Too late. Cage stumbled forward as his foot met nothing but air. He grabbed at her skirts, but the woman was solid as a rock, unlike her house. He muttered an apology as he righted himself and a grim smile flashed across her face.

They reached the first floor without further incident and she led him to a nearby door. It was ornately panelled, the craftsmanship evident. The woman unlocked it and Cage followed her into the room, squinting around while she worked to light another lamp. It was a surprisingly large space, high ceilinged, and the wide mullioned windows let in a shaft of pale moonlight that sliced across a polished floor.

'Here.' She placed a tall lamp on the desk in the centre of

the room and turned up the flame. 'I'll be in the kitchen if you need me. I need to prepare dinner.'

'How many tenants do you have here?'

'Just the one, now Pickering's gone.' She was at the door, having retrieved her own lamp. She held it close, and he could see her face clearly for the first time. Despite her age, her skin was unlined.

'I shall find you when I am done.'

She closed the door behind her and he turned to examine the room. It held a certain majesty – was this the very chamber that had once perhaps housed the corpulence of the Prince of Wales? The large, high bed was carved from the same wood that panelled the walls, and seemed sturdy enough. It had been made neatly, and the jaunty paisley quilt that covered it was new and made of expensive silk: a Pickering touch, no doubt. He could see exactly why the place had appealed to Moses now, the romance of its history and the light that would come through those windows on a summer's day would have been fodder to his artistry.

Cage opened the armoire beside the bed. It was laughably oversized for the few items it contained: a summer suit in sage-green linen, well made and perfectly pressed, which Cage remembered from the trial. It was joined by three crisp white shirts, a black morning jacket that smelled slightly of camphor, and a pair of dress shoes, polished to perfection. The only thing that seemed out of place were the four empty hangers on the rail.

He crossed to the desk and sat down. The surface was uncluttered: an ivory box of perfectly sharpened pencils, a large pad of thick canvas paper and a rosewood cigar box embossed with the East India crest, containing assorted stubs of charcoal on a lining of wax paper. He thought of his own chambers, the mess Cross's men had created in a few short minutes. There was little evidence here of a thorough police search, but then Moses had few belongings, nothing extraneous, with which to cause such chaos.

Cage pulled open the single drawer that ran the length of the elegant desk. As expected, it was neatly organised: paperclips in a round tin, a sheaf of bankers' letters, and a slim album of family photographs. Cage took it out and leafed through it. There were no pictures of Moses himself, but that didn't surprise him. Moses was a slim man, and dapper in his dress, but he took care of his appearance more to blend in rather than stand out. He hated attention.

Cage found a single photograph of the aunt that Justin had mentioned. An old woman stared back at him, looking uncomfortably hot. She held a parasol stiffly in one hand as the other grasped the back of a wicker chair, the real star of the show being an abundant rose bush that towered beside her. Pickering's printed label said merely 'Aunt Lucille, Kent, 1873.' Cage dug around further, but he could find no letters from this Aunt Lucille. He could only conclude that Cross had taken them already.

He slumped back in the chair. It had been foolish to think he would find anything here. Cross was a full day and a half ahead of him in the game. How on earth could Pincott expect him to find Pickering first?

Weariness overwhelmed him. A goose chase was what it was. He needed a drink.

A crystal decanter glittered atop the bookcase below the window, the amber liquid glowing within. What the hell – Moses wouldn't begrudge the imposition.

He half-filled a tumbler and took a sip – a fine-quality

single malt, but with a musty aftertaste. Pickering was not a big drinker, said he liked to be in command of his faculties at all times. Or was there a deeper reason? A need to control his darker impulses, perhaps?

Cage crouched down and looked over the bookcase, tumbler in hand. The top shelf was mostly taken up with past editions of *Poetica Veridica*, filed in date order. He thumbed through them, reaching automatically for the edition in which 'The Sacrifice' had been published, intrigued perhaps to see it in its virgin state, crisply printed, unmarked by his own self-pity and regret. He pulled the pamphlet from its place and opened it to page nine, but to his surprise it wasn't there. The page had been neatly torn out.

Randomly he pulled more pamphlets out, and leafed through them – three, four, five, no pages missing. But the sixth had been similarly defaced, a single page torn out. What had Pickering done with those pages? Cage put the pamphlets back in their rightful places, respectful of Moses's obsession with order, then dropped to his knees to explore the bottom shelf. It mostly contained books about various artists, perfectly aligned by height, rather than alphabetically. He pulled out a thick volume – reproductions of Da Vinci's drawings – which he knew would have cost several months' salary. It was in beautiful condition, the leather spine unlined. The pages crackled as he opened them. Had Moses even read this book? Or had it been enough to simply possess it?

As he went to replace it on the shelf, Cage noticed a plain Manila folder sandwiched against the next book. When he picked it up, several pieces of paper fluttered to the ground – poems ripped from *Poetica Veridica*, the same neat scoring that had severed them from their binding.

Cage counted them: thirteen in total, including his own. He skimmed them quickly, looking for some kind of connection: there was a poem about the stoic heroism of the Crimean peoples, written by a retired brigadier in a most romantic style; an anonymous contribution that ran to two pages in tribute to the Scottish countryside; several of course on the subject of love; and one dedicated to a dead spaniel called Margaret. Some were better than others and the style varied hugely, so what had made them all stand out to Pickering so that he tore them to form a new collection? As Cage laid them out on the floor before him, the connection became obvious. None of the poems had been illustrated by Pickering: all the pages held words alone.

He shuffled everything away and stood up to refill his tumbler. His stomach growled, unhappy to be fed more alcohol when it really needed sustenance. The wall between the window and the bed was hung with Moses's small art collection – ten or so illustrations, placed without symmetry but no doubt with much thought and precision. But Cage barely focussed on them as his brain fought to make sense of the file of poems. Had Moses simply not *liked* them? Was that his reason not to illustrate their appearance in the magazine? Or did they represent some kind of personal deficiency on Pickering's account, a file of failures that he kept in the hope that he would one day unlock new inspiration and complete the illustrations at last?

Cage shook his head. However intriguing, it was not the mystery he was here to solve. He glanced around the room quickly once more. There was nothing here that was going to help him find Moses Pickering.

He shrugged down the last of the whisky, then reached for the lamp on the desk. He had to lunge quickly to catch the glass lantern that slid sideways as he lifted the thing up. He secured it precariously beneath his chin as he grabbed the door handle and turned to see the room one last time.

That was when it hit him. It should have been the first thing he noticed. He lurched back towards Pickering's art collection. The illustrations had, in fact, been arranged symmetrically, but three of them were missing, their previously occupied places marked with brass hooks.

The Rubens drawings weren't there. The most valuable possessions Pickering had owned. Had Mrs Chappelhow purloined them, perhaps? Or Cross? Or one of his men? But no, Jack Cross was not a thief – he was far too fond of the moral high ground. And the drawings were not obviously worth a small fortune compared to other, larger and more striking prints in the collection. Cage thought about the four empty hangers in the armoire, and the conclusion seemed inescapable. Moses Pickering had taken the drawings. He had returned here that night, packed some clothes and treasured possessions, then left.

Where the hell had he gone?

On his way back down the stairs, Cage only just avoided the missing tread. Keeping both hands on the lamp, he followed his nose to the kitchen, a surprisingly fine aroma of cinnamon guiding the way. God, he was hungry.

The kitchen was well lit, and the range gave off a powerful and welcome heat. Bessie Chappelhow nodded to him but continued pounding spices with a mallet, holding it with both hands. The scent of cloves and braising apples added to the heady mix and made him salivate. He thrust the lamp down and walked towards her, wanting to see her eyes when she answered his next question.

'When did you last see Moses Pickering?'

But her gaze returned to her work as she answered. 'I already told 'em. Monday morning after breakfast.'

'What did he take with him?'

She shrugged. 'Don't know. Didn't see him go.'

A door stood open to a cosy parlour beyond. An old man in a smoking jacket was reading a newspaper and filling a pipe at a table laid for one. Mrs Chappelhow caught his line of sight and moved hastily to shut the door, her eyes still cast down.

'And you are certain he did not return that evening?'

She picked up her mallet, giving him only a brisk nod.

'Might I talk with your other guest?'

She looked at him then, a flash of fear in her eyes before she recovered herself. 'Mr Manners is not to be disturbed. Besides, he's not all there these days. He can't tell one day from the next.'

Cage leaned down, his hands on the table, and asked a question he'd asked a hundred times before. 'Why are you lying, Mrs Chappelhow?'

She dropped the mallet and rubbed her hands on her apron. 'What did you say your name was? You don't look like no officer of the law to me.' She stared up at him, not so easily intimidated as he had hoped. The silence continued for a few moments, but he could see he would get nothing further from her on the subject.

'I shall see myself out.'

A smirk was all he got in return.

Cage stumbled in the dark towards the lobby, feeling his way along the panelled walls, certain he could hear the rustle of rodents' claws across the cold stone floor. He pulled back the stiff bolts on the main door, and waited for the dusting of old plaster to fall before stepping outside.

He was grateful to see the moon as it guided his way through the compacted ice to the New Inn a mile or so back along the road. He dined there partly to spite the lying Bessie Chappelhow, although he was not able to resist ordering the apple pie. The place was cheap, thankfully, and he tried not to think of his dwindling resources. A man had to eat, for God's sake.

The food helped to clear his head. The mysteries of the evening – the file of poems, Moses's deliberate departure, the landlady's lies – were mere distraction from the task in hand. Pincott's words replayed themselves: *find Pickering, prove him innocent, or point the finger elsewhere.* Nothing he had found had altered those stark choices.

So what next? As far as Pickering was concerned, he had to hope that Cross might find the man for him, and that Cage could work his magic in the courtroom once more. Cage still could not believe him guilty of such a crime, but even if Pickering came to light, pointing the finger elsewhere would play the vital role, either way.

If today had been about finding Moses, tomorrow was about something else entirely. Who had really killed those boys?

Cage had his suspicions.

CHAPTER TEN

Cage woke to the sun, bright yellow in a blue sky, ready to shine its light on the truth. He took his time making tea, heaping in four spoons of crusted old sugar as a kind of breakfast. Then he took out his strongbox and forced himself to face the uncomfortable reality: three pounds, ten shillings and three pence.

As he slammed his front door behind him, the cold air bit deep. His first stop was to purchase a pair of ugly workman's mittens that set him back almost two shillings, but it was still cheaper than hiring cabs everywhere. It was the omnibus and his own boots from now on.

His second stop was the Farrier's Arms. He needed to get an urgent note to Pincott, and only a few were trusted to know where he could be found. Message safely dispatched, he stood in line on the freezing Whitechapel Road and waited for the omnibus that would take him into the city, where he could catch another towards Holland Park. The last leg of the journey saw him wedged on the knife plate of the top deck, his earlobes aching with cold and his eyes blinded by the sun.

The wealthy Crewler family had never forgiven Cage for the role he had played in the aftermath of their youngest son's demise. Moses Pickering had been their tenant, and they were the first to call suspicion down on his head when their precious boy was brutally murdered in his own home. Edmund Crewler, the dominating patriarch who had made his fortune importing silks and other luxuries from the Far East, had died two years after the trial. With the sole surviving son, Leland, no doubt at work in the Crewler company offices in Threadneedle Street, Cage saw his opportunity.

It took him some time to find the entrance to Sheldrake House, the Crewler estate. He wandered the street several times looking for Moses's gatehouse, but failed to find it. Realisation finally dawned – the gatehouse had been demolished and in its stead stood a modern mews, the previously imposing entrance now reduced to a modest driveway. One of the iron gates was propped open with a servant's basket full of groceries, and Cage slipped through.

The brick façade of Sheldrake House was bathed in sunlight, but Cage could immediately see that the grounds had been significantly curtailed. A straight line of spindly plane trees to the west did a poor job of disguising the chaos of building work beyond. The mammoth house now sat disproportionately in its plot. It had only been a few years since the old man had died. Was Leland's management already driving the once-thriving Crewler name to penury?

Cage removed his mittens and shoved them into his pockets as he approached the portico. The iron bell pull was cold to the touch as he tugged hard. The first time he had visited here had been with Emma, in the very first days of their acquaintance, a meeting that had come to nought in pleading Pickering's innocence with the dead boy's pompous father and entitled elder brother. Leland Crewler had turned whatever grief he felt into one single, strident emotion – anger. It had seemed a curious alchemy to Cage.

He heard footsteps, then the door swung open. He recognised the butler immediately, a man with coiffed grey hair and a barrel chest puffed out like a frigate bird. He just had to hope the man would not be able to place his own face.

'Good morning, my name is Charlie Dossett, my father was an old friend of the late Mr Crewler's, from India. We visited here just the once on our travels several years ago. Perhaps you remember me?'

The butler smiled. He'd have welcomed Satan over the threshold rather than admit to a failing of memory. 'Of course, Mr Dossett, do come in.'

The hexagonal hallway was all angles, shiny and hard with a marble floor and dove-grey walls, the panels picked out in purest white as they towered towards the dome overhead. Cage shivered, although it must have been warmer in here than it had been outside.

'Is Mrs Crewler at home?'

'Indeed, sir. I'm sure she will be delighted to see you. She has little company these days. Dossett, did you say?'

'Indeed. Charles, although she will know me best as Charlie, I think.'

'You mustn't mind but I'm afraid Madam's memory is not what it was. Do not be offended if she doesn't recall you at first.'

Cage was counting on it.

'Might I suggest you remove your coat, sir? Mrs Crewler spends most of her days in the hothouse, she finds it eases her pains.'

'Maybe when I have warmed up.' The last thing Cage could imagine right now was feeling overheated.

He followed the butler. The opulent high ceilings and pastel walls continued through a maze of rooms stuffed with delicate tables, shimmering silk drapes and sofas not meant for sitting on. Every piece of furniture looked as if it might shatter the moment you touched it. If he were Harriet Crewler, he wouldn't spend any time in this ice palace either.

The garden room was attached to the rear of the house. As they approached, condensation ran in branching rivers down the glass doors and puddled on the polished floor. Beyond he could see only a haze of green. When the butler opened the door, he stepped gingerly to the side as a cloud of steam billowed through.

The heat was initially welcome as Cage followed the man inside. Their path led them through a forest of palm trees, their upper fronds flattened against the ceiling of glass some twenty feet above them. Cage could feel his cheek grow wet, and he pushed his hair back, certain it was growing more lively by the second in the humidity. The smell was foul and sickly, as if the air itself was rotting around him.

At the end of the path, he saw her. A tiny, crooked figure wrapped in blankets and sunk into a bath chair far too large for her. She was dozing: one hand curled like a claw in her lap while the other lay atop a pile of books stacked on a small table beside her, fingers splayed as if to prevent someone stealing them while she slumbered. The woman must be barely sixty years old, but the early dementia, already in evidence five years earlier, had eaten away at her body as much as her mind.

The butler touched her arm gently, but she bolted awake, her shoulders hunching forward as if expecting a blow. The man whispered in her ear and her eyes looked up and about, squinting towards Cage without really focussing.

Cage seized the initiative. 'Charlie Dossett. James's son. You remember James, do you not?'

She paused, studying only his boots, then nodded.

Satisfied, the butler straightened. 'May I get you anything, sir? Some water, perhaps?'

Water would have been much appreciated in the sapping heat, but Cage didn't wish for further interruption. 'No, thank you, I shall just sit with her for a while, if I may.'

'Very well. If you need anything, just ring.' The man indicated a cord that hung down beside her, then backed away.

Cage pulled up a cane chair, which he planted firmly in front of Harriet Crewler. He unbuttoned his coat and wiped his brow with a handkerchief. All the while her eyes remained focussed on his feet.

'It is wet outside.' Her voice was soft and young.

'Snowing. Almost two days now.'

'So cold, everywhere.' She huddled her hands beneath her blankets, pulling them further up her skeletal form.

'The last time I was here, your dear husband Edmund was kind enough to show me around, but we had no time to explore this place. Astonishing, I have to say. Quite the collection.'

Her eyes finally reached Cage's face. 'Edmund does not like it here. The smell, it is too much.'

'It is most strong.'

She smiled. 'The Devil's snare. They say the odour can drive one to madness. Although the flowers themselves smell like paradise should.'

He looked around. 'Which plant is it?'

'Right there.'

He turned sharply in his seat. Behind him was a bush, about chest height. The leaves were brackish, as jagged as holly.

White trumpet flowers bent the branches down, like heavy fruit. At the base he could see a profusion of seed pods, heavily armoured with long spines.

'The Amazon Indians use it to poison their spears and fishing hooks. Hindu monks use it to distil a broth that brings their ancestors to them in dreams.'

'Should we be sitting so close?'

A laugh caught in her throat and he turned back. 'Men can kill far more easily than a plant. Perhaps I should not sit so close to you?'

He saw his opening. 'Men can be cruel. They can take what we love from us.'

She held his gaze, her countenance unchanged, as if she had not heard. He was about to speak again, but he saw her eyes glisten, and a single tear roll crookedly down her wrinkled cheek: condensation in a cold world.

'Nathaniel. My boy.'

He nodded. 'I was sorry to hear of your loss.'

Her hand wandered back to the stack of books beside her. The topmost volume was an old compendium of exotic species. She picked it up, and opened it to a marked page. The paper was curling and damp, despite the wax inserts that sought to protect the plates. He had lost her, he thought, until he saw that the bookmark was in fact a photograph. Her hand shook as she handed it to him.

Cage examined the image of Nathaniel Crewler. Five years ago, he had been of no mind to reflect on the victim, so pre-occupied had he been with his client's defence. And when he had last been to this place, the grief had felt so raw and churning it was as if the boy yet lived, running through the corridors, just out of sight, as if he were simply part of the game Cage was playing. All he had known were the bare facts: Nathaniel Crewler had been a lively and artistic child, born late to his almost elderly parents. When the new tenant, Moses Pickering, had moved in, Nathaniel had befriended him, showing an interest in his work. It was this creative friendship with the boy, and Pickering's lack of masculine presence, that had really been the key evidence against him.

The portrait before him now was elaborately composed. The teenage Nathaniel stood proud, a toga wrapped loosely about him and a wreath upon his head in the style of a Roman emperor. His skinny arm held a spear, jabbed into the podium on which he stood. The boy appeared to be smiling, his lips pressed together as if he had been told not to. But Cage could discern nothing more. The image was fading, the chemicals casting the boy in shades of green, like a corpse.

He passed it back to her. 'A vignette?'

She nodded happily. 'The boys like to play. Leland loves his new camera. But the smell, my word! Edmund hates the smell. The whole world would be a better place if it didn't *smell* so much, he says.'

Her mind had jumped to happier times, and it felt cruel to bring her back. 'What happened to him, Harriet? What happened to Nathaniel?'

She put the photograph back in the book and closed it, before replacing it with care on the table beside her. Beneath it lay a thick leather volume, the words *address book* emblazoned in gold.

'He went to bed one night, and never came down again.'

'Leland must miss him terribly. All the fun they had.'

She grew more animated. 'Ask Leland to show you his *cartes de visite*! They are in his study, a whole wall of them! One year, it was our midsummer party, and all the guests came as faeries, or goblins and other etherea. I dressed as a wood nymph! Leland had us all pose in various tableaux, just where the garden meets the park. Such a time we had – and the portrait was spectacular.' She looked up at him, eyes shining. 'But you were there, were you not? I remember you, and your lady, striking, with dark hair—'

Cage jumped in quickly. 'Titania and Oberon. We did our best at such short notice for we had just returned from India.'

'Shakespeare! Leland loves to use the Bard for his muse. He even made his father pose as King Lear, last Christmas I think. The rest of us dressed as his daughters. Edmund was not amused, but mostly it is Nathaniel who joins in, Ophelia to Leland's Hamlet, Desdemona to his Othello—'

Cage leant forward so suddenly that Harriet Crewler jumped.

He put out a calming hand. 'Desdemona, you say?'

She twisted her blankets in her gnarled hands. 'Who?'

'Leland – he had Nathaniel dress as Desdemona?'

'Nathaniel, my dear sweet boy, I . . .'

Her hands turned to the book by her side once more. 'I have a photograph here.'

'I know, Harriet, I have seen it.'

But his words fell on deaf ears, and she held out the image towards him again with a shaking hand.

He took it, his heart moved by her predicament, trapped in this cycle of remembering and forgetting, the loss felt anew each time.

He looked once more at the image of Nathanial Crewler, dressed up for his brother's entertainment. Had all this been known, he wondered? Would Cross not have explored such family dynamics? An elder brother with a passion for staged vignettes that involved his younger sibling masquerading as women. One woman in particular should have struck a chord: Desdemona, strangled to death in her own bed by her jealous lover.

He needed to find a way into Leland's study, so he could examine this wall of make-believe.

'I should leave you now, to rest.'

Her eyes had drifted down once more, her previous show of energy now depleted.

He stood up, which roused her again. 'Some tea, perhaps? Edmund will be home soon.'

She reached for the cord but he stayed her hand.

'I have no time, sadly. Perhaps before I go I should update my details in your address book, then we may find each other easily again?'

He reached down to the table. It was a long shot, but worth a try. As Justin said, the Crewlers had held the address of Pickering's aunt at some point, and the book did not appear to be a recent acquisition.

Harriet Crewler's eyes had closed, and her mouth had fallen open. He grabbed the book and began to flip through; a few pages fell to the ground but he ignored them. The heat was dizzying now that he was on his feet, and the stink of decay even more noxious.

He found the pages for 'P' and scanned them quickly. No Pickerings. Damn. Did this Aunt Lucille even have the same surname? He started back at 'A', looking for a Lucille, and a Kent address, a needle in this haystack of disremembered acquaintances, who in turn had no doubt forgotten the sad old woman now snoring gently in her bath chair.

'What the hell are you doing here?'

Cage dropped the book on the table and spun around to see Leland Crewler marching towards him, the butler in tow. Crewler was a short man with a boxer's build, his beard carved to a point, like a knife.

Cage held one hand up in defence, while the other stuffed the photograph he still held of Nathaniel Crewler into his coat pocket.

Leland shouted, 'Get out of my house!'

'What little there is left of it. Struggling to pay the bills without your father's help?'

Leland Crewler shoved him hard and Cage almost toppled into the old woman's lap, causing her to stir once more.

'Leland! Look, James has come for tea!'

Leland's voice was low, but deadly, as he leant close to Cage. 'Telling lies to a dying woman. How low can you go, Lackmann?'

Cage straightened up. 'As low as I have to go to find the truth. Tell me Leland, where were you this Monday night past?'

There was a flash of uncertainty in Leland's eyes as he said, 'That is none of your damned business. What has my mother been saying to you?'

Cage smiled. 'Now, how does it go? "Beware, my lord, of jealousy; It is the green-ey'd monster, which doth mock the meat it feeds on."'

Leland's face was cold and blank. 'Get out of my house.'

CHAPTER ELEVEN

The Farrier's Arms was busy when he returned to Whitechapel. He took what was offered – a jug of ale and a mutton pie – and retreated to a corner table.

Once he had eaten, he pulled out the stolen picture of Nathaniel Crewler. He slipped the other photograph from his breast pocket and placed them side by side, hoping to see something new. But they were impossible to compare, one a blurred image taken at a distance, the other a brutal close-up: the black lashes, the painted mouth. Would Nathaniel Crewler, dressed as Desdemona or Ophelia, have looked like this?

'Afternoon.'

Cage hadn't seen the pharmacist approach. He shuffled the pictures away as the dwarf pulled himself into a spare chair. Once settled, he slid a piece of paper across the table with one finger, always fond of a little drama.

'That was quick.' Cage unfolded the note, and for several moments stared at the name and address written there. 'It's not what I expected.'

'Too close to home.'

Literally. The dead boy's name was Baxter Spring, and he had lived in Weaver Street, less than half a mile from Cage's own house. It was known to be one of the more dangerous streets in Whitechapel – even Pincott struggled to exert any authority there. Poor Baxter Spring, growing up there, dying there. At least Cage had a name now.

'Tell him I'm grateful for this.'

The pharmacist smiled. 'It comes with a message. Do I need to deliver it?'

'Please don't. What's your name, by the way? I never asked.'

The smile was colder this time. 'People rarely do. Until they're in trouble.'

Fair enough.

'There is something else. I went back to the Crewlers' this morning. We need to send someone in. Find some photographs.'

'We?'

'It's not exactly my speciality.'

'I'll ask.' The little man pushed himself away from the table and slipped to the floor. 'It's Merriwether, by the way.'

Baxter Spring of Weaver Street. It was a disappointing revelation. How could there be any connection to the Crewler family, who lived ten miles and another world away? Maybe the scene of the crime would reveal something – anything, for God's sake. He didn't have to build a watertight case against Leland Crewler, but he needed more smoke than this to compose the spectre of someone other than Moses Pickering hovering over the dead bodies of those two boys.

Weaver Street. As he approached the corner, he saw three men loitering in the cold, a fire glowering hopelessly in some makeshift brazier. He sauntered past, ignoring their stares, but the crunch of ice told him he was being followed.

He had to guess the numbers of the houses, counting up

from the only one he could see which identified itself with a tin plaque. Part of him admired the defiance of it all – no visitors wanted or required here. Finding what he hoped was the right one, he knocked on the badly fitting door, held in place only by a top bolt on the inside that was visible through the rotting wood.

There was no answer so he knocked again, louder this time. Immediately he heard a window slam open above.

'What the hell do you want?'

Cage stepped back and looked up. The face leering down at him was fleshy and pink, a sheen of sweat visible on the man's cheeks as he scratched at the black stubble across his head and jowls. Cage could almost smell the alcohol.

'I'm sorry to bother you. I work with Detective Cross. I have more questions.'

The man stared at him through unfocussed eyes, then retreated back from the window. Minutes later, the bolt shot back and the door opened. Up close the man was huge, towering over him on unsteady feet.

'Show me.'

'I don't carry identification. I'm a crime-scene expert. A doctor, not a policeman.' Was this going to work?

'Too late for a bloody doctor.'

'Still. The sooner I come in the sooner I will be gone.'

The man seemed open to basic logic in his current state. He stepped back, still leaning on the door for support, and Cage squeezed past him into the dingy little house. The front door slammed, leaving them in virtual darkness, the only light coming from the landing above.

'You'll want the attic.'

Cage went first, climbing the narrow stairs as the man

lumbered behind him. On the first floor, the door was open to the front room. A filthy mattress lay directly on the boards, an impressive number of empty bottles lined up beside it.

The staircase wound up further to a tiny attic door, but the man was no longer following him. One set of stairs had been enough as he made for the front room and slumped onto the grubby mattress. Cage followed him in.

'You're the boy's father? Mr Spring?'

The man laughed as he rolled onto his back. 'Who knows? His mother said so, but she was a conniving little bitch. Just like him.'

The grief was overwhelming.

'And it was just the two of you living here?'

'Kicked his sister out years ago. Whore.'

'When did you last see Baxter?'

'No idea. He stayed up there. I stayed down here. Worked for everyone.'

'And you heard nothing? Saw no one?'

The man sat up and grabbed a bottle. 'I've told you lot all this.' He waved the bottle in the air. 'So why don't you fuck off?'

'Did you raise the alarm? How did you know he was dead?'

'Something dripping on my face. That bitch's piss and shit all over me, coming through the ceiling.' He took a swig from the bottle, his face briefly haunted by the memory of such inconvenience.

Cage looked up at the ceiling. Chunks of plaster had rotted away, leaving only bare boards above them.

Twice the man had called his son a bitch, which meant only one thing to men like Spring.

'Did Baxter have friends? Men friends, perhaps?'

'This ain't a molly house! Ask that do-gooder priest that always hangs around.' The man lay back down, an arm across his face.

This was going nowhere. Cage turned back from the doorway and towards the stairs.

'Fucking Poet.'

He stopped in his tracks. Had Spring recognised him from somewhere? He looked back over his shoulder, but the man was falling asleep, the bottle tipping over in his hand.

Cage climbed the final flight of stairs and opened the door to the attic. He immediately recognised the room from the photographs, although the furniture had been righted, and the bed had been stripped. It was a neat space, the fireplace recently swept and the window free of grime – not the work of Scotland Yard but rather the previous occupant. Cage walked around the bed towards the window. There was no sign now of where Baxter Spring had lain in a tangled sheet.

Cage sat down on the bed, allowing the silence of the room to envelop him. There was a calm here, a stillness, some kind of peace. It was not what he expected to feel in a room that had seen a life taken so brutally. He looked down to the floor once more, tried to imagine the boy's body, broken and cast aside, but he could not. The serenity of this room did not belong to death, for death was never serene, not to Cage. Most of us go brawling and howling over the abyss; only a few lean forward willingly, like Charlie Moore, whose grave he would visit once more tomorrow with his mother. But there had been no peace in Charlie's death, only despair.

There were few places to search and he started with the bedside chest. The top drawers were empty, the bottom containing only some worn undergarments and two nubs of candle, almost useless but hoarded nonetheless. A fold-out table had been swept bare, leaving just a single broken pencil that had become wedged in the fold.

That left the wardrobe, a small affair with one knob missing. It was empty – presumably Cross had cleared the place out. The frustration of it all roiled within once more. Cage was no detective – what the hell was he doing? With more aggression than was required, he pulled the table into the room, not caring about the noise he made. Nothing had fallen behind. The chest scraped across the boards as he yanked it forward, but he found only a dusty handkerchief beneath. With a final effort, he shunted the bed aside with his knee, and this time the grind of metal produced a shout from below.

'Shuddup!'

Cage looked at the square of wall he had revealed and dropped to his haunches. The words were written in a neat script, the pencil marks gouged precisely into the plaster.

Beauty is truth, truth beauty – that is all
Ye know on earth, and all ye need to know.

He recognised the poem. Keats's 'Ode on a Grecian Urn'. What comfort did those hidden words offer Baxter Spring? Truth and beauty were rare qualities in Whitechapel. Perhaps he carved them here after a particularly savage beating from his father, a rebellion of sorts against the world he found himself in. But they were only words, and they hadn't saved him in the end.

Cage stood up and went to the window, staring up at the fading sky through the sparkling panes of glass. The boy would have stood here, Cage knew, silent in the dark as he waited for dawn to come. He had come here for answers, but was leaving only with another question.

Who were you, Baxter Spring?

CHAPTER TWELVE

Outside, the light had all but gone and the cold bit deep in Cage's lungs. The man who had followed him earlier was leaning against the wall opposite, arms folded in easy intimidation. Cage smiled and walked directly across the road towards him. The man straightened, the approach unexpected.

'A do-gooder priest?' asked Cage. 'Can't be many of them around here.'

'Bugger off.'

'Happily. Just point me in the right direction.'

The man nodded tersely towards the south. Cage turned to look, mentally mapping the city streets towards the docks.

'St Thomas?'

Cage took the man's silence for assent.

Ten minutes later, Cage stood in front of the church of St Thomas. He must have walked past it a hundred times, a solid medieval structure hemmed in by the slums of the East End. A row of tall cypress trees and a strip of graveyard either side guarded its boundaries, the dead keeping the living at bay.

He found the sexton in the newly built porch, a single gaslight casting a bucolic halo around him as he sharpened his scythe with slow, patient strokes. He directed Cage to the vicarage, no more than an end-of-terrace house a few streets away. The sexton gave him a name too – the Reverend Archie Weston. So not a priest, but a reverend – and not Archibald, but Archie. That told Cage what to expect: one of those young, earnest reformers who sprinkled his sermons with communist epithets that would have even the atheist Engels applauding, if such a thing were allowed in church. Cage didn't know – he'd seldom been in one.

His foresight proved accurate when the blue door of the vicarage was opened and a tall, ginger-haired man, complete with freckles, greeted him with a jaunty, 'Afternoon! How can I help you?'

'Good afternoon!' The man's enthusiasm was infectious. 'I'd like to talk to you about Baxter Spring, if I may. I am working with Detective Cross on the matter.'

The smile remained, effortlessly morphing to a thoughtful, bittersweet sadness. 'Of course. Do come in. It's Mr Lackmann, is it not? You've been pointed out to me on the street a few times.'

Caught in a lie, he could feel the flush of humiliation rise. But there was no judgement or sense of victory in the reverend's benign gaze, and Cage felt a rare compulsion to honesty.

'You have caught me, sir. In the last few days, lies about my interest here have been easier to tell than the truth.'

'They always are.'

'Indeed.'

The man stepped aside. 'Please.'

Cage entered the hall and followed the reverend into a study. The walls were lined with books and framed photographs. The room was warm without being stuffy, a fire snapping happily in the grate.

Cage's eye was immediately drawn by the photographs – vivid portraits of Whitechapel life. He recognised the streets and their people, captured without artifice. In one image, three prostitutes looked over their shoulders directly at him, no attempt to hide their profession, their thin faces smiling with reckless defiance. In yet another, a young girl sat on the pavement, head resting on her hand, her steady gaze as old as the hills.

'You took these?'

'Yes. A hobby that has become quite an obsession.'

'It seems quite the thing these days.'

Reverend Weston stood beside Cage as he continued to examine the faces he had seen every day of his life, as if seeing them for the first time. 'They are quite something, I will admit.'

'My grand project,' the reverend said with a smile of self-effacement. 'I hope to document the East End. I am planning a book, to tell the world of this place: the strength of character, the privations, and yet Christ still lives here.'

'Does the world want to know?'

'Probably not.' Archie Weston moved to one of the chairs by the fire and sat down, waving Cage towards the other. 'There have been books published, of course, describing how people live, but words can never be the whole truth. The author is ever present, judging what he sees, whether he wishes to or not. The very words he chooses draw the veil one can never quite penetrate. A camera tells the truth always.'

Cage sat down and warmed his hands at the fire. 'But as you know, I make my living painting pictures with words.'

The reverend smiled. 'And are those pictures truthful?'

'Sometimes.' Is this what confession would feel like? 'These people, the ones who pointed me out to you, they no doubt had an opinion.'

'They did.'

Cage pressed no further. He was of no mind to hear the church-going residents of Whitechapel's judgements on himself. 'Tell me about Baxter Spring. I have just come from his home. His father, quite the character, pointed me to you.'

'Reggie Spring. Resident drunk and bully. I knew the mother before she died, must be three years ago now. She had been cleaning for us here since we arrived seven years ago; Reggie drank her wages so we fed her too. Baxter would come sometimes. We have always run a small ragged school, most recently from the new parish room. Baxter used to attend until his mother died – a fearful bout of pneumonia took her – the winter of seventy-eight. Reggie stopped Baxter coming to school, but he still managed to defy his father once in a while. Baxter had quite the thirst for knowledge, and my wife and I were fond of him. Even at a young age, he had a certain intensity.' The bittersweet smile had returned, fond memories battling with the grief of a wasted life.

'How old was he?'

Archie Weston shrugged. 'Not sure. Fifteen, maybe? He was small for his age.'

Cage thought of the photograph he carried, the barely-there stubble of a boy on the cusp of the manhood that might have saved him. 'I found some lines of poetry, written on the wall behind his bed. Truth is beauty. Keats.'

'Ah, he loved that poem! He found it in the anthology I leant him a few years ago.'

Cage nodded. 'He had good taste, for a young boy.'

Archie Weston sprang to his feet suddenly. 'Quite a fortuitous comment, you will see!' He began to rummage through a pile of papers on his desk. 'Once the authorities had left, I took the liberty of removing some of Baxter's things. The idea of Reggie Spring getting his hands on Baxter's . . . well, his thoughts shall we say . . .' He held up a notebook. 'Here it is!'

He passed it to Cage. It was a small, cheap thing, the cardboard cover rough to the touch, the pages as thin as tissue. On the front were printed the words *Favourite Poems*. Cage held it in his hands for a moment. So here was the soul of Baxter Spring he had been unable to locate in the little attic room.

He opened it, his eyes struggling to adjust. The script was tiny and neat, the paper obviously precious. There were many more poems by Keats, Wordsworth too, and Blake. Others Cage had never heard of, but he read them carefully, wanting to respect the young boy's choices, although how they could help him in his worldly task he did not know.

The reverend interrupted his thoughts. 'It is near the middle. I think you will be surprised, gratified maybe.'

And there it was. 'The Sacrifice' by Cage Lackmann. Cage stared at the tiny letters, carefully copied, the poem fitting neatly on one page. Something inside him lurched. He was moved, obviously, but something else, too . . . the heavy clang of coincidence.

Cage looked up at the smiling reverend. 'Is this why you let me in?'

Archie Weston held his hands up. 'No. I did not intend to play a trick. I let you in because . . . I suppose I felt sorry for you.'

The man's pity was as surprising as it was unwelcome. Cage stood up and placed the notebook on the desk. 'Why on earth would you feel sorry for me?'

The man looked bewildered. 'I assumed you were looking for comfort, to understand Baxter and make amends, to deal with any sense of responsibility you felt—'

'Responsibility!' Cage shook his head in disbelief. 'I am sorry for his death, but I feel no responsibility for it. Moses Pickering did not kill Baxter Spring! He didn't even know him!'

Archie was on his feet, eyebrows raised. Then he said, 'You don't know, do you?'

'Know what?'

'Baxter was a poet too. A fine poet. He was to be published in the next edition of *Poetica Veridica.* He met them here, one day last week: Mr Kenward and Moses Pickering. They met in this very study to discuss the editing and illustration process. I had allowed him to use our address for correspondence. Baxter was so excited, as if his life was beginning. But it wasn't, was it?' The man's eyes glittered.

Cage put a hand on the back of the chair, saw that his knuckles were white. Why had Kenward said nothing? He looked down at his arm to see Archie Weston's hand there, dotted with freckles and fine red hairs that sprang across his tapered elegant fingers.

'Please, sit down again, I'll ask my wife to arrange some tea.'

Cage slumped into the chair as Archie briefly left the room. When he returned, he sat down beside Cage, his movements noiseless and graceful.

Cage said softly, 'You must think me quite the fool.'

'We are all fools. I am sorry to have told you the truth if it is the first time you have heard it. You must have been holding out hope this was some kind of misunderstanding.'

Cage closed his eyes. 'Detective Cross does not like me very much. No doubt he thought that if he withheld information, it would go worse for me.'

'Pickering was your friend?'

'No. He was a client. But I liked him.' God, this man was easy to talk to. He should have been a lawyer.

'You thought him innocent. I can tell.'

For Archie Weston, Cage's motivation seemed purer than it really was. 'You are someone who sees the best in people.'

The reverend's face turned earnest once more. 'We are not fixed as one thing or the other. There are only the choices we make.'

'And what about the choices that are made for you?'

'They can be harder to bear, and harder to forgive.'

Can't they, indeed. Cage stared into the heart of the fire, watching a log crumble slowly to ash. 'So, reverend, what did you think of Pickering, when you met him?'

'Please, call me Archie.' The man shrugged his shoulders. 'He made little impression, if I'm honest. It was Mr Kenward who did most of the talking, asking Baxter questions about his work, his inspirations. Mr Pickering simply listened, and observed. He took some notes, I believe, or was sketching, I'm not sure.'

The door opened and a female version of Archie Weston bustled into the room with a tray of tea and some buttered scones. Suddenly it seemed quite ridiculous. He should leave. It was degrading to sit here, wallowing in his failed career with a man he had never met.

'This is my wife, Elizabeth.'

She looked like an Elizabeth, with quick movements and an open face, and even her pale hair, pulled into a practical bun, looked capable of something. She poured two cups of tea with swift efficiency, smiled and left the room. They seemed a formidable partnership.

Cage drank and ate, although he wasn't particularly hungry; the scones would save him the expense of buying dinner. He took the last one from the plate.

'You have other clients?' his companion asked.

Cage put the scone down. Archie Weston was an observant man. 'Not really. Not after this.' Cage smiled to avoid his face doing anything else.

'In time, things will change.'

'Why are you being kind to me?'

Archie pointed at his collar, a wry look on his face.

Cage laughed and shook his head. He stood up. 'Thank you for your time, and your . . .' He waved his hand in the air helplessly.

'Sustenance?'

'Indeed. Do thank your wife for feeding me. Every little helps right now.' It was meant to be a joke. Cage put his hat on and pulled the mittens from his pockets – no point in hiding them now.

'Perhaps,' said Archie, 'if you wouldn't mind, I would very much like to take your photograph, to add it to my collection. I can also make a print for you, to keep. You have a strong face, noble, a portrait that should be taken.'

Cage opened the door and smiled back at the reverend. 'I'm not sure what the camera might have to say about me. If it always tells the truth, as you say.'

'Why don't we see? And I can pay. I always pay my subjects. Shall we say a sovereign?'

The sting of charity – a pound for sitting still. 'Maybe. I shall think on it.'

Archie Weston smiled. 'You know where we are.'

Cage looked around the room once more. His eyes fell on

Baxter's notebook; the desire to take it with him was as palpable as it was incomprehensible.

Archie followed his gaze. 'It seems you were no longer the only poet in Whitechapel.'

I never was, thought Cage.

CHAPTER THIRTEEN

That night, the ghosts returned. Emma, or the shape of her, the feel of her skin, her hands fisting in his hair as he grazed his teeth across her neck. And the sound of her, too, her laughter, low and intimate as she teased him, eyes wide with mischief at her own daring. But the laughter changed, its dimensions shifting, growing into a howl of yearning, until her cry of *do not leave me* was all he could feel or smell or even taste.

Charlie too, came to him, his back strong and shoulders down, silhouetted on a ledge against a masochistic ocean that whipped itself across the rocks below. He held the hand of a small, dark boy, the breeze ruffling his hair where a mother's hand should have been. The sky washed to black until there was just the man and the boy, and the ledge that led nowhere. It was the boy who stepped forward first; he always did, Charlie following half a pace behind. That half a pace, that momentary reluctance, felt like the whole world was breaking, and Cage woke once more.

His sweat was damp and cold against the sheets and he threw the blankets back, the freezing air a welcome relief. Dawn was almost come; Cage could feel it stalking behind the thick snow clouds, looking for an opening. After the revelations of yesterday, it had been all he could do to stop himself from going straight to the Kenwards. But there had been sufficient calculation left in his lawyer's brain to know that little would come of a late-night altercation with Justin Kenward, and the dangerous territory his anger might lead him towards.

He would walk there now this morning, a few hours to clear his head, some strong coffee along the route, and surprise them at breakfast.

A fresh covering of snow greeted him as he stepped out, but it seemed less cold than it had in recent days. His boots crunched as he stamped towards the west of the city, his purpose clear and focussed, even if his thoughts were not.

What have you done, Moses? Round and round it went, but still he could not believe it. Gentle, fastidious Moses Pickering, the murderer of two young boys? Surely not. Both crimes had involved artifice, and control, a kind of tyranny in what those boys had been forced to do that sat so ill with Pickering's apparent nature. Yesterday, he had been undone by the revelation of Pickering's connection to Baxter Spring. Maybe it was the warmth of Archie Weston's hearth and home, or the man himself, or the empathy he had felt for the boy poet, but he had temporarily forgotten his real purpose. It mattered not whether Moses was innocent, the only thing that mattered was what could be proved. He could destroy any circumstantial case, and hint at another's involvement.

Until Cross could place Pickering with his hands about the boy's throat, all was not lost.

He knew he needed to see Cross again – the man was not above holding Moses in custody without communication with his lawyer, hoping to sweat a confession from the frightened man. But Cage was due to meet Honor later that morning to make their annual pilgrimage, and she would not be short-changed of his time.

The sky was blushing pink by the time he reached Notting Hill. The house on Elgin Gardens was just waking up. He waited until the drapes were pulled back in the front window before ascending the steps and knocking on the door. To his surprise, the maid was unperturbed at such an early visit, as if she had been expecting him.

'Morning, Mr Lackmann. Mr and Mrs Kenward are just at breakfast. Will you join them, sir?'

'I think I will.'

Justin Kenward emerged from the dining room. 'Cage! Come in. I tried to reach you yesterday but to no avail. You got my note?'

What note? 'I'm here because I found out that you and Pickering knew the dead boy. Yet you neglected to tell me.'

Kenward threw his hands up in the air. 'I did not know the boy's identity when you were last here! Cross had said nothing, you know what he's like. Looking to catch me out, no doubt. He returned yesterday, and it all came as quite a shock, let me tell you. Please.' He took Cage by the arm, 'Come in. Join us.'

Cage allowed himself to be led into the dining room, temporarily wrong-footed by Kenward's explanation.

It didn't matter how much time he'd had to prepare himself, the shock of seeing her face hit again like a sledgehammer to his gut. The maid fussed about, laying a place for him while Justin poured out some tea and filled a plate with scrambled eggs and smoked mackerel from the buffet. Emma remained seated, her eyes wide and watchful as she sipped from her teacup. He stared back, the silence between them twitching with discomfort. Justin seemed oblivious as he bustled around Cage, alternating explanations with the serving of breakfast.

'Cross had hoped to lay a trap, I think, to see if we knew more than we did, but it never crossed my mind that the dead child would be poor Baxter. Why would it? There are thousands of children in this city, hundreds of thousands, and he had told me nothing of the boy's age or whereabouts. I hadn't asked. Maybe I should have done. Would you like some pepper? Emma, could you pass the pepper?'

'It's all right, thank you. This is perfect.' Cage lifted a forkful of mackerel to his mouth and tried not to choke on it under Emma's blank gaze.

'Of course, it made sense, I suppose, why Cross took some of Moses's paperwork away with him, although I think I told you, Moses was struggling to find the right approach for Baxter's poem – he had yet to make a start.'

Cage thought of the file of unillustrated poems he had found at Pickering's apartment, his own included. Would Baxter's contribution have also found its way there eventually?

'What else did Cross say? Is he any closer to finding Moses?'

Justin shook his head. 'He didn't say in so many words, but I don't think so. He made a big point of ensuring we contacted him if we heard from Moses in any way.'

Cage put his knife and fork down. The eggs were dry and the mackerel was greasy. Emma's plate remained empty. 'Tell me about this meeting, Justin. You, Pickering and the boy.' *The boy*, not Baxter: an attempt to keep his distance.

'We met at a vicarage, some reverend who had employed Baxter's mother and taken an interest in the boy. I was surprised at how young Baxter was – I mean, I knew he was young, under twenty, say, but his submission had not mentioned he was little more than a child.'

Emma poured herself another cup of tea. Cage watched her as Justin talked on: the long, pale fingers that held the lid of the teapot in place, her slim wrist, tendons straining, impossibly strong as it lifted the heavy pot to her cup and poured, turning sideways at the last moment with practised art to avoid a familiar drip, the quick movement of the milk jug, a splash and no more, then the stirring of the spoon, slow, habitual and thorough.

'The boy was most promising – unusually so. He had this quiet intensity that all poets aspire to impress upon you – present company excepted, of course! But with Baxter it felt genuine, without artifice. That such a talent should exist unnurtured struck me as a marvellous thing . . .'

Emma raised the cup to her lips and she blew gently across the surface before taking her first sip, her head dipping down, her eyes looking up to his as she did so.

Cage interrupted Justin's monologue. 'And Pickering? How did he behave during this encounter?'

Justin sat back in his chair. 'As I said to Cross, there was nothing untoward that I could see. As always, Moses said very little. He likes to observe sometimes, read the man behind the poem, or in this case the boy . . .'

Cage could imagine Pickering, taciturn and unobtrusive, allowing Kenward to prattle on as if everything that mattered could be articulated, and that which could not was therefore of no consequence.

'And what of the boy? What did you make of him? Any sense he was scared of something, or even someone?' Cage was clutching at straws now.

Kenward paused and looked up to the ceiling. It was obvious he recalled much of what he himself said in that meeting, but little of Baxter's responses. 'We talked about the publication process, some minor edits for scansion and punctuation, that kind of thing. He was relaxed about that, I remember. In fact, he seemed happy just to be published, didn't even ask about payment; it was the vicar who asked on his behalf. Baxter wanted the fee to be paid to him in cash, something about an untrustworthy father, I believe?'

'You could say that.' Cage smiled at Kenward's understatement. The man was a fool. He wanted to ask more: what sense did Kenward have of the boy's sexual maturity, his inclinations? Had there been any time for a brief private moment between Baxter and Pickering? But he might as well have asked the bloody mackerel. Its glass-eyed stare would capture more truth in this world than Kenward's inability to see beyond his own fascination with himself, like a puppy constantly surprised and delighted by his own tail.

Emma said to him, 'You're smiling.'

Thanks, Emma.

'I met the father, is all. A drunk and a bully.' They were Archie's words but he felt no need to change them. 'Untrustworthy indeed.'

Kenward shook his head. 'What a sorry show.'

'May I have a copy of the poem?' Cage asked. 'Then I should take my leave.'

'Hmm? Yes, of course!'

Justin was on his feet and halfway out of the room. Stupid, Cage should have made the request when he himself had already been at the door.

The thought of the silence they would make together was

too much to bear. He turned to Emma, looked at her full on. 'You think Moses did this?'

She smoothed a stray lock of hair into place. 'I asked you that once. Five years ago. You said it was a pointless question, that it didn't matter. All that matters is what can be proved.'

'So, it's a stupid question, but I want to know: do you think he did this?'

Her shoulders sagged briefly and a softness returned to her features. 'I know you're a poet, Cage, but sometimes a spade really is just a spade. I'm sorry for it.'

He nodded. 'I'm sorry for it, too.' Cage stood up, the sound of his name on her lips fluttering inside of him. 'Thank you for a lovely breakfast.'

Emma rose to her feet also. 'It was a terrible breakfast, but thank you for lying.'

He laughed softly, the old intimacies intact. He turned around. She was there, right behind him, all he could see. From down the hallway, he heard the study door open. He wasn't sure who moved first, whose hands reached out, whose mouth found whose.

'The copy I found is not the latest version with all the corrections. Cross took those, sadly.' Kenward lumbered back into the room.

They had pulled apart at the last moment, not even time for their eyes to meet and find intention or meaning.

'Thank you, Justin.' Cage's hands shook as he reached out and took the proffered page.

Emma had retreated. He heard the clatter of plates being cleared. Were her hands shaking too?

Kenward ran his hands through his hair. 'Perhaps I could ask you a question? I could do with your counsel here.' The man's face looked genuinely concerned on some matter.

Cage was already moving into the hallway. He couldn't look back.

At the front door, Kenward retrieved Cage's hat and coat for him. 'You see, I'm really not sure what the protocol might be. But I would very much like still to publish Baxter's poem. Would that be the right thing to do? Or the wrong thing? What do you think? I wouldn't want to do the wrong thing.'

Cage shrugged on his coat and took his mittens from his pockets. 'I'm not sure it really matters now.'

'Doesn't it? Oh well. In which case, I think that I shall. As a kind of memorial. Only who shall I pay? I wouldn't want to profit from it.'

Cage couldn't care less. 'Why not ask Archie Weston?'

'Who?'

Cage wanted to hit him then. 'The reverend. Baxter's friend.'

There, I finally said your name.

CHAPTER FOURTEEN

The Graves of Whitechapel
By Baxter Spring

I travel further, my feet relentless in their tread.
My journey is young, the ground still fresh
The journey is I, and I the journey;
The one impossible without the other.
Dandelion and velvet grass sigh beneath me,
The oaks my constant companions
Until they give way, by and by
To cypress and yew, to grass like thorns.
A chapel in white, its doors clamped shut
To lock me out or else to keep him in.
A graveyard stretches across the hill,
Liberal and wide, with space for many more.
First I find Joy, her gravestone tells of how
She died young, brittle-boned and afraid.
Then comes Love, whose death was expected,
By everyone else but she.
And here lies Hope, who perished quietly,

An illness that crept o'er her for many a year
Silent and disregarded, until it was too late.
My feet resume, steady in their stride
Until the last stone, whose tenant I am pleased to see,
The one I would gladly bury, if all the rest are dead:
For here lies Remembrance, the last to fall.
I yearn for the end of my journey,
Not for what it will bring, but to know
That all will be lost, in this place, one day.
And I might find peace once more.

'What are you reading?'

Honor held a compact close to her face as the cab rocked and rolled on their journey north to Highgate. She was attempting to powder her face despite the drifts and sudden potholes, although her complexion looked as perfect as ever to Cage.

'It's a poem.' He folded the paper once more and put it away. 'It can wait.'

Granger leant forward in his seat. 'How marvellous! You are writing again?' His jowls wobbled in time to the cab's rhythm.

'Me? No. It was written by another.'

Baxter. Baxter Spring.

He wondered why Moses had struggled with the poem's illustration. The imagery was clear, he thought: the trees, the graveyard, the graves themselves. Maybe Pickering had eschewed the obvious, and was reaching for something more profound.

But why did any of it matter? The boy was dead, his voice silenced. Nothing could bring him back, including the conviction of the rightful killer, whether that was Moses or not.

And nothing Cage could do would change Baxter's ending: his poem or his life.

The priority remained simple. Cage needed more mud to sling at Leland Crewler.

He turned to Granger. 'The make-up you use, wigs and so on. If money was no object, where would you go?'

'My dear boy, what a bizarre question. What interest have you in this?'

'A case.'

Neither Granger nor his mother had mentioned the coverage in the papers of the new murder. They had always lacked any real interest in what was going on in the world.

'Ah! Well, money or no, I would go where I always go: McKerrell and Hampton, on Long Acre, the only place for quality. There are inferior suppliers, but I wouldn't put that slap on my face.'

'We are almost there.' His mother spoke quietly, her eyes gazing out at the brightening sky. 'Look, the sun has almost appeared!'

Granger reached out with both his hands and took Honor's fingers in his. He smiled at her, forever her willing conspirator.

Cage's mother had always held to the belief that the sun appeared whenever they visited Charlie's grave, but her memory was selective. Cage remembered one visit in particular when he was about eleven; the puddles were so deep that the water had come over the top of his boots and frozen his feet so he could no longer feel them. Honor had knelt down at the grave despite the rain. A purple dress, he remembered, darkened to the colour of old blood by the sodden earth.

Today she wore the same black garb she had worn as Winnifred Latham in court, although it could not have looked more different on her. The scarf she had wrapped beneath her neckline was gone, her smooth décolletage now visible. But it was the change in posture that made it seem like a different dress. Her mother's shoulders were back and down, her neck long and proud, but there was something of Winnifred always behind her eyes.

When they reached the gates of the East Cemetery, the snow had been cleared from the main pathway. Honor walked ahead of them, her pace sombre, as if each step held meaning. Granger and Cage walked in silence behind.

The final part of their journey involved turning onto a smaller path, which had not yet been cleared. Honor held out her hand and lifted her skirts with the other. Cage stepped forward and linked elbows, manoeuvring her through the perilous peaks and troughs of the compacted snow.

The grave was plain, a simple stone surrounded by its more ostentatious neighbours. It must have cost his mother a small fortune nonetheless as she had bought the neighbouring plot also, ready for the day she would join him. Cage often wondered if the debt his mother took on to buy his resting place had been behind her motivation to sell Cage's own future to Obediah Pincott some years later.

Granger grasped his mother's other elbow and they gently lowered her to the ground before the gravestone.

'What do you remember of him, Cage?' she asked.

Always the same question. Every year he had to search for a new answer, grasping at wisps of something, pushing ever outwards into the darker reaches of his memory, avoiding the vivid truths that took centre stage.

'His inkwell – do you remember that? The lid that flipped up, with the tiny catch. I used to play with it, tip it upside down, roll it around the table, but it never spilled. He was so proud of it, but still I was allowed to play.'

His mother was smiling – he could tell by her voice. 'He liked his things, looked after them, but he was generous, too. He didn't have much, but the quality was always first rate. Do you remember his notebook? The finest leather, always making notes. He was going to write one day.'

Cage reached out a hand and laid it on her shoulder. It had begun to shake, as she called her grief forward with a spiritualist's ease.

One hand gripped Cage's, as the other traced the name carved plainly on the stone with her index finger. Charles Edgar Moore. Charlie. Uncle Charlie. The best man Cage had ever known.

A breeze moved through the trees, and the branches of the huge cedar that overhung them shivered in the cold.

'Why, Cage?'

This question, too, always the same. Was she hoping that as he grew older, he would be inducted into some special knowledge of what it was to be a man? The reasons they stayed, and the reasons they left? With a start, he realised he was now the same age as Charlie had been when he died. Thirty-three.

Honor ignored his silence. She was in full flow now. 'One day he was there. The next he was gone. Six months I waited, not a single word. Until that day, that awful day.'

Cage remembered it. The letter that came from the coroner's office in Scarborough – his mother's address had been the only one to be found in Charlie's lodgings. His mother's howls of grief had been the most shocking thing he had ever witnessed. She clung to his small body, overwhelming him, but he had stood it, holding her close, relishing her love. It gave him the strength to withstand the onslaught of her sorrow.

Honor had been allowed to claim Charlie's body, what the Scarborough rocks and the North Sea had left of it, since no one else had come forward and it saved the town the expense of a pauper's burial. His death had been deemed misadventure, in the absence of a suicide note. None of Charlie's things were returned, purloined no doubt by a rogue clerk or opportunistic landlady, and Cage had been glad of it, for he could not have borne to see anything of Charlie again.

His mother wept on, both hands atop the gravestone. Cage read the familiar inscription, Shakespeare, naturally:

Life's but a walking shadow, a poor player
That struts and frets his hour upon the stage
And then is heard no more: it is a tale
Told by an idiot, full of sound and fury,
Signifying nothing.

The inscription was chiselled simply, the money spent on the number of words rather than their quality. His mother had chosen them, although Charlie had been nothing like Macbeth. He had lived and died a romantic, desolate maybe, like Baxter Spring, but he had never been a cynic.

His mother's grief was waning, releasing itself into the indifferent air. She stood without assistance, her gaze remaining on the headstone. Cage stood alongside her, the least he could do.

'Love is a curse, Cage.'

'I know it.'

She half-turned. 'You have seen her again? As part of this –' she waved her hand in the air '– Pickering issue?'

Issue? It was a calamity. 'Yes. She is unchanged – outwardly, at least.'

His battered heart was the least of his problems at the moment. He grasped her hand. 'I'm in trouble, Mother. Pincott, he is refusing to employ me until I can clear Pickering's name and restore my own. I don't know that I can do it.' Her hand dropped but he kept hold of it all the same. 'I will try, obviously. I have some ideas, but I lack resources. The pipeline was cut off so suddenly, I had no chance to plan. There are debts . . .'

She pulled her hand from his and placed a finger on his lips. She was smiling, and the tears were drying on her cheeks. 'Did I not teach you to survive?'

'Yes. Yes, you did.'

'So survive.'

She put her arm through his and gently pulled him back to the path. 'Let us return home before it turns. I don't like the look of this sky. I think this is the coldest it's ever been on this day. Do you remember the time it was so warm the daffodils had bloomed early? When was that?'

Their feet crunched through the snow as they followed Granger back to the main driveway. Their pace was shiftless, a mother and son, strolling arm in arm through a cold land.

CHAPTER FIFTEEN

They rode back into town in silence. His mother slept most of the way, her face as peaceful as it was perfect. The cab dropped Cage in Covent Garden and he did not wake her to say goodbye. He and Granger exchanged friendly nods, then he climbed down into the slush of St Martin's Lane.

Meltwater ran freely through stubborn canyons of ice as he made his way towards Long Acre, but when he reached the shopfront of McKerrell and Hampton, a sign announced they were closed for lunch.

Cage loitered outside, exploring the window displays. One side of the double-fronted shop was given over to their work as artist's colourmen: a large easel held a half-finished painting, a bucolic scene of trees and fields that invited the passer-by to imagine how they might complete the image, if only they stepped over the threshold and purchased the fine array of brushes, palettes and paints. On the other side, their theatrical supplies were presented. A backdrop of Swiss mountains was artfully painted in every shade of grey. An elaborate regency wig dusted in silver was set on a waxy, featureless mannequin. There was a white mask, too, perfectly contoured, the eye holes lined in black and the lips coloured red. Was this the inspiration, he wondered? To turn the faces of those boys into masks, to hide the human souls that cowered beneath?

It occurred to him that both boys must have been willing participants in some element of the charade – it would have been impossible to paint their faces so without some co-operation. Were they threatened? Or were they lulled initially, sold on the idea of an innocent game?

A sprightly youth in a dapper red hat was unbolting the door from the inside. He flung it open and smiled at Cage. 'We are open now, sir.'

Obviously.

Cage stepped over the threshold and into the shop.

'Please, do look around.'

In truth there was little to see – the walls were mostly lined floor to ceiling with shelves and drawers. Cage could see some of the labels, but they made little sense to him – *duck primed* and *base XV*.

'Perhaps you could help me?'

'But of course!' The man immediately leapt forward. 'What are you looking for?'

'I've recently taken up photography, and my family and I are enjoying our evenings creating various tableaux. Our ambitions are growing and we thought we should perhaps invest in some stage accoutrements to inspire us?'

'Ah! 'Tis a popular pastime these days! We have many such requests. Theatre is no longer just for the professionals. Something many are sad about, but I say good luck to you, sir! What had you in mind?'

Cage stepped closer. 'Actually, it was a friend who made the suggestion I should visit this place. He uses you regularly, I believe. Leland Crewler?'

The man's expression of eager helpfulness remained unchanged so Cage pressed on. 'He thought I might wish to replicate one of his more recent orders, to help us get started.'

'Ah! Let me check for you. Leland Crewler, you say?'

'Indeed.'

The man scurried into a small office behind the counter. Cage found himself holding his breath as he waited for the man to return. The assistant's guileless behaviour implied that Detective Cross had yet to pay a visit here. But then why would Cross bother? He was already convinced he had his man in Moses Pickering.

The assistant returned, carrying a thick ledger. 'I thought I didn't recognise the name. The last order placed by Mr Crewler appears to have been in the summer of seventy-six.'

Five years ago. Nathaniel Crewler had died that autumn.

'How typical of Leland! He made out his order was recent but his timekeeping can be more than erratic.'

The man smiled, not really accepting that a man's calculation could refer to five years ago as recent.

Cage continued. 'Perhaps it was my mistake and I misheard. Either way, it would be jolly useful to know what my friend purchased – it's as good a place to start as any. I cannot go home empty-handed, my wife and children would be most disappointed. Not to mention my grandmother.'

The thought of a sale had the assistant looking down at his ledger once more. 'Let me see . . . There was the Leipziger Stadt make-up box, a full Austrian goatherd costume, a trident and assorted wigs.' The man looked up. 'Not quite a starter kit I would say, although the Leipziger box would fit the bill.'

'Excellent! And assorted wigs, you say? Does it mention which ones?'

The assistant shook his head. 'I'm afraid not. They come and go. All bespoke, quality wigs are rather dear to make. Mostly we sell on after a particular production has finished with them. I can show you our current selection, however?'

Cage acquiesced and the man took him to a large cupboard and threw the doors open with a flourish. Nothing inside resembled the blond tresses lying beside Baxter Spring.

'Thank you for your time. I shall just take the make-up, if I may.'

'I shan't be a moment.'

The assistant scurried away to the storeroom and Cage made a break for it. Once he was outside, he trotted as fast as he dare along the icy street, not putting it past the man to chase him abroad.

He turned towards the market and slowed down. Although he had nothing solid, the circumstantial case against Leland Crewler was raising itself from the ground. Smoke and mirrors. Now all he needed was to create the possibility that somehow, somewhere, Leland Crewler might have stumbled upon a boy called Baxter Spring.

He walked back to Whitechapel. His route took him past Threadneedle Street, and he paused outside the Crewler company headquarters, built thirty years previously. The façade was blandly classical, with Doric columns either side of the arched entrance. The keystone above the door was some ancient deity or other, with swirling beard, a jutting jaw and a laurel wreath of stone. No doubt a man such as Edmund Crewler had seen a reflection of himself in some apocryphal story of triumph, a parallel to his own success, a Victorian Caesar reborn to conquer the East with ships once more.

As Cage left the city and headed for the slums, the snow

began to fall heavily. People scurried off the streets, and the Whitechapel Road was almost silent, the snow dulling his steps to a soft thud. The world was white and blinding as he turned into the street where Archie Weston lived, the snowflakes light and gentle on his frozen skin.

It was Elizabeth Weston who answered the door, wearing a striped apron spotted with flour as she wiped her hands vigorously. Her smile was polite, her eyebrows raised in enquiry.

'Cage Lackmann. I visited with your husband yesterday.'

'Come in, come in. Archie is due any moment. I thought you were him – he forgets his key most days!'

Cage stepped into the warm house, lit by the soft amber glow of gaslight. A young child stood near the stairs, similarly attired to her mother, with daubs of flour on her face and in her curly red hair.

'Ursula and I were just making cakes.' Ursula stared at him with a child's unnerving gaze. Her mother continued, 'Perhaps you'd like to wait in the study, unless you wish to join us?'

'The study will be fine, thank you. My skill at cake making is somewhat rusty.'

Elizabeth Weston smiled and took him through to her husband's study. She took up the poker and began to prod at the sleeping embers in the grate.

'Please, let me do that. It shall keep me occupied.'

She happily handed over the poker and returned to the kitchen. Once the fire was revived, Cage perused the bookshelves, finding many of the titles he would expect Archie Weston to possess: John Stuart Mill's *On Liberty*, Hobbes's *Leviathan* and Karl Marx's *Das Kapital*. Some of the other books were more of a surprise: the full Brontë collection, for example.

He heard the front door open, and an exchange of words

in the hallway, voices too low to comprehend. Moments later, Archie himself appeared, his face red with cold.

'I hope I haven't called at an inopportune time.'

'Not at all! I am sorry to have kept you waiting.' The reverend indicated the bookshelf Cage had been examining. 'If you wish to borrow anything, do say. It's an eclectic collection.'

Cage's eyes returned to the first edition of *Wuthering Heights*. 'You have a romantic streak, I see.'

'Once, perhaps.' Archie clapped his hands and raised an eyebrow, keen to get to business.

'I wanted to let you know I have decided to take you up on your offer and sit for a portrait. I am intrigued to see the results, I must admit. I thought we might arrange an appointment?'

'Excellent! Well, there is no time like the present I say!'

Cage was taken aback. 'But aren't preparations required? I would not impose on you without warning!'

Archie Weston was in his element. He opened a large cupboard and flung the doors wide. Cage could see a whole array of equipment within. Archie withdrew a small mahogany box, the brass hinges gleaming in the pale daylight. He placed the box on the desk and began to release a series of catches. He talked as the box transformed itself, flowering to reveal a bellows made of black leather, crisply folded like an accordion.

'This is a very new model. I have had it only since Christmas. It is a beautiful contraption, is it not?'

Cage concurred. 'Quite miraculous.'

'Genuinely portable, too. It weighs very little. I can have it set up within minutes. It is so simple – my whole family are learning to use it! The light here is perfect just by the window. Perhaps you might pull over the chair?'

Cage had not planned for this. He had intended only to

pump Archie Weston for further information. 'Your parish, it is well funded I imagine? The great and the good give generously here, I presume.'

Archie Weston stood up and looked at Cage, his cheeks reddening once more. 'I can assure you that this hobby of mine is paid for purely from my own private income.'

Cage leapt forward and placed his hand on Archie's shoulder. 'Forgive me! You misunderstand my intention. I did not mean to imply such a thing. I was merely making conversation. I'd like to understand more of your work here. I've been impressed with what you have told me so far, the ragged school you mentioned, for example. I can see you are a good man—'

Archie Weston cut him off. 'It is I who should apologise, my friend.' He ran his hand across the tiny bald patch at his crown. 'We are proud of what we do here, but we have our critics. Not everyone believes in making such an investment in the poor. You know the argument: they have only themselves to blame, etcetera. I can be defensive, I suppose.' He laughed at himself, and began to assemble a folded tripod.

Cage moved the chair from the desk to the window as requested. 'I am still intrigued, however. Does the church have a few key patrons or do you fundraise more broadly?'

'I wish it was but a few. Elizabeth and I spend more time in the city trying to fill the parish coffers than we do running the school these days. The number of donors for the school itself ran to hundreds – their names take up a whole wall of the parish room, recorded for posterity on a very expensive oak panel. The money would have been better spent on books, but there you have it.'

This was good news. 'I would like to see it, the parish room, if I may.'

'Of course! But first, to business.'

The camera had been assembled, and Archie spent some minutes arranging both Cage and the chair into the best position to capture the light at just the right angle. 'White light is the best! I avoid using anything artificial, the results are so often soulless I think. They are experimenting with magnesium now, but I prefer the natural approach.'

'Will I need to be still?'

'Yes, a few seconds will give me a fabulous exposure. Now, let me insert the plate.'

'Should I look at anything in particular?'

'Into the lens, just here. It's all about the eyes.' Archie disappeared under a black hood and leant over the camera, his face replaced by the brass lens.

'It is a disconcerting process.'

'Is it?'

Cage shuffled in the chair.

'Please don't move, I need you to be perfectly still. On One. Three, Two, One. Now hold, please.'

Cage wanted to blink, the scrutiny of the lens making him uncomfortable. He thought about the photograph in his pocket, the detail of Baxter's face that had been so brutally captured, like no other photograph he had seen – but then, the dead can't move. The question of who had left the image for him to find burned once more. And where had they obtained it? Maybe he should confront Cross.

'Done!' Archie emerged from beneath the hood and removed the plate, sliding a cover across it to protect the image.

'I shall develop the negative later and make the prints.'

'The negative?'

Archie began to disassemble the camera. 'We call them

negatives. It's the calotype process, where light and dark are swapped over on the plate itself.'

Cage stood up and stretched. 'A vicar's worse nightmare, I would have thought?'

Archie laughed, eyes gleaming with humour. 'I like you, my friend.'

The statement seemed genuine. Cage wasn't used to being liked: admired, desired or despised, but never liked. He didn't know what to say in return.

'I suppose you'd like to see a photograph of Baxter?'

Cage hadn't thought about it.

Archie took his silence for assent. 'I only have photographs of the whole class, none of Baxter on his own, although I have one somewhere of his mother.'

Cage was keen to get to the schoolroom, but Archie seemed in no rush. Cage took a chair by the fire. It was seductive, this place, this fledgling friendship.

Archie emerged from another cupboard, carrying two heavy albums. Taking the seat next to Cage, he leafed through them carefully.

'Here you are. It's not the best, I'm afraid. Taken three years ago.'

There were two lines of boys and girls. The youngest sat cross-legged on the floor, the oldest stood behind. Some of the girls were in Sunday-best pinafores; others were wrapped tightly in scratchy wool shawls, the uniform of Whitechapel, hiding the truth beneath. He spotted Baxter immediately in the front row, his dark hair a black mark in a sea of grey.

'This is him. He would have been twelve, maybe.' Archie's finger pointed unnecessarily.

The face was hard to distinguish, although it was

clear that Baxter was smiling. Had this been before the death of Joy?

Archie turned his attention to the other album and opened a page. 'This was his mother, Alexandra. She was known as Allie.'

The picture was taken in a kitchen, presumably here at the vicarage. She was holding a mop, one hand on her hip, clearly interrupted in her task. One eyebrow was raised and her smile was lopsided; Cage had rarely seen such informality in a photograph. Allie Spring was young, alive, dark-haired and beautiful.

'It is hard to believe such a woman was married to Reggie Spring.'

Archie removed the albums from Cage's lap. 'I don't know the story, but it was a tragedy, for sure.'

'Baxter took after her?'

'The spitting image. There was little of his father in him.'

'Maybe if there had been more, he would still be alive.'

Archie put the albums away and opened a drawer of his desk. 'Now, sir, a deal is a deal.' He produced a sovereign and held it out towards Cage.

Cage threw his hands up in the air. 'I couldn't! Not for so simple a task.'

'Please.' Archie grabbed his hand and folded the coin into his palm. 'As you will have noted earlier, I like to be scrupulous in these matters. Let us be honest with each other, Cage. You may yet be standing in court, with Pickering in the dock and myself in the witness stand, on opposite sides of the situation. I would have no imbalance between us before then.'

It was a flimsy argument and they both knew it, but Cage took the money gratefully.

'Perhaps I might see the parish room now?'

The snow had stopped by the time they left the vicarage.

The parish room lay to the back of the church – built simply to mirror the brutal lines of the church itself. The stone plaque above the entrance revealed that the building had been officially opened by the lord mayor several years previously. The room itself was of good size, and freshly whitewashed. The ceiling was open to the oak rafters and the temperature was barely warmer than the graveyard without. Chairs and dismantled trestle tables were stacked along one side. The back wall held a blackboard on which the remains of an algebra lesson could be seen.

'The room has many purposes, as you can see – the school, mainly, but we hold all sorts of gatherings here. There is a mother's group, adult reading classes . . .'

As Archie chattered on, ignorant of Cage's real interest, Cage approached the wall of panels that held the names of all the donors: individuals, companies and charities, hundreds of them. He started at the first, determined to take his time. He only needed the vaguest of connections to build on. He could spin the rest.

The As and Bs alone took up the first panel and he moved to the next, hope quivering inside as he scanned down the column of names.

'Yes!' he blurted, louder than he had meant to, but Archie Weston had not heard and was continuing his monologue on parish room activities.

'. . . so, as I tell our donors, it has been money well spent.'

Archie's eyes shone in his open face, and Cage felt the tiniest stab of guilt at his own subterfuge, but it was nothing compared to the excitement leaping within him at his discovery. If he could, he would have dug up the corpse of Edmund Crewler and kissed him for his pious, self-serving generosity.

CHAPTER SIXTEEN

It was almost four o'clock when Cage left the church, promising to return to the vicarage in a few days to collect a copy of his portrait. His mind was spinning with plans. It felt good, to be on top of the situation: Cage Lackmann, ahead of the game once more. He tried and failed to hail a cab – hang the expense – but the roads were treacherous and there were few about. No matter: his boots carried him quickly towards Dodd's Lane, where the crowds began to build as the streets narrowed and darkness came. A barrow of roasting chestnuts greeted him outside the Pestle and Mortar, as if Christmas had returned unexpectedly, and maybe it had.

The bell clanged as he pushed into the pharmacy. Merriwether was already there, rearranging some jars on a shelf, as committed to the illusion as ever.

'Is he here? I have news.'

'You know the password system is as much for your protection as his.'

'I know, dear chap.' Cage flashed what felt like his first genuine smile in days. 'But is he here?'

The dwarf led him back through the shop and out into the yard. Pincott was not in his usual quarters, and Cage followed

Merriwether up several flights of crooked stairs and along a rope walkway, the smooth planks slippery with ice. They entered a corridor on one of the upper levels of the compound. Cage could hear a baby crying somewhere, an incongruous sound.

Merriwether knocked at a door and went in before him, leaving Cage outside, hat in his hands. Was this an inner sanctum of some kind?

The dwarf emerged and told him to go in. Cage braced himself: he had good news, did he not?

The greeting died on his lips as he entered. He was taken aback by how exquisitely the room was decorated, like some grand apartment, with heavy drapes shielding the window. The polished sideboard shone in the glow of a crystal chandelier, and Pincott himself reclined on a delicate gold chaise longue, wearing of all things a pair of spectacles, as he perused a copy of *The Times*. The greatcoat he normally wore had been replaced by a green velvet robe, although it too fell open to reveal the disconcerting tattoo on his bare chest.

Clifford Chester sat opposite, stuffed into a delicate club chair.

'Sit,' Pincott said.

Cage did as he was told, taking the only other seat in the room, a dark leather wingback chair of exceptional quality. 'Your apartments are extraordinary, Obediah, I had no idea.'

Chester cut short the pleasantries. 'Why are you here, Lackmann?'

Cage addressed Pincott. 'I wanted to thank you for furnishing me with the boy's address. It has yielded results, I believe, along with my own enquiries.'

'You have found him?'

'Pickering? No, but maybe I have something better. Leland

Crewler. He was the elder brother of the first victim, Nathaniel Crewler. I went to his house, to see his mother, and—'

'Whose mother? Why you tell me all this?'

Cage took a deep breath. Obediah Pincott cared only for outcomes, not the story behind them.

'I have enough evidence, I believe, to cast serious aspersions on Leland Crewler as the murderer of both boys. He was brother to the first, and liked to pose as fictional characters and historical figures, often casting his younger brother in female roles. He was a customer of the main supplier of theatrical paraphernalia, and bought make-up and wigs there. The boys were found wearing both. I have also found a connection between Crewler and the second boy, Baxter Spring. Leland's father donated to the school which Baxter attended. It is therefore entirely possible they encountered each other there.'

Pincott removed his spectacles and rubbed his nose. The gesture made him almost human. 'You have nothing.'

Cage ignored his own disappointment. 'If it were a trial in a court of law, then I would agree, for the burden of proof falls to the prosecution. But that is not the goal. I need only to cast serious doubt on Pickering's guilt, and to do so in the papers, not in the courts – not yet at least. But if the press themselves are less convinced of Pickering's guilt, if they have the scent of another man to pursue, then public opinion will follow. That is the goal, after all!'

'Is it?' Pincott's eyes bored into him. 'What is the goal, exactly?'

'To . . .' Cage hesitated. His own goal was clear: to win back his reputation and Pincott's favour, to start earning money again. Was there any point in pretending otherwise?

He sat forward in his seat, leaning into the full glare of

Pincott's scrutiny. 'Look, Obediah, you have invested much in me, we have invested much in each other. It is my reputation, built carefully over many years, that has borne fruit for both of us. We both know it is a ruse, hard won and so easily lost, but I am the master of it, you know I am. There is enough here, with a bit more work, to get us back to where we were.'

'To get *you* back to where *you* were.'

'It is the same thing, Obediah. What else will you do? Pull another child from the gutter, send him to school, send him to university, apprentice him in chambers, watch him learn his craft over many years and still he might not be what I have been. Dub and all the rest will have swung by then, you know it.'

Silence greeted Cage's words. Were they sinking in? He glanced at Chester but his face was unreadable. He ploughed on. 'All I ask for is a quick search of Leland Crewler's study. There is a specific photograph I need, his brother dressed as Desdemona. Then I have enough to spin a yarn that will have Fleet Street chasing their own tails in excitement and hailing Pickering as no more than Cross's whipping boy, whether he turns up or not.' Cage sat back in his chair. 'You won't find another counsellor like me, Obediah. And the search will take you years.' It was as good a closing line as any.

'But I have found one.'

'Pardon?'

Pincott stood up and removed his gown, throwing it carelessly to the floor. He took has greatcoat from the back of the door, and swung it about his shoulders, the leather snapping in its own draft. Cage turned to Chester for an explanation.

'I've hired another barrister,' the solicitor said, struggling to his feet. 'Young, I will admit, but with cheaper tastes in wine and women than you.'

Cage stuttered, trying not to drown. 'A stopgap, that makes sense.' He turned back to Pincott. 'But I will do this, Obediah, I will restore myself, I promise. And it will be quickly done.'

Pincott shrugged. Could the man really not care either way? A shrug was not what he came for, but it was something. Everything Pincott did or said meant something.

Cage stood up. 'Just the loan of one man, tonight, will make all the difference. It is low risk; I can brief him exactly. Then I can make the deadline for tomorrow's papers.'

As if he hadn't spoken, Pincott opened the door and slammed it behind him.

Cage turned to Chester. 'Was that a yes or a no?'

'Low risk, you say?'

'Yes! Absolutely. I guarantee it.'

Chester wedged his hat on his head. 'Then do it yourself.'

CHAPTER SEVENTEEN

It was a ludicrous notion. Cage had not the first idea how to go about breaking into a property such as the Crewler mansion. Perhaps if he went straight to the Farrier's Arms, he could hire the right kind of criminal, but there would be no guarantee of discretion, or that the mission would remain focussed on the photograph alone. Besides, it would cost him money he didn't have.

Cage headed to Fleet Street. It was still early evening, and he knew there was plenty of time before the newspaper deadlines.

But did he have enough without that photograph? Crewler had money, which meant he had power. Some of the papers were more courageous than others at risking a defamation claim, but even so they would need to stick to the facts: their report justified as news, not gossip. He looked once more at the photograph of Nathaniel Crewler on his podium. Someone would publish it now that the boy's death was back in the news. But the key information had to be the connection between the Crewler family and Baxter Spring. To his knowledge, the papers were still unaware of the connection between Pickering and the boy. Pickering's disappearance had been all Cross had needed to damn him in the press.

He was just going to have to use what he had. If the tide began to turn, maybe he could persuade Pincott to action, and keep the fire burning beneath Leland Crewler with another photograph.

The Old Bell Tavern on Fleet Street was rammed, smoky and damp with ale and sweat. The paraffin lamps burned, and the shadows of men danced across the blackened walls. Cage pushed through the crowd, head high, meeting the eyes of those that recognised him, hearing the words '*I say, isn't that . . .*' more than once as he forged his path. He'd spotted Finian Worthing from *The Times* through the window before he entered, and the purpose of his current passage was not to find him, but to be seen finding him.

Finian sat alone at a small table, his walking stick propped to one side. His was the only chair, the others having been removed by bigger groups at other tables. Cage caught his eye, and Finian attempted to rise, a difficult task when he was hemmed in on all sides.

'Please, Finian, do not get up. Let me find another chair. I have urgent news to share.' This said quite loudly.

Cage made a show of casting around for a spare seat in the congested room. Within seconds, another hand grabbed his arm and pulled him close, and a gnarly voice whispered: 'Lackmann, talk to me. Worthing's on his third, maybe his fourth. He won't remember what you tell him, the old fart.'

It was the response he had hoped for, and it came from Dylan Walsh, one of the senior crime reporters at the *Morning Globe*, a publication with an obsession for the lurid and the extreme. The pantomime with Finian had been to strongly indicate that what he had to share would withstand *The Times*'s journalistic rigour, which of course it would not.

Cage sighed to convey an inner struggle. 'I know, Dylan, but it's a risk I think I must take. It's vital that what I reveal reaches the widest audience, and with absolute credibility. A miscarriage of justice, a cover up in the highest of places, these are serious matters, not entertainment.'

Dylan Walsh actually licked his lips. 'Our circulation is the same as his.' He took out his pocket watch. 'We have time. My editor never leaves before nine.'

The bait was taken. Cage looked wistfully at the bemused Finian before turning to his companion and nodding. 'Very well. You will need a drink, and so will I.' He took some coins from his pocket. 'A bottle, perhaps? I shall find us a table at the back.'

Dylan Walsh took the money and grabbed his arm again. 'Don't talk to anyone else while I'm gone.'

Cage nodded reluctantly.

As Walsh elbowed his way towards the bar, Cage fought his way to the back of the pub, where the crowd had thinned. By the time Walsh returned with a bottle and two glasses in hand, a table had come free. Cage took his time pouring the wine, building the tension effortlessly.

Walsh let his impatience show. 'They've found Pickering? What did he say?'

Cage looked at him square. 'No, it's bigger than that, Dylan. Pickering is a sideshow. I've found the connection between the dead boys, between Nathaniel Crewler and Baxter Spring, the second boy.'

'What?' His eyes were wide.

Cage leaned in, his voice low. 'Leland Crewler.'

Dylan Walsh sat back. 'Well, I'll be damned.'

'I'm afraid there is more. There was evidence at the time of

Nathaniel's death, some of which I have with me. The rest I can attest to seeing with my own eyes.' He took the photograph of Nathaniel Crewler from his pocket and placed it face down on the table. 'Evidence that the police ignored at the time, and kept from Pickering's defence, photographic evidence that . . .' Walsh was leaning in so close that Cage could see the thread veins on his cheeks. 'Well, there's only one way to say it. Leland Crewler frequently dressed his younger brother in girls' clothes and took photographs of him.'

Walsh sat back in his chair. 'My editor needs to hear this.'

The rest was plain sailing, almost. The editor of the paper initially offered up some objections, but enthusiasm eventually won out. An office junior was immediately dispatched in a hansom to check the names on the panels in St Thomas's parish room, and an engraver was stopped from leaving the building at the end of his shift and set to work on transferring the blurry image of Nathaniel Crewler into print.

It wasn't to be page one, but page three, a sop to the possible legal ramifications of slinging dirt at someone as rich as Leland Crewler. But the man could deny none of the facts, only the implications that the paper would stop just short of spelling out.

Cage left Walsh to put the whole thing to bed. A flood of victory washed through him, and he balled his hands into fists, just to redirect his energy. The snow was melting already, despite the late hour – the temperature was at last rising. His feet carried him quickly towards Whitechapel, but he wasn't tired enough to go home – he wasn't even sure he would sleep at all before the paper was published in the morning. He would go to the Old Bailey early, find some pretext or other to present himself and judge the temperature of the place.

As he reached Whitechapel, he knew where he was going without having reached a conscious decision. Archie's sovereign was snug within the fold of his breast pocket. He wouldn't spend it, but the coins that jiggled in his hand were another matter.

The brothel where Agnes worked masqueraded as a simple taproom off the unhappily named Christian Street. Two girls greeted him as he entered, breaking off their sharing of confidences by the fire to flirt in his direction. When he asked for Agnes by name, they seemed visibly relieved that their services were not required. Cage tried not to feel offended. One of the girls fetched him a drink before leaving him alone to wait for Agnes to *become available*. At first, he tried not to think of her, upstairs in that tiny box room with an oversized bed, some man's pudgy hands kneading and grabbing, but it seemed childish. Didn't he pride himself on his mature relationship with reality? He saw the way the world was, without wishing it otherwise, for as his mother had always said, that is how one survived it.

He finished his wine, just as someone began to step lightly down the stairs. He looked up, expecting Agnes, but it was the man who appeared first, a young fellow like himself, slim and well dressed, his hat and coat already in place. As the man walked past, he tipped his hat towards Cage in some kind of acknowledgement.

Cage stood up. He threw a penny on to the table – it was all the wine was worth, after all. He pulled his mittens from his pockets.

'Well, well. The poet has returned.'

He hadn't heard her footfall on the stairs. She wore a loose silk robe that swamped her and her hair hung about her shoulders. She looked at his gloves. 'Were you going or coming?'

He laughed at her innuendo. 'Going, actually. And I'd like it very much if you came with me. My wine is better, and my bed is warmer.'

'Not sure I agree about the wine. Have to charge you more, though, and I'll need ten minutes to dress.'

'Why? A coat will do.'

She pulled at her gown, revealing pale pink slippers. 'They weren't made for snow.'

'I can carry you if you like.' Why was he flirting? It was foolish.

She dipped into an elaborate curtsy. 'How gallant of you, sir.'

'That's me.'

It was another ten-minute walk to his street, and she chattered most of the way, her voice easy on his ear, a comfortable sound. He liked her laugh – there was no affectation in it. Cage kept a distance from her, head down, avoiding whatever looks came their way. He must have walked with her like this the other night, but then he had been drunk. Maybe he had even pushed her into a doorway, his hands lifting her skirts as his mouth sought hers, both of them alive with their shamefulness. But he lived in what was considered to be the nicer part of Whitechapel, where honest traders and their families outnumbered criminals, if only just.

It was another matter once they were through the front door. He threw his hat to the floor, hers too. Coats followed, and she tugged him towards the stairs, her hand in his waistband, the tips of her fingers cold against the hardness in his groin, making him burn even more at what was to come.

Upstairs, she removed the last of her clothes with ease – he supposed they were made for that purpose. He lit a candle and placed it beside the bed, still unmade from his restless night before. She was behind him now, hands on his shoulders, her breasts pressing close against his back. He turned, circling his arms about her, his hands sliding down to grab her buttocks. Bracing, he lifted her up and she wrapped her long pale legs about him, her thighs gripping his hips with a young girl's strength. With one hand, he freed himself. She held his head close, the moonlight illuminating one half of the smile on her face, the rest cast in shadow: was it smiling too? As he entered her he forgot, for the tiniest of moments, to think about Emma.

CHAPTER EIGHTEEN

He woke suddenly, his dreamless sleep shattered by the banging on the door.

'Bloody hell!' Agnes raised her head from his chest, one eye still closed with sleep. She wrinkled her face against the morning sun that was pouring into the room. She had freckles. He hadn't noticed before.

The banging came again.

'Does he do this every morning? Or just when I'm 'ere?' She leveraged herself up, her limbs heavy as she collected her clothes together.

Cage swung himself out of bed. A part of him had been expecting this, although he had planned to visit Scotland Yard later that day on his own terms, and fully attired. Ah well.

He dressed quickly, focussing his thoughts on the encounter to come. Last time he had been unprepared and addled with drink. Not this time.

'Your money, please.'

He turned to see her fully dressed. She was smiling, despite the demand in her voice, a phrase learned young and now produced by rote.

He fumbled all the change from his pocket into her outstretched hand. 'Remember—'

'Yes, I know.' The coins disappeared into a purse. 'Scullery to the right, not the left.'

'Close the door when you leave.'

'Of course.'

He followed her down the stairs as the banging started up again, although there were no shouts this time to accompany the ferocious sound.

She grabbed her hat and coat from the floor. 'Bye, then.'

She pushed past him and into the back room. What did he expect? An affectionate gesture? A compliment? He was getting old.

'I'm coming!' he yelled.

He waited for the scullery door to shut before approaching the front door. Then he yanked it open, with what he hoped was a warm welcome on his face.

A small army greeted him. Five constables in blue, and a thin man in a black coat and hat. But no Jack Cross.

The man in black had a folded piece of paper in one hand which he slapped repeatedly into the palm of his other hand, as if he really wanted to whip it across Cage's face.

'Cage Lackmann, I have a warrant for your arrest. You're coming with us.'

Cage almost laughed. Cross must be even angrier than he had anticipated. 'One moment. Let me retrieve my things.'

Cage left them waiting on the threshold. He could see the police cart behind them, its thick black steel gleaming in the sun. He took his time arranging his cravat in the mirror above the fireplace. He smoothed his hair and donned his coat and hat, then took his time finding his keys and checking his pockets to make sure he had everything one might need for a short spell in the holding cells of Scotland Yard. He would have liked a cup of tea but that would be pushing it.

'We need to go now, Lackmann.'

'One moment, I must lock the back door. Just in case a real criminal should appear.'

The thin man nodded sharply at one of the bobbies, who followed Cage through to the scullery as he locked up and tested the door was secure.

'There's quite a few of you here, and that's a large cart for only one man.' Cage beamed at him. 'I shall be no trouble.'

The man refused to look at him or engage.

Cage returned to the front door, the constable one pace behind.

'Right. I am done! Shall we go?'

The thin man grabbed his hands and held them out before him. Handcuffs? Really? The iron was tight about his wrists, and the chains were heavy. The man grabbed one of his arms, signalling the constable to take the other. A light rain was beginning to fall as they muscled Cage to the back of the van, despite his lack of resistance.

Some of his neighbours had come out to see the show. Cage shouted towards the tailor who lived a few doors down, 'You might wish to buy the *Globe* this morning, then you'll understand.' He turned to address the neighbourhood in general. 'Page three!'

His head was pushed down as they bundled him into the van. No one got in with him and they slammed the door. Was his company really so bad? The wooden seat was hard and the small barred window at the rear let in little light. But despite the smell of stale piss, it was warm in here. He could hear the others clamber up on the knife plate above his head, and he knew where he would rather be.

As they rumbled away, someone on the street shouted: 'Leave him alone! Crooked bastards!'

It was music to his ears.

Cage took his watch from his waistcoat pocket. It was almost ten o'clock. It had been a long time since he had slept so long without the aid of several bottles of claret. Maybe adversity was good for him, the physical and mental exertions of the last few days a reminder that a good night's sleep had to be earned.

It was a quick journey, and he could hear the whip crack as the horses drove fast through the streets. The odd curse from above told him his companions were none too happy at their speed.

Finally, they came to a stop. The cart rocked as the men dismounted, and Cage could smell the horses relieving themselves. He sat up straight as the door was flung open and the man in the black hat reached in.

'Out with you.'

The handcuffs were yanked sharply and Cage stumbled into the yard. The iron doors that led to the cells were open already and Cage was dragged through, the cohort of constables marching behind. Other officers stood to one side as they led their prize through the maze. Cage nodded and smiled at them, even risking a 'Good morning!' that saw the chains being jerked harder. If Cross was this angry, the ruse must have had some effect.

To his surprise, they passed the last of the open cells and he was pulled instead towards a metal staircase. Three storeys they climbed, before he was pulled through a heavy set of doors and out into the main room of the Criminal Investigations

Department. He had been here only once before, and he recognised the huge clock that hung on one wall, a reject from the building works at St Pancras a decade earlier. Up close the second hand lurched visibly, a reluctant witness to time's relentless march.

He was led to a glass-framed office. The thin man pulled him triumphantly towards the door like a farmer delivering a prize cow to the fair.

He knocked once, a sharp rap, and a voice called them in.

Jack Cross stood at the window. He didn't turn around as the man forced Cage into a chair opposite the large metal desk.

'Shall I remove the cuffs, sir?'

Cross turned then, his face pale and cold, not red and flaring as Cage had expected. Cross simply nodded and the cuffs were removed. They exchanged no more words as the man silently left the office, closing the door behind him with a click.

'Hello, Jack.'

Cross ignored the greeting. He pulled out his chair and slowly settled into it, the lines in his forehead deep and unmoving.

'You look tired.'

'Fuck off, Lackmann.' A burst of steam from a sleeping volcano. Cross gripped the arms of his chair, his hands splayed like spiders. 'You know why you're here?'

'I can guess.'

'Then guess.'

Cage sat back and rubbed at his wrists, more for effect than anything else. 'Impersonating a police officer.'

'Did you? I wasn't aware.'

'Mrs Chappelhow, the landlady. She's lying, by the way.'

'Anything else?'

'Let me see. Gaining access to the Crewler mansion under

false pretences. I'm not sure if that's illegal or simply morally dubious.'

'It's both. That's one of the crimes on the warrant.'

'I can't think of anything else.' And he honestly could not.

'Perverting the course of justice.'

Cage laughed. 'That's ridiculous and you know it. I have done nothing to hinder your blind persecution of Moses Pickering. I have merely assembled some facts about the Crewler family. There is a case to answer there. In fact, there was clearly a case to answer five years ago and you did nothing.'

Cross leapt out of his chair and Cage shrank back in his, convinced he had pushed the man too far. But Cross merely marched over to a small table in the corner and retrieved a folded newspaper which he slapped hard into Cage's groin.

The detective spat at him. 'Have you even read it?'

Cage unfolded that morning's copy of the *Globe*. The photograph of Nathaniel Crewler in his toga had been faithfully reproduced at full size, but it was the headline that grabbed Cage's eye first. It read, IDENTITY OF SECOND VICTIM REVEALED. It was disappointing – he had hoped for the Leland Crewler connection to hold centre stage. But the content of the article as he scanned through was all he had hoped for: the photograph, Leland's patronage of McKerrell and Hampton, and the Crewler donation to the school which Baxter had sporadically attended. The lines were drawn deniably thin, but they were there.

Cage looked up at Cross, who was back in his chair. 'So, why were you keeping Baxter Spring's identity a secret?'

A muscle twitched in the detective's face. 'That is none of your business.'

But Cage was beginning to piece it together. 'You haven't found him, have you? Moses?'

Cross said nothing, so Cage continued. 'And, what's more, you have no evidence to go on other than Pickering had met Baxter. Once, and in the company of two other men. You've only got the one shot, is that it, Jack? Find Pickering and trick him into a confession by making him mention Baxter's name first. It's pathetic.'

Cage expected the rage to come down on him then, but Cross remained in his chair.

The detective rubbed at his eyes, as if willing them to see something new when he opened them again. When he spoke, his voice held something Cage hadn't heard in it before, a kind of sorrow. 'Don't you care?'

The question was unexpected. Cage was tempted to ask, 'About what?' but he wasn't that callous. Cage put his hand over his mouth, a gesture he recognised in others to be an attempt to stop them telling some fundamental truth. And what was that truth for him? That his own fortunes mattered more to him than solving the murder of two young boys? The image of Baxter Spring came unbidden, dark-haired and grinning.

Cage leant forward. 'Jack, I honestly do not believe Moses Pickering is responsible for this. I know it doesn't look that way, but something is going on here. Pickering is some kind of scapegoat, both then and now.'

Jack Cross shook his head, unconvinced, but at least he hadn't shut him down, so Cage continued. 'There are other photographs of Nathaniel Crewler in Leland's study, one of him dressed as Desdemona, for God's sake, and you know how it ended for her. At least look into it, and whether Leland ever met Baxter Spring.'

The detective looked at him, his face pale and cold once more. 'How do you live with yourself, Lackmann?'

'I don't.' The words were out before he had a chance to cover his mouth.

'You said the landlady was lying. What about?'

Cage's conviction that Moses had returned to his lodgings that night and packed up his things was not necessarily in Moses's favour, so he decided to keep it to himself for now. 'I'm not sure it signifies. Maybe visit her again and check the story is all I'll say.'

The meeting had run full circle, and Cage felt tired of it, of being who he was in the detective's eyes. 'I take it I am free to go? Unless you want something else from me?'

Cross stared at him with outright disgust. 'I won't beg for your help, Lackmann. If you knew where Pickering was, you'd have produced him to the press by now, got them to print some story of persecution and innocent misadventure.'

Cage let the comment go, for it was true enough. He retrieved his gloves from his pocket. 'His aunt in Kent yielded nothing, I suppose.'

Cross laughed. 'Kent is a large county to search when you only have a name.'

Cage paused for a fraction of a second, before resuming his task. He took his time, pulling his cuffs over his mittens, his eyes darting towards the files on the desk before him. A name: Cross had a name for Pickering's aunt. Cage needed to see those files.

'Before I go, I have a crime of my own to report.'

'Tell the locals. I'm sure they'll be eager to help such an upstanding citizen.'

Cage took the photograph of Baxter from his pocket. He would be glad to be rid of it: the white face and dark lashes, the mouth serene in repose, as if the boy were simply sleeping. 'Someone left this on my desk.'

Cross took the photograph and stared at it for some time.

Cage wanted him to look up, to read his expression and see what he already knew.

'Turn it over.'

Cross did so, and he smirked immediately when he saw the word *murderer* written there. 'Crude, but an understandable sentiment.' He threw it to one side and the photograph landed on top of the files Cage was so desperate to see. 'I'll divert all my resources into an investigation.'

'Fuck you, Jack. That's one of your photographs.'

'Maybe. A lot of people are involved in the process. External print houses, freelance photographers. You understand. And murder makes people angry.' Jack Cross rose behind his desk, his face reddening. 'It's not right, you see.'

Cage looked up at him. 'I shall need a chit.'

'A what?'

'An evidence chit, for the photograph. Signed, please.'

Cage smiled innocently as Cross loomed over him. Would a punch be thrown? Quite possibly. It was worth it if he could just see those files.

Cross flexed his fingers, restraint battening down his rising fury. 'Wait there,' he smouldered.

The moment the door closed, Cage was on his feet. What did he have? Thirty seconds? Maybe less.

He grabbed the files, pulling them towards him, and flicked open the first, the pounding in his ears making it hard to see. *Focus. Just one name is all you need. Lucille Somebody.*

He scanned one form, then another – witness statements written in faint pencil. *Lucille, Lucille, where are you?*

He glanced back at the door, the frosted glass throwing shadows from beyond. There would be no warning, just the twist of a handle and the crack of Jack Cross screaming in his ear.

Cage dragged his gaze back to the files and grabbed at another, fingers fumbling to release the seal. Baxter's poem lay on top, then some of Moses's drawings.

How long had Cross been gone? Cage tore open another folder. More forms. The word Kent flashed before his eyes. This was it! He forced the build-up of air from his lungs. *Slowly does it.* Why do policemen have such bad handwriting?

The door shuddered and Cage looked back. The handle was turning and a large shape loomed beyond the glass. A low murmuring – Cross was talking to someone.

Cage wrenched his eyes back to the file. Desperately, he flipped forward through the pages, his hands shaking.

There it was! Printed neatly in type: Lucille Barrett.

Cage tried to shovel the pages back into the file, but it was too late.

The door flung open.

'What the hell are you doing?'

Cage turned and smiled as his nervous hands shuffled the papers into order. 'A breeze. The papers flew everywhere. I thought I'd make myself useful while you were gone.'

Burly hands grabbed his collar and dragged him towards the outer office, the papers in Cage's hands flying upwards. He stumbled and hit the floor: an inelegant plunge that almost pulled the detective with him.

'Your chit!' Jack Cross flung the receipt towards him with a grand ferocity, but the flimsy paper merely floated gently through the air like a lover's kiss. Cage almost felt sorry for him: all that hatred that had nowhere to go.

Cage made no attempt to rise. 'Look into Crewler, Jack.'

'Get out.'

CHAPTER NINETEEN

When he got home, Cage lit the fire in his office and began to sort through the piles of paperwork still strewn about the room, but his mind was elsewhere.

Lucille Barrett.

He just had to hope Justin Kenward's throwaway remembrance was correct, and that Harriet Crewler did indeed have Pickering's aunt's details scrawled in her address book. It now seemed certain to Cage that Moses had gone to Kent, to his aunt, and was likely there still, for if Cross had not taken his aunt's letters from Moses's apartment, then Moses himself must have done so, to prevent himself from being followed and found. Again, the mystery of why Moses had run in the first place lay awkwardly with him, but hopefully he was now a step closer to asking the man himself.

He stood up. Dare he return to Pincott's and seek help with what he now had to do? Chester had been clear in his instruction: *do your own dirty work.* The thought of breaking into Leland Crewler's study in the heart of the Crewler household had been too much, but how hard could it be to get in and out of a building made entirely of glass? He could leave Leland's photograph collection to Cross.

A knock on the door interrupted his thoughts. His heart beat with the thought that Hazel Smythson might have returned, faith restored. He straightened his necktie and smoothed his hair, then opened the door.

Emma Kenward stood on the threshold, a scarf wound tightly about her neck and her hat pulled so low that he could not see her eyes. But he knew it was her. He could have picked her out in a crowd at a hundred paces.

He retreated into the room, saying nothing.

She paused in the doorway, regret and fear, maybe both. Then she too was inside. Without turning, she pulled the door closed behind her and finally raised her eyes to his.

Cage stumbled, treading on a pile of documents as he backed into his desk. The room, snug at the best of times, felt too small for both of them. Slowly, she unpinned her hat and laid it on a chair. The scarf followed. She began to undo her coat and the action drew him to her, his arms reaching out, circling her waist as she pulled the garment from her shoulders and let it fall to the floor. His lips found her throat. Her skin was warm, the life within vibrant and strong. Her fingers were in his hair as he lifted her up and turned back to the desk. With one hand he swept aside all that was on it. Emma gripped the edge of the desk as he pulled at her skirts and myriad petticoats. He grasped the belt at her waist to release her from her dress but she stopped him.

'No. Like this. I want it like this.'

Her skirts billowed around her as he reached for her hips and pulled her towards him. He ground into her as her hands fumbled to release him. He slid a hand beneath her, his fingers searching. She groaned as he found what he was looking for, her head dropping against his shoulder as he stroked her, over and over.

'Now,' she mumbled into his chest. 'Do it now.'

She met his thrust with equal savagery, head up, eyes blazing as she cupped his head in her hands. That is how it was, faces inches apart but not touching, seeing nothing but each other, unblinking and brave.

When it was over, he looked away first, dropping his head onto her shoulder, her small pearl earring scraping against his scalp. She stroked the back of his neck, and he felt all tension slip away. He pulled out of her and shifted back, his hands grazing the skin of her thighs all the way to her knees, but she pushed him away and began to tug her undergarments into place. She no longer held his gaze as she rearranged her skirts.

'Wine?'

'Yes, please.'

'Shall we move upstairs?'

'No,' she tucked a stray strand of hair behind her ear. 'It's warm enough here.'

'One moment.'

He went upstairs and quickly retrieved his last bottle of claret and two glasses. Returning, he took the stairs two at a time, half fearful she might not be there any more.

As he walked into the office, she was crouched down, retrieving the fallen objects and replacing them on the desk.

'There is no need.' He didn't want his desk returned to order. For when she left, it might feel as if this hadn't happened.

He poured the wine, his hand unsteady. 'You know, I'm not sure I have ever seen you naked, not entirely. Something always remains.' He handed her a glass.

'There was never time.'

'Maybe so.'

She took a long draft from her glass. 'There might have been though.' She smiled, but not at him. 'If you hadn't left.'

'Emma—'

'I'm sorry. I told myself I wouldn't do that.' Her eyes were glistening as she spoke. 'I told myself there was no point in recrimination. I came here to feel you once again, to feed something in myself, to know it was real and not just something I made up to make my sad little life not feel quite so sad, or so little. How can we know to trust our memories? Surely they aren't always real? They are made of what we wish for, or of what we can stand.'

The pain in her voice was almost too much to bear. Cage thought of the line in Baxter's poem: *remembrance, the last to fall.* But maybe it wasn't. Maybe Emma was right and it was the first to fail us.

He wanted to sit down, but he couldn't, not with her standing there, holding her glass so tightly it might shatter. 'I wasn't worthy of you. I would not have made a better husband. I was undeserving of your love.'

She snorted, an ugly sound full of disdain. 'I thought that maybe, in five years, you would have thought of something new to say. You're a liar, Cage, to use the same words, lines you learned off by heart because they don't *come* from the heart, do they? And that poem. God, that poem! We were still together when you wrote it, and it was beautiful, and so, so, noble. I didn't know it was about me until you left! Such calculation on your part.' She finished the last of her wine and slammed the glass on the desk, the tears falling freely now. 'Did you intend to leave me all along? Were those words supposed to be enough to make me understand? Did you expect admiration? The noble Cage Lackmann, brought low by his carnal love for another man's wife, finds the strength to finally do the right bloody thing—'

He moved fast towards her, crushing her to him, as if he could squeeze the life out of the lies he'd told that had taken root so deep in her soul. 'I would change it if I could, Emma. All of it. No poem. Nothing lost! Then I could be the man you wanted me to be.' Did that sound like another empty lie? Or could she hear the awful truth of it bouncing off the walls?

He held her until the sobs lessened. Then they pulled apart, her energy spent. She bent to retrieve her coat and he leant down to help her. 'Let me.'

'No. I can dress myself.' She wiped her face with the back of her hand and sniffed away all that had happened between them. 'I saw the paper, by the way. Justin was impressed. No doubt the others will pick up the trail soon enough. You really think Leland Crewler might be responsible?'

The change of tack unnerved him for a second, but returning to the murders, the thing that had thrust them together once more, seemed as good a way of ending this inexplicable encounter as any. 'He is a more likely villain than Pickering.'

She nodded vigorously to herself. 'Yes. Poor Moses.'

The words were out before he could consider them. 'I know where he is.'

She looked at him sharply. 'You do?'

'I will do. Later tonight, I think.'

'That's marvellous. What can we do? Justin and I?'

Justin and I. Said without irony. But who was he to judge? Her care for Moses clearly ran deep, sufficient to override her earlier passions.

'I shall think on it.' And he would, when sanity returned.

She wrapped the scarf carefully about her once more,

obscuring the mouth he had not kissed enough in their brief and frantic union. The hat completed her disguise: a woman of repute, communing with a Whitechapel reprobate. And so it was.

She was at the door. 'Goodbye, Cage.'

He said nothing as she left. Of all the countless words he had tumbled in her direction, true and untrue, 'goodbye' had never actually been one of them.

CHAPTER TWENTY

When Emma had gone Cage took what was left of the wine and retreated to his apartment upstairs.

A familiar despondency wormed within, the sense of worthlessness he had felt so keenly every day of their affair five years earlier. To see his passion for her mirrored back to him, his love returned so ardently, was always too much to take. That those enquiring eyes could not penetrate his façade and see the counterfeit beneath left him feeling lonelier when he was with her than at any other time of his life. He had never wanted to leave her, just the prison she had placed him in, iron walled and unbreakable.

He slumped onto the sofa, pulling his coat over himself against the cold. He closed his eyes although he wasn't really tired – anything to push the thoughts away.

When he awoke it was dark. He checked his watch. If he walked, he would reach Holland Park by dinner time, the best time to strike. He had not noticed dogs on either of his two previous visits to Sheldrake House, but if they kept them, they would unlikely be released to roam the grounds until all the occupants were abed. Just thinking of their potential existence made him feel sick.

He stood up, and made to prepare. What does one wear to break into another's house? Not a mohair coat, surely? But the streets around Holland Park were universally grand: to dress as anything other than a gentleman would incur curiosity after dark. He donned his coat and wrapped a muffler tight about his neck and face. He would be anonymous, at least. In the scullery, he retrieved the hammer he had purchased several years ago to hang Pickering's gift on his office wall. He grabbed a small towel, too: all those years defending Pincott's rabble against burglary charges had taught him something, at least. Besides, was it really burglary if he didn't plan to steal anything? He opened his briefcase, untouched for days, and removed the assorted documents within. Then he placed the hammer and towel inside.

The sky was black, the new moon a tiny slash of silver like an artist's mistake. The thaw had continued all day but the sudden drop in temperature made the pavements treacherous. Where he could, he kept to the roads, but his boots were thick with mud by the time he reached the west of the city. The few people he passed were hunched like him against the cold, hands in pockets and eyes cast down.

The newly planted trees that marked the altered boundary of Sheldrake House, separating it from the building of the terrace beyond, did not yet provide any real protection. He walked around until he reached the new street that had mushroomed from the Crewler estate, eerily quiet and still. There was not the slightest breeze, and the canvas that hung from the windowless façades were like the eyes of the dead, milky grey in the mean light. The only thing he could hear was his own breathing, shallow and quick.

At the end of one terrace, there was a gap that led to the

back of the houses. Pallets of bricks were stacked up, sagging into the mulchy ground. He stepped forward, wanting to light a match to illuminate his path, but not daring to for fear of discovery. He moved slowly, his boots sinking deep into the mud. As he neared the back of the houses, the line of trees came into view, and he could see a dim light beyond: the mansion itself, he hoped. As he picked up his pace, his left foot splashed deep into a puddle and he had to drop his case and put a hand out to steady himself, grasping at the planks stacked against the side wall. They tumbled forward, one after the other like dominoes, crashing onto the bricks and scattering them into the soil. It was over in seconds, the uproar deadened immediately by the muddy ground. He held his breath. Was there a watchman on site here? His boot squelched as he pulled his foot from the earth, freezing water soaking through his stocking as he retrieved his briefcase and stumbled towards the trees. He grabbed at the safety of a trunk and squatted down.

Sure enough, a light began to move across the back of the houses. Someone was coming.

'Anyone there?' a voice shouted.

Cage shifted his weight and a twig cracked beneath him. He cursed silently, thinking what on earth he would say if he was discovered. Something about a lover perhaps, making a quick escape before a husband returned, and finding himself lost in this ghost town of the future.

The light had reached the passageway where Cage had fallen, but then stopped, the watchman probably assessing the damage. Cage waited a few more minutes, then heard the sound of the planks being hauled back into place and stacked against the wall.

Cage wiped his briefcase on the grass, to little effect. It

had cost a small fortune, a gift to himself for Christmas a few years ago. The black leather was soft, not made for dropping in muddy puddles while attempting to break into someone's house. It had been a ludicrous decision to bring it with him.

He waited a few more moments to be certain he had not been followed. Then he slid beneath the tree and out into what remained of the manicured grounds of Sheldrake House. Only a few lights shone from the windows that ran across the rear façade. The mansion hulked against the iron sky like a giant spider, its eyes half closed. At the rear, the hothouse glowed a sickly green, and as he approached he noticed the tiny panes were alive with trickling water, like a witch's cauldron on All Hallows' night.

He paced the full perimeter, taking care to stay away from the few tentacles of light that reached out from the main house. It took time to find the doors, as they were continuous with the main structure of glass, the only clue to their existence the small cast-iron handles and a thickening of the window frame. He paused in the dark, his hands gripping both handles, as if he were his mother preparing for her grand entrance. The metal was cold; if he held them much longer his skin might burn.

He turned both handles and pushed inwards. Nothing. He tried again, pulling the doors towards him. They gave slightly, metal groaning on metal, but remained closed. At least he could now sense where the bolts were, at the top of the doors, the bottom pulling loose from the frame. He'd need something to stand on.

He turned back to the main garden, searching the thick border of bushes that grew beneath the main terrace. Above him, he could see a cast-iron table and chairs, abandoned to the snows. But was the light too strong for him to risk it? He peeked over the rampart. There would be no cover if he stepped onto the terrace, but the shutters along the doors to the main drawing room were half drawn. He could be quick.

Cage crawled towards the terrace steps. His heart was pumping – he could hear it like a percussive accompaniment. He wanted to smile at all the theatrical allusions spinning through his mind – they were his only reference point for this insane act of criminality.

He left his case beneath a bush, took a deep breath, then darted forward, keeping low as he made for the terrace, his feet slippery on the ice. He reached the chairs and grabbed at the first one. It was heavy, and his mittens made it hard to gain true purchase. Then the light changed, a sharp glare hit his eyes and he ducked to the ground, hunched beneath the table, knees drawn to his hammering chest.

Someone emerged onto the terrace, silhouetted against an open door. Had he been seen? Should he run or keep to his hiding place? He had nothing to draw on to help make the decision, and the fear kept him immobile.

Something reached his nostrils. Cigar smoke. Leland Crewler was enjoying his after-dinner ritual. How strange we are, thought Cage, to be such creatures of habit. There was no one left to object to Leland's smoking in the house. His father and brother were dead, his mother lost in a swirl of disconnected memories and confined to her chair. Yet still he roamed the terrace on a freezing night in order to indulge, the ghost of a disapproving father ever present.

Had Leland read the papers that morning? Of course he had, and would know who was responsible for their contents. No doubt he had been plagued by journalists all day. Cage couldn't begrudge him his cigar.

The man's idle pacing turned to a quick march as he retreated to the open doors. Cage waited until he heard them bolted shut, then stood up and made quick work of heaving the leaden chair down the terrace steps. Stopping only to retrieve his case, he worked his way across the lawn and back to the glass doors. He set the chair down and wiped at the beads of sweat on his forehead, their appearance less to do with his physical exertions and more to do with the anticipation of what he was about to do. So far, there was no harm done, a minor trespass, a relocation of an item of garden furniture. His lawyer's brain churned away.

He grabbed his case and retrieved the hammer, then wrapped the head in the towel. He stood on the chair and brought the hammer to the topmost pane, where he could see the long bolt that ran across the inside. Was he really doing this? What if his efforts came to naught, and Harriet Crewler's address book yielded nothing? What if it wasn't even in the same place any more?

He tapped the hammer against the glass, but nothing happened. It was not much of a blow. He gripped harder, and braced himself against the doors. This time he took a full swing, and the dull thud was followed by the crack of glass. He dropped the hammer to the floor but kept the towel. The pane had broken neatly, the cracks reaching to the corners of the frame. He was able to remove one piece, and then another, the warm air within billowing through. Finally, his hand reached in and touched the bolt.

The metal was unyielding, and the angle was all wrong. He moved the chair again, his fingers struggling to grasp the catch. With a sharp tug, the bolt snapped open. He jumped down from the chair and tested one of the doors, opening it just an inch. He was in.

He returned the chair to the terrace. Back at the hothouse, he propped his case by the door, ready for a quick getaway if required. He could outrun the butler, but what of the other servants? Or Leland Crewler himself?

He grabbed the handles of the doors and pushed into the warm, wet air. All was dark around him, but up ahead he could see the soft glow of gaslight. He trod carefully towards it, remembering Harriet's warning about the Devil's snare. The plants reached out to him on either side, tickling his face as he stepped past. Some stuck to his hair with gluey fronds as if they might prevent his passage. The light was stronger now – just around the next corner. Tentatively, he leant forward.

Harriet Crewler was asleep in her bath chair. Did she never move from this place? He crept forward, each step exaggerated as he placed his feet carefully on the slippery tiles. It was funny, a part of him thought, like a pantomime villain, arms out and hands like claws to help him balance. The noxious smell of the plant at her side grew stronger, but as he drew closer, he could see the pile of books on the table next to her. She was snoring softly beneath the blankets, one withered hand clasping them to her. He reached down and moved the top two books aside.

There it was, the address book, the same pages he had dropped a few days ago spilling out where they had been hastily stuffed back in.

He picked it up and leafed through until he came to 'B'. The writing was tiny, and faded in places. He would need the light to see. He shuffled forward, placing the book as near to the light as he dared. He was so close to her now, he thought he could feel her breath against his arm where her head lolled to one side. His own breath was locked in tight, his chest willing him to exhale, but he would not risk it lest the sound wake her.

His fingers scanned down the first page, then the next. Had this been a fool's errand? But then he saw it, and the moment forced the air from his lungs. Lucille Barrett. Highland Cottage, Rouge Lane, Gravesend.

He had him. He had Moses at last.

Suddenly, Harriet Crewler's hand shot out and grabbed his arm. Her grip was unfeasibly strong, the gnarled fingers digging deep into his flesh. Her eyes were wide and staring. It was a ghoulish sight. His heart pounding, he raised the index finger of his other hand to his mouth.

'Shh, Harriet. I was simply tidying your things. You remember me, don't you?'

'Do I?' The uncertainty in her voice gave him hope.

'Yes. I'm James's son. I am staying with you and Edmund for a few days before I depart for India once more.' How easily he lied, he realised.

She looked at him, her eyes searching. Then it was as if the light went out. 'Edmund is dead.'

His stomach plummeted to his boots, but his brain was slow to catch up. She let go of his arm and yanked the cord at her side twice in ferocious succession, her lips pursed, her face mean. She was attempting to rise, as if she might throw herself atop him to prevent his escape.

He stumbled backwards away from her, and turned to run, but his foot slipped on the tiles and he fell instead into the nearby border, his hands landing painfully on the spiny pods of the Devil's snare. The smell was overwhelming and he scrabbled forward, pushing through the foliage to the other side. He felt his watch fall, then something caught in his eye. He cried out, pushing blindly on. He could hear a man's voice behind him. The butler? Leland? Reaching the pathway he spied the doors ahead of him and ran, his boots sliding about as he struggled to reach them. He exited with a crash, his feet going from under him. He daren't look back to see who was giving chase. Out in the cold he grabbed his case and ran for the line of trees. All the doors on the terrace were open now and the light flooded out; more voices, too. Would there be dogs? Please don't let there be dogs.

He had not planned an escape route other than the way he had come. Stupid, he now realised. But the time for thinking and caution was gone. He had only his legs to save him now.

CHAPTER TWENTY-ONE

He was drifting on water. An ocean, perhaps? Or something smaller – a sea, or a lake. His vision was obscured. There was something caught in his left eye and he rubbed and rubbed. Was the water warm? Maybe, he wasn't sure, he couldn't feel it, couldn't feel anything, other than what was troubling his eye. He rubbed harder. Maybe the water would help. He took a breath and sank beneath the waves, then opened his eyes, but the water stung like fire and he pushed upwards again, kicking his legs, once, twice, three times, but still he did not break the surface. He kicked harder, desperate . . . surely he had not sunk so deep? His chest strained with the effort, his breath almost gone, only moments left until his body betrayed him and he sucked down a lungful of water. It was coming, any moment now, inevitable. He stopped kicking, hanging onto a precious few more moments of life, as if they could make a difference. Then his chest heaved, and his mouth opened, and his empty lungs gorged themselves on sweet air.

'Oi!' A rough hand shoved him. 'Go die somewhere else.'

Cage looked around. One eye was swollen shut and all he could see with the other were bricks, above and beneath him, moist in some faint light. He was frozen. How could he have thought the water was warm? But he wasn't in the water any more, he was somewhere else.

He could smell the man next to him, rather than see him. He was wrapped up like a swaddled babe in layers of blankets.

'Where am I?'

The man sniggered and shook his head a few times, reaching for a witty answer. Instead, he settled for, 'Vauxhall.'

Vauxhall. The railway arches. What was he doing here? He leant back against the wall and closed his one good eye, but within seconds the water had churned around him once more and he jolted himself awake, his hand reaching out and grabbing the man's beside him.

The man edged further away. Cage's nose was grateful.

'You taken something?'

Cage made to stand up, but his legs wouldn't work properly and he slipped back to the floor. 'The Devil's snare.'

'I'll say. Time to piss off, though.'

Cage crawled forward and pushed himself to his knees. Pins and needles came first, then the cramps, so painful he cried out. But at least the feeling was returning. He leant forward, his hands touching something soft and muddy. His briefcase.

His brain ached. He remembered running towards the park. There was a wall, he thought, a wall he had climbed over, and then more running, but then the memories stopped. Vauxhall was miles from Holland Park, the other side of the river. Which bridge had he crossed?

The cramps were lessening now and he hauled himself up, then leant back against the wall. He raised a hand to his eye, feeling the swelling there. Harriet Crewler had said that some men used the plant as a drug in order to see their ancestors in their dreams. Cage had seen no one, his hallucination had been bereft of anything but the churning water.

'Thank you for your hospitality.'

The man grunted as Cage hobbled away, his feet unsteady.

He needed to get a grip of the situation. He had been discovered, that much he knew, but obviously no one had been able to follow him. Lucky too that he had weaved his way like a drunk through the breadth of the city without being stopped by anyone. But had Harriet Crewler been able to identify him when she raised the alarm? It had only been a few days since his previous visit. Had the dots been joined already?

He stumbled forward, stepping over other sleeping bodies. Eyes watched him in the dark as he made his way out into the street. The city was empty. What time was it? He searched his pockets for his watch but couldn't find it, remembering then that it had fallen at Sheldrake House. More importantly though, he realised that every last penny he had in the world was also gone. He turned back towards the archway he had just left, but what was the point? He was lucky enough that he had been allowed to leave with his life and the clothes on his back. He still had his briefcase.

He turned up the Albert Embankment towards Waterloo, his legs beginning to firm up as his mind cleared. He couldn't go home straight away in case the authorities were waiting for him. He needed an alibi for this night, and a decent explanation for the injury to his eye, before he dared show his face.

Would Agnes lie for him? Probably, if he paid her enough, which he currently could not do. He would visit Shanksy's pawnshop in the morning. The man owed him a few favours, did he not? Although there was little left to put in hock. His briefcase, maybe, if he could clean it up. An alibi and a trip to Gravesend would have to be funded somehow.

Gravesend! But what was the address? He stopped abruptly by the gardens of Lambeth Palace. 'No, no, no . . .' he muttered.

He rubbed his face, took a deep breath. It had been like this always for him in exams, willing himself to retrieve some small morsel of case law or precedent from the filing cabinet deep in his mind. It was impossible unless he remained calm, subverting the self-fulfilling anxiety that hopped about his brain.

There was a cottage, and a lane, that much was easily remembered. But the rest was in darkness, for now at least. He quickly closed down the inquiry, knowing that trying too hard would drive the knowledge deeper. He was still suffering the effects of the plant's poison. Maybe in the morning the address would come unbidden.

It was still dark when he reached Agnes's place of work, but the brothel appeared locked shut for the night. Dawn could not be far away. He knocked lightly, and it was the madam herself who answered the door: a still-attractive widow whose left arm ended below her elbow, an injury said to have been obtained by an encounter with a lion in the circus ring. His heart sank, however – the madam would be more expensive to bribe.

She told him Agnes was already abed, but that she would wake her and see if she was able to receive another visitor. He was allowed over the threshold, to wait in the taproom downstairs, and he sagged gratefully by the dying embers of the fire. He felt the swelling around his eye – was it already receding? That would be something, at least. He leant his head back against the settle. The wood was hard, but he was grateful for the support. With his eyes closed, the world swam only a little, then went still.

'What happened to you?'

He looked up. Agnes was alone; the madam had gone. She held a lamp with one hand, the other securing the wrap about her shoulders. In that moment, she looked like Florence Nightingale.

'Ah. I had an encounter with a dangerous plant.'

'Plant, you say?' She sat beside him and raised her hand to his eye. 'Do you need me to bathe it for you?'

'That would be nice.'

She left him briefly, returning with a bowl of water and a cloth. The water was cool on his skin.

'I should be honest. I have no money with me. It was taken. Tomorrow I should be in funds again.'

She paused only briefly in her administrations. 'You've had a bad night.'

'I need to ask you a favour.'

'To say you spent the night with me.'

Clever girl. No wonder he liked her. 'I can pay you tomorrow.'

She turned his head to look at her. His bad eye was beginning to open again. He felt vulnerable, his head and his fate in her hands.

'Forget it,' she said. 'You overpaid the previous evening.'

'Thank you. That's kind.'

She shrugged. 'Just business.'

Of course it was. He stood up. 'I should get home. See what is waiting for me.'

'Not your Mr Cross again, I hope. Come into the kitchen, we can brush your coat and boots.'

Half an hour later, he stepped out into the dawn, his boots clean and his grateful stomach full of tea and toast. His eye was fully open now, if still puffy. He was tired, but otherwise the plant's effects seemed to have worn off. His mittens were gone. Had he dropped them at Sheldrake House along with his watch? The memories were still fuzzy of those final moments. No matter, he swung his newly cleaned case onto his shoulder and plunged his hands into his pockets.

Once inside his own house, he ignored the fatigue in his bones and set about examining all his possessions. The Dartford decanter, with its silver stopper, and set of four crystal glasses was an obvious choice. They alone should raise enough to fund another week of existence. Find Pickering, bring him back, construct alibis and explanations, a few days at most. Maybe an interview then with the *Globe*, the wrongful persecution of Moses Pickering, Cage Lackmann to the rescue once more. Surely that would turn the tide enough for the Pincott tap to grind back on?

He found a small crate in the scullery and carefully packed up the crystal in old newspapers. Ignoring the Rubens drawing, he removed his bar certificate from its gilt frame and added the frame to the crate too, then his ebony inkwell for good measure. All these things he had bought himself, pointless compensations that had provided a fleeting justification for a pointless existence. Maybe when he was back on his feet, he would start saving in earnest, buy himself a new life, free of chains. But that was for the future, not for now.

It was too early yet for the pawnshop to open. He fired up the stove and heated a pan of water, then stripped naked and washed himself clean.

He emptied his strongbox of the last of his savings, then returned to his office and checked his eye once more in the mirror above the fireplace. Swollen, yes, but no longer unsightly. Coat on, he slung his case over his shoulder, lifted up the crate and made for the door. Once he'd procured more funds, he would go straight to London Bridge and take the first train to Gravesend. The address eluded him still, but there would be time to dig deeper when he was on his way.

His hands were red with cold before he reached the end of the street, although the sun was blinding as it peeped above the rooftops.

A familiar form waddled around the corner ahead of him, but his mind was still sluggish and he had no time to avert the encounter before she saw him. The way she picked up her pace, her arms pumping herself forward, he knew he was the sole reason for her appearance here. And there he was, carrying his most valuable possessions, his motivation and intention painfully clear.

'Beautiful morning, Mrs Castan!'

'Four shillings and three pence you owe me.' Utterly charmless.

'You catch me at an unfortunate moment. I was robbed last night. Every penny taken.'

She stared at the crate, her rapid calculations pinching across her face. 'Shanksy's?'

'Sadly, yes. Just for a few days. I have several bills owing to me.'

'I'll come with you.'

The thought was an appalling one. But what choice did he have? He could make a scene, but it would embarrass him far more than it would embarrass her. 'Very well.'

She stuck to his side as he walked the quarter mile to the pawnbroker's.

Shanksy was just opening up shop as they arrived, pushing aside the metal grates that protected the merchandise.

'Mr Shanks! I hope you are well?'

Shanksy was a small man, barely reaching Cage's shoulder. His hair sprang up in grey curls and the glass within the frames of his black spectacles was so thick his eyes appeared like two giant fishbowls. Which was appropriate – Shanksy missed nothing.

The man turned around at Cage's greeting, seeing the shadow of Mrs Castan beside him. She nodded her head tersely in his direction. The pawnbroker decided against comment – the situation was after all rather self-evident. 'One moment, Mr Lackmann.'

'Certainly.' Cage busied himself looking in at the nearest window while Shanksy removed the last of his padlocks. The display was always well laid out, the items changing frequently. Today, a large doctor's bag took pride of place, the clasps pulled open to reveal a full set of gleaming instruments. It was stolen, no doubt, probably by one of Pincott's goons, for what doctor would pawn the very tools he needed to do his work? Behind the bag was a mannequin wearing a white wedding dress, after the fashion of Queen Victoria, although it looked all wrong – the mannequin was of male build, flat chested, and the gown bagged across the décolletage.

'Please, come in.'

Cage stepped towards the door. Mrs Castan made to follow him but he turned and muttered sharply: 'Mrs Castan, you will be paid. There is but one way in and out of the shop. But I must ask you to allow me to conduct my business in private.'

She shrugged, her faced unmoved. As he entered the shop, she took up position, guarding the entrance, her hands folded across her bosom. He imagined running her from behind, taking her down then scarpering away with his proceeds untouched by her grasping hands.

Inside, he stumbled through an explanation for his current state of affairs: a big case, a poor client most wrongly accused but without the means to pay.

Shanksy held up his hand. 'It is of no concern to me, Mr Lackmann. Let us see what you have brought me.'

Cage watched as Shanksy's thin but elegant fingers danced among the hastily packed luxuries, moving the paper to one side just enough to evaluate the wares within. Then his attention turned to the briefcase, inspecting the workings of the catch and exploring the lining within.

Those big eyes looked up at Cage, and a number was mentioned. It wasn't nearly enough.

Cage began to rattle through the list of favours he had done over the years: charges averted, connections hidden. Shanksy reminded Cage that he had always been well rewarded for his services, then the man's eyes drifted down to the box before him, eyes that said *and this is where my money went?*

Exhaustion thrummed at his temples and Cage closed his eyes. He had no energy for this.

Shanksy leant forward, a hand reaching out to touch Cage's arm. A new number was mentioned, barely higher than before. It would have to do. He needed to get moving, keep up the pace. If he returned home to sleep now it would be for days. He watched as the money was counted out, including a separate pile of four shillings and three pence for the hound of tub and mangle waiting for him outside.

'Oh wait, I need gloves.'

Shanksy nodded, and began to rummage through a drawer behind him as Cage shuffled the coins he had been given into his pockets.

'On the house.' The gloves were surprisingly good quality,

lined with sheepskin. Cage muttered his thanks, shy of the man's charity when he had only wanted a fair deal. But that was how the engine of Whitechapel worked, the scales forever grinding one way or another.

Outside, he slapped some money into Mrs Castan's meaty hand. 'Here are your thirty pieces of silver, Mrs Castan.'

She smiled, an expression which really didn't suit her. 'Take your business elsewhere from now on, and I hope you get what's coming to you.'

'And what would that be, dear Mrs Castan?'

Her eyes shone up at him as she said one of his least favourite words: 'Justice.'

CHAPTER TWENTY-TWO

At London Bridge, Cage bought a third-class ticket, but returned to upgrade to second when he saw the numbers waiting at that end of the platform. Soldiers mostly, making their way to Milton Barracks, the final staging post before they were shipped to the Transvaal or Afghanistan. There were emigrant families here too, perched on cases and trunks, small islands of stillness around whom the soldiers ducked and danced with boyish bonhomie. The parents looked thoughtful, the children uncomfortable, bundled up as they were in most of the clothes that they owned. Would he want to be one of them, heading to a new life in Australia or America? A new start, the possibility to be anyone he wished. But the bonds that tied him would drag across the ocean. He could not leave behind the two burdens he most longed to escape: the past and himself.

When the train pulled in, he found an empty carriage and settled himself in the corner. Cage watched the passing landscape as the factories turned to slums and then to countryside, the fields green once more, with only a trace of frost still remaining on the outstretched limbs of naked trees. They passed a graveyard, sweeping up and over a hill, a tiny church in the distance. A small boy meandered past the headstones, carrying a large bundle of sticks. Cage took out Baxter's crumpled poem, buried deep in the pockets of his coat, and read it once more, the boy's voice so clear in his mind, as if he were sitting beside him. He had inherited another ghost.

The address came to him all of a sudden, landing like a letter upon the doormat: Rouge Lane. The name of the house itself was lost, but he should have enough to find Lucille Barrett and her errant nephew.

The train switched back towards the river, and the factories returned as they neared the Gravesend Docks, the chimneys belching acrid smoke that hung in dark clouds on the horizon. Cage was sorry to see the green fields disappear, knew too that it would not be long before the city swallowed them whole, slumping outwards like a pile of rotting fruit.

At Gravesend, he followed the general flow out of the station and north into the bustling town. A light rain was falling and the air was cold and damp. The main street was lined with taverns, coffee shops and hostelries, all offering a warm welcome. It was tempting, but Cage resisted. Instead he walked into the post office and waited his turn to be served by the postmistress. Her instructions on how to find Rouge Lane were vague, accompanied by limp hand gestures that pointed nowhere in particular.

'Beneath Windmill Hill, you say?'

'Yes, you can't miss it.'

'And why is that?'

'On account of the windmills.'

It was as good a direction as he was going to get. Back out on the street, he wandered closer to the Royal Terrace Pier, where two huge steamers sank low in the water. He climbed the steps of the Mission House and looked back towards the town. In the distance he could see the spokes of one windmill turning in a lazy arc against the bleached sky. It looked to be a fair distance away.

The clock tower struck twelve as he ambled back towards the station and into the streets that lay to the south, looking up now and again to ensure he was still heading in the right direction. On the Wrotham Road, he gave in to temptation and ducked into a small tavern. The place was cold and empty and he had the bar to himself. The ale was strong and the oyster pie too salty for his liking, but at least the attendant's directions were clear and easy to follow.

As he found the turning into Rouge Lane, he pushed the thought of failure aside. Moses was here. He knew it. The lane was narrow and twisted upwards along the hill. Most of the houses he passed were obscured by trees, but their names were attached to the gateposts out front. None of them rang a bell as he trudged forwards, the rain falling in earnest the further he got from the town.

Up ahead, he could see a cottage peeping through the hedge. It was a tumbledown affair, the main roof drooping like a scolded mongrel, its belly almost scraping the floor. The fluttering in his stomach grew stronger as he approached the entrance.

The low gate was wedged shut. The slate plaque attached to the post was covered over with moss which Cage had to scrape away. Highland Cottage, it said.

This was the one.

The garden was overgrown, but clearly had once been splendid. The rose bush that had been cultivated to trail around the door had taken to the windows as well, needy tendrils searching for the care they had once known. The gate had clearly not been opened for days, as the last vestiges of ice glued it to the post. The only sign of occupation were the muddy footprints that snaked along the mossy cobbles from the front door to a woodshed beyond.

Cage looked up at the chimney, but all was still. He grabbed the gate with both hands and lifted it as far as it would go, then walked it backwards across the pitted ground, careful not to make a sound as he squeezed through. He crept over to the woodshed first and peered in: it appeared to be well stocked, and some of the timber was green, the sap still rising. He walked the perimeter of the little cottage, taking care to duck beneath the small windows as he passed them. At the rear of the house, he found another entrance: a stable door, the jolly yellow paint now flaking. There was a small terrace here, with a decrepit wooden trestle and two chairs leaning against it, their rattan weaving beginning to unravel. As quietly as he could, he moved the table in front of the stable door and piled the chairs on top.

He made his way to the front of the house again and approached the main door. A rose thorn snagged his coat and pierced his finger as he removed it. He sucked a bead of blood, cursing Moses silently, everything he had suffered in the pursuit of his client coming to mind.

He knocked on the door, softly he hoped, the kind of knock that announced friend not foe. Then he stepped back and waited. There was silence at first, then he heard something: footsteps, perhaps? But the sound was retreating, not coming towards him. Cage circled back around the house, arriving on the back terrace just as the chairs he had piled up crashed to the ground. Cage ran forward. Whoever had run into the obstacle had escaped back into the house.

Cage clambered over the table and through the stable door into the gloomy cottage. He darted through the kitchen and into the hallway in time to see the back of Moses Pickering fiddling with the locks and bolts on the front door, his fingers clumsy with haste.

'Moses! Stop running!'

Moses turned around, his face a picture of fear and his mouth half open, ready to scream. His arms flattened against the door in abject surrender.

'It's me, Moses. Cage Lackmann. I'm here to help you.' He approached slowly, his hands up to show he meant no harm. A guinea pig, that's what Moses reminded him of: receding chin, narrow face, long nose and wary eyes set too close together. Cage could see his thin frame trembling as he neared.

He stopped a few feet away.

'I know you didn't kill them.' Did he, though?

Moses relaxed, his hands falling to his sides. 'How did you find me?' The voice was delicate, and resonated with the quiet dignity Cage so vividly remembered.

Cage smiled, hoping to put him at ease. 'With great difficulty, old chap.'

'The police?' Moses had not yet moved from the door.

Cage shook his head. 'Just me.'

Moses nodded at this, still wary.

'We need to talk, Moses. Some tea, perhaps?'

Moses nodded again but made no attempt to move. Cage gestured to the kitchen. 'Shall we?'

'Yes, yes, of course. How rude of me.' Moses moved past him, giving him a wide berth as if Cage might yet tackle him to the ground.

Cage followed closely as they returned to the kitchen. It was a bright room, well maintained compared to the exterior of the house. The walls were freshly whitewashed and the table Cage sat at was scrubbed clean. Moses shut the door against the cold and busied himself with the stove.

'The last of the milk is gone, I'm afraid, and I daren't go out again, but I have lemon and sugar. The lemons are from the garden – my aunt was always green-fingered; she could grow anything in this soil she said, although apricots were a struggle, I recall.'

'Where is she?'

Moses had his back to him, but Cage could see his shoulders slump briefly. 'Gone, last winter.'

'I'm sorry.'

'Earl Grey or Assam?'

'Either.'

'Earl Grey, I think. I couldn't bring myself to sell the cottage, not yet at least. But I haven't been able to come here as often as I would have liked, a few times last summer is all I have managed. The garden, she would be horrified, but I daren't attempt anything in this weather.'

Pickering rattled on, something about wisteria and frost. Cage could see his hands shaking as he sliced a gnarly green lemon into a dish and placed it on the table. Then came two cups and saucers, and a fancy silver sugar bowl with matching tongs. Any moment some biscuits would appear.

'Would you like a biscuit? I have shortbread and oatcakes.'

Cage smiled as four biscuits were arranged on a dainty plate.

'We should stay in the kitchen, if you don't mind. The stove is the only heating I allow myself during the day as the smoke cannot be seen. The parlour is unbearably cold, I'm afraid.'

'The kitchen is fine. We need to talk, Moses.'

He nodded. 'Tea first, I think.'

Cage let him continue the charade of a tea party. What harm could it do? Finally Moses settled, a large teapot before him. 'Shall I be Mother?' His hands were now steady as he poured.

Cage added a slice of lemon to be polite and took a sip. The tea had an earthy aftertaste, like mildew, and the biscuits were stale. But the china was nice.

'Moses. I have so many questions. But first, you have to tell me, why did you run?'

Pickering cocked his head to one side, bemused by the question. 'Because you told me to.'

CHAPTER TWENTY-THREE

The letterhead was his.

He'd had five hundred printed a few years ago on expensive cream paper, an enormous quantity that had seemed financially prudent at the time. Most were still in a box beneath his desk, some he kept at Chester's grubby offices on the Whitechapel Road, others had been left in court as he doodled, pretending to write notes.

The words written beneath were in anonymous block capitals, neatly printed in black ink.

BAXTER SPRING HAS BEEN MURDERED.
I CANNOT HELP YOU THIS TIME. ESCAPE
WHILE YOU CAN.

There was no signature.

Cage read it again. And then again.

'You didn't send it, did you?' The blood had drained from Pickering's face.

Cage shook his head, his voice temporarily locked away.

'Oh. I see.' But the man obviously couldn't see anything. None of this made sense.

Cage cleared his throat. 'Who gave this to you?'

Pickering's hands were shaking again as he raised his cup and drank. It rattled in its saucer when he placed it back down. 'My landlady. When I came home from work, an envelope was waiting for me. I didn't ask her any more about it. After all –' he looked up at Cage, his eyes like a beaten puppy '– I thought it was from you.'

'Mrs Chappelhow denied seeing you that night.'

'Did she? I packed very quickly. I was terrified, understandably. I fell down the stairs, put my foot through one of the treads, made a dreadful crash. Mrs Chappelhow had to help me down in the end. Even hailed a cab for me to the station.'

'Very helpful of her.'

'I must admit to not having a very high opinion of her always. But if she lied for me, maybe there was some kindness in her. Perhaps she read your note and trusted her instincts about me.'

Cage didn't see it that way. Her lies had nothing to do with helping Moses out. 'Tell me what you did then.'

Pickering shrugged. 'I got the first train I could. It must have been midnight by the time I arrived. I thought no one would find me here.' He placed his trembling hands on the table. 'How did you?'

'Harriet Crewler. She still has this address in her book. No one else thought to look.'

'You saw Harriet? How is she? I always liked her, even when she called me "murderer". She had a gentle soul, I think. Too gentle for this world.' His voice drifted off, as if he had been talking about himself.

They sat in silence for a while, contemplating the same question. It was Moses who finally articulated it. 'Who sent this note, Mr Lackmann?'

'I don't know, and please, call me Cage. We are beyond formalities now.' Pickering nodded as Cage continued, 'So someone else killed Baxter Spring, and was hoping for you to catch the blame.'

'Hoping?' Pickering's eyes were desperate. 'They need hope no more. Their plan was successful. I am undone. Only the guilty run.'

Cage reached across and grabbed Moses's hand. It was a tiny thing, the bones like twigs beneath his grasp. 'I have found other connections between Nathaniel Crewler and Baxter Spring.'

Moses looked up, his face the picture of astonishment. 'Justin? You cannot mean . . .'

'Not Justin, no. Leland Crewler.' Cage explained all he had discovered – the photographs, the donation to the school – but Moses seemed unimpressed.

'That is all most tenuous.'

Cage sat back. 'It is all I have – for now, at least.'

'Of course. And I thank you for trying, Mr . . . Cage.'

Only I didn't do it for you, thought Cage. He picked up the note once more, wondering at its authorship. Anyone who had a mind could have procured his stationery, he hardly treated it like the Crown jewels. He thought of the possible intruder a few days ago, or had it simply been the wind? And then there was the photograph of Baxter that he had since handed over to Jack Cross. Maybe someone had stolen into his office before?

He slapped the table as the thought came to him. Hazel Smythson, the potential client: he had given her his letterhead in place of a business card the very afternoon that this note was sent to Moses! But she couldn't have expected that, surely?

Although a card attached to a plain piece of paper would have done the trick also of convincing Moses that the note was from him.

His mind reeled. If she was behind this note, why turn up at his office the very next day? He needed to find her again.

Cage's cup was empty. 'Do you have something stronger?'

Pickering returned to the role of host, but with less energy than before. There was a stoop to his back as he shuffled into the pantry. How old was he now? Sixty, perhaps? He returned with a plain bottle, which a homemade label announced in spidery handwriting was apple brandy. Dubious, Cage took it and pulled at the musty cork, which broke in his hand, so he pushed the remains into the yellow liquid as Pickering watched, horrified.

'I shall fetch some glasses from the parlour.'

'Don't worry,' Cage filled his cup. 'This will do.'

The brandy was sour, but strong.

'Do you have enemies, Moses?'

It was a ridiculous question, and Pickering's eyes grew wide at the thought.

'Of course you don't.' Cage took another sip. 'But I do.'

Pickering shivered, as if he could shake everything away. He didn't fit the story that was unfolding, – a kitten caught in someone else's trap. 'You think someone wished to bring *you* down? But you are not in the frame. No one has accused you of murder!'

Oh yes they have. Could it be that Cage was the intended target here, and Moses Pickering no more than the stick to beat him with? But no, that was a delusional idea. A boy was dead, and there were easier ways to ruin Cage's reputation than that. His mind circled around to Leland Crewler once more. And what of Justin Kenward? Interesting that Moses had mentioned him as the only other connection he knew of between the two boys. But Justin had only met the Crewler boy a few times when he had followed Moses to work, and he had been away on business in Manchester when the child was killed: it had been one of the reasons Moses had no alibi spanning several days. Harriet and her husband had sworn blind that the only other people in the grounds that night had been the servants, Moses and Leland.

'Poor Baxter. He was an astonishing child, a man almost. An old soul, as they say. It is hard to believe what happened. He had a strength to him, not physically, maybe . . . but to be duped like that, to put himself in that position . . . It must have been for money; the boy was clearly penniless. Was the crime really . . . the same?'

'I have seen the photographs.'

Pickering wrapped his arms about himself. 'I still wake up sometimes, you know, and wonder how you did it, how you talked that jury out of convicting me. The evidence—'

'Was circumstantial, and the police investigation was lazy. Once they had you in their sights, they had their perfect suspect.'

Moses's smile was grim, almost cynical: it looked odd on his face. 'A *bachelor* you mean. A man who prefers the company of men.'

'And an artist to boot.'

Pickering waved the description away. 'I would not name myself so. I am an illustrator. I reflect back what is there, I do not create.'

Cage took another slug of brandy, appreciating the effect if not the taste. 'I went to your apartment, to pick up the trail. I looked through your things, hoping to find your aunt's address—'

Moses interrupted. 'I brought her letters with me for that reason.'

'Quite. I found something that interested me. You kept a file, poems torn from various editions, poems that you had not illustrated.'

Pickering looked away, and dusted a piece of lint from his jacket. There was no reason for Cage to ask, but something compelled him. 'Why?'

'Why did I keep them, or why did I not illustrate them?'

Cage shrugged. 'Both.'

'I suppose I would have to say it was because I could not find the truth of them. That is what inspires me at least, for there are many possibilities always, this line or that, many options for the image that might make sense. But normally there is one that emerges somehow, some fundamental certainty that the poet believes in. Something solid, that anchors everything else.'

'And these poems do not have it, this anchor?'

Pickering shook his head. 'Not necessarily. It is that I cannot see it. I could always make a choice, of course – this image, that metaphor – but that would be a disservice to the poem itself.'

'I had not thought there was so much to it.'

Moses stared out of the window, as if the truth were hidden there. 'Maybe there was not. But it was how it worked for me. So I kept them, and Justin always said he would republish if I ever found what I was looking for.'

Cage leant forward, coming closer to what he really wanted to know. 'And was the failing yours? Or the poet's, for not making himself clear?'

'Sometimes I think it's neither. Sometimes I think it's

deliberately obscure, that the writer wants no one but himself to see the truth.'

'And my poem? "The Sacrifice". What truth was missing?' Cage knew the answer, but could not help but wonder if this unassuming man, facing the gallows, might now see it too.

Moses looked at him then. 'Let's just say something did not make sense to me.'

He knew. Moses Pickering *knew*, but somehow the roof had not fallen in. He was still here, drinking apple brandy in a cottage at the end of the world. Cage merely nodded, a truth acknowledged. Time to move on. 'And what of Baxter's poem? Had you found the heart of it? Justin said you were struggling, but the poem seemed straightforward to me, if brutal and unbearably sad.'

'Did it? I thought it was neither. Poor Baxter.'

'Really? What was it then?'

Moses looked out of the window again. 'A secret, buried within somewhere.' He shrugged and returned to his tea. 'It doesn't matter now. Nothing does.'

Cage sat back. 'Moses, all is not lost.' He picked up the note and folded it into his pocket. 'I will find who sent this.' It was said with more confidence than he felt, but he had to try.

Moses laughed, an unpleasant sound. 'I'd have hanged the last time, if it hadn't been for you. But then we were only fighting circumstance, and prejudice. Now, there is someone out there, someone who is putting quite some time and effort into ensuring I am condemned for this. It is too much; it is too much to fight.'

Cage could hear the emotion rising in Pickering's voice, a level of despair he had not heard even in their darkest days. 'Moses. I have fought worse.'

He hadn't, but the lie was necessary.

Cage got to his feet. 'Now, you stay out of sight and I shall go back into town and return with provisions. I shall make for London this evening. I will need a few days at most, and the tide shall turn, Moses. It is already on the cusp – the *Globe* ran an article yesterday, questioning Leland Crewler's involvement. Even Cross intends to look into it. I have some leads, and this note will certainly help. We are further forward than we were yesterday. Have faith.'

'In you?'

'In justice.' Cage wanted to laugh at himself, but the man needed reassurance.

Moses pressed some coins into his hand and a wicker basket was found. It took an age for Pickering to unlock the bolts on the front door, his fingers slow, and he tore his skin on the rusted iron, although he seemed not to notice.

'Any special requests?' It was a bizarre situation, buying groceries for a client.

Pickering shook his head. 'I do not need much. You might purchase some stiff brandy, I think. And thank you, Cage.' Moses gripped his arm. 'You are a better man than you think yourself to be.'

CHAPTER TWENTY-FOUR

The light was fading as Cage trudged back into town. He felt more than a little ridiculous, carrying the basket like a housewife. So much for not drawing attention to himself. Maybe it didn't matter now? He didn't feel as confident as he had implied to Moses. The man was right – the real killer was actively working against him. What other evidence might have been planted? As well as tracking down Hazel Smythson, he needed to find out exactly what the police thought they had against Moses. A new thought occurred: maybe he would be better off bringing Moses back to face trial? That at least would force Cross to reveal his hand, and this case could be played out where Cage was at his best. He needed to be back in a courtroom, not scurrying about the streets of Gravesend buying milk and cheese.

On his way back, he stopped off at the tavern on the Wrotham Road to buy brandy. Knowing Moses's tastes, he chose a good one, the coins from Pickering more than enough to pay for it.

The lane that led to the house was dark, the moon hidden behind a bolt of clouds. He passed the cottage once before realising he had missed it, and retraced his steps, stumbling and cursing. The milk was leaking, but the brandy was at least secure.

When he knocked on the front door, there was no answer. Moses was being cautious again.

He knocked louder. 'Hello! It's Cage. You can open the door.'

There was still no response, so he found his way to the back of the house. A paraffin lamp flickered in the kitchen and the stable door was unlocked, but there was no sign of Pickering. He dumped the basket on the kitchen table and went into the hallway. There were no other lamps, and he struggled to see anything as he yelled up the stairs, 'Moses, I've returned!'

Still nothing. Cage cursed. Had Moses slipped through his fingers again? He took the stairs two at a time, despite the dark. The curtains were open in all the bedrooms, and there was enough light to see that they were all empty. He ran back down the stairs and into the parlour, tearing open the dainty drapes at the front window, but Moses was nowhere to be found.

Cage slumped into an armchair and leant his head back against the flowery chintz, grey in the meagre moonlight. He closed his eyes. He should have expected this: Cage's bluster had been no salve to Moses's fear. For all his sophistication, Pickering was driven by the same instincts as any cornered animal. Fight or flee, and, as Moses had said himself, he was no fighter.

There was no point sitting here, he should go to the station. Pickering must have known a shortcut to avoid Cage's path to and from the house. Maybe someone there would remember him and which direction he had travelled in, assuming he had left town at all.

Cage stood up, then yelped as he caught his shin on the table in the centre of the room. *Damn you, Moses.* His eye caught on something: lined up across the table were the three Rubens prints. Surely Moses would have taken them with him?

Another thought settled like lead. Cage ran to the kitchen and searched for a spare lamp, but found only matches. Outside in the garden he took a match from the box, but it refused to light against the damp tinder. He tried another, then another before giving up and throwing the whole box to the ground.

The garden surrounded the house and he searched randomly, panic rising as he pushed vines and bushes to one side. A sharp memory of the moment he fell into the Devil's snare at the Crewler hothouse returned, but he stamped it down. This was not about him; it had never been about him.

He found himself at the front of the house, looking back into the parlour like a ghost. Had he been wrong? Had Moses simply decided to travel light? He turned, and his eyes fell on the woodshed. The door was ajar.

Please God, no.

His legs were reluctant to move. Minutes seemed to pass before he reached the hut. He placed his hand on the latch and paused, half knowing what he was about to see. The world was silent, just his own breath, and something else coming from within.

The creak of rope on wood.

Cage thrust open the door and faced the horror of it. Moses Pickering hung from the rafters, shoulders slumped, his back towards Cage. His toes were mere inches from the floor, like a ballet dancer's in mid-flight. A taller man could not have done it. Logs scattered around the floor – Moses must have stacked them up then kicked them away, a final act of bravery.

Cage grasped the man's legs and lifted him up. Pickering's head fell forward as if in prayer. He could just reach the beam and with fumbling hands attempted to untie the knots, trying not to look at Moses's face, trying not to think of the body he embraced in death, his left arm encircling Pickering's waist and holding him close, this man he had left to die by his own hand.

Finally, the knot came loose and Pickering's body slumped into his arms. Cage carried him outside and laid him on the ground, the rope trailing from his wretched neck. Cage stood up and looked around. The world was as he had left it, which seemed wrong, somehow. He wiped the sweat from his forehead on the sleeve of his coat. He needed a drink, to wait for his thoughts to return, wait for an idea of what the hell to do now.

He returned to the kitchen and grabbed the brandy from the basket. He opened it, took a slug, and then another, then collapsed into a chair. His eyes wandered, waiting for his brain to catch up. The blue gingham curtains were faded at the bottom, years of sunlight stripping them of colour. The cups they had drunk from were neatly stacked on the drainer. Who washes the dishes before taking their own life? Moses Pickering, that's who. Moses Pickering, whose body now lies on the ground, dust to dust.

Cage's vision was hazy. He wiped at his eyes. They were wet. He looked back at the basket of groceries, ordered in the knowledge that they would not be eaten. He hadn't seen it before, but a single crystal glass stood in the centre of the table, drops of water within, as if recently washed.

The brandy had been for him.

CHAPTER TWENTY-FIVE

He wasn't sure how long he sat there, how much brandy he drank from that elegant little glass. He thought he was waiting for his mind to return, to figure out what to do next, but it was the memories that came first. Charlie, facing the swirling sea, the little boy holding his hand a figment of the child's own imagination. Charlie had been alone in the end, just as Moses had been.

He should return to the town and find the police station, report the death. His lawyer's brain half-heartedly considered options and possibilities. What web might be spun from this? But in truth, he could find no angle, no alternative strategy to pursue. Moses had said it himself, hadn't he? Only the guilty run. And only the guilty hang themselves in a woodshed.

The game was up. He would be a fool to protest the innocence of a dead man who had already condemned himself to a gallows of log and fisherman's rope. The papers would lynch Pickering all over again, and Cross would seal shut the case of Baxter Spring and Nathaniel Crewler, tied with a nice red bow. Then life would go on, for everyone except Cage Lackmann. He wouldn't return to Pincott, he wouldn't beg again. His days in a courtroom were over, but what else could he do? He shook his head, as if the ghost of Moses Pickering had been the one to ask the question.

He pulled himself to his feet. His body felt heavy, devoid of will. He forced himself to return to the front of the house. He was almost surprised to see Pickering's body where he had left it, as if the man might have one last twist in the story to offer. Cage knelt down. Should he remove the rope from around Pickering's neck? Or would the coroner need it as evidence? Cage knew he should make haste to the police station, but he was reluctant to leave Moses alone. Instead, he took Pickering's hands and laid them together on his stomach: neat, just as the man had liked it.

Pickering's notebook had fallen from his pocket as Cage had laid his body down, and he retrieved it now. Fine leather, the pages dry and almost furry to the touch. He flicked through: in the moonlight he could make out countless shapes, some crossed out, others circled or highlighted with stars. He pushed the notebook deep into his coat pocket, where it met the crumpled page of Baxter's poem and the note written on his own stationery.

I will have something of you, Moses, he thought. *Another man I didn't save.*

The walk into town seemed to take an age. He had no concept of time any more. The police station was closed when he got there, but the coffee shop next door was still open and doing a roaring trade, the shouts and barks of laughter that greeted him as he entered sounding cruel to him, taunting the dead.

An attendant directed him to a nearby tavern where a Sergeant Downing could almost certainly be found. The place was close to empty, and the man in question was still in uniform, sitting alone with a pint of ale and reading the paper by the fire. After an initial frown, he took the interruption with a professional grace. Cage wondered how he would begin to explain what had happened, how there came to be a dead man lying in the grounds of a cottage a mile outside of town. When had the story really started? Five years ago? Or before that, forged in the malevolent flames that also wrought a child killer?

In the end he simply said: 'My name is Cage Lackmann, a lawyer from Whitechapel. I visited a client here today, but he has taken his own life. I took the body down, and came here.'

Sergeant Downing stood up. 'You are sure he is dead?'

'Quite sure.'

A notebook appeared in the man's hand. 'What was your client's name?'

'Moses Pickering.'

The sergeant stopped writing and looked up. His expression said everything.

'You will no doubt want to telegraph Scotland Yard. Detective Jack Cross.'

The man was efficient, demanding details in a quiet, clear voice. The tavern faced out onto the quayside; a huge steamer sat solid in the water. Cage wondered where it was going. Might there be a place for him somewhere in this world, even now?

'Stay here. I will send someone for your statement.'

Cage slumped into the chair the sergeant had vacated. He was glad the policeman wasn't a fool. Moses deserved better than that, some dignity in death. For a moment, Cage felt a wave of guilt for leaving Moses outside on the ground. He could easily have taken his thin body indoors, laid him on the chintz sofa, kept him warm. He made a noise then, like a howl that had to be swallowed down. The barman took it as a demand for service. Cage wanted a brandy so badly, he could feel himself shaking.

'Some water. Thank you.'

More hours passed, the fire offering comfort as it smouldered kindly beside him. Cage took out his wallet and counted the loose coins in his pocket, now swelled by the change he had been unable to pass on to Pickering. He should have left it there on the table, with the milk and the bread and the cheese. Had Moses left a will, he wondered? Who would now inherit the cottage with the blue gingham curtains and the roses grown wild about the door? Justin would know. Cage realised that Moses Pickering was not his problem any more, and there was some relief in it.

It was past nine, the clock on the wall announced. The few patrons that remained were supping their last. The trains to London ran until eleven but it was unlikely he would make the last train now. No one had yet appeared to take his statement.

Cage took out Pickering's notebook. He would give it to Kenward, to Emma maybe. The thought of breaking the news to them was unpleasant. One of them was bound to ask why he had left Moses alone. He opened the notebook to distract himself from what he might say.

The first page announced that the book was the property of Moses Pickering, and gave the address in Kilburn. Beneath this was written a plea:

This notebook, and the drawings within, are of huge value to me. If you find it, please return it to me at the above address and I shall pay a suitable reward.

The book was barely a quarter full, but the pages that had been used were densely covered: the titles of poems, and various lines written in quotation marks above a series of illustrations, most unfinished. The process Moses had described to him was evident. For most poems it would seem, he had eventually circled a quote and its accompanying illustration. What had Moses called it? The anchor? The heart of it? Or maybe those had been Cage's words as he tried to grasp the idea.

He turned to the last few pages, knowing what he would find there. 'The Graves of Whitechapel' was neatly written and underlined with a flourish. Cage recognised many of the lines Moses had pulled out: *a graveyard stretches across the hill . . . First I find Joy . . . Here lies remembrance*, and so it went on. Below each line was a series of literal illustrations: the cypress trees, the gravestones, a path that stretched into the distance where a tiny tree marked how much further there was to go.

Some of the illustrations were unfinished, others crossed out, or with asterisks against them, even a question mark. The final drawing was a simple chapel with a single door and two windows, the stark lines leaving it creamy white against an ink-black sky, a reference to the poem's title. Had there been a white chapel there once? Is that how the name came into being? It was hard to imagine the East End as green meadows and ancient oak, but he supposed it had been at one time. Everything that is spoiled was perfect once.

He looked up. It was ten o'clock now and he was the only one who remained. Even the attendant was nowhere to be seen. He stood up and stretched his legs. He'd seen others head through a door the other side of the bar and followed in their path. The outhouse was at the end of an enclosed yard. The temperature was well below freezing as he stepped in, grateful to see a paraffin lamp hanging from a hook in the ceiling and a jug of water set on a washstand.

The knock on the door startled him. 'Sir? Are you in there?'

'Yes! One moment.'

'There's someone here to see you, sir.'

Finally he could give his statement and leave. He suddenly felt a desperate urge to be away from here. Whitechapel at least was home, even if there was nothing else there for him now. Moses was dead, forever branded a murderer, and Cage's career would be buried with him.

He returned to the empty bar. Empty except for one man, who sat at Cage's table, his back turned, his hat still rammed low on his head as he warmed his hands by the fire. Maybe it was the cut of his shoulders, or the gnarly hands that gave him away, but Cage recognised him in an instant.

He turned back to the attendant, who had followed him in. 'A brandy, if you please.'

Cage walked over and took his seat across from the man. 'You got here quickly.'

'The wonders of the modern rail system.'

Cage looked at the untouched glass of red wine on the table. 'And you're a claret man? I'm surprised.'

'Why?'

'It's not a man's drink.'

Jack Cross raised his eyebrows a little. 'You have quite the taste for it, I thought. You don't consider yourself a man?'

'We both know what I am.'

'Ah.' The detective's smile failed to reach his eyes as always. 'You are feeling sorry for yourself.'

Cage shrugged – there was no point lying any more. The attendant brought a glass of brandy to the table, then left them alone.

'Brandy. You are still in shock then?'

'I left him. To buy provisions. To keep him going while I returned to London. But it seemed he wanted peace more than he wanted toast and jam.'

'You're a damned fool, Lackmann.'

Cage slammed his glass back on the table. 'Jack, what's the point? Pickering is dead. Case closed.'

Cross frowned then leant forward. 'How long have you known he was here?'

Cage rubbed his eyes. God, he was tired. 'Since this morning, give or take.' There was no point confessing to his break-in at the Crewler house. It was bad enough that his career was over, but he'd like to keep himself out of prison, at least. 'I realised his aunt's address would be in my paperwork somewhere, and so it was. I came this afternoon.'

'And what did Pickering tell you?'

Cage thought of the note burning a hole in his pocket, the note that told Pickering to run, written on Cage's own stationery. But it didn't help Moses now; all it did was implicate Cage in the whole damned sorry mess. Whoever wanted to frame Moses had succeeded.

Cage leant back in his chair. 'Why are you interested, Jack? The truth doesn't matter. You've got your man, as you say.'

'Only I haven't.'

Cage laughed. 'You wanted to hang him yourself, personally – is that it?'

Cross suddenly looked as tired as Cage felt. 'I would have done, gladly. There's just one problem.'

'I don't care about your problems, Jack. But it appears I have nothing better to do than to listen to them. So tell me, what's your one little problem with this gift of a solution that poor bastard has just delivered to you with his life?'

Cross sipped his wine. 'Moses Pickering didn't kill Baxter Spring.'

The words hung in the air for a moment. Cage wasn't even sure he'd heard the man correctly.

The detective slid a ticket stub across the table. It was for a single first-class journey from London to Gravesend, dated the day that Cage had last appeared in court, the day Pickering had run, the day that Baxter Spring had died. The time read 6.14 p.m.

'We found this in his wallet. A driver at the station remembers picking up a man who matched Pickering's description at seven-thirty and taking him to Rouge Lane that night.'

'Where's the punchline, Jack?'

Cross reclaimed the ticket. 'Baxter Spring wasn't killed until much later that night.'

'How can you know that?'

'*Science*, Lackmann. Poetry is very last century.'

They sat in silence for a while, Cage thinking of how that tiny detail, the time of Baxter's death, could have saved Pickering's life if only they had known. But it hadn't happened that way. He wondered how he would answer the next question when it came.

'Why the hell did Pickering choose that very evening to abandon his life and come here?' continued Cross. 'What did he tell you?'

Be careful, thought Cage. Moses is exonerated. The unachievable goal has been achieved. He could get his life back now. He could get his life *back*.

'It was simply a horrible coincidence. He'd been struggling for a while. The grief at his aunt's death, you know how it is. That day, he decided to come out here, just for a short while.

He kept some things at the cottage, clothes, paintings and personal effects.' Lies, all lies. Cage looked steadily at Cross. 'Then he saw the papers, the boy's death, the way the tide was flowing. The man was too terrified to return.' He shook his head. 'Poor Moses.'

It wasn't too late, was it? To take that note from his pocket and lay it before Cross, tell him the truth. But where would that go? Would Cross believe he had not written it? Or would he simply assume Cage was protecting someone else: a grand ruse from the master of the grand ruse.

Cross was looking at him, waiting for more. Cage filled the silence with the only honest thing he had left to say. 'Leland Crewler. He is the only other connection. Unless you think Kenward—'

Cross interrupted with a wave of his hand. 'Not Kenward. We investigated him five years ago. He's not a man for secrets.'

'Crewler, then. Does he have an alibi for that evening? One you can trust?' Cage thought suddenly. 'And the photograph, the one that was left in my office – that must be a lead of some kind, unless it was one of your own personal jokes?'

Cross pulled back from any further confidences, and the old enmity returned. 'Why do you care?'

'Last time we saw each other, you asked me why I didn't.'

'You've got what you wanted, Lackmann. Your precious reputation will be restored. Champion of the innocent, isn't that what they call you?'

'Can I go now?'

Cross stood up and threw some coins on the table. 'You still have to give a statement to the thorough Sergeant Downing. I, on the other hand, will make the last train.'

'It's been a pleasure, as always.'

Cross seemed undaunted. 'It's coming, Lackmann, your comeuppance, one of these days.'

Cage couldn't bring himself to disagree.

CHAPTER TWENTY-SIX

After Cross left, a message arrived to meet Sergeant Downing at the station at nine in the morning. Cage was sent to a clapboard bed and breakfast beyond the furthest quay. The attic room was basic and cold, but spotlessly clean, with white bedlinen that froze around him as he climbed in.

He shivered through the night despite keeping his coat and boots on, and was still awake when the dawn came. He rose and went down to the breakfast room. He was the first one there and chose a seat as close to the newly laid fire as he could. His eyes began to close again in the growing warmth, and he laid his head on the table, sleep coming almost immediately.

The chatter of other voices grew and eventually he was shoved awake by the sharp elbow of the man who had sat next to him. 'You won't want to miss the breakfast, laddie, trust me.'

Cage muttered his thanks and signalled to the proprietor. Minutes later he was sipping a mug of hot, sweet tea and eating curried eggs with thick buttered toast. It was his best meal in days. The food made him sleepy all over again, but the day had to be got through first.

Thankfully, the sergeant was waiting for him when he

arrived early at the police station and he gave his statement without interruption. He signed his name and wrote down the Kenwards' address when asked for information on Pickering's next of kin. They were the closest thing he had to family since the aunt had died, and himself too, he supposed.

As he was about to leave, he thought of a question. 'Is it still the case that suicides cannot be buried in consecrated ground?'

Downing shrugged. 'Think it depends on the church. There is discretion, I believe.'

He'd have to ask Archie – not that there was any real reason to return to the vicarage now that Pickering was no long implicated. Having his portrait taken had been a subterfuge, and he was not so interested in seeing the results. But he had liked Archie, with his warm study filled with books and pictures and a life well led.

He made the 10.20 train, buying a second-class ticket before remembering that everything had changed and he could now upgrade to first. He had his life back after all. Maybe it was just the tiredness and the shock of Pickering's death that was stopping him from feeling any satisfaction just yet. He had heard the expression *a hollow victory* many times. And now he felt it, a vacuum in the pit of his stomach, where something else should have been.

If Pickering had trusted him enough to stay alive, would Cage have found the proof of his innocence without the help of Jack Cross? He would not have thought to check the timings of that night: the facts, in other words. Facts had never helped his clients before. Facts were normally arranged on the opposite side of the bench, stern-faced and reliable witnesses. The only facts that had ever served him were the ones he manipulated, or fabricated completely from scratch, a currency to be traded. By the time he reached London, the vacuum within was beginning to clot with self-revulsion.

At the station, he hired a hansom to take him to Notting Hill. After the quiet of the country, the noise of the city assaulted his ears: he'd left a part of himself back there, lying next to Pickering on the heartless ground.

It was well into the afternoon when he finally arrived at the steps of the Kenwards' house. The same maid he had met before opened the door. Her eyes were pink and she gave him a sorry smile: the news had already been broken to the occupants of the house, and some of the burden lifted, but not all.

He was shown into the parlour. Justin and Emma Kenward sat at either end of the Chesterfield, their hands joined across the space they had left between them. Justin rose to greet Cage, red-rimmed eyes still filled with tears.

'Cage, what can you tell us? A constable came a half hour ago but he had only the bare facts. Moses is dead? By his own hand?'

Cage took a chair near the fire, although he wasn't especially cold. He was attracted to fire these last few days: the spit and the crackle, the sheer life of it even as it turned everything to ash.

He told them the truth, or most of it, anyway, leaving out the break-in at the hothouse and the note squirrelled away in his coat pocket: Justin was not a man born to keep secrets. As he talked, he tried to avoid Emma's gaze. Both of the Kenwards rippled with grief, but somehow hers was harder to take.

Unexpectedly, they seemed to accept his explanation of why Moses had gone to Gravesend. He had obviously stumbled upon a credible lie.

Justin said: 'He had mentioned a few times that he was thinking of taking a break from it all, although he had said nothing of his aunt's passing, or that the house was now his. He was a private man, but the well ran deep.'

Emma rang the only note of scepticism. 'But why did he not tell us of his plans?'

Justin shrugged. 'We were not due to meet for another few days. He had been struggling with Baxter's poem – maybe he thought it would help, and that he would be back before we knew he was even gone. Then, when he read the news and saw his name in print once more, well, that would have changed things.'

Emma stood up suddenly, and strode to the window, one hand tight against her stomach as if to hold something in. With her back turned she said, 'I can't bear it!'

Justin rose and followed her, placing his hands on her arms and pulling her back to his chest, his head resting against hers, a gesture of husbandly comfort. Cage tried to look away but couldn't.

Emma's hands went to her face, wiping the tears away. She turned back to Cage. 'What did Cross say? Will he pursue Leland Crewler?'

Cage shook his head. 'I have no idea. He wouldn't share those kinds of confidences with me. But the truth won't bring Moses back, or Baxter, or Nathaniel.'

Emma returned to her seat. 'Justice is always too late, even if it comes swiftly.'

The words hung over all of them.

Kenward stirred first. 'I should go to my lawyers. They prepared Moses's will and I am executor. And there will be a funeral to organise . . .' He looked at both of them, 'Although—'

Cage interrupted, 'It's discretionary, apparently. Depends on the diocese.'

Kenward nodded, a lost little boy. 'It must have been awful, to cut him down like that.'

'Worse for him.'

'I can't imagine the pain that drives a man to such a place.'

'I can.' Emma spoke softly, her eyes on her feet, which was something at least.

'Yes, well, I can't sit here. I need to do something.' Justin wiped at his face in the mirror above the mantel and rearranged his necktie.

Cage stood, grateful the meeting was at an end.

Emma grabbed his hand. 'Perhaps you would stay with me, Mr Lackmann, and talk some more. I am not ready to be alone just yet.'

Kenward intervened before Cage could react. 'Oh, my darling, if you would rather I remained . . . ? It is unfair of me to think only of my own needs at this time.'

Emma looked up at him. 'It's fine, Justin, I know you need to take action. I would hear more from Mr Lackmann on those last few hours; it will help me, I think.'

Her eyes turned to Cage, bright and clear. She was still holding his hand, her fingers strong against his.

'Very well. I will be quick, I promise.' Kenward bent and kissed her cheek, which she proffered to him at an angle, like a tennis racket meeting a ball.

When Kenward was gone, Cage reclaimed his seat by the fire.

Her eyes were on him, and impossible to read. 'So, how many lies did you just tell us? I counted one, but I suspect there are more.'

'You tell me.'

'Very well.' She sat up straight. 'You didn't find his aunt's address in your papers. You told me so the other day when we . . . met, you said you were going somewhere that night to find it.'

Maybe a confession is what he needed, and who else could he really tell but her? They held worse secrets between them. 'I went to Sheldrake House. Harriet Crewler had the details for Pickering's aunt in her address book.'

She looked bemused. 'And they let you in?'

'Not exactly.'

She slumped back in her chair and a smile flashed across her face. 'You're a rake.'

There was nothing to say to that. 'So that was one lie. Where are the others, do you think?'

'Then there is at least one more?'

'One big one.'

'Ah.' She smoothed her skirts, the ghost of their former relationship haunting the room, for they would tease each other like this, put their minds to battle, before reaching out and ending it with a fevered touch.

'So, Mr Lackmann, your story lacks plausibility in one key element, I believe. Moses was alive when you came to him, or so you say; his predicament was already known to him through the papers. And yet within hours of your arrival, the poor man decides to end it all, and quickly too.' The playful tone fell away as she spoke, the grief too strong to keep down. 'Something happened to change things, to change his decision that life was still worth living. How did you snuff out that hope, Cage? What did you do?'

He said nothing for a while. The accusation hurt, although his failings were not in what he did, but in what he didn't do.

'I need to get my coat.'

Her voice was suddenly ferocious. 'You *cannot* leave me without answers!'

'Nor will I. The answer is in my coat.'

She leant towards the table at the side of the sofa and rang the bell impatiently. The shrill of it made him jump.

The maid appeared and his coat was requested. Emma turned back to him. 'The brandy glass – was that true?'

'Of course. Why would I embellish that?' He was almost offended.

She shrugged. 'Isn't that what they say about lies? They beget each other, like rabbits.'

It was not what he felt at all. If anything, he was beginning to wonder if we didn't all have a store of them, a certain number of falsehoods we were allowed to tell in our lives, and he was fast running out of them. One day, he would open his mouth, and all the truths inside of him would spill out.

The maid returned with his coat, and he took out the note that Mrs Chappelhow had given to Moses. Cage handed it to Emma without explanation.

Her brow furrowed as she read the message again and again. Then she stood and went to the window, as if some invisible words would be revealed in the light. She was silent for a while. He watched her, seeing her mind spinning, fracturing apart all the possibilities. 'What the hell is this, Cage?'

He stepped her through all that Moses had told him. How he believed the note was genuinely from Cage, and that the realisation it had not been sent by his lawyer, but rather by someone looking to frame him for a murder that had yet to even take place, had put an end to any hope he had.

Throughout the whole story she had stood in the fading light, staring at the darkening sky. Now she folded the note into her pocket and came to him, kneeling at his feet and placing her hands to the fire. 'So that is what made up his mind.'

'I begged him to have faith. That I would find whoever wrote this note. But I think he was out of faith at that point. We had beaten circumstance once before, but deliberate malice, that is something else entirely.'

'And do you have any inkling? Who would do this?'

He shrugged. 'My stationery is hardly held under lock and key. But there was a woman, that afternoon, a potential client. Hazel Smythson. Maybe there is a connection there, if I can trace her.'

'Don't.'

The single word surprised him. 'Why not?'

'Did you tell Cross about this?'

He was immediately defensive. 'I couldn't! Moses wasn't there to corroborate his story. All Cross would think was that I was implicated somehow in Baxter's murder. That I was hanging Moses out to the winds to defend somebody else. The man hates me; his judgement is more than clouded.'

She placed a hand on his knee. 'Then you have to let this go, Cage. Moses is dead, your reputation is no longer threatened.'

He grasped her hand. 'That's all I wanted. But I'm not sure it's enough any more.'

'Why?' Her eyes searched his.

'Do you know what Moses's last words to me were? He said, "You're a better man than you think you are."'

She laughed. She had a right to. Besides, was it really Moses's words that had cut so deep? Or was it that other crumpled paper in his pocket? The words of the dead boy poet of Whitechapel, and the dark-haired boy in his dreams that wore both faces, himself and Baxter Spring. Weren't they the same once?

He slumped back in his chair and rubbed his eyes. He could feel the dreams dancing in the wings, waiting for the lights to dim. 'Baxter Spring's death was planned. In cold blood, arrangements were made. If I can find out anything—'

She sat up on her heels and reached out, hands grasping his face as she pulled him forward and kissed him, long and deep. He could feel the tears falling hot against both their cheeks. When she spoke, their lips were still almost touching, as if she could breathe the words into him. 'Do not risk yourself, not for this, I couldn't bear it. Maybe there is hope for us yet?'

He covered her hands with his. 'Maybe.' And in that moment, the maybe felt real.

She pulled back from him and stood up, then turned to the fire. She pulled the folded note from her pocket and before he could stop her, threw it into the flames.

'The future, Cage. Let us make it all that matters.'

He watched the scrap of paper curl and disintegrate to nothing. If only he could believe the past could be destroyed so easily.

CHAPTER TWENTY-SEVEN

Cage returned home. With the rise in temperature, the Whitechapel stink had returned: the hum of sewage and yesterday's ale, a concoction that whispered of something rotten. The fog, too, had come back, a yellow swirl that had magnanimously yielded the stage to the snow, but not for long.

On the corner of his street, the elderly newspaper seller was crouching awkwardly, untying the string from the bundle of evening papers that had landed carelessly on the pavement, his fingers quick as his knees strained. Cage approached him and purchased a copy.

The article was on page three: MOSES PICKERING FOUND DEAD. It was sketchy on the details: no mention was made of the cottage in Gravesend or even that Moses had taken his own life. But the quote from Jack Cross was clear: 'Mr Pickering is no longer suspected, and our work continues to find the killer of Baxter Spring.' Next to the article the paper had reprinted the image of Nathaniel Crewler, dressed up and photographed by his brother Leland.

It was everything Cage could have wished for, but his feet still trudged towards his front door. As he fumbled for his keys, he turned back to the street, his eyes finally catching what should have been unmissable: the black carriage of Obediah Pincott parked at the crossroads up ahead. Other pedestrians were giving it a wide berth, as though if they came too close the Grim Reaper himself might cast his scythe and snatch them in.

Cage had no stomach for a meeting with Pincott right now. But maybe that was a good thing: he was too tired to play their usual game. He ambled towards the carriage. In all the years he had known Pincott, the man had not once set foot in Cage's place of residence. Their meetings had always taken place in the compound, or in the velvet dark of this vehicle, as if Pincott were a spirit unable to break the chains that bound him there.

He knocked on the nearside door. Moments later, it swung open. Cage grabbed the rail and stepped up, still clutching the newspaper in one hand.

Pincott sat next to another man, his face cast in shadow, but judging by the smell, it was Clifford Chester. Cage took the seat opposite, the cold leather stretched and buttoned across horsehair as hard as stone.

'Evening, Obediah. Some light would be nice.'

Cage's eyes had adjusted. He could see enough, in truth, but he was growing weary of the dark.

'I am told congratulations are in order.'

With this, Chester broke his composure and leant forward, slapping Cage hard on the thigh. 'A triumph! And Pickering gone too, forever innocent. The dead can't let you down. It's perfect. Well done, old chap.'

Pincott's eyes shone in the gloom. 'Did you kill him?'

'No.' It felt like a lie.

'I'm glad to have you back, Lackmann,' said Chester. 'I have missed you. This other chap –' he waved his hand dismissively '– not so good. Not so *inventive*.'

'I need some time,' said Cage. 'The last few days have been a challenge.'

Pincott gave a nod to Chester, who hurriedly pulled his case onto his lap and removed a wallet. Cage could see the wad of notes as Chester's chubby thumb leafed through them, wondering where it should stop.

'What is needed?' asked Pincott.

'Time. That's what I said.'

'Ah. I do not have it to give.'

Pincott took the wallet from Chester and removed half the contents. He leant forward and Cage ignored the instinct to shrink back in his seat as the Ukrainian took his hand in his and folded the notes within.

'A bonus.'

How much was there? Maybe a hundred. He'd never in his life felt less grateful to see such a sum, as if Pickering's blood was fresh upon it.

'Thank you.'

Chester rifled through his case. 'Tomorrow. We are third up. One of Dub's men. Assault and violent affray.'

A thick file was handed across. Cage took it without a glance, his eyes still on Pincott, who had slunk back into the shadows.

'Why me, Obediah? All those years ago, what did you see?'

'You want compliments?'

Cage shook his head. 'I'm not expecting the answer to be complimentary.'

'And there it is. Self-hatred. It makes a man ambitious.'

Cage scrunched the notes into his pocket and clutched the file to his chest. 'Goodnight, Obediah.'

He reached for the handle and wrenched open the door. Chester flung him a set of instructions for the morning as he stepped back into the night, but he didn't respond. By the time he reached his front door, he could hear the clip clop of the carriage departing.

As he entered his office, the air was thick with smoky residue from where the fire had burned itself out, and the tang of stale claret. He looked at the detritus the last week had wrought: papers strewn across the floor, his desk stained with spilled wine. He had no energy to re-lay the fire; the stock of coal was already running low. He tried to make a mental list – hire a charwoman, a maid even, visit the grocer's – but the fog was too heavy for it. He thought of Shanksy and the box of possessions he had left there. But he wasn't sure he wanted any of it back. Not now.

Upstairs, he emptied his pockets: the banknotes, Baxter's poem, and Moses's notebook, which he had forgotten to give to Emma. He pulled his strongbox from beneath the bed and stuffed most of the notes within. He would count them another time. Increased security: that needed to go on the list too. So much to do, but sleep was the priority.

His bed was cold at first, but the pillows were soft as he wrapped himself within the eiderdown and curled up like a child. He panicked for a moment, thinking sleep might not come, but the panic was the last thing he remembered.

He woke only once during the night, the dream shaking him awake. Charlie at the cliff's edge once more, holding the hand of the dark-haired boy, only this time they were not alone. The thin silhouette of Moses Pickering held the boy's other hand.

They stepped forward together, their feet defiant against the turbulent, spiteful sky.

Cage lay in the dark, his breathing calm and a promise on his lips.

I will find who killed you, Baxter Spring.

CHAPTER TWENTY-EIGHT

The next morning he took his time to wash and dress, managing to remove two days' worth of beard without a nick.

Downstairs, he ignored the mess, grabbed his trial wig from its stand and stepped out into the hazy sunshine, clutching Chester's file of notes to his chest. He called first at the coal merchant's, paying his debt and arranging a new delivery that afternoon. At the grocer's, he was greeted with suspicion at first, but the smiles returned when he withdrew the coins from his pocket. A slice of fresh pound cake was freely given, and Cage wolfed it down as he marched towards the Whitechapel Road and hailed a cab.

Grateful for the traffic, Cage flipped open the file Chester had given him: Connor MacGregor, a familiar name. He shuffled through the papers and found Chester's notes on the man's previous offences. He had served two years for grand larceny several years earlier. Cage remembered the case well. Pincott had been displeased that Cage had been unable to exonerate him completely, but MacGregor had been lucky not to be convicted for killing a man called Ormond, the manager of the ship's merchants he had robbed at knifepoint. Cage had blamed a mysterious cohort of MacGregor's for the murder: a ring leader who had fled the scene and cruelly left his naïve young colleague, one Connor MacGregor, to face the consequences of his murderous actions. It was Granger who had provided the evidence, playing the part of a bystander who witnessed a thick-set negro holding a knife and running across the rooftops as the victim lay bleeding in the streets. It had been a performance of pure ham: Granger had added a stutter and a limp. But it worked: Connor MacGregor, the real culprit, got off lightly. Ormond's widow had been present every day. Cage had avoided her gaze for the duration of the trial.

The current charge levelled against MacGregor involved a street brawl outside a tavern in Islington. Three others had been arrested on the same charge and it wasn't clear who had been fighting whom: a victimless crime. Today was a bail hearing only, but Cage would need to get a semblance of the story from MacGregor first.

Cage alighted a few streets from the Old Bailey steps, hoping to make a quiet entrance. It had not even been a week since his previous appearance there, but he felt nervous to be returning, as if he had forgotten what to do, or what he was.

He climbed the bail dock and pushed through the great doors into the main chamber, his eyes searching for Clifford Chester like a port in a storm, but various colleagues and court cronies were on him in seconds.

'Lackmann, good to see you back. Bad business, eh?'

There were back slaps and arm squeezes, even a ruffle of his hair. He smiled sadly at them all, muttered the odd *thank you*, dignified at the death of his innocent client. Even some of the establishment barristers nodded in his direction, acknowledging one of their own returning to the fold. He had always seen them as a different breed, honour and a regard for the law running through their privileged veins. But maybe they were not so different to him: their paymasters may have smelled more fragrant than Obediah Pincott but they all clambered over the truth, crushing it into the ground to put food on their tables.

He needed to speak to one of the clerks but the three on duty were all occupied with other enquiries. The court was busier than usual. He looked around once more: he couldn't see Chester anywhere but Finian Worthing, the *Times* reporter, caught his eye.

'Quite the turn of events, Lackmann.'

'Indeed.'

'The investigation is turning towards Crewler.'

That was something, at least. 'Pickering hanged himself in his aunt's woodshed.'

Worthing nodded. 'It is not enough, to be innocent, if the world thinks otherwise.'

Cage could see over Worthing's head that one of the clerks had come free. 'Excuse me, Finian.'

Cage rushed across to where the clerk hunched over the papers on the lectern before him. As he approached, the clerk looked up and smiled.

'Welcome back, sir!' The man looked down at his schedule. 'Bail court is running late. You'll be delayed an hour at least.'

'Actually, I was hoping you could help me. I met a client here last week but in all the distractions of the last few days, I have misplaced the details. Might you look out an address for me? I know this is unorthodox, but I would hate to let her down after she approached me for help.'

The man blinked through his glasses several times. 'What was the name, sir?'

'Thank you! Hazel Smythson. Her husband is due in court on a forgery charge, I believe. I do not recall his first name, but Smythson is unusual enough, I think.'

The man promised to check the court records at luncheon. Cage thanked him once again, then turned towards the prep room. He had not gone three steps before a hand grabbed his arm.

'You're late, Lackmann. I was about to make contingency plans.'

'We're delayed, apparently. An hour at least.'

'Come then.' Chester waddled forwards. 'Let us go and see our boy.'

The Old Bailey was linked to Newgate Prison by a tunnel. Although public executions had not occurred for over a decade, the tunnel was still referred to as Dead Man's Walk. This morning, it was busy. Lawyers strode in and out of the prison, and wardens led the accused into the courts and, if they were unlucky, back again. Clifford Chester was greeted with furrowed brows by some of the wardens, but warmly by others, palms greased and ready to help in any way. Within ten minutes, they were squashed into a small room with a trestle table and a single chair.

Chester took the chair as Cage thumped his file of notes onto the table and slouched against the wall.

'You have read them?'

'Yes.' In truth, he had barely taken more than a glance.

Connor MacGregor was led in. Even with chains about his wrists and feet, he brought a palpable air of danger with him. He was not a large man, but everything about him seemed hard. His shoulders still rolled as he walked, a swagger that announced how lightning-quick with his fists he could be if provoked, and how easily he could be so.

Chester signalled for the warden to leave them alone, then asked, 'What's the story, Connor?'

MacGregor blessed them with the bare facts, in a thick Irish accent. His voice came in jabs and hooks, fast and brief, his eyes on Cage as if sizing him up. Not that the man bore him any ill will, it was just a primal instinct, to figure out how to take someone down if it came to it. Cage found himself trying to imagine MacGregor as a boy, vulnerable and afraid. There must have been a time when those eyes cried in helplessness, but any evidence was long gone, covered in scar tissue and muscle as hard as stone. Why did that happen to some and not others? Why had Baxter Spring turned to poetry and not violence? Whatever lines he had written on his bedroom wall, it had not protected him from his killer as well as fists might have done.

Cage was aware that Chester was now looking at him. 'Any questions, Mr Lackmann?'

There were so many. 'No, I have what I need.'

The warden returned and MacGregor winked at him as he was led away, as if they were conspirators, which Cage supposed they were: players in the game of the English court system, keeping each other busy while their victims stood silent in the gallery.

Thirty minutes later, Cage found himself at the barrister's bench of Court Number Two. Whitaker was leading the prosecution once more, reading out a list of previous crimes committed by the defendant. Cage looked across to MacGregor. He had forgotten to brief the man on how to act in court, one of the basic principles he normally drummed into them. MacGregor was looking down, a smile on his face as each arrest or skirmish with the law was noted, as if they were all here to toast his career.

Then Whitaker began the speech Cage had heard a thousand times before: a danger to ordinary citizens, a trigger temper, known affiliations to a criminal collective, etc. It was almost midday according to the large clock above the Lord Mayor's crest. Would the clerk have been able to track down the Smythson case by now, he wondered?

'Mr Lackmann?'

Cage looked up at the judge who gazed back expectantly from beneath angry beetle brows. What was his name again? Cage had forgotten.

He stood up. 'Yes, indeed. I apologise, your honour. So, my client, Mr MacGregor, has you will have noticed turned quite the corner over the last few years. Despite Mr Whitaker's long list of previous offences, Mr MacGregor has not been any trouble to anyone for, well, for some years now. He was unlucky enough to be set upon while out drinking a few nights ago with his colleagues after a long week at work. He defended himself and nothing more, something we shall prove beyond a doubt when we come to trial. Not to grant bail at this juncture would be an unnecessary waste of precious resources.'

That would do. Cage sat down.

The judge leant forward, his eyebrows now more quizzical than angry. 'Is that it, Mr Lackmann?'

Cage stood up again. 'Yes, your honour.'

'Very well. Bail is denied. Next case!'

The gavel came down: a sharp rap that almost made Cage jump.

Cage looked across to the dock. MacGregor was resisting the warden's attempts to take him away, his eyes murderously focussed on Cage.

Whitaker shuffled past him, patting his shoulder. 'Stunning performance, old chap.'

Cage followed Whitaker towards the main hall. At the last moment he looked up to see a woman leaving the public gallery. She turned, and their eyes met.

Hazel Smythson.

It was seconds only, then she bolted for the door.

Cage pushed roughly past Whitaker and ran straight into Clifford Chester, his beady eyes full of recrimination.

'I don't have time for this!' Cage squeezed past and ran into the hall. The entrance to the gallery led out towards the bail dock. He rushed forwards, but the hall was busy. He ran straight into one of the clerks, knocking him to the floor, his papers spilling everywhere.

'I say!'

Cage apologised, spinning back towards the great doors just in time to see the back of Hazel Smythson as she emerged from the gallery steps. He cried out, 'Mrs Smythson!'

Everyone turned but her. She was out on the bail dock now, running down the steps to the street. He made it to the doors in time to see her leap into a cab.

He ran after her, taking the steps two at a time, his wig flying off behind him. Her cab pulled out into the road and he cast around for another to follow her.

He stepped out into the street and waved his arms. He was causing a scene he knew. But the traffic moved past him, indifferent to his predicament. Someone yelled at him to get out of the road. Frantically he turned around, just in time to see her cab turn into Ludgate Hill.

She was gone.

An arm grabbed at his and he was pulled back towards the pavement.

Cage caught his breath, as Clifford Chester spat into his ear, 'What the hell has got into you?'

Cage saw his wig had rolled down the stairs, and now lay in a grimy puddle on the bottom step. He picked it up and wrung it out. What a pointless thing it was: a symbol of civility made of dead things.

'And what was that performance in the courtroom all about?'

'I think they call it justice. Shall I spell it for you?'

Chester's voice was low as he yanked Cage towards him. 'Don't be a fool, man. Pull yourself together.'

'I want out of this.'

'I'll pretend I didn't hear that. There is no *out*.'

Cage knew it was true. He'd just wanted to say it aloud. 'Who were you, Clifford? Before Pincott bought you.'

'Nobody. Absolutely nobody.'

Cage nodded. He wished it were true of himself too, but he knew it wasn't. He had been somebody once.

He walked back up the steps and through the main doors, ignoring the glances and questions. Chester remained at his side, still awaiting guidance on how to handle the storm that was coming their way.

'Tell Pincott it was the judge,' said Cage. 'He was against us from the start.'

'And MacGregor? I think he might say something else.'

'Sour grapes.' Cage looked about for the clerk he had spoken to earlier and saw him at his lectern. 'I have to go. Another case demands my attention.'

Chester puffed himself up. 'Be careful, Cage. Final warning. The dead can't pay.'

The clerk looked up as he approached. 'Ah, Mr Lackmann. I did as you asked.'

'You have an address for me?'

'No, sir. We have no record of any Smythsons, Hazel or otherwise. Nobody called Smythson is standing trial here.'

CHAPTER TWENTY-NINE

The cab journey to Kilburn passed quickly once he was out of the city. The horse's hooves held a steady pace as he looked out at a bright, clear sky of liquid blue.

He wished he still had the note with him – it would be far easier to confront Bessie Chappelhow with the evidence in hand. He should have snatched it from Emma's fire, but he had been too tired to react, too caught up in her belief that something could be salvaged for them. Had he done the right thing in not sharing the note with Jack Cross? The urge for self-protection sat ill with the altruistic mission to find who killed Nathaniel Crewler and Baxter Spring.

At the entrance to the George Inn, he remembered the falling plaster and stood to one side as he launched the iron knocker against its plate. He heard the bolt snap back, then the blackened door opened.

The moment Bessie Chappelhow caught sight of him, she heaved the door forwards, but Cage was ready for her and leapt into the gap. She let go and stepped backwards, moving surprisingly fast to grab something from behind the door frame. Cage caught her hand and seized hold of the long wooden cosh that was hiding there. It was an inelegant struggle, their relative sizes utterly mismatched. He admired her spirit if nothing else. She panted for breath as she stood away from him, her blank eyes waiting for his next move.

'Quite the welcome, Bessie.'

'I've got nothing to say to you.'

'That is no problem. I have plenty to say to you. You see, as you may well know, Moses Pickering is dead. I found him myself, hanging from the rafters of his aunt's woodshed. She lived in Gravesend, but then you knew that, didn't you? In fact, Moses told me before he died how very obliging you were in helping him take his leave that night. All part of the service, I'm sure. Tell me, did you open the note before you gave it to him that evening? Did you take a peek? You must have been curious why somebody would pay you so handsomely to pass a message to your tenant and then to deny to the authorities when they came asking that Moses had even been here. How much did they pay you? Five pounds? Ten?'

The woman's face was impassive.

He placed the cosh on a large oak sideboard, next to the visitors' book. 'Shall I leave a comment? I have a number of suggestions.'

Still she said nothing.

'I do know what you're thinking, Bessie. You've been promised more, have you not? Another handful of gold if you say nothing after a certain time has passed.'

He saw her eyes flicker briefly.

Cage moved closer. 'But the problem is, the game appears to be up. The police know that Moses did not kill Baxter Spring. Whoever *really* did, well they need a new strategy to protect themselves. Your silence can't help them any more, so why would they keep paying for it?'

Bessie Chappelhow's tiny mouth worked silently as her brain evaluated her situation. Finally she spoke. 'What do you want?'

'All I've ever wanted. The truth.' *Very funny, Cage Lackmann.*

'And the police?'

Cage shook his head. 'They don't know what I know. They won't come here.'

She was silent for a moment, the wheels turning. 'It will cost you.'

'The truth should be free, Bessie.'

Her smile was ugly: they both knew better than that.

Cage took a banknote from his pocket and placed it next to the cosh.

The landlady folded her arms across her chest. 'A woman came. That afternoon. She gave me the message in a plain envelope. Told me to give it to Mr Pickering when he returned from work. Said that he would want to leave very quickly soon after, and to help him, but say nothing afterwards, as if he had never come home in the first place.'

She lifted her head up proudly, waiting for Cage to challenge her on why she would do such a thing.

'Tell me more about the woman.'

'Young. Simply dressed. Good manners but determined.'

'You should have been a detective, Bessie – that is quite the description.'

She ignored the compliment, her eyes now on the sideboard where the banknote lay.

'You may take it now.'

She shuffled forwards and folded the note into the pocket of her apron, patting it afterwards for good measure.

'If this woman returns to make further payment – I doubt she will, but if she does, find out as much as you can. Send a boy to follow her if it's possible. You can get word to me at the Old Bailey. My name is Cage Lackmann. I will pay of course, and always more than her. Always that.'

Bessie Chappelhow gave a sharp nod. The deal was sealed: honour among thieves.

'I shall keep you no longer.'

Cage turned towards the door, still ajar after their earlier tussle.

Her voice followed him over the threshold. 'I didn't read it! The note.'

He slammed the door behind him and brushed the resulting debris from his shoulders and hair. It was worth it for the blasting thud it had made: a verdict handed down.

His driver was still waiting for him as requested. 'Where to, sir?'

'Whitechapel.'

As they drove away from the late-afternoon sun, Cage could see the city laid out before him, a coal-fuelled haze attempting to shield its secrets. Somewhere in those streets, amid the lies and delusions, Hazel Smythson was waiting for him to catch up with her.

CHAPTER THIRTY

Darkness had come by the time he reached the east of the city, but the afternoon rush of the streets had yet to abate. He jumped out on the Whitechapel Road and joined the throng.

Outside the establishment where Agnes worked, one of the floormen the madam employed was sweeping the gutters to remove the Whitechapel muck from the path of their wealthier patrons. A thick leather apron protected his shirt, more appropriate to a slaughterhouse than a brothel. As Cage approached, a rat squealed towards him, escaping the swish of those stiff bristles.

The man looked up at him. 'Not open for another hour, sir.' The word *sir* was pronounced with a mocking emphasis.

Cage ignored him and rapped on the door.

'Oi!' the man said, more exasperated than threatening.

Moments later, a young girl answered the door. She couldn't have been more than ten. She was dressed in white and wore ribbons in her hair, as if prepared for a Sunday school outing. Her blue eyes stared at him, reserving judgement.

Cage stuttered through his explanation. 'I wish to see Agnes – only to discuss a private matter; I do not intend to . . .

avail myself.' On every level, the one-sided conversation was deeply uncomfortable.

Thankfully, the madam stepped forward from the shadows, sliding her last few hair grips into place using her elbow to hold her unruly curls taut. Cage started his explanation afresh, his eyes still drawn to the girl. He shuddered to think what she was doing in such a place.

The madam's stare was as hard as the child's. 'What have you given her?'

'I beg your pardon?'

'Syphilis or the clap?'

'You misunderstand! That is not why I am here. I genuinely seek her advice only. As a friend.'

The madam placed her hand on the young girl's shoulder. 'You can have a quarter hour. But you stay down here.'

He was led into the taproom, and the girl brought him a jug of ale while the madam trod the creaking stairs to fetch Agnes down. Cage wished the girl would leave, but she sat across from him on the other side of the fire, eyes steady as her slippered feet swung back and forth, unable to reach the floor. The image conjured Moses to mind, his body twisting in mid-air.

When Agnes appeared, she was dressed in all her finery, her red silk corset catching the light of the flames. Tendrils of hair artfully escaped the black ribbons that held it haphazardly in a knot at her crown. She smiled at him as she took a seat, blocking his view of the girl.

'You look well. Better than the last time at least.'

'And I must still thank you for taking care of me that evening. I am forever grateful.'

She leant back. 'So, it seems like you prefer talking to fucking now.'

He hastily swallowed down his beer, shocked at her speaking so in front of the young girl. His face must have given him away because Agnes turned around and spoke to her. 'Lucy, you can leave us now.'

The girl launched herself to her feet and skipped towards the service door, closing it softly behind her.

'Who is she?'

'Lucy? She is Mrs Bennett's niece. She is learning the trade.'

'Yours or her aunt's?'

Agnes frowned. 'Is one so much worse than the other? The money comes from the same deed.'

Cage felt stupid in his concern. 'Were you like her once?'

It was Agnes's turn to splutter. 'Lord, no. At Lucy's age I was sleeping in a storeroom, wearing boys' clothes and picking pockets on the Old Kent Road. That was before these came.' She thrust her breasts forward, brief and inelegant, and Cage could glimpse the little scamp she had once been. 'What do you want, Cage Lackmann?'

He held his hands up in surrender. 'What I want is a maid. I wondered if you might know of a local girl in need of such a position. I would rather help someone who needed it.'

She laughed. 'Liar! You've come to rescue me. Put me in a uniform and make me respectable.'

He reddened, for it was mostly true.

'Do you know what a maid earns?'

He shook his head. He had not worked through the details in his own mind.

'A fraction of what I make. A tenth, maybe. I wouldn't be surprised if some weeks I earn more than you.'

He had to laugh at his own crassness. 'Our jobs have much in common, I think. Maybe it is I who needs rescuing.'

She touched her hand to his hair, brushing a curl from his eyes. 'Maybe you need a wife.'

'Why? Are they cheaper than maids?'

'I suspect not. But they can give you other things in return.'

'Sex.'

'Love.'

The word stumped him for a moment. Did Agnes believe in love? Believe it had any currency for her?

'I love another man's wife.'

'Ah.' She shook her head in mock consolation. 'A maid it is, then. I shall ask around; that is the most I can do.'

'And what do you want, Agnes? It cannot be this life, not for ever.'

She smiled, searching for something playful to say, before her face settled on the truth. She leant forward once more, her voice low, as if scared the world would overhear and ruin it for her. 'I want a shop one day. Haberdashery – ribbons and lace, pearl buttons and beads, pretty things. Bond Street, perhaps. I'd travel to Paris, import the very latest, negotiate with the merchants. I'd be good at that, I think.'

'I think so too.'

'Two more years, maybe three.'

He took her hand and clasped it in his, like a handshake, cementing the idea of their mutual futures: the fallen who might just climb again.

She pulled away and stood up. 'A quarter hour, or else I have to charge.' She smiled as she said it. 'I'll find you a maid. Allow me a few days.'

'I would happily pay, to hear more of your plans. It inspires me, and I'd like to help the cause.'

She tapped him on the cheek. 'My dreams aren't for sale, love.'

Out in the alley, the floorman had disappeared. The temperature had dropped suddenly and the moon was nowhere to be seen. The Whitechapel fog had begun to retreat as the frozen air cleared a path for the snow that was surely stalking from above. He pulled his coat tightly about him and tugged his hat low. He almost tripped over the solitary small boy at the end of the street, who was methodically bouncing a bright red ball against the back of a grocer's shop.

Cage stopped at a quiet tavern on his way home, demolishing a plate of liver and onions. By the time he turned the corner of his own street, the first few flakes were falling, fat and slow as they landed in the dirt. The tailor's son was hastily dismantling the awning outside of his shop, standing atop a rickety ladder as his father held it steady.

At his door, Cage fumbled with the keys through his thick gloves.

'Steady!' the tailor's son cried out.

Cage looked back. The young man had almost fallen but his father had secured the ladder in time and all was well.

But something else had caught his eye. A hundred yards behind him, a small boy was throwing a ball against the side of a house. A red ball.

Cage ran towards him as fast as he dared across the dusting of snow. It had been the wrong approach. The boy turned at the sound of his boots and snatched the ball in mid-air before he too took off at pace, head down as his spindly legs pumped fast. The boy turned the corner and picked up his pace, heading straight for the Whitechapel Road, where the traffic would be busy.

Cage skidded clumsily, his ankle twisting. He scrambled back to his feet and pushed on. The boy had a great head start, but on the straight stretch of road Cage began to close him down. Fifty yards. Thirty. It wasn't enough. Up ahead, the doors to the coal merchant's at the corner of the main thoroughfare swung open and two men led a dray cart through the narrow opening.

'Stop! Thief!' Cage yelled.

One of the men dropped the reins of the carthorse and made his move, blocking the boy's escape. Immediately the boy came to a halt, wise to his situation and conserving his energy. He turned to face Cage.

Panting for breath, Cage came to a stop in front of the boy, hands on his knees. The man from the coal yard approached from the other direction. Cage thanked him for his help and waved him away, then lurched forward and grabbed the boy roughly with both hands.

'Oi!' He was a confident little bugger.

'Why were you following me?'

'Five bob and I'll tell you.'

'You'll tell me now. Or I'll take you to the nearest copper.'

The boy was unimpressed. 'Following ain't illegal.'

Smart boy. Maybe he should hire him as an assistant?

Cage let go with one hand and rummaged through his pocket, pulling out half a crown. He held the coin to the boy's face, as if it could dazzle him with its shine, but in truth it was hopelessly grubby.

'There's another one for you if I like what I hear.'

The boy snatched the coin and bit it with his teeth before shuffling it into his pocket. 'A lady.'

'What kind of lady?'

The boy seemed bemused at the idea that there might be more than one kind.

Cage helped out. 'Tall or short? Young or old?'

'Not young, not old neither. Pretty.'

'You have a name?'

'Smith something.'

Cage's stomach leapt at the mention of her name. 'Where were you going to meet with her again?'

'That's another question. It'll cost more.' Snowflakes had caught in the boy's lashes and he blinked them away.

Cage was too desperate for information to haggle. He rooted around once more but found only banknotes. He switched hands to try his other pocket, but in that split second the boy darted to his left. Cage lunged blindly, but the boy was too quick for him.

He hobbled after the boy, his ankle painful and beginning to swell. Desperately he picked up his pace, finding his stride just as the boy turned left into the busy Whitechapel Road. Cage followed, his eyes grimly focussed on the boy's bobbing head as he ran through a group of dark-skinned sailors, but where the boy had weaved between them, Cage barged against shoulders and suffered their own shoves and curses in return. He tried the same tactic, yelling at the top of his voice. But to point out a thief on this particular street brought no assistance, only affronted stares.

The boy was getting away. The pavement was jammed with the usual flotsam and jetsam: streetwalkers and dirty children, round-bellied thugs and weaving drunks. Cage passed under a great brazier outside a tavern, shards of flaming straw landing on his coat and hair. He thought he'd lost sight of the child, until he saw the boy step out into the road, timing his run perfectly between an omnibus and a rag and bone cart. Cage followed, his boots squelching through horse shit as he rounded the cart. The driver of the hansom behind yelled at him to get out of the way and Cage only narrowly missed the trotting hooves as they bore down. The horse's flank brushed against him, spinning him around, leaving a trail of greasy sweat across his cheek.

Finally he made the other side of the road, but the boy was gone, rolled in the undertow of the Whitechapel sea.

CHAPTER THIRTY-ONE

The next morning, Cage woke early, having struggled for sleep most of the night. Why was Hazel Smythson watching him, stalking him, just as he was stalking her? Was he getting close, perhaps? Maybe she had been watching for who returned to see Bessie Chappelhow. Jack Cross or someone else?

He was beginning to regret not telling Cross about the note when he'd had the chance. The police had the resources to find her, but they would be focussed on Leland Crewler now. And for sure, he was still ultimately the right target. Whatever Hazel Smythson's role had been, she could not herself be the murderer, could she? More likely an accomplice, an ally of some kind, an enabler. What kind of woman would be capable of that, and for what reason?

Love or money. Everything came down to that in the end.

Another lead opened up in his mind. If money was her motivation, then her role had been to act a part, to pose as a potential client. Maybe his mother or Granger would know of such a person, someone like them, happy to treat the courtroom as a stage. It was worth a try.

His main task for the day ahead, however, was to find a

connection between Hazel Smythson and Leland Crewler. If he couldn't find the one, he would need to explore the other.

He left the house the moment the dawn came. The snow was only a few inches thick and not yet turned to ice. He walked in the opposite direction at first, stopping on the corner to turn back and see if anyone was following him, but the street was empty apart from a lone milk cart, the elderly driver grim-faced as the horse ambled through the virgin snow. Cage went left, then left again, meandering along a circuitous path towards Aldgate, but there was still no one behind him as far as he could see.

He picked up the pace, reaching Threadneedle Street just in time to enjoy the rush of clerks and secretaries marching importantly to their places of work. This was the heart of the Empire, where the flourish of a pen could buy a whole country and sell it on for a profit before the day was out. And at the centre of it all was the Crewler Corporation.

Cage found a tiny coffee house further down the street. He ordered coffee and toast, then settled in at a table near the window to observe the comings and goings at the Crewler building. He had no plan, not yet at least, and he hoped something would occur to him. His whole life had been invention and schemes, deployed in the service of criminals. Now his cause was honest, the lies came harder.

A grand carriage pulled up outside the building. Cage craned to see Leland Crewler step down, a tartan scarf wrapped luxuriantly about his neck, his beard protruding above like a serpent's tongue. Two men descended the coach behind him, identically dressed in the uniform of the city. As Crewler slipped briefly on the steps, they rushed forward to take an arm each, but Crewler shook them off and they stepped back smartly as if they'd put their hands too close to the fire.

Cage finished and paid for his coffee. The sky was growing white again and Cage's eyes strained against it, a false promise of sunshine before the heavens opened again.

As he approached the Crewler building, a group of four men were just ascending the steps and Cage fell in behind them. Their leader was a small, barrel-shaped man, the creases in his trousers ironed to such sharpness they flapped about his knees.

Cage followed them through the doors into the great marbled hall. He recognised the same icy look of white panelling and shining metal balustrades that he had seen at Sheldrake House. Old Edmund Crewler had clearly been a man of limited taste.

A long reception desk ran the width of the lobby, guarding access to the staircase behind that swept up five storeys to a glass dome above their heads. Two receptionists patrolled the desk, and one of them greeted the party of four with a professional smile. 'Good morning, Mr Grant. Mr Crewler has just arrived.'

'Thank you, Armstrong.'

A ledger lay open on the desk and Grant took the proffered pen to spell out his name. A visitors' book – that would do nicely.

As the other men signed in, Cage quickly looked around the hall. There were two sets of doors either side of the stairs. Head down, he peeled off to the right and walked with purpose to the door nearest to him, waiting at any moment to be summoned back by Armstrong or his other officious colleague. Thankfully, the door swung open at his approach and a clerk came through, holding the door open for him impatiently. He muttered his thanks and rushed in.

Beyond was a long room, panelled in dark wood, quite

different in style to the grand entrance hall. The high windows let in a mean stream of daylight that just missed the polished desks that ran in rows across the width of the room. Most of the occupants were typing, the clack and whirr a constant hum beneath the gasoliers that ran along the ceiling in a single row. Cage kept walking, a man with important things to do, a man not to be interrupted. Just before he reached the end of the room, he saw a doorway to his left. Without hesitation, he marched in.

A cloakroom: perfect. He peeled off his outer garments and hung them on a hook, then checked himself in a small mirror at the back of the door. Would he pass for a Crewler employee? He pushed his hair back as neatly as he could and rearranged his necktie.

Back in the main room, he strode past a row of filing cabinets. Choosing one randomly, he opened it and rifled through as if searching for something. He grabbed a manila folder from within and shut the cabinet, then made his way back to the main hall, pausing briefly to take a breath before yanking open the door.

He approached the reception desk, almost breaking into a run. Both men turned towards him, frowning. He waited until he was close before speaking in a low voice. 'Armstrong, Mr Crewler sent me down urgently. Mr Grant has arrived with a number of other guests, one of whom Mr Crewler has met several times before but for the life of him cannot remember his name. I need to check the register.'

Cage reached for the visitors' book without asking permission, exuding all the confidence in the world. He could see the two men silently conversing with each other with furrowed brows and open hands. Cage scanned the most recent names, making a show of not being able to read the writing for one of them.

'Might I help, Mr . . . ?'

Cage faked a barely masked effrontery that the man didn't know his name. 'Dossett. Sir James is my father. I am recently returned from India. Can you recall when Mr Grant was last here, Armstrong? Perhaps a previous entry will be easier to read.'

'A week ago perhaps, Mr Dossett.'

Excellent. Cage flicked back through the pages. Thankfully, the book had a separate column for title. A Miss or a Mrs would stand out a mile in a sea of men. He had to go back five days to find a woman's name: a Mrs Angela Whitworth, written in a spidery hand.

'Ah, Mrs Whitworth was in I see!' He looked up at the quizzical receptionists and smiled. 'A family friend. We are most fond of her. She was well, I hope?'

Armstrong cleared his throat. 'She was with her grandsons. Her hearing is not what it used to be I understand.'

Not Hazel Smythson then. Cage continued flicking backwards, well beyond the time frame he had been given. Armstrong was leaning in, and suddenly his finger shot out and halted Cage's progress. 'There you are, sir. Mr Grant's previous visit. Let me read the names.'

The receptionist gripped his precious ledger and turned it around. The game was up as he clearly announced the names of all those in Mr Grant's party. Cage tried not to sound too lacklustre. 'Ah! Robert Grantham. That was it. I will let Mr Crewler know how helpful you have been.'

Armstrong smiled pleasantly and took the ledger away. Cage turned away, disappointed. If Hazel Smythson was connected to Leland Crewler, the evidence wasn't here. He returned to the cloakroom, dumping the stolen folder on the floor.

What now? He had to find the connection somehow. If he couldn't find Hazel Smythson, maybe he could entice her to come to him? And if Leland Crewler was the man she was protecting, there was only one way to do that. He grabbed his coat and hat. It was time to scare the horses.

Back in the main hallway, he checked that Armstrong and his colleague were busy before slipping behind them and ascending the first flight of stairs.

There was no obvious indication of where Leland's office lay. He would have to ask. Turning left, he knocked on the first door he came to and went in. A solitary young man hastily removed his feet from the desk and shuffled a newspaper clumsily to one side before standing up and stuttering, 'Can I help you?'

Cage simply demanded directions to Crewler's office without explanation. One disapproving glance at the newspaper had the young man offering to deliver him personally to Mr Crewler. Cage turned the offer down. There was no point landing anyone else in the trouble he was about to cause.

Leland Crewler's office was in the far-right corner of the second floor. The corridor turned into a plush and welcoming waiting area, with handsomely carved dark wood chairs and tables, and faded Persian carpets. Two huge stone elephants guarded the fireplace, their trunks and ears worn with age, stolen from a temple, no doubt. The whole room was as exotic as anything he might see at the British Museum: a shopfront for the Crewler empire. Beside the doors to the inner office was an empty desk where an appointment book lay open.

Cage could hear voices on the other side of the doors, coming closer now. Hopefully Mr Grant and his cohorts were leaving. Cage stood to the side as the talk turned to laughter and the doors swung open, keeping Cage out of sight for now. He watched the backs of the men as they were escorted out of the waiting area by Crewler's secretary.

There was only one way this was going to go and he needed to prepare himself. He slung on his coat and moved the notes and coins into his breast pocket where they would be secure, along with Baxter's poem – close to his heart once more, a place it had never really left.

He squared his shoulders, and walked in to Crewler's office.

Leland Crewler was standing by a floor-length window, gazing out at the white sky beyond. He puffed silently on a pipe, his mouth moving like a fish, a picture of serene contemplation. He did not look like someone under serious investigation for the murder of two boys. Maybe he wasn't? The thought allowed Cage to muster the required amount of righteous anger.

'I know what you have done, Leland.'

Crewler whirled around to face him, his eyes turning to angry slits the moment recognition came. 'What the hell are you doing here?' Crewler dropped the pipe and stormed towards him. 'Get out right now!'

Cage stood his ground as Crewler shoved him in the chest.

'What happened, Leland? Did you lose control of the game, or did they fight back?'

Crewler shoved him again, harder this time. Cage stepped back, but used the momentum to push Crewler with a force that surprised even him. The man stumbled, landing awkwardly on the arm of a chair. As he attempted to right himself, Cage stood over him, hindering his progress.

'How many boys have there been, Leland? Was Nathaniel the first, perhaps? And ever since, you are compelled to recreate him, to bring him back to life? Your very own Desdemona, your very own little bitch.'

Crewler had stopped twisting. The look in his eyes was something like grief. 'I loved him.'

'Too much!' Cage yelled, the rage no longer fake. 'You can love too much!'

The words shocked them both to silence. Then Cage remembered why he was there. He stood back, his eyes on the fallen man, his voice colder now. 'I know about her. Hazel Smythson. I know about the note. And I know where to find her.'

Did Crewler's eyes flicker? Or was it a trick of that brutal light?

His job was done. He'd said what he had needed to say to set the wheels in motion, to make them come for him. But somehow, he could not bring himself to leave.

'You chose him, didn't you? Baxter, Baxter Spring. Did you know he was a poet? Of course you did. A connection to Moses, that's what you wanted. Nathaniel was an accident. But Baxter, that was deliberate. *That*, you meant to do.'

'No!' Crewler was shaking his head violently, whether to deny the veracity of his words or to tremble at their appalling truth unclear.

'The boy deserved more, Leland. Much more.' There was such relief to say the words out loud, although suddenly he wasn't sure who he was really talking about. 'I know what it is to be chosen.'

Leland Crewler's eyes darted behind him and Cage turned just as two men grabbed him by his arms: the same men who had helped Crewler to his feet on the steps outside. This time they didn't let go when Cage tried to shrug them off. They dragged him backwards as Cage struggled to find his feet. He kept his eyes on Crewler, still slumped on the floor, until the wide-eyed secretary ran towards his employer and slammed the doors closed behind him.

Cage was dragged into the corridor and down the stairs, then past the astonished receptionists.

On the steps outside, Cage received a sharp push that saw him slip in the snow and skid forward into the gutter. No one came to help him as he pulled himself to his feet. He brushed the icy grit from his hands and pulled his gloves from his coat. His hat had been lost somewhere. Slowly he seemed to be losing everything, and only a tiny part of him cared.

CHAPTER THIRTY-TWO

He was halfway to Whitechapel before he thought to slow down and make it easy for someone to follow him.

Cage turned down the Commercial Road and headed towards St Thomas's. His ankle still hurt, and the wind had picked up, carrying the sharp stink of the Bermondsey tanning factories across the river: fresh dog urine and decaying offal, a witch's brew of awfulness. He was glad when he could turn north again and come once more to the welcoming blue door of the Reverend Archie Weston. He paused before knocking and cast around, but there was no obvious sign yet that Crewler or Smythson had sent anyone to observe him.

He knocked on the door but no one answered. He turned around and walked the few hundred yards to the church itself. He was struck again by the narrow lines of graves to either side of the building, imagining their occupants lying coffin to coffin like orphans in a cramped dormitory. It was far removed from Baxter's fantasy of a cemetery that stretched across the hill. He thought of Moses's drawing: the simple white chapel etched against a black sky. But here the vision was reversed, the soot-smoked building shadowed against clouds and a watery sun.

The door to the church stood ajar. Inside, the temperature dropped once more. At first, Cage thought the church was empty, but as he walked towards the altar across the uneven stones, he spotted Archie Weston in a pew towards the front. Cage approached silently, as the man had dropped one knee to the floor, his eyes closed in a half prayer, his mouth moving gently. Cage turned his attention back to the altar: it was simple but neatly kept, raised high beneath the mullioned window of three stained-glass saints, the only remnant of its Catholic past.

Cage crept into a pew on the opposite side from Archie, unwilling to interrupt his conversation. It was so quiet, Cage could hear himself breathe. He closed his eyes, wondering if God was really here. He'd spent precious little time in his life contemplating the existence of a deity. It seemed a remote and almost laughable idea in the slums of Whitechapel. But here, one could almost believe that God was present, shielding his eyes from what his world had become. Had Baxter Spring been a believer? He doubted it. For religion thrived on hope, which Baxter had consigned to an early grave.

'Mr Lackmann! Cage! I did not hear you enter.'

Cage opened his eyes and stumbled to his feet to greet the rising figure of Archie Weston. 'Apologies, I did not wish to interrupt.'

Archie grinned. 'Ah, I can talk to God any time. Visitors are far rarer for me.'

'I knocked at the rectory, but there was no answer.'

'My wife's sister, Amy, is staying for a few days and they have taken the children out now the weather has cleared. Come, let us return, this is not a warm enough place to converse sensibly with anyone but Himself.'

Cage followed Archie out of the church. The reverend walked

briskly, his thin legs energetic in their rise and fall. At the gate he turned back. 'I should offer my condolences for Mr Pickering. I was sorry to hear of his death.'

Cage nodded his thanks, wanting to save the details and the questions they would give rise to. Instead he filled the short time it took them to reach Archie's house by feigning interest in his portrait, ostensibly the reason he was there.

The reverend was enthusiastic. 'I am very pleased with it! I hope you shall be too. I have captured the essence, I believe.'

What essence would that be, Cage wondered?

Archie's study was still warm when they entered, but the fire in the grate was burning low. Archie stoked the embers with more wood, and apologised for the lack of refreshment. 'Elizabeth says I am accident prone and not allowed in the kitchen unsupervised.' He went to his photography cupboard and retrieved something wrapped in brown paper. 'Now, I hope this will excite you, to see yourself as never before.'

Cage took a chair by the fire. 'I have looked in the mirror countless times. Does it not reveal the truth?'

'Only if you know where to look.' Archie unwrapped the paper and handed the portrait to Cage.

Cage stared at himself for a few moments. The image was well captured, each curl of hair perfectly defined in the light. His face was more rounded than he thought, his cheeks full and the bones in his face not as chiselled as he might have hoped. But it was his eyes that held his gaze now, looking back at himself. 'It is me, but it is not me.'

'Exactly!' cried Archie, as if that were the point. 'When you look in the mirror, you see a familiar friend, but the camera sees only a stranger. So now you see yourself as the same, as someone you have not met before.'

Cage looked at the photograph again, fascinated and a little horrified. 'I look frightened. Or nervous at the very least.'

'It is the eyes that do not lie, not the instrument itself.'

Cage handed it back.

'This copy is for you.' Archie wrapped it again in the paper and set it on his desk. 'Make sure you frame it behind glass and keep it away from direct light. You will be glad of it in time, to show your grandchildren what a handsome and important man their grandfather was.'

'I am grateful, genuinely. It has been a difficult few days.'

Archie took the seat opposite and clasped his hands together. 'Detective Cross returned here yesterday. He gave me little information about Pickering's death. Do you know more?'

'I was there.'

Archie leant forward, his hand reaching out to touch Cage's arm. Cage waited for him to ask his questions, but the vicar was silent, the only interrogation a sympathetic enquiry in his pale blue eyes. Cage's words tumbled out – Gravesend, the woodshed – but he held back on any mention of the note. When Cage mentioned the single brandy glass, he heard the break in his own voice.

Archie shook his head. 'Some men are destined to give more than they take. Their tragedy is to the benefit of the rest of us.'

'Tell me, where does the Church stand on suicide these days? Is it still a crime?'

Archie smiled grimly. 'In doctrine, at least. But the crime is ours, I think, for a man to feel that alone.'

'Would you bury him?'

'In principle, yes, I would. But our yard is small, and plots are necessarily expensive. But I would be happy to preside at an alternative location, somewhere close to his home, perhaps.'

'And what of Baxter? Will he be interred here?'

Archie nodded. 'When the time comes, the parish will fund his burial. But Cross will not release his body yet, poor child.'

'And how was Detective Cross?' It was the real reason Cage was here, after all.

Archie seemed hesitant. 'He asked a lot of questions, mostly about Leland Crewler, and what opportunities he might have had to encounter Baxter. It was not a connection we had made ourselves until the papers dug up the Crewler contribution to our parish room.'

Cage reddened slightly, grateful that Archie had not seen his hand in the newspaper coverage. 'And what did you say?'

Archie shrugged. 'I did not recall meeting the man, but Elizabeth was not so sure. We had dealt with a manager at the corporation itself over the donation. When we held the opening festivities, I could not remember who, if anyone, had come to represent them. Elizabeth thought he might have been there, but it was a busy day for both of us. Baxter was present, of course; all the children were. But Leland Crewler? I do not know.'

'Could Baxter have met him in another context? Was he, I don't know, *active* in some way? There is money to be made. I saw how Baxter lived . . .' Cage drifted off, it was an awkward subject to discuss with a vicar.

But Archie took it in his stride. 'Cross asked the same question. We cannot know for sure, but my instinct is not. His father believed he inclined a certain way, but that was more a judgement of his interest in poetry. Then again, money, as you say, is tyrannical in its absence. It has driven men and boys to worse.'

Cage made a mental note to ask Agnes about brothels in

the area that specialised in boys – he should have thought of it before.

'I cannot offer tea, but a brandy, perhaps?'

Cage assented. Once again, he found himself reluctant to leave this man's house. He muttered his thanks as the glass was put in his hand.

Archie too had taken a glass, smacking his lips after the first sip, although Cage suspected the man was not given to daytime drinking.

'I have to ask, Cage, why are you still so interested in Baxter's case? Surely you have a life to return to? A career to pursue?'

Cage swirled the brandy in his glass. 'I made a promise.'

'To whom?'

'I'm not really sure.' Cage smiled.

'There is something else I should tell you.'

A blush appeared on the man's cheeks and Cage felt a tiny lurch within. 'Oh?'

'Detective Cross. He asked other questions too. About you.'

Cage sat forward.

Archie continued. 'He asked whether I had ever met you before or knew of any connection you might have had with Baxter. He also asked me about your character.'

'And what did you say?'

'The truth! That although I knew of you, I had never met you before your visit here in the days following Baxter's death. Nor was I aware of any contact you may have had with Baxter himself.'

'And what of my character? What did you say of that?'

Archie held his hands up. 'That I did not know you well enough to form a true opinion. But that you appeared to have a concern for Moses Pickering beyond the mere impact of the accusations against him upon yourself, and that you appeared genuinely affected by Baxter's poetic ambitions and his admiration for your own work in that regard.'

'Ah, did he ask to see Baxter's notebook of favourite poems?'

'He did. He has taken it with him.' Archie blushed once more. 'I am sure it is nothing to be concerned about. Detective Cross struck me as a thorough man, that is all.'

'Thorough is a good word. There are others, too.'

Archie Weston sat back in his chair and ran his hand through his hair. 'Ah, Cage, I am as wary of pride as any of the other sins, but I do believe I am a good judge of character. I see many things written on your heart, but murder is not one of them.'

The brandy was sticking in his throat. The thought of Cross turning his investigations on him was at once ludicrous and sickening. 'I am almost scared to ask what those things are.'

'There is a sadness. Regret, maybe. Anger too, I think.' Archie shook his head at his own pretensions. 'But it is not for me to press you into a discussion of your soul.'

'I'm not sure I have one.'

'We all have a soul, even the man who kills. And something weighs on yours, I can see. Not just Pickering and Baxter. Something deeper.'

'We all have our burdens to carry. I have been sinned against for sure, but I am no Lear. I cannot claim those crimes outweigh my own.'

'Our own condemnation is often worse than what the world would offer us, if only it knew the truth.'

'My mother . . .' Cage stopped himself. No good would come of this. He was in the confessional again, this warm room and Archie's kind enquiring eyes like a balm that drew out the sickness. But Archie Weston was wrong. The world was a cruel place, and the past was even crueller, its unchangeable judgements already cast in stone.

Cage drained the rest of his glass and stood up. 'I should go. Thank you for the portrait, and for your hospitality.'

Archie too was on his feet. 'I am sorry if I have caused any difficulties for you with Detective Cross.'

Cage shook his head. 'We have a history. That is all.' He hoped it was true.

Cage took his leave and walked out into the cool afternoon. Before he turned the corner he bent to tie his laces, taking the opportunity to cast around for anyone who might be loitering in wait for him, but the only people he could see were two women and two children a few hundred yards further back along the road. The elder child was skipping, a flame of red hair escaping her cap. It must have been Elizabeth Weston and her sister returning with the children from their walk. They walked slowly towards the house, heads down against the stirring wind.

When he reached his own street, he made a point of greeting his neighbours, those who were abroad, at least. If someone was waiting to hear of his return, he wished it to be known far and wide.

He dug his keys from his pocket and fumbled the right one from the chain.

Inside, he bent immediately to the fire in his office. It was damned cold in there. Colder than it should have been. The moment the thought hit, he looked up sharply. Dropping the coal scuttle, he ran through to the scullery to find the back door gaping open and one of the bolts standing out at right angles where it had been ripped from its hinges.

He immediately thought of his strongbox, freshly filled with most of Pincott's notes. He took the stairs two at a time.

The box was still in its place beneath his bed. He tore off his gloves and with shaking fingers found the key and opened the lid.

The money was still there. All of it.

CHAPTER THIRTY-THREE

A locksmith arrived just as the skies darkened, and set to work.

Nothing else seemed to be missing, and the Rubens drawing was still there. His altercation with Leland Crewler that morning had been intended to heighten the man's curiosity about what Cage did or did not know. Was the break-in an attempt to find some real evidence that Cage might have against him? He looked across at his paper-strewn desk, and the untidy piles of documents on the floor that had yet to be returned to their rightful place. Had someone been through them, he wondered? It would be hard to tell.

Once the locksmith was done, Cage went upstairs and lit all the lamps. His plan was to leave for Richmond in a few hours and to catch his mother before the evening's performance at eight. He lay on the bed and stared up at the ceiling, but his thoughts were not at peace. What the hell was he doing? This promise he had made, to see Baxter's killer punished, was like a rock that had crashed through the ceiling of his life, a stubborn, immoveable thing. But what then? Whether the crime was solved or not, Cage had a life to live, as Archie himself had said, and as Emma had said before him.

He had not allowed himself to dwell on his last meeting with her, but now her words returned. *Maybe there is hope for us yet?* Tomorrow perhaps he would go to see her, on the pretext of returning Moses's notebook. He picked it up from the nightstand and began to thumb through it again. His eyelids grew heavy but a knock on the door summoned him downstairs once more.

He opened the door to see Merriwether, the diminutive pharmacist from the Pestle and Mortar.

'He wants to see you.'

Cage had barely thought about Obediah Pincott, not since his lacklustre performance in front of Chester at the Old Bailey.

'Tell him I shall call tomorrow.'

Merriwether smiled: his face said *I don't think so.*

'A few minutes, then.'

Cage invited the man to wait in the office. Upstairs, he gathered his things and turned down the lamps. He took all of the money from his strongbox: it was a lot to carry on his person, but it felt like the safer strategy. When he came downstairs again, he found Merriwether warming himself at the fire.

Cage swung his coat on. 'Right.'

The little man didn't move, his hands still stretching to the flames as if he could catch them. 'A few more moments will not matter.'

Cage remembered the freezing rooms of Pincott's compound, where warmth was seen as an unnecessary luxury. Sadly though, he had little time for this detour as it was. 'I need to make Richmond by seven.'

Merriwether smiled. 'Ah well.'

Cage moved the guard across the fire, then pulled on his spare hat before following the dwarf outside. He took his time locking his front door, casting his eyes up and down the street in the hope of spotting a new follower, but again there were few obvious candidates.

It was a ten-minute walk to Dodd's Lane, and they spent most of it in silence, Cage's concern too wrapped up in the break-in, and furtive glances behind him, to put too much thought into the meeting to come. It was only as they turned into the lane itself that he thought to ask the question. 'Do you know why he wishes to see me?'

The little man looked up. 'A message came from Newgate Prison.'

So, Connor MacGregor was unhappy with his performance the previous day. So be it.

At the Pestle and Mortar, he was invited to find his own way out into Pincott's compound. 'Good luck, Lackmann.'

Cage pushed out into the yard. A large number of crates were piled in the middle, wet with slush. He skirted around them and marched across to the other side.

Before he reached the door, Dub emerged from the gloom, his normally red face pale with indignation. 'Lackmann, you bastard.'

'That's me.' Cage brushed against him as he pushed into Pincott's den, noticing the strong stench of garlic and ale breathing down from the man's nostrils as he puffed hatred like a dragon.

Inside, he found Pincott alone, settled in a chair at the head of the table, one long leg out to his side, the other slung across the table itself, his huge military boot covered in a dusting of snow. A mean fire skulked unobtrusively in the grate in the far corner. The room was cold, but Pincott's greatcoat flapped open as usual to reveal his two faces.

Cage took a seat. 'Good evening, Obediah. You had something urgent you wished to discuss?'

Pincott shook his head. 'I have nothing to discuss. Dub, on the other hand, has a point to make.'

Cage turned just as a massive fist thumped into his shoulder, sending him spinning to the floor. Pain splintered through his back and he yelled out, but the cry was silenced by a boot that caught him in the stomach, sucking the air from his lungs as he crouched on his hands and knees.

'That's for MacGregor.' Dub's voice was calm as he slumped into the chair Cage had reluctantly vacated.

Cage couldn't move as he struggled for breath. The wheezing in his throat sounded to him like a pig at slaughter, the indignity second only to the screaming pain in his shoulder. Time moved slowly as his breath dragged in and out. It was curiously intimate, both men watching him with not even a mild curiosity as his body began to find some order from the chaos of Dub's attack. He sat back on his heels and focussed on Pincott, surely the more rational of the two, although Pincott did not return his gaze, his eyes fixed solely on a cigar that he rolled between his fingers.

'I am sorry I could not do more.' Cage coughed, bringing on another spasm of pain in his shoulder.

Pincott waited for the coughing to subside. 'I heard you did not try.'

Cage stayed on the floor, figuring he was safer there. 'I am sorry. It won't happen again, I promise.' The words felt cold and alien in his mouth. A part of him was looking down at the scene, watching himself kneel at the feet of Obediah Pincott, the brittle straw that littered the floor pressing deep in his palms while Dub's boots swaggered before him, ready to punish him once again. He was a dog to them, a whelp, his fancy clothes and the money in his pocket simply the chains they used to bind him.

Pincott stood up suddenly. Cage tried not to flinch as the man reached down and almost gently took him by the arms and raised him to his feet.

The two men faced each other in silence. Was Cage supposed to say something else? Some magic words that would make everything all right between them?

Pincott said: 'I do not understand men like you. You have never known war in this world, so you do not know peace. You make your own war. Inside.'

'I will try to be a simpler man.' In that moment, Cage wished it for all the world.

CHAPTER THIRTY-FOUR

Cage headed south to the river. The pain in his shoulder and ribs was building and each swing of his arm was excruciating.

The threat of violence had always been there in his relationship with Pincott, never overtly stated, just a constant presence in those cold, blue eyes. Maybe his performance in court had been a deliberate testing of the boundaries, to see if after all these years the threat was real. Well, now he knew. There would be no amicable separation from the man. As he crossed London Bridge, he looked into the darkness beneath: to leave Pincott's employ would be to find himself broken at the bottom of the river.

At Waterloo he bought his ticket and a good scarf in black wool from one of the vendors who lined the concourse. Once on the train, he fashioned a sling with the scarf, accepting the offer of help from a genial companion and gaining sympathy for his story of slipping on the ice as he crossed the bridge.

The King's Theatre was on the north side of Richmond Green. He found the old, red brick building in a state of some disrepair. Richmond itself was a prosperous town, and clearly felt it deserved better: the theatre was scheduled for demolition the following year. Cage thought of Bessie Chappelhow, sinking into the earth with the building she loved. This was one of his mother's favourite stops on the touring itinerary and she would be sad to see it go, not least as any new building would be grander, and far less likely to be impressed by Granger's economical approach to staging.

The lamps were already lit outside the theatre, but when he entered there was no one manning the shabby box office. At the stage door, he was told it was too early for the cast to have arrived, and they could most likely be found in the White Swan down on the river – but that he should be careful of the tide.

Approaching the tavern from the rear, he could see the inky black water licking the building's foundations. He entered through a side door, tiptoeing through the river's icy tendrils, and was immediately greeted by the familiar, raucous, smoky atmosphere of a troupe of actors having a Good Time.

Cage could see Granger at the bar, already unsteady on his feet. Over the years, his pre-show pick-me-up had expanded to include one-for-Saint-Vitus, one-for-luck and one-for-the-road – although, Cage had to admit, he had never seen him drunk or slurring on stage.

Granger spotted him as he pushed through the crowd. 'Cage, my dear boy!'

Cage yelped as he was enveloped in an enthusiastic hug. Granger's mouth fell open when he saw the sling. 'What on earth!'

Cage gave him the same story of ice on London Bridge and was immediately pulled into another embrace. He winced, but there was something comforting about Granger's show of affection.

He asked after his mother but was told she had yet to come

down from her room. 'She's not one for drinking before the show these days. Better things to do.' Granger tapped his nose, temporarily forgetting he was talking to Honor's son.

Cage asked for her room number, promising to return for a brandy before they departed for the theatre. The rooms were on the attic floor, and he hauled himself up the stairs, still wary of his bruised ribs and aching shoulder.

As he approached her door, he heard a girlish giggle, his mother's special laugh that was reserved only for the men in her life. Cage paused outside. His intrusion would be unwelcome, but he was past caring. He knocked, not as lightly as he could have done.

'Off with you! We'll be down in ten minutes. 'Tis only seven!' Freddie Southgate's voice could project through ten walls if it had to.

'Mother, it's me. I need to talk to you,' he shouted back.

There was movement then, the whine of bed springs and the rustle of clothing.

Moments later, the door opened and his mother greeted him in a silk dressing gown of garish purple. 'Darling! I had no idea you were coming.'

She kissed him on each cheek, her lips shy as butterfly wings, then stepped back into the room. 'Do excuse the mess.'

Cage walked in. The room was tiny, and what little floor space there was around the canopied bed was littered with clothes. Southgate lay back on the bed, the lazy smoke from his cigarette masking his face. He had at least pulled his trousers on, but stopped short of doing them up.

His mother collapsed into the only chair, leaving Cage to stand. 'Been in the wars, I see.'

No Granger-style concern here.

'I fell on the ice.' Not that she deserved the lie.

She cocked her head to one side and smiled at him. 'I heard about Pickering. All is well again. I'm glad.'

Cage said nothing, so she continued. 'Anyway, I'm delighted you're here, darling. The houses have been poor, we could do with the boost.'

'I'm not staying for the show.'

'Oh.'

'I need to ask you something.'

Cage kept the story simple. A woman had been to see him, masquerading very convincingly as a potential client, but her intention had been fraudulent. Her performance had been convincingly professional. Perhaps Honor knew of another woman who plied the same trade in legal matters?

'What did she look like?' It was Southgate who asked the question.

Cage shrugged. 'No more than thirty. She dressed very plainly, but well. A dull, dutiful wife, but if you looked a while, you could see she was pretty. Forceful too. In another role, I would imagine she could be striking.'

Southgate smiled. 'I love the sound of her.'

Honor didn't like that. She stood up. 'So, I have competition.'

Between Southgate's lasciviousness and Honor's monumental narcissism, the room felt crowded. 'It's a simple question.' Cage spoke to both of them. 'Do you have any idea who she might be?'

Honor looked at him then. 'It's important to you.'

'Yes.'

'Well, it could be any of us, although I cannot think of someone specifically. I can ask around though. I *will* ask around.'

'Thank you.'

'If that's everything?' Southgate eyed him from the bed, his hand resting on his belly, moving lower.

A deep loathing unleashed itself and Cage bent down, picked up Southgate's shirt and threw it at him. 'Get up and get out.'

Honor's voice was sharp. 'Cage!'

Cage kept his eyes on Southgate. Slowly he rose from the bed and stretched, before pulling his shirt over his head. He was smiling to himself as he sat on the edge of the divan and put his shoes on, taking his time to tie the laces.

Honor tried to regain control: always the leading lady. 'Freddie, you don't have to go. Cage, if you want to talk further I will meet you in the saloon in five minutes.'

'No.' Cage turned to her. 'We'll talk here. But he needs to go.'

She bristled. 'Do not talk to him like that.'

'Don't give me orders. I am tired of them.'

She stared him down but Southgate had already reached for his jacket and was making for the door. He circled his arms around Honor's waist from behind and bent like a vampire to kiss her neck. The smile didn't leave his face.

It was too much for Cage. As Southgate pushed past him, he grabbed the man with his free arm and slammed him into the wall. Cage ignored the pain as he pressed his injured arm across the man's neck. Cage could feel Honor behind him, the ineffectual flutter of her hands on his shoulders trying to pull him away. Words tumbled through his head, the things he wanted to call this man. But Southgate's smile had slipped, and all they were left with was a mutual derision.

Cage let go. He turned and opened the door. Southgate needed no further encouragement and slipped through without looking back.

'What was that?'

Cage closed the door. 'Anger.'

'At him or me?'

Cage spun around to face her. 'I'm leaving him,' he said. He didn't need to say who.

She seemed confused at first, then comprehension dawned. 'You can't.'

'Can't or shouldn't?'

She looked horrified. 'It's the same thing.'

'No!' he shouted. 'It's not!'

Her eyes travelled down to where Cage's hand was rubbing his shoulder. 'He did that to you, didn't he?'

Her own hand reached out but stopped in mid-air as if a barrier prevented her from comforting her son. He knew what that barrier was: a thick wall of irony. To touch him now would be a sick joke, a denial of responsibility that even she could not fake.

'How much did he pay for me? Was it worth it?'

Her eyes hardened. 'You don't understand.'

He grabbed her then, shaking her by the arms, a pantomime gesture. 'One day I was free, and then I was not. I was a child, Mother, a child! I wanted to write, to . . . live. But you killed all that. You sold me like a fucking whore!' The words ripped from him, landing on her face like spittle.

He let go suddenly, as if his hands had been burned. She fell on the bed, her wrinkled fingers grasping her robe about her. All her years were in those hands, and nowhere else.

She looked up at him, her eyes wet with the tears he had only ever seen reserved for Charlie. Her voice was barely a whisper. 'Don't do it, Cage. Stay alive.'

He grasped the handle of the door and laid his head against

the unyielding wood of the frame. He was so tired now, deep in his bones.

'Death is not the worst thing.'

He heard something catch in her throat, but he left without turning back.

CHAPTER THIRTY-FIVE

On the train home, he felt his eyes closing, sleep dragging him under. He was almost at a dead end with his investigations. He would revisit Agnes, explore what he could of the male brothels in the borough – although he, like Archie, doubted that he would find a connection to Baxter. He had failed the boy spectacularly. Perhaps the only thing left was to carry out his threat to his mother and leave this life behind. Did he really have the gall to do it? Just how far could Pincott's fingers reach?

At Waterloo, he took a cab home. He had no energy to visit Agnes tonight. All he could see was his mother's face, the tears in her eyes as he'd said those vicious words. The guilt was brewing: who was he to accuse her? He had destroyed her life long before she returned the favour.

The cab entered his street. Two dark carriages were stopped outside his house, a group of men huddled around them. As his cab drew closer, Cage saw the iron bars at the back of the first carriage. Realisation dawned too late as one of the men stepped out in front of his cab.

Cage sank back in his seat, enjoying a few last moments of peace and freedom. Then the door was yanked open and a pair of hands reached in. He stumbled out of the carriage, his shoulder bumping the frame painfully. He landed awkwardly, the sling coming loose. When he stood up, he came face to face with the thin man in the black hat: Cross's man.

'Cage Lackmann, you're under arrest.'

Cage smiled at him, about to banter, but the constables that now circled him dragged Cage towards the police cart before he could even think of something to say. He was bundled inside and two constables followed him within, squashing him between them on one of the wooden benches. He heard the others clamber atop the vehicle, then a sharp whip crack as the cart lurched away. There was an urgency to it all, a seriousness that belied the crime of his escapade at the Crewler Corporation. He thought of Archie's warning: *Cross was asking questions about you.*

The agony in his shoulder and ribs, squashed between the two men, was too much to bear. Every bump in the road sent fresh waves of pain rolling through him.

His voice ragged, he explained his predicament to the men either side of him. They said nothing, making it clear they didn't care.

He tried a different tack. 'I think I'm going to be sick.'

One of the men leapt up, his head bumping the steel roof.

The constable settled onto the bench opposite, and Cage was able to reattach his makeshift sling and haul himself into the corner, the pain beginning to lessen with each breath he took.

At Scotland Yard, he was hustled once more through the iron doors and into the maze of corridors on the ground floor, the thin man striding purposefully in front of him. Expecting to be taken once more to the offices of the CID, Cage was surprised when the man stopped and flung open the door to his left and shouted, 'In here!'

Cage was thrust forward into a small room, lurching to a halt as the door clanged shut behind him. There was no window, but the light from the corridor reached in through an iron grille set in the door, a measly opening meant for looking in, not looking out. The only furniture was a steel table bolted to the floor and two wooden chairs: an interview room rather than a cell. In the dim light, the walls were a sickly khaki green.

Cage flopped into one of the chairs and waited. Then he waited some more. Maybe they would leave him here the whole night? He pulled himself closer to the table and, using his good arm as a pillow, leant over in an attempt to sleep. His mind should be churning with possibilities, readying itself for another encounter with Jack Cross, but the exhaustion he had felt on his journey from Richmond had returned.

His brain shut down. He didn't sleep, exactly. All he could feel was an emptying out, a stasis of being, not thinking. Hours passed. Eventually, he heard the key turn in the lock, but still he was reluctant to move. Something was slapped down on the table beside him, but before he could raise his head, the door had slammed closed again.

A bowl of porridge. Cage stared at it for some time. There was no steam to be seen and when he touched the steel bowl it was barely warm. His stomach rumbled, and he answered its call, spooning a lump of grey mush into his mouth. He ate it all joylessly.

Now he was awake, his mind returned to him, the memories too, everything crushing in like a disorderly multitude at the gates. He heard the grate of steel on steel, and the lock turned once more. Cage sat back and pushed his hair from his eyes as

Detective Jack Cross entered the room with a single constable trailing behind.

Cage waited as Cross took the chair across from him and placed a brown folder on the table. Someone had typed a label on the front: 'Cage Lackmann.' So he had his own file, and it was not exactly thin.

The constable had taken up position by the door, staring ahead into nothing. Cross meanwhile was looking at Cage's sling.

'I slipped on the ice.'

'Bollocks. I heard you gave a rather tame performance in court. The boss was unhappy, I suspect.'

Cage shrugged and the gesture caused him to wince. 'Perhaps. It's been a difficult few weeks.'

Cross sat back in his chair. 'You're braver than I thought, Lackmann. Playing with fire.'

'Why am I here, Jack?'

'Take your pick. Breaking and entering, assault, impersonation. The list keeps getting longer.'

'And you have hard evidence, I suppose? I'd hate to think of you trying to get a conviction on Crewler's word alone.'

'You mean other than the watch you left in the Crewlers' conservatory with your name engraved upon it? Lying next to a hammer?'

Damn.

'And what particular blend of crimes will you charge me with? Or is it all of the above?'

Cross looked undecided, as if he were having to choose from a particularly mouth-watering menu.

'And what of Leland Crewler?' asked Cage.

Cross laughed, a hearty, genuine sound. 'Leland Crewler has an alibi! He always had.'

'Alibis are easy to fake. Trust me.'

Cross turned to the man behind him. 'Remember that statement, Constable. Cage Lackmann says alibis are easy to fake.'

'Come on, Jack! You must have investigated him. The photographs in his study? His brother dressed as Desdemona? You've convicted on less.'

Cross was still smiling. 'Yes, they are all there, just as you said. But Leland Crewler did not kill Baxter Spring. He was attending a dinner at the Guildhall that night; more than ten witnesses of good standing can attest to it. They broke after three in the morning, and Leland Crewler went to a nearby hotel. A waitress served him breakfast at seven the following morning. She remembered him being worse for wear.'

'What was her name?'

'I'm sorry?'

Cage leant forward. 'There is a woman, in league with him. An actress he uses.' Cage knew how mad it all sounded, particularly as he had no evidence to back himself up.

Cross furrowed his brows. 'Lackmann. You're describing yourself.'

'No! This woman had me followed. She used the name Hazel Smythson. She visited, pretending to be a client. I'm sure there is a connection—'

Cross pushed his chair back and lurched to his feet, his face angry now. 'Stop it, Lackmann. Stop lying.'

'What the hell do you think I have to hide? Moses Pickering is dead. There is no one left to protect!'

Cross sneered. 'Other than yourself.'

Cage laughed then. 'You cannot for a moment think I am involved in this.' Cross remained stony-faced and Cage laughed even harder. 'Jack, this is ridiculous.'

'The boy had your poem. Written out in a book of favourites.'

'A coincidence! Come on, man. This is low, even for you.'

'Do you have an alibi?'

'What! Yes! A girl called Agnes. She was with me all night. But Jack—'

'As soon as the first judge walks through the door of the Old Bailey this morning, I will have a warrant to search your house. And I will, properly this time.'

The laughter had died away. 'All because of a poem in a book? What are you hoping to find, for goodness sake?'

Cross rubbed at his temples. 'You're connected, Lackmann. Somehow you're connected.'

And he was, wasn't he? Beyond the note he had withheld from Cross, there was a missing piece, something he wasn't getting. If only he could trust Jack Cross to be objective, between them they might find an answer.

He dipped his toe in the water. 'This woman. Something about her was familiar. I saw her again, at the bail hearing for MacGregor. Maybe—'

'Stop,' said Cross. His face was determined but his voice was weary.

So much for sharing. 'You have nothing, Jack. This is desperation; you are simply shaking the tree. You and I both know that Leland Crewler did this. You might have enough to procure a warrant to search my house again, but you will find nothing there. Now, you have to let me walk out of that door.'

The two men stared at each other until Cross broke the silence. 'What was this woman's name?'

Cage swallowed down a sigh of relief. 'Smythson. Hazel Smythson.'

He gave a detailed description of what had transpired

between them, hating that he had to leave out the forged note sent to Pickering, for without evidence it would only complicate matters. He ended with, 'She is at the heart of this, I know.'

Cross wrote down her name on the inside of the brown folder, then stood up. 'As soon as I have that warrant, you can go.'

CHAPTER THIRTY-SIX

It was another few hours before the thin man returned to release him. A great palaver of paperwork ensued, and Cage handed over the key to his front door, asking that it be left with the tailor when the search was done. He noticed the charge sheet had marked his arrest as 'suspicion of breaking and entering', confirming that Cross had no grounds for his inference of murder. The search of his home was likely just an attempt to find some Crewler stolen property. Without it, a charge would not stand up to scrutiny. He could always claim he had dropped the watch there on his previous visit.

Had Leland Crewler told the detective about Cage's appearance at his office the previous day? Cage should have asked. If Crewler had failed to mention it, was that not a further sign of his guilt? He had to hope that Jack Cross would have more luck finding Hazel Smythson than he himself had done. If they could only track her down and find her connection to Crewler, Cage could bring Bessie Chappelhow and the note back into play. But he couldn't risk telling the detective about that yet, not when the man had doubts about Cage's own role in the death of the two boys, outrageous though the idea was.

He headed back to Whitechapel, and to Mrs Bennett's house.

The pain in his shoulder had settled to a dull, stiff ache and he removed his sling, tying the scarf around his neck instead.

He knocked on the brothel's door and, within moments, it was flung open by Mrs Bennett herself, fully dressed already despite the time of day. She looked none too happy about it. She opened the door wide to let him in, following behind as he entered the small saloon. The few chairs were piled up on the tables as the floorman, with desultory enthusiasm, mopped the brick tiles in semi-darkness.

Cage opened his mouth to speak but Mrs Bennett interrupted him. 'You'll have to wait. She is with another body right now. Got us all up a half hour ago.' She gazed at the sky out of the one tiny window. 'Maybe spring is coming, something to do with the sap.' She sounded unconvinced. 'A glass of wine for you, sir?'

He shook his head. 'Actually, you might be able to help me in her stead?'

'What exactly do you take me for?'

She had misinterpreted him, but even so her reaction bemused him: propositioning the owner of a whorehouse, whoever heard of such a thing? Even the floorman had stopped his mopping and was staring at him as if he'd just shat on his clean floor.

'I simply wished to ask Agnes for some information – in return for payment, of course.' Cage considered his words carefully. 'I am trying to locate someone. A young lad who is missing. It's possible he's found his way to a local molly house, or that someone might at least have seen him there recently. I know nothing of these things but was hoping you could point me in the right direction. Somewhere local, within Whitechapel perhaps?'

She moved towards him, her shrewd eyes weighing him up. 'You going to cause trouble for them?'

Cage offered his assurances: just a private enquiry, all confidences to be respected, etcetera. He shuffled through the coins in his pocket and produced half a sovereign. He placed it on one of the tables, rather than handing it over directly, uncertain now of how her pride lay in such matters.

She nodded but made no move to pick up the coin. 'There's several. But if it's a young lad you're after –' Cage winced at her words '– then there's really only one place.'

He waited for her to say more, before comprehending her tactic. He put his hand in his pocket again, peering at the coins in his hand to find another of the same value. He placed it on top of the first.

She folded her arms. 'Mother Molly's. White's Row. Blue door to the left of the Paul's Head Tavern.'

He thanked her and made to leave.

'You'll need the password.'

He turned back. She came towards him and stood on tiptoes to reach his ear. Evidently, she didn't wish the floorman to hear. Not that he appeared interested.

'Victoria and Albert,' she whispered.

Cage smiled. Queen Victoria was a known prude – that her name and that of her beloved dead husband was a password to a notorious male meeting house would not have amused her.

'Give my regards to Agnes.'

White's Row lay in Spitalfields, to the north. He knew the street – he had once had a client who lodged in one of the many boarding houses there. A transient population made good neighbours, no doubt, for an underground gentlemen's club. He wondered if the name was a nod to Mother Clap, the only person he knew of to have been prosecuted for running such an establishment. But that had been over a hundred years ago, and Cage wondered how such a case would make headlines now. Or would the whole thing be brushed aside to protect the sensitivities of the age?

He arrived at a flat-fronted four-storey house with a glossy blue door. There was nothing to indicate its nature – not that he expected a brass plaque.

He knocked on the door and waited. He caught the eye of a few passers-by, but no one seemed overly interested in the place. If it was such a well-kept secret, Cage wondered if a boy like Baxter could even have known of its existence.

He was about to knock again when the door was opened, a few inches only. Cage couldn't make out who stood behind, but judged their silence to be an invitation to share the password. Feeling slightly foolish, he leant forward and muttered the words he had been given.

The door pulled back further, just enough to let him enter. He walked into a dark, narrow hallway. The door slammed behind him and the darkness grew more intense. He turned back to greet the man behind him, but could see nothing but shadows, a faceless shape, black on grey. The effect was disconcerting.

'May I take your coat, sir?' The voice was elderly and the hand that reached out shook with age.

'No thank you, I shan't stay for long.' Cage's eyes were adjusting: the man before him was small, although he stood upright, his chest proud in his butler's uniform.

'The dining room is not yet open, sir, but a few gentlemen are already settled in the library. If you prefer a quieter place, I was about to light the fire in the Arbuthnot suite?' It sounded just like any gentlemen's club.

'The library, thank you.'

The butler manoeuvred around him to the stairs and began to climb, his hand gripping the banister like a claw. Cage followed, the pace so slow it made his calves hurt.

The library was on the first floor at the front of the house. As he followed the butler's funeral march along the hallway, he had plenty of time to look around him. The panelled walls were dark grey, scuffed in places but enlivened by many artworks, mostly smaller illustrations, portraits of men and boys, some appearing to be quite antique, the glass bulging in faded gilt frames. How long had Mother Molly's been here, hidden behind that blue door? A single gasolier lit their way, but as the butler opened the door to the library, light poured through.

They entered a large space that ran the width of the house. Two generous sash windows lit the room. At one end, a marble fireplace was doing a roaring business. There were only a few bookcases along the back wall, but the arrangement of elegant club chairs casually gathered around a number of small tables and a profusion of antique rugs certainly spoke to the room's name.

A group of three men sat near the fire. They looked up at Cage as he entered, but otherwise continued their amiable conversation. The only other occupant of the library was a man who had his back to the door. Cage could only see the crown of his head as he lounged comfortably in a wingback chair, reading a book.

'Can I bring some coffee for you, sir?' The butler looked up at him.

Cage thanked him and made his way to a group of chairs by the window, where he could more easily peruse the room. He noticed that two of the men by the fire were sitting close together, holding each other's hand casually, as they continued the conversation with their friend. It was far from what Cage had expected: a male-only version of the many brothels he had frequented over the years, where sex was bought and sold with hard-nosed vigour, as if it were oil or tin. But these men, at least, were here for another reason, to express their essence in the most ordinary of circumstances, to hold hands with the person they loved while simply drinking coffee and passing the time of day with an acquaintance. Cage had grown up in the world of theatre, so was not uncomfortable with the sight. Others, he knew, would find two men holding hands like sweethearts to be more shocking than if they were found tumbling naked in a bed. Moses would have found peace here. Had he ever come?

Cage realised he was being stared at. He turned to look at the man who was sitting on his own. His appearance was startling: much younger than he first appeared, barely twenty, if that. He wore an elegant suit, his thick auburn hair brushed to one side, but his face bore the telltale signs of enhancement – nothing compared to the image of Baxter that was seared on Cage's brain, but a shadowing around the eyes, a certain clarity to his complexion, perhaps.

The butler arrived at that moment with his coffee on a silver tray, balanced precariously on one hand. Once he had left, the young man rose from his chair and sauntered across to where Cage was sitting.

'May I?' His voice was deep, despite his young face.

Cage nodded, eager to broach his real purpose here.

The young man settled into the chair opposite and placed his book on the table between them.

'Ah,' said Cage, '*The Return of the Native*. A controversial choice.'

'I'm a controversial type.'

'I have not read it. What is it about?'

'Boy meets girl, boy falls in love with girl. No one gets what they deserve. Love is blind, etcetera, etcetera.'

'You are not enjoying it then?'

'Quite the contrary! It's marvellous.' There was the merest hint of drama in the man's voice. He was intelligent and charming: quite the catch.

'I should explain why I am here.'

'No explanations are necessary. It is your first time?'

'First and last, I'm afraid. I'm looking into the death of a young boy. It's possible he might have come here.'

The man's eyes grew wide so Cage rushed on. 'I am not with the authorities. I am a lawyer; my investigations are private only. That someone trusted me with the password should be testament to my integrity in this. Growing up, I knew many with such proclivities. I am a tolerant man.'

The young man relaxed and gave a wry smile. 'But you do not share such *proclivities*?'

'No. Although maybe life would be simpler if I did.'

'Trust me, it would not.'

It had been a stupid thing to say. Love and desire were the complications, not the object of their determinations. He needed to get to the point. 'You have read no doubt of the murder of Baxter Spring? Similar in nature to another death five years ago, a boy called Nathaniel Crewler.'

The man nodded. 'When it happened, we talked of little else.'

'Then you will know my next question. Is it possible Baxter came here?'

The young man ran his hand through his hair. 'It is possible, of course. The description given was hardly unique. Boys do come here, sometimes as young as twelve; no one is turned away. The name rang no bells, but then I am not sure I know the real name of *anyone* who comes here. Most lie. I do not.' He lifted his chin to match the challenge in his voice. He was brave or foolish; Cage wasn't sure which.

'Baxter was a poet. A promising one.'

The young man considered. 'That does not make his end any more woeful. Nor does his poetic ability bring anyone specifically to mind. I'm sorry. I would help if I could.'

'How does the system work here?'

The man's brow furrowed. 'The system?'

Cage cleared his throat. 'I mean, the purchase – the purchase of someone's time.'

The face before him visibly hardened. 'You misunderstand. This is not a brothel. Men and boys come here to meet each other, to express themselves, to be free, at least for a short while.'

'I apologise. I press for information so as to find the truth, not to pass judgement.' Cage sat forward to emphasise his point. 'Whoever killed these boys had a certain approach, shall we say: the boys were dressed alike, their faces painted theatrically, both wearing wigs of women's hair. It is possible both boys did so willingly, at least at first.'

The man seemed to judge his words carefully. 'It is true to say that many men who come here celebrate both youth and beauty. It is in all men's nature to do so. Women too. But all relationships that are struck here are entered into willingly, with respect, even love, if you can comprehend that. Anything less would not be tolerated.'

'I see. But not everything can be policed with such scrutiny.'

'Perhaps not. But tell me, what is the boy to you?'

'It's a long story.' What would the ending be, he wondered?

He pressed on. 'I must ask about a specific name. I know you must hold everyone's privacy in the highest regard, and whatever you have to tell me will be said in confidence without the police knowing the source, but I would ask you also to think of those two boys, not so much younger than you.'

The man raised an eyebrow at Cage's blunt strategy, but asked nonetheless, 'And the name?'

'Leland Crewler.'

Cage could sense himself holding his breath as he waited for an answer.

The man shook his head. 'If you had a photograph, perhaps.'

Cage bit down the disappointment, but it should not be too hard to obtain one. Another visit to the Old Bell would do it – any one of the papers should have an image of Crewler in their files. 'I could return with one another time. And you would help?'

The man nodded. 'You might also view the portraits in the hall. Those who cannot live honestly as who they are sometimes ask for their picture to be hung here even before they die, a small act of bravery. Or a large one, perhaps.'

Cage thanked him. 'If I return, what name should I ask for you by?'

'Mother Molly.'

Cage stared at him, slightly at a loss.

The man smiled. 'An inheritance. I was considered the most deserving.'

Cage smiled back. He had underestimated the man. 'Thank you for your help.'

'What little I could give.'

The group by the fire were laughing heartily at some joke. Cage looked across, and Mother Molly followed his gaze before saying, 'Our world has its darkness, but there is light too, if you know where to find it.'

Cage stood up. 'How do I pay for the coffee?'

'Ah, we have a strange ritual involving chickens and garters.'

Cage stared blankly.

The man laughed. 'Money will suffice. There is a bowl by the door. Pay what you can afford.'

With a promise to return once he had procured the necessary photograph, Cage left the library, depositing a shilling in a majolica dish on his way out.

The hallway was empty, the butler nowhere to be seen. Cage took his time exploring the myriad portraits on the walls as he ventured back to the stairway, his eyes searching for Leland Crewler. The young man he had spoken to must have been the latest in a long line of Mother Mollies. It was a romantic idea, a secret meeting place passed down through the ages, the torch passed on to the brightest, or simply the bravest, of the next generation.

Cage thought he recognised one of the larger portraits, which bore a clear resemblance to a prime minister from the reign of George the Third. Could it be him? It seemed odd at first, that men who strove to keep their homosexuality a secret all their lives would take the risk of having a portrait hung in this place, even after their deaths. But perhaps that was the point: a daring revelation of the truth, still hidden from the world but pointing a silent finger of accusation. Sadly, if Leland Crewler was indeed a visitor here, he had yet to find such mettle within himself.

At the head of the stairs Cage paused to find his gloves. Had he dropped one? He turned back just as his hand found it buried deep in his pocket. But his eyes had caught on something. A photograph on the wall. A few years old, maybe, the frame in simple wood, the face unmistakable.

Mother Molly was wrong. Love did not make you blind, but jealousy did.

Cage started running.

CHAPTER THIRTY-SEVEN

At the corner of his own street, Cage ground to a halt. Hands on his knees, he leant forward, the sound of his own tortured gasps crashing in waves through his skull.

He spied two constables further up the street, leaning against a police cart. The search was bound to be over by now: had they stayed behind to harass him on his return? He would speak with Cross before the day was done, but on his own terms.

He cut through the alley at the back of his house, fumbling for the keys that would open the door into his yard and then the new lock into the scullery.

When he entered his office, the place was a mess: the hastily stacked piles of documents now lay scattered across the floor once again. Even the chimney had been searched, black chunks littered the hearth and motes of coal dust swam lazily in the air, not yet ready to come to rest. Cage ignored it all and climbed the stairs, not caring about the trail of black footprints he left behind. In his apartment, he opened the armoire and took his travel bag from the top shelf – a green tweed affair that smelled of camphor and collapsed in on itself through lack of use.

He packed quickly, throwing in Moses's notebook, and the crumpled copy of Baxter's poem he had left on his bedside table. In his office, he grabbed the Rubens from the wall and slid it carefully into the bag.

He was ready: ready to do what he should have done five years ago. In the yard, he slammed the scullery door with a final thud. He was halfway to the Whitechapel Road before he found a cab.

'Elgin Gardens, please.'

The pace was painfully slow. It had begun to rain, fat drops spanking the tarpaulin roof as the cab moved west through the city. He huddled back into the warm leather, feeling more awake than he had in years. He had found the identity of Baxter Spring's killer, and the discovery had brought him something he had never thought could be truly his.

He had the fare ready in his hand before the cab even stopped. The carriage rocked as he jumped down, almost forgetting the half-full travel bag he had slung on the rack above his head.

The rain was coming hard now, washing the steps clean as he leapt towards the Kenwards' front door. He raised the knocker, then paused before he brought it down on the plate. What if she was not alone? Stupid, he had not thought about that until now. But he was Cage Lackmann, Poet of Whitechapel, the best lawyer in London and the absolute king of deception and guff. If Justin was there, he would think of something.

He knocked, and within moments the starched maid had opened the door. He wiped his feet quickly, stepped across the threshold, then looked up into Emma's face.

She was midway down the stairs, silhouetted cleanly against the window, her mouth open in a perfect 'O'. He smiled up at her with everything he had to give: the love of his life.

'I'm afraid Justin is out just now.' She came towards him, her features growing stronger. He longed for her to keep walking, not stopping until she was in his arms at last.

'It is you I have come to see.'

Her eyebrows half raised before they remembered themselves. 'Of course.' She gestured towards the parlour. 'Do come this way.'

'After you,' he said, enjoying this display of chivalry and decorum, the last time it would ever have to be this way between them.

He followed her into the room, his eyes on the wisps of hair that had come free from the dark abundance piled atop her head. He shut the door behind himself. He had no words prepared, no idea of the order in which he should offer up what he had come to say.

She stood formally by the fireplace, her hands clasped together in symmetry. Cage closed the distance between them. She tried to back away but there was nowhere to go. He grabbed her hands in his and pulled her close. She looked up at him, her eyes registering alarm. He forgave her fear; he just hoped she would offer forgiveness in return.

'I've come to ask you to do what I refused to do all those years ago.'

She searched his face. 'I don't understand.'

His hands cupped her cheeks. He could feel the silk of her skin and the delicate bones beneath. 'Run away with me. Now. Today. I have money. Some, at least. It will be enough, we can make it enough.'

Her hands were on his arms, her grip tight on his biceps, whether to pull him closer or push him away he couldn't tell. 'Why now, Cage? Why the hell do you ask me now?'

'I know who killed those boys. I am sorry for it, but at least we can be free now.'

Her eyes had grown wide. 'Who?'

This was the hardest part, telling her the truth. 'My love, I believe it was Justin. I am sorry, but I found his photograph, at a place called Mother Molly's, where men go to meet younger men.'

She said nothing, but her face was anything but silent as his words sank in.

He carried on, mercilessly. She had to know the truth. 'There are only three men that connect the two boys. Moses we know was not guilty, he was set up to take the blame. Leland Crewler has an alibi. But Justin? Where was Justin the night Baxter was killed?'

She stared at him. He could only imagine the turmoil within. She managed to whisper just one word. 'Out.'

He grabbed her hands once more. They were cold as ice. 'I know he claimed to be in Manchester the night Nathaniel was killed, but someone lied for him. Maybe this Hazel Smythson, who has to be some kind of accomplice of his. You may even have met her under another name?'

She looked at him as if he were mad, and slowly shook her head.

'You're in shock, I know. Come with me now, we can take a room somewhere. I shall speak with Jack Cross and tell him everything I know, then we can leave. For ever. When is Justin due back? If you pack quickly, can we be gone before he comes?'

She looked down at her hands, small and pale against his darker, rougher skin.

'I am sorry to bring this to you. But I am not sorry for what it means.'

Her eyes flitted back to his and he wrapped his arms about her waist.

'I was always so jealous of him, so scared I could not compete. I couldn't destroy your perfect life.' Cage laughed a little. 'I wasted all those years for both of us, thinking he was the better man. I was wrong.'

She let out a tremendous sob, her body rocking into his with the violence of it. Fat tears began to roll down her cheeks, a storm arriving without warning. He cradled her to him, his mouth making soothing noises. 'I'm sorry, I'm so sorry. It will all be all right.'

She found her strength and pushed away from him, her feet catching on the hearth as she stumbled and seized hold of the back of a chair. She gripped it with both hands, her knuckles turning white as she breathed her tears away. 'I would have given anything to hear that promise five years ago.' Her voice dropped to a whisper. 'Anything!'

How could he explain? It was not all about Justin and his discovery. 'I couldn't let myself have you. Couldn't let myself know love. But I dreamt about you. Every night for five years.' Charlie too, and the boy he had once been.

She surprised him then. She laughed: a genuine sound, not hysterical, just amused.

His shock continued as she pulled her chemise from her waistband, her eyes glistening still from her tears and her laughter. She reached behind her neck to undo the buttons there.

'We should leave first. In case he returns.' He sounded prudish to his own ears.

She ripped her shirt over her head: he heard it tear. Her hands reached behind as she undid her skirt. It fell about her ankles, her petticoats following in a puddle on the floor before she ripped her stockings from her suspenders, tearing them away with an anger he had never seen. She stepped out from behind the chair and walked slowly towards him, only her corset and underwear covering her. He had never seen her revealed like this, except in dreams, but what he saw now was nothing less than a nightmare.

The bruises started around her throat, black and ugly. A ridge of livid scar tissue slashed across the skin of her left breast. Her knees were red raw, the skin puckered as if the threads had been pulled too tight.

Cage tore his gaze away, back to her face. She had almost reached him now, and he saw that the gleam in her eyes was neither laughter nor tears, but triumph. He wanted to reach for her, but she had never seemed so far away. 'I didn't know.' Pathetic, but he said it anyway.

'Still want me now?'

'Yes!'

He fell to his knees before her. Her hands reached out and held his head, tipping his face to look at her.

'Is it absolution you want, Cage Lackmann?'

Cage blinked rapidly, the tears stinging his eyes. The scar on her chest was close now, the skin so badly sewn you could see where the stitches had once been. Had she used the needle herself? Or had Justin done it, contrite and tender after the event, on his knees before her as Cage was now. 'I am so sorry. Emma, my darling, if you had told me—'

'Five years you left me to rot in this marriage. Five years! I have paid the price every night.' Her fingers dug into his skull as she leered down at him. 'Nathaniel Crewler –' she spat the name '– was a sideshow. I was the main attraction. Always he came back to me, to this.'

She bent her head and kissed him savagely, her lips pulling

his mouth into hers. Then she broke away, her voice cracking on her words like a ship on the rocks. 'I loved you! I thought you would take me away, rescue me.' The laugh came again, hard and brittle all at once. 'Well you taught me a valuable lesson all those years ago, Cage.' She let go of his head as if she were dropping it over the side of a bridge. 'Save yourself, because no one else will. That's what she taught you, didn't she?'

Emma turned her back and walked away. He saw more bruises, and a round black patch on her calf like a burn from the butt of a cigar. She grabbed at her skirt and pulled it back on roughly, her torn chemise too. The show was over. His head burned with a million things to say, but just one question.

'When did you know about Nathaniel?'

She shook her head. 'I've always known.'

Cage swallowed down her reply. 'When Moses was arrested?'

'Before. The very night the boy died.'

'How?'

She looked at him as one might a stupid child, failing to grasp the basics of addition. 'He confessed. It was the third time they had been together, in Nathaniel's room. The boy liked to dress up. Justin said he was seduced, the boy made a play for him, hinted that he liked what Justin had to offer, which in case you haven't guessed is brutal, like a dog in the yard.'

'Your neck . . .'

She was putting her stockings on now, her voice a monotone. 'That too. Supposedly heightens pleasure. Not sure for whom. With Nathaniel it went too far.'

'An accident then.'

'When Justin came home, he was so scared, like a little boy.

He was bleeding. Nathaniel had scratched at him wildly when he knew he was dying. I held Justin all night and we made love, the proper way, like you and I once did. It was the only time we had done so since our wedding night.'

Cage nodded, as if any of this made any sense. 'You lied for him. Said he was in Manchester. Did Cross even check?' He swallowed down on the next question. 'And Baxter?'

She closed her eyes, like a brave invalid facing down a chronic and familiar pain. 'I asked him, but I simply received this in return.' She pointed to the burn on her calf before pulling her stocking higher. 'He doesn't share such secrets any more. I've learned to hold my tongue, then it's not so bad. Just this.' She touched her neck.

He held her gaze, bearing witness to her suffering: it was all he could do.

She nodded to the floor in front of the fire. 'This is where it happens. Mostly.'

Cage looked down at the carpet: the faded pattern, the threadbare patches where the weave was now visible.

She snapped her suspenders into place and pulled her skirts down, looking for all the world as if the last five minutes had not happened.

Cage found his voice once more. 'I thought I knew him, knew what he was.'

'No one knows anyone.'

She was right. He didn't know Justin, and he didn't know her. The awfulness of it was too much. 'Damn it, Emma, why the hell didn't you tell me?' It was the same question over and over, but he could not stop asking. 'It would have changed everything!'

'Would it?'

'Yes! Why didn't you tell the police when it happened? Why lie for him? Why not go to them now? It makes no sense!' He knew he was shouting, angry at the world, and yes, angry at her.

She laughed his fury away. 'And ruin my life? I've made do. I will do so again. If Justin was exposed, my life would be unliveable, the wife of a murdering degenerate.' She wrapped her arms around herself, as if she were cold. 'With you, there was a chance, just to leave it all behind, but that's gone now.'

He rushed towards her. 'No, it's not—'

'Stop!'

'I could go to Jack Cross. I *will*.'

'They won't listen to you.'

'With your evidence, of course they will!'

She shook her head so vigorously her hair came loose. 'You shouldn't have come here. It wasn't supposed to happen this way. Just go, leave now, I'll give you that.'

'I don't understand.'

Her back was against the wall, as far from him as it was possible to be. She didn't meet his eyes when she spoke. 'Cross has everything he needs now. I have made sure of it. The note was the very last thing. It will damn you completely.'

He was floundering. 'The note?'

Her back stiffened suddenly, like his mother's did before she stepped out on stage. 'The note you sent to Moses, telling him to run, to cover up your foul crime.'

'What! Emma this is ridiculous. Justin must have sent that note, using this Smythson woman. Besides, you burned it!'

'Did I?' Her eyes were full of challenge, daring him to hate her for what she had done. 'Or was that merely a shopping list I threw on the fire?'

He couldn't believe what he was hearing. His mind was chasing itself in circles, he couldn't think fast enough. 'I have an alibi. A girl—'

She shook her head. 'Not any more. I was with Agnes this morning. Such a delightful girl, and so ambitious. I suggested a little town in the West Country for her adventures in haberdashery. With the money I gave her, she has more than enough. I told her not to waste any time, and that more would follow in six months if she stayed away.'

Would Agnes really sell him out so easily? 'How did you even know about her?' It wasn't the biggest question but it was all he had.

'I had you followed, to see what I could find. I used the name Smythson when I hired the boy. I don't know who she really is but you gave me her name so I used it.'

This was madness. 'And Justin knows what you are doing?'

The wild shake of her head again, her hair flying across her face, as if she could release something trapped in her head. 'Just me.'

'What else have you done?'

'Oh, there's more.' She wiped a hand across her mouth, as if the words were poison to her too. 'I wouldn't wait to find out. I just need Cross to *believe* it was you, whether he has you or not. Run, Cage Lackmann. Run like you always have, you fucking coward.'

He strode across the room and grabbed her arms. 'For goodness' sake, Emma, you'd blame me for Justin's crimes, just to avoid scandal?'

The scream tore from her body. 'You murdered hope, Cage! If the world won't damn you for that, I will have it damn you for something.'

Baxter's words again: here lies hope, a quivering fragile thing he had crushed beneath his boot more than once. The grave need only be shallow, for it would not rise again.

There was so much more he should ask. But he looked at her face again. If this was the death of love, then Baxter had been right again.

He had not seen it coming.

CHAPTER THIRTY-EIGHT

The rain fell with a new ferocity as Cage stumbled towards the station at Ladbroke Grove. He tried to assess the evidence against himself dispassionately, but all that stirred within him was Emma's betrayal, his mouth scabby dry as the shock of it settled in to stay. He had always rationalised why he had never seen her entirely naked: modesty, perhaps, a discomfort with their illicit lovemaking, or simply the practicalities of their snatched moments together. To think that he had kissed her, touched her, and all the while that horror lay beneath his fingers. He had felt her bones, her muscles, through gossamer layers. Why had he not felt those bruises and scars, why had their miserable heat not burned the skin from his hands?

He was soaking wet when he arrived at the station.

She said she had given the note to Cross that morning. He thought back to a few days ago: she had entreated him not to pursue Baxter's killer and opened the door to a possible future together, but all that time she had planned this. The moment the door slammed on the possibility of Moses's guilt, Cage himself had opened the gateway to another option

He ran his hands through his hair, willing the fog to clear.

He was in trouble, serious trouble. That was what he had to focus on now, not this howling for lost love. He needed the lawyer, not the poet.

Agnes was critical. If she was still in town, then there was still a chance. Whatever evidence Emma had stacked against him, even the alibi of a whore would act as counterweight. He couldn't believe he had to think like this. Despite their mutual enmity, surely Cross would see he had no motive? And no connection at all to the two boys other than through Pickering and Kenward. He had to cling to that.

Perhaps Cross would find Hazel Smythson? The key to the puzzle, he was sure. Though it was doubtful whether he would even still look for her now that Emma had served up the note and whatever else she had cooked up. That was why the police had remained at his house after their search. They had found something, after all, and Emma had put it there: the break-in a few days earlier, which had been her doing. How delighted Detective Jack Cross would be to have Cage Lackmann behind bars, however illegitimate the cause.

Agnes first. He bought a ticket to Farringdon, and climbed the steps to the platform, as the callous rain slanted down the steps towards him, as if it meant to seek him out. He huddled beneath a canopy, flat to the wall, grateful for the blast of steam when the train shuddered into the station.

He found a seat by the window and stared out at the merciless, grey city as the train rumbled eastwards. He would be anywhere but here, in this bitter, broken place. It was all he had ever known, a city built of stone and shit, the rot steaming beneath them all.

At Farringdon, he struggled to find an empty cab. He had almost reached the London Wall before a driver stopped for him. Even then, the man refused to take him all the way to Mrs Bennett's, the rain tipping the laws of supply and demand in his favour. Cage accepted his decision without a fight, and got out at the Whitechapel Road. He offered a tip, determined to see kindness somewhere, even if it was his own.

Cage pulled the collar of his coat up and pressed forward into the rain. The streets were mostly empty; even the whores and peddlers had found refuge from the storm. He pushed all brooding thoughts away and tried to focus. Emma must have been the visitor Agnes had received that morning. To think he had been under the same roof as she opened her purse and spilled its contents into Agnes's lap. Had Agnes known who she was, he wondered? The woman he had once told her he loved? Had Agnes seen iniquity in that beautiful face?

He banged on the brothel door, but had to wait, the rain at his back like needles.

Finally the door whined open, and one of the floormen let him inside.

'I need to see Agnes urgently. Now. It is most important.' He had almost said a matter of life and death, but it would have sounded foolish, even if it were true.

He waited in the saloon while the man despatched a kitchen girl upstairs. Cage looked across to the steps, willing Agnes to walk down them.

At last he heard noises above, then the rustle of skirts as someone descended. He ran across to the stairwell, but it was only Mrs Bennett coming down the steps, the girl Lucy trailing behind her.

Cage spoke first. 'She's gone.'

Mrs Bennett merely nodded, her mouth pursed in anger.

Cage grabbed a chair and slumped down as Mrs Bennett

ranted: 'Five years I invested in that girl, then she leaves without a word of thanks. Tried to take her dresses too. I put a stop to that, left her in the clothes she stood in. Arrogant little bitch didn't care. Someone's made promises though, promises they won't keep. Thought it was you until I saw the look on your face.'

He looked up at her, with no attempt to disguise his misery.

'There are other girls, you know. I've taught them all the same things.'

Cage laughed. She thought he had fallen in love with Agnes. Maybe part of him had, what little of himself that had been going spare. The hole within him where love had lived grew wider, and he thought he might collapse in on himself, like the bag at his feet.

'I don't suppose she left an address.'

Mrs Bennett shook her head. 'Why would she? Something about the West Country, I think. Why would I care? Gone is gone.'

'I was here, a Monday night, the night I met Agnes, the night I first came. The end of January—'

She interrupted him with a gentle touch on his arm. 'Not for all the money in the world, love. Even if I could remember, which I can't. So don't ask.'

That was that, then. No alibi.

'I'll fetch you a drink. Red wine, wasn't it? Then best be on your way.'

She left him there. Cage stared at the floor. A puddle was forming around his boots, as if he were melting. Something white flashed in the periphery of his vision and he looked up to see the girl, Lucy, standing there, clenching something in her hands.

Now she had his attention, she stepped forward and handed over a piece of paper, folded tight in a tiny square. She placed it carefully into his hand and pleated his fingers around it, as if it were a fragile thing. She just had time to raise a single finger to her lips before her aunt returned with the promised glass of wine.

Cage stood up. 'Thank you, but no. I should go.'

The woman looked relieved.

He stepped out into the storm once more, although it was beginning to exhaust itself. He pulled his collar up and hunched his shoulders.

A whistle sounded up ahead, muted by the rain. He looked up: two policemen at the end of the alley, running towards him.

Cage spun around and banged his fist on the door. The alley was a dead end, he had nowhere else to go. He banged again, as if he could splinter the wood with his bare hands.

The door swung open and he ran inside. A hand grabbed his and the young girl dragged him towards the kitchens with surprising strength. He needed no encouragement and sprinted through into a warren of unlit rooms. Her grip was firm as she pulled him this way and that. Then the knocking came, thundering through the brothel like the crash of a giant's boot.

'Police! Open up in there!'

The girl ducked left into a scullery and stood on tiptoes to reach a key on a shelf above her head. Then she turned to a low wooden door and fumbled the key into the lock.

'Thank you,' panted Cage. He was out of breath, not from the brief run through the house, but from the shock of it all. The moment had come. Emma's work was done. He was a wanted man, a felon on the run. He was guilty of so many things, maybe it didn't matter in the end what he was condemned for. Isn't that what Emma thought?

Finally, the girl thrust open the door and stood aside to let him pass. Her face was unreadable, but he had no time to question her motives. He ran past her and out into a cluttered courtyard beyond, hearing the door close softly behind him.

On the back wall, a shed leaned against the bricks. He crept forward. The shed was hopefully sturdy enough to take his weight. His shoulder groaned as he slung his bag upwards. It landed wetly on top of the shed. He grabbed at the ledge of the roof, but the slippery wood resisted him.

He took a breath. Then another. On the far side of the courtyard was a wheelbarrow: it was all he could see that might help him. But there were windows in the back of the house and he would be visible from all of them. How long could Mrs Bennett and the girl wait before answering those hammering blows on their front door? He ducked down as low as he could and crept across the yard. He tipped the barrow backwards and retraced his steps, the single wheel shrieking like a banshee.

He pulled it level against the shed. He hoisted one leg into the barrow, tested its robustness, then launched himself in. He could just reach over the roof now and grab the central timber. One foot lodged on the windowsill, offering barely a few inches of purchase. It would have to do. He hauled himself upwards.

The shed groaned beneath him as he lay spread-eagled upon its roof. The wall was within his grasp. He seized his bag and crept forwards, imagining the roof giving way beneath him, his belly exposed to the tools no doubt housed below. Death by rake, or chisel, perhaps. It was funny. It should be funny.

He reached the back wall and pulled himself on to it. It was a straight drop down to the alley below. Eight feet perhaps?

He flung his bag downwards and dangled his legs forward. He couldn't resist one last look back at the brothel. There was no sign of anyone on the ground floor. His eyes snagged upwards. The girl's face looked down at him, opaque behind the glass of a bedroom window. She lifted her hand in a single wave. To hell with it. He waved back.

Then he jumped.

CHAPTER THIRTY-NINE

He felt his right ankle give, but he couldn't think about that now. West or east? He chose east, where the sea waited. The sea and ships and liberty.

He ran until he reached the next junction. Another alleyway lay before him, but maybe being out in the open afforded a better chance? If only the weather was fine, and there were more people about.

He turned north. The street was empty. If he could reach the Commercial Road, there was bound to be more activity, maybe even a cab. He limped on, pulling his long hair inside of his coat and turning the collar up. He crossed over to another street, as deserted as the one he had left.

Then he saw it. Up ahead, a small black carriage moving towards him, two rows of constables hunkered atop the knife plate, their rain cloaks shrouding the carriage as they walled their backs to the rain. He slowed his pace. If he turned around now they would notice him, if they hadn't already. But he could not risk getting closer. The houses to his side were closed up against the storm, the doors slammed against him.

Then a whistle sounded. The constables splashed down from their perch: eight of them pouring towards him.

Cage turned on his heel and ran. Back the way he had come, then taking a road to the east once more. His ankle hurt, his shoulder hurt. He ignored it all and pounded on.

He snubbed the first turning north in case any of his pursuers found an alleyway to cut off his path. At the next corner he swung left. Five men were loitering outside a pub up ahead. They turned at his approach.

'Coppers!' he shouted.

They spilled in all directions like marbles.

Cage kept to a straight line, a quarter mile from the main road at least. The rain silenced everything around him. They could be twenty or two hundred yards behind him, he had no idea. Running became everything. He felt he could run for ever, all the way to the sea if he had to.

Finally the Commercial Road was in sight: carriages, carts, people. It would be busiest on the stretch that ran towards the city: that was his best option if he could make it that far. His legs carried on; he could no longer feel the pain in his ankle, could no longer feel anything any more.

At the corner he swung left and immediately slowed his pace. There would be other police here, guarding the main artery of valuable traffic through the lawless East End. Up ahead a hansom cab had come to a stop, and two gentlemen were descending. Cage jogged towards it, his hand raised at the driver.

He could see another man with two suitcases waiting at the curb. The man stepped forward, his moustache twitching in agitation that his ride might be stolen out from under him.

Cage spoke quickly. 'Please. We can share. My wife is in labour!'

Without waiting for an answer, he hoisted himself within.

The other man was indecisively loitering on the pavement. *Come on!* Cage yelled within himself.

After a few agonising seconds, the man grabbed the door, and began to load his heavy cases within. Cage grabbed them from him.

'I say!' the man sang out as two constables buffeted past him.

Cage stared in horror as the man turned and began to remonstrate with them, calling them back. One constable stopped and Cage retreated into his seat, one hand on the other door, ready to leap out into the traffic if he had to.

The constable walked towards the man with the moustache. Cage shrank back still further.

'Sorry, sir.'

Cage could hear the policeman's breathlessness and blew out his own sigh of relief. The constable was merely exhausted, content to have a reason to stop running. Me too, he thought. Me too.

Eventually the man climbed in and slammed the door.

'Where to?' the driver called.

The man looked at Cage: he was the expectant father after all.

Cage calculated rapidly. 'Liverpool Street, please.'

The man smiled. 'Myself also. Where do you live?'

Nowhere. 'Gravesend.'

Now the man frowned. 'Would London Bridge not be the quicker route?'

'I have luggage at Liverpool Street.'

Satisfied, the man nodded.

Cage looked away. Keeping back from the window, he closed his eyes, his breaths slowly deepening.

Then he remembered the note the girl had given him. Frantically he searched his pockets, and found it balled up, sodden from his wet coat. Impatiently he unfolded it, tearing one corner. Just two sentences, not hard to forget. He read it just the once, the ink streaking across the page.

I'm sorry. It seems my dreams were for sale after all. I hope you understand. Ax

So, gone was gone. Good for her. Good for Agnes. He couldn't find it within himself to be angry. She would have her freedom and her ribbons and her pearls: he had been worth something in the end.

What would he do now? Cage pulled his sodden travel bag onto his lap and covertly counted the crumpled banknotes within. More than one hundred pounds, he calculated. It was a decent sum. Enough to leave the country, or at least hide himself well. Isn't this what part of him had always craved? A fresh start, a new life. Become a carpenter. Bury Micajah Lackmann in Baxter's graveyard on the hill. *I let you go.*

He felt a pang of regret at allowing Archie Weston to take his portrait: he was bound to be compelled to hand it over to Jack Cross. But Cage could change his appearance if needs be. A beard was fashionable, after all. His brain skittered about the place. The West Country, perhaps? Wouldn't that be ironic.

As the cab pulled up outside Liverpool Street, his anxiety returned. Cross had anticipated his visit to Mrs Bennett's, no doubt acting on information Emma had given him. Still, sending men there had been a punt on the detective's behalf. How many other bets would he place? Did he have the manpower to cover the main stations that led out of the city? The will would be there, that much was for certain.

Cage settled up with the driver then waited as his insistent companion meticulously counted out in pennies and farthings precisely half of the fare. They parted ways and Cage descended into the station, hat jammed low, just another commuter in a perpetual rush.

The subterranean concourse echoed around him: a thousand feet and a hundred conversations bounced around the cavernous space. He scanned it quickly: two bobbies loitered at either end of the ticket barriers – a standard posting, he hoped, nothing to be alarmed about.

He hurried towards the ticket office and took his place in the queue. Behind him, the huge board announced various arrivals and departures. He had no idea where to go. The end of the line, that was for sure, but which one? He settled on Colchester. From there he could reach Harwich and cross to the Continent. Amsterdam, or Germany perhaps? His mind danced once more. Was he really doing this?

He purchased his ticket. His train would leave in twenty minutes. He found the men's room and emptied his bladder, then braved a glance in the mirror. He barely recognised himself: his hair was wild, his eyes wide and startled. He washed his hands and face, then patted down his curls, pushing them beneath his collar. His boots were caked in mud, at odds with his still smart coat. He pulled the worst of the mud away from his boots, then washed his hands again. There was nothing he could do about the look in his eyes. They screamed *fugitive*, as if it were someone else entirely who lay trapped behind them.

He left the men's room and made for the ticket barrier. Five booths only: he chose the middle. The queues were building. It was rush hour, which was good. He kept his head down, not daring to glance left or right and risk catching the eye of either constable.

Finally, he was through. He climbed the stairs to his platform, the rain pounding onto the great roof above, offering him a standing ovation.

The train had yet to pull in, but the platform was already busy. Men huddled in groups, lining up to the precise spot where the door to their favourite carriage would open. He joined the back of one such gathering. No one spoke, for all the familiarity they must have had with each other. Another thing he hated about this city, and he had yet to even leave it.

Nerves jangled now he was still again. Other men were reading their papers. He should have bought one. Instead, he reached into his bag and withdrew Moses's notebook. He flipped idly through, his fingers still numb with cold. He came to the pages where Moses had sketched out and then scratched through his thoughts on Baxter's poem. Here was the graveyard, the bleakness of the hills, and the simple white chapel against the sable sky. He stared at the images, as good a thing as any to distract him from the tortuous wait. He could hear the train pulling in, its laboured breath like a dying man as it sank to a stop. Only then did he allow himself to put the notebook away. A lone man stood behind the carriage window nearest to him, waiting to open the door, his form a dark shadow against the fading daylight behind. Something sparked within Cage, something he had missed, perhaps? He reached for Pickering's notebook once more, and as he bent down, felt the shock of a hand clamp onto his shoulder.

'Cage Lackmann. You are under arrest!

A moment's hesitation was all it took. A pause between freedom and death. Had Charlie known that too?

A second hand landed on his arm, then a third. A whistle sounded, although he had offered no resistance. His fellow travellers parted around him, a silent receding tide. Still Cage had not turned around. Three men held him now, maybe four. The hands of strangers, but they might as well have belonged to Pincott or Emma.

The carriage door opened. He was mere steps away. How close he had come. But the city would not let him go. Why had he ever thought it would?

CHAPTER FORTY

Two days and two nights. That is how long they left him for.

For the first hours only, he had paced: a tiger in a cage, his body still wound for motion as if it might yet pump itself across the sea. He thought through his arguments, preparing for the visit from Jack Cross that was inevitable. A two-day wait: that was unethical, illegal even. But he was determined not to be sidetracked by procedure, when the truly monstrous matter was the charges laid against him.

When he had first arrived at Newgate, the thin man had been summoned. Cage's wrists were chained as the man loudly recited that he was detained on suspicion of two counts of murder: the victims Nathaniel Crewler and Baxter Spring. Cage literally had not known whether to laugh or cry. In the end he did neither.

His bag and coat were taken from him, the various articles itemised. He watched as the guard counted out the money, his lips mouthing the words as he did so. When the guard pulled Baxter's poem from the folds of damp tweed, he laid it flat on the desk.

'"The Graves of Whitechapel". By Baxter Spring.' Each word

laden with censure. Surely proof of an unhealthy obsession with the young lad? In a way he was right. Cage had been obsessed.

On the third day the door to his cell was unbolted and he was taken to the interview rooms behind the Old Bailey that he was more familiar with. His feet were chained for the march and he was led through the tunnel towards the court. The 'graveyard' it was sometimes called, or Dead Man's Walk. Here, the executed had been buried until only recently, interred beneath the flagstones in lime-filled coffins.

The room he was taken to was freezing; his cell almost balmy by comparison. His chains were unlocked and he sank into one of the chairs, the metal whip-cold through the fabric of his grubby clothes. He anticipated a long wait and closed his eyes the better to keep his focus. But within minutes, the door slammed open again.

Cage kept his eyes shut, hearing the squeak of another chair being pulled up on the opposite side of the table. A muttered *thank you* told him that Jack Cross was finally here. He pictured the detective's face. Would he see a smile? A glint of victory? Or something worse. Condemnation, perhaps.

He opened his eyes. There was no smile, no judgement either. The lines on the man's forehead had deepened and the skin beneath his eyes sagged with fatigue: stress, that is what he saw – and confusion. Please, thought Cage, be as bewildered by this as I.

'The charges have been officially laid this morning. The evidence has been deemed sufficient to prosecute. Whitaker is keen to lead.'

Cage said nothing.

'Do you require a lawyer, or do you wish to represent yourself? The bail hearing is in the morning.'

They both knew bail was not a possibility. He had been caught attempting to flee the city and faced two charges of murder. He wouldn't even go to court, wouldn't fan the flames of the journalists in the gallery. Not yet, at least.

'I won't contest bail,' he said.

Cross nodded, a kind of professional approval. How had it come to this?

'What will you do?' Cage asked.

'Pardon?'

'While I rot in here, wrongly accused, what will *you* do? Pursue the real killer? Or just move on, job done. It's Justin Kenward, in case you're interested. I put it together, which is why I'm here.' It wasn't, but the real reasons were too obscure, and not his to own.

Cross leant forward. 'Tell me what you have, Lackmann. What evidence?'

Cage laughed. 'None. I wasn't as clever as them. I have his confession of course, as told to his wife, and then related to me, but that is not admissible, just second-hand confirmation. Then there is a photograph of Kenward in a secret establishment where men go to meet younger, more beautiful men – but wait, that only speaks to proclivity, is too circumstantial, and anyway I doubt it is even there any more. The only hard evidence to speak of is Emma Kenward's naked body. Years of marital abuse stitched to her skin. I only saw it for myself a few days ago, but if you hurry, I'm sure the bruises will still be there. Although I'd like to see you get a judge's signature on that particular warrant. So no, on second thoughts, far better to stick with prosecuting me. Anything else would be foolish, don't you think?' The anger was rising; he stood no chance against it.

Cross shook his head. 'Evidence is everything, Lackmann. You know it.'

'And what of motive? Come on, man, you don't believe it any more than I do!' He had promised himself he wouldn't beg.

'Then explain that note to me! Whoever sent it murdered that boy.'

'Of course they did! But if it was me who sent it to Pickering, why on earth would I not destroy it? Have you spoken to the landlady, Bessie Chappelhow? She'll confirm the description of the woman, the same one I described to you as Hazel Smythson. She took the notepaper and came to my office, some collaborator of Kenward's. I kept that note from you precisely for this reason, Jack. Until I knew who had sent it, I daren't share it with you. You'd use any reason to—'

Cross's face grew livid. 'To what, Lackmann? See you get your just deserts? If I added up the time that should have been served by all those fucking villains you've returned to Pincott's service, I'd need to lock you up for the next millennium to see justice done!'

They both drew a breath.

'Then do it, Jack. The truth doesn't matter, does it? Not here. And not in Whitechapel. It doesn't matter anywhere.'

They stared at each other, the detective's jaw working silently. He raised his fingers to stop the pulse, to no effect. Eventually he spoke again.

'Mrs Chappelhow has sworn it was you who delivered that note.'

The Kenward fortune had been busy, it would seem. 'And how exactly did Emma Kenward say she came by it?'

Cross stared him down, his face inscrutable. 'It dropped from your pocket. When you visited them.'

'How careless of me.'

'When she challenged you, you confessed to the crimes and threatened her.' It was hard to tell if the man believed the words he was saying. 'She showed me the bruises. Said they were from you.'

Cage slammed his fist on the table, so hard the room seemed to shake. The guard stepped forward but Cross waved him away. Cage looked down at his hand, still clawed, the nails biting into his own flesh, as if there was something it might yet achieve. But he was done, wasn't he? He didn't look up as he asked, 'What else do you have?'

'The photograph.'

'The one *I* brought to you.'

'And the watch you left at the Crewlers'.'

'A week ago. Not five years ago.'

'Who's to say?'

Cage looked up, his face incredulous.

Jack Cross closed his eyes and rubbed at them. He looked as exhausted as Cage felt. 'We found other evidence. When we searched your house.'

The temperature seemed to drop still further, as if hell were freezing over. This time he could see it coming: the killer blow. 'Shall I guess?'

But Cross was in no mood for games. 'Other photographs. Nathaniel Crewler, posing, wearing the same clothes we found him in.'

Cage said nothing; he would know it all first.

'And a blood-stained handkerchief. Monogrammed, the initials NC.'

A handkerchief – how apt. 'Desdemona,' said Cage.

'Exactly so.' It appeared they shared the same Shakespeare references. What else did they share, this man and him?

'Surprising you found none of these things on your previous visit.'

'Ah. I wasn't really looking then.'

'She must have kept it, the handkerchief, that night Justin returned in such a state. Maybe it was her insurance against him. Until I came along, that is.' Had she ever really loved him? Or was he simply her way out, one way or another?

'So, Jack, whose story do you like the best?'

'It doesn't matter, Lackmann. It's what a jury will believe that counts. You know that better than anyone.'

Cross stood up. 'Any advice for me, Jack?'

Cross smiled, thin-lipped. 'You might want to think about confessing. Avoid the death penalty if you can.' The smile grew wider, just in case the joke hadn't landed. Abruptly, it disappeared. 'I shall keep investigating. Everyone.'

It was the best Cage could hope for. Cross knocked on the door and a key sounded in the lock. He turned at the last moment. 'You are sure you do not wish for a lawyer?'

Cage shook his head. 'No, but I should like to see my mother.'

Cross was right about one thing. It was time to confess.

CHAPTER FORTY-ONE

The days passed. The pacing stopped, until one morning he found himself unwilling to even move from his cot. He seemed to have grown used to the thin mattress and the scratch of the blankets.

Twice a day he was taken into the yard for a half hour of exercise, which was no more than a relentless shuffle with a dozen or so others around the perimeter. The walls of the prison rose up on either side, rusty and damp as if the bricks were weeping. It was a different group each time, and he only saw a few faces repeated on his outings. Most, like him, wore their own clothes, as was the rule for prisoners on remand. You could always spot the new ones: their shirts still deserving of the word *white.* Occasionally he would start at the sight of a man that might be Connor MacGregor, a meeting that was best avoided.

Mostly he kept his eyes on the floor. To view the sky involved craning one's neck backwards. Even then, the view was mean and hardly worth the effort. One morning a pigeon had flown down, thrashing its wings in horror to have landed in such an abyss. Cage watched as it flew about in circles, letting loose a stream of brown fluid as it battled the fear it might never escape. Eventually it rose, the circles of its arc tightening until it swooped across the rooftops once more. The bird soared away and he had to clear his throat at the sight of it.

On the fifth day of his incarceration he was visited by the matron, a young woman almost as tall as him with hips that barely squeezed through the door. He was given his spare suit and a clean if crumpled shirt and underwear from his bag. Clean sheets and blankets were also handed across wordlessly. She stood outside the door as he changed, a surprising act of modesty. When he was done, she picked up his old suit and shook it out, folding it neatly over her arms, like a maid. Strange to see the social order intact in such a place.

The door clanged shut once more. He gazed about, amazed at how familiar it had all become. He knew the strange workings of the water tank and the basin, knew the best time to use them was in the evening before the prisoners were all fed. There was a stool and a table, the wood pitted and split so badly his fingers were full of splinters. His plate, chipped but functional, and a tin mug sat high on a shelf along with an unread bible, just beneath the arched window that looked out on the yard below. Not that he could see anything without standing on the untrustworthy stool, and even then, just another window in another wall.

The dreams were a constant now, growing richer. He even caught a glimpse of Charlie's face before he stepped over the cliff; Baxter's too. One morning Cage awoke to the peal of the chapel bells. It was his second Sunday here, and still his mother had not come. Had their argument torn the relationship entirely? Or maybe Cross had failed to reach her, or perhaps made no attempt at all.

He took his place on the landing, ready to walk single file towards the chapel. The march slowed as the men reached the chapel yard, the most expansive of the outside spaces, with walls one could almost see over and windows that were meant for looking out of.

Inside the chapel, Cage took his place on the lower pews, huddled up between two ripe-smelling fellows. Once they were all seated, they waited for the female prisoners to be led onto the balcony above. Most of the men looked up as the herd of angels stamped through, even though the chapel was designed for neither sex to see each other. There was a bump overhead, followed by a robust curse: naughty angel. The men sniggered, but the guards looked on stern faced from their own benches, close to the communion table and, more importantly, the stove.

The matron entered the room and, to Cage's surprise, took her seat at the harmonium. She pulled and pressed at various knobs, then paused with eyes closed and her hands raised above the keys. The sound that eventually came was thin and discordant, not the fault of her passion, evidenced by her swaying shoulders, but rather because the instrument was old and in need of tuning.

Finally, the governor and the chief warden filed in and took their seats in their special box. They were followed by a rake-thin priest, with naturally tonsured white hair. Behind him, Cage was astonished to see Archie Weston.

It couldn't be a coincidence, surely? Archie sat at one of the pews where the guards had made space for him. He looked straight ahead, but his cheeks burned under Cage's gaze. He was here for him. He had to be. The thought lifted Cage's spirits momentarily, but the more Cage looked, all he could really see were the bars between them.

The other priest climbed into the pulpit, an inelegant exercise as the steps were tall and narrow. They were exhorted to sing a hymn, and shuffled to their feet. Cage picked up the hymn book from the shelf before him and flicked through to find number 307. Someone had defaced the book with charcoal, scoring their name and a date: John Street, 1848. Any memorial was better than the scarred initials of Dead Man's Walk.

The man to his left had a lusty voice, but Cage didn't know the tune so stayed silent. Wasn't he Jewish, anyway? His eyes stayed trained on Archie, willing him to turn and see him.

Then Archie was on his feet. He walked to the reading desk before the pulpit. He held a small bible, his thumb marking a page. Finally, he looked up at the pitiful congregation, his eyes finding Cage immediately.

He smiled, and Cage smiled back.

Archie began his reading. Something dense and incomprehensible: there was a father, and a son, some kind of sacrifice that sounded like a penny dreadful. Cage's feet were numb with cold inside his boots. He thought of Archie's study. A million miles and worlds away.

Archie's sermon ended with the words, '"Come now, let us settle the matter," says the Lord. "Though my sins are like scarlet, they shall be as white as snow, though they are red as crimson, they shall be like wool."' Archie paused and looked around at the faces before him. 'That is how forgiveness works. We cannot half forgive, or forgive only the smallest infractions. We must forgive the worst, turn the scarlet to white with the power of God in our hearts. Anything else would be the greater crime.'

Cage could see the governor was frowning, and Archie ended with an abrupt 'Amen.'

He caught Cage's eye again as he returned to the bench. Cage nodded his head to show support, but what Archie Weston really knew about crime could be written in large letters on the back of a stamp.

There was another hymn, and then the service was over. The dignitaries filed out into the yard, then it was the women's turn to be led into the light again. Cage fidgeted impatiently. Would Archie be gone by the time he made it outside? Would there even be a chance to talk?

The sun was blinding when he finally left the chapel. For the first time that year, it warmed his face: it meant spring was coming. Were the daffodils out yet? It had never mattered to him before.

Archie stood in the line that greeted the prisoners as they shuffled past: a stern nod from the governor and a kind word from the priest handed out on a weekly basis like wages. Archie spotted Cage as he emerged, then broke from his position and whispered to the chief warden. The man nodded and strode over, grabbing Cage's arm and pulling him from the line. Archie had fallen back into the shadows of the outside wall and Cage was led towards him.

As they approached, Archie leapt forward and clapped his hands on Cage's shoulders, but the warden intervened.

'No touching!'

Archie apologised and the warden slunk back, leaving the two of them facing each other, a respectful yard between them.

'Thank you for coming,' said Cage. As though he was having a tea party.

'I had to call on a few favours, and I spent an hour at breakfast with the governor and his dreadful wife, persuading them to let me see you here. But it is only for a few minutes, I'm afraid. I can return, though, another time, in normal visiting hours.'

He was gabbling, so Cage interrupted. A few minutes was not long. 'Justin Kenward killed Nathaniel and Baxter. His wife, my former lover, intends for me to take the blame instead.'

'Oh, Cage.' Archie shook his head. 'I know what they have against you. Although I don't believe a word of it.'

Cage nodded. Should Archie's belief mean something to him? He felt numb.

'Why would she shield him and blame you?'

'Because I abandoned her. Five years ago. It doesn't matter why.' Oh but it did, it mattered so much.

'What evidence do you have against Kenward?'

'Not enough.'

Cage told him of the photograph at Mother Molly's, and Emma's confession. When he got to the mysterious role played by Hazel Smythson, Archie ran his hand across his brow. Cage was glad to know it was not just him who struggled to make sense of anything.

'Who is she?' asked Archie. 'An accomplice to Justin Kenward?'

'She has to be. Emma, if she was telling the truth, only knew about Baxter after the event. And Justin refused to discuss it with her.' He thought of the livid burn on the back of her leg.

'So Kenward planned to kill Baxter and blame Pickering. Your . . . his wife suspected him, but let his plan unfold. When it failed, they decided to target *you*?'

Cage was glad for the incredulity in his voice. He could only hope Jack Cross would feel the same way. 'I think this part is Emma's plan alone. The motivation is hers. She used Hazel Smythson's name when she hired someone to follow me, but she heard the name from me, not Justin. She is no longer in his confidence, and he knows nothing of our affair. I think he would kill us both if he did.' The words sounded strange. Beneath all of this, the truth was still hard to grasp. Justin Kenward, bumbling dilettante, the murderer of men.

'Why would Kenward plan to kill Baxter?'

Cage shrugged. 'Who knows what depravities drove him? Nathaniel may have been an accident, but if he revisited that moment, re-enacted it over and over, at some point the desire to do it again might have been overwhelming.' Exactly the accusation he had flung at Leland Crewler, an innocent man.

Archie had grown pale. 'To think the seeds of such a deed were sown in my own house, on my watch. I should have seen it!'

The man looked wretched and Cage said: 'Do not blame yourself. It is only sad that my escape failed. Colchester. It has a nice ring to it, don't you think?'

Archie stepped forward. 'I am not sorry your escape failed. I know the evidence is strong but you must take the opportunity now to clear your name. Then you can start again!'

Oh, Archie.

When Cage failed to answer, the reverend continued. 'It is all circumstantial. Even Cross admits to that.'

'You have seen him?'

'Several times. He is still investigating the case. Anomalies, he said.'

Cage was intrigued despite himself. It was best not to have hope, to leave it buried. 'Anomalies?'

'I'm not sure what he meant entirely. He talked about first principles, and the dangers of assumption. He said often the key to a case was to challenge the things you believe to be true and see where it takes you. That was it, but it shows he is still considering.'

The warden must have signalled behind Cage's back. Archie

said: 'I have to go. This was meant to be a meeting about your welfare only. Can I bring anything for you? Help in any way?'

A long list began to form in Cage's mind but there was really only one thing that mattered. 'I need to see my mother.' He gave Archie her name and details of the tour.

Archie nodded solemnly. 'I will find her and I will bring her to you.'

'She might prove hard to persuade. We had a falling out, you see.'

'Ah.' Archie smiled confidently. 'I can prove hard to resist.'

The warden interrupted them, his hand firm on Cage's shoulder.

'Goodbye then.'

Archie pumped his fists together. 'Have hope.'

But Cage would rather it stayed away.

CHAPTER FORTY-TWO

A few days later, his laundry was returned and he was allowed to keep the change of clothes in his cell. As expected, the shirt had been washed to a dull grey, quite an impressive achievement in just one attempt. His suit was stiff and smelled of lime, but everything was neatly pressed. He thought of the matron, her fervour at the harmonium, and wondered at her story. He had time for that now, to think and to wonder.

He hoped Agnes was doing well in the West Country. He couldn't blame her, not really. Then he thought of Emma, the monster that was half his creation – he could see that now. But the look on her face at the end of their last meeting had been unmistakable. She would not deviate from this path. The Emma he had loved was gone, already disappearing before he had even met her. Not all victims lay down in their shrouds: some returned, the lessons they had learned more ghastly than even their aggressor could know. Was Justin even aware of her hand in this, or the real reason she had chosen Cage to blame for his crimes?

His trial date was set, three weeks away. The case against him would be fully disclosed in the next few days. That was more than enough time to prepare his defence. He wondered how the papers were dealing with his arrest. Sensationally, no doubt: he was glad he could not see them in here. Maybe he would reach out to Finian Worthing or Dylan Walsh before the trial started, run some kind of line, spin a yarn, do his thing: but it all still felt too far away.

Then, one afternoon, a fist banged on his cell door. What time was it? Too early for supper. He barely knew these days.

'Visitor for Lackmann.'

He stood up and took the position as chains were fastened to his ankles and wrists. He was led down the landing, clanking like the ghost of Christmas Past. All unnecessary, of course. The visitors' box was as well guarded as any other space within these walls. The chains weren't there for him, but for the visitors. *See what can happen?*

The visitors' room was barely occupied. He recognised one fellow prisoner, whose visitor was a thin woman of indeterminate age: two children climbed about her as if she were a tree. Their little hands reached out across the table and she slapped them away. The prisoner himself slumped forwards, eyes down, as if the sight were some kind of torture.

Then Cage saw his mother. Honor was in the black dress she had worn to Charlie's grave. How appropriate. As if she knew.

Her eyes conveyed her sorrow as he approached the table, darting from his face to the chains and back again. He was probably quite the show, he thought. He hadn't shaved in several weeks.

Her hands moved across the table towards him.

'No touching,' he said.

Reluctantly, she pulled her hands away.

He didn't know where to start. *I have something to tell you. Remember when?*

'I had no idea, Cage. The papers, I don't read them, you know that.'

Just the reviews, he thought.

'Your friend found me yesterday. Archie? A good man. He told me everything – the Kenward woman, the evidence against you. I came as soon as I could. Pernilla is going on for me tonight.'

'Quite the sacrifice.'

She stared at him.

'I'm sorry. I mean it. Thank you for coming.'

I'm sorry. Should he start there?

She was crying. 'I can't bear to see you like this. What's to be done, Cage? What can I do? It's clearly ridiculous!'

'Yes.'

She seemed relieved at the word. Had she doubted him? She didn't know him. He hadn't let her know him.

'Then what can I do?'

'It's not why I asked you to come.'

'But you need help! We have to get you away from here!'

He shook his head. 'Maybe it's where I belong.'

'What?' Bewilderment made her seem half her age. 'Why?'

Say it. Say the words. 'Because I killed him.'

'The boy?' Her eyes widened.

'Charlie. I killed Charlie, Mother.'

She blinked. Pain and confusion. But no words came out of her mouth.

It was like diving into a glittering pool, magnificent and shocking.

'The day he left, I was there. A telegram came, calling him north for work. The opportunity he had hoped for had come through. He had to leave that night, before you would be home.'

Cage paused to allow her to catch up, to see where this was going, but still she said nothing.

'He wrote a letter for you, explaining, promising to send a forwarding address, promising to return in six months, promising he loved you, promising he loved *us* . . . I tore it up, tore it into pieces and cried and threw it away.'

Pain and confusion were turning to rage, hardening the lines of her face into stone. He pressed on.

'Many more came though. But I always rose before you. Every day a letter, and every day I tore them up. Didn't even read them, not at first. Then they grew more sporadic, every week, every two weeks. I started to read them when they came. I couldn't stop myself. He didn't know why he had heard nothing back. He still loved us. I realised what I had done, but there seemed no way back from it. All I knew, or thought I knew, was that one day Charlie would return, and my crime would be known, failing to give you that first letter. I would be punished and I was scared. I just wanted to put it off for as long as I could.

'Then the final letter came, just a poem. The last line seemed obvious to me. He was letting you go. He was letting us go. Starting again. I wouldn't be punished after all. But I was wrong, you see.' Cage could taste salt in his mouth: that he was crying appalled him. He had no right. 'It was life he was letting go of. It was a suicide note, I see that now. Moses did too, that's what he saw, *the heart of it*, he said. And so he knew it wasn't mine, but he said nothing.'

'Charlie wrote that poem? Not you?' Her voice was that of a stranger.

Was that the worst of it? Perhaps it was.

'After we heard he was dead, I read it over and over, kept it hidden beneath my bed. I knew the words off by heart in the end. I'd always planned to tell you. When you stopped crying, when your heart mended.'

'But it never did.' Cold as ice.

'No. Then I burned the letter a few years later, when you sold me to Pincott.'

She winced at his words.

'That was my punishment, I thought then. A crime for a crime. But one hole can't fill another. I know that now.'

Rage had turned to horror in his mother's face.

'Years later, I met Emma when I took the Pickering case.' He closed his eyes, allowed the memories in. 'Then I finally knew what love was, this thing I'd killed as a boy. And I knew what I had to do. I had to leave her. Leave love behind. Smash my own heart to pieces in return for breaking his. That was the punishment that befitted the crime. So I let her go.'

Honor covered her mouth with her hand.

'I published the poem. I called it "The Sacrifice", but the words are his, written for you. It seemed the right thing to do. To honour him in some way, to acknowledge what I had done. I couldn't keep his words to myself any more, and they were the only words I knew that could justify what I had done to her.'

'You're a liar. You're a fraud,' she said in barely a whisper.

'Yes.'

'The Poet of Whitechapel,' she spat.

'Not me. Charlie. Baxter, too.'

She was biting the pad of flesh beneath her thumb, her fingers shuddering against her cheek as the tears rolled down. He refused to look away. *I did this.*

She pulled her thumb from her mouth, a string of saliva keeping the connection. 'Why?'

'I was a child. A jealous boy.'

'He loved you!' she screamed. Everyone turned to look.

'But I didn't want his love. I wanted yours.' There it was at last. The heart of it.

She bent forward and moaned like an animal, so low and guttural that not even the guards could hear. Her fingers crept across the table, reaching for his bound hands. He thrust them forward to meet her, but all she would feel were his chains.

'I am so sorry. I know it's too late to say that. I am here because of what I did to him, one way or another. The world will damn me for something, at least.' They were Emma's words, but he owned them now.

After a few more moments, she let go of his hands and sat back, her eyes avoiding his gaze. She took a handkerchief from her sleeve and with brisk movements dried her face and blew her nose. She patted her hair into place, straightened her back and smoothed her dress.

Then, without sparing him a glance, she stood up and walked away.

CHAPTER FORTY-THREE

What would he dream of now, he wondered? What demons would his confession unlock? In the end he dreamed of nothing, his mind a blank space. Charlie was at peace now, perhaps. But what of Baxter? If Cage's own incarceration here was retribution for a crime committed long ago, how could Baxter's killer still walk free? How did that work, in God's grand scheme?

He could have asked Archie, who returned to see Cage the day after his mother visited, but Cage had been in no mood for discussion and refused to see him. The papers for his trial also arrived, a slim folder of depositions. He'd been allowed paper and pen. He opened the folder and flipped through, seeing the names on the witness statements: Bessie Chappelhow, Leland Crewler, and Emma, of course. Hers was the longest by far. He slid the folder underneath the bible on the shelf, as inclined to read the one as the other.

That left just the pen and paper, staring at him from the table, a shaft of sunlight illuminating the tableau. Maybe he should write a poem.

Outside in the yard, the air had grown warmer. He no longer missed his coat as he shambled across the flagstones. He had started counting his steps, reaching a thousand one day, or so he thought. It was hard to keep the numbers in his head. Sometimes his mind drifted. Would he ever see his mother again? It was an idle speculation, for he had gifted the entire thing into her hands. Her judgement was all that mattered now. If she wished him to save himself, then he would try. If she didn't, then so be it.

This was peace, he thought. Surrendering control to someone else so entirely. But what of the boys? Who would fight for them now? *I tried, Baxter, I tried my best.*

Then another visitor came. Jack Cross this time. Cage refused him too, but the guard soon returned.

'It wasn't a request.'

He was led out to the landing, no chains this time. Maybe he had proved himself docile enough. How long had he been here? Two weeks? Three? He really needed to get better at counting.

The same interview room, warmer this time. Cross was already waiting for him.

'Sit down, Lackmann.'

Cage did as he was told. Such a good boy these days.

'That's quite the beard.'

Cage rubbed the fur across his jaw. 'An experiment. While I had the time.'

Cross sat forward and placed a single sheet of paper on the table between them, the words facing Cage.

His eyes scanned the document at first, then darted back to the top to read it again. Finally, he looked up and met the detective's gaze.

'I was expecting more of a reaction.' Cross sounded genuinely disappointed.

Cage looked down at the paper once again. A release form. *His* release form. 'How?'

Cross rubbed a hand across his hair. His own stubble looked more than a few days old. 'Justin Kenward has been arrested on two counts of murder.'

Cage sat back. So the truth had come to light. Miraculous. Had it appeared of its own volition? Or had someone thrashed it from the undergrowth. He cleared his throat. 'Has he confessed?'

Cross nodded. 'He killed Nathaniel Crewler. An assignation gone wrong, consensual at first, then the line was crossed. Before he knew it, the boy was dead, he said.'

'And Baxter?' Cage spoke the name softly.

'Kenward says no, claims he was haunted by the Crewler boy. I believe him.'

'Why?'

Cross was silent for a moment, his eyes looking upwards, his words spoken to himself as much as to Cage. 'I have thought it ever since you found Pickering. Nathaniel Crewler and Baxter Spring, they were not killed by the same person.'

Anomalies, Archie had said, Cross believes there are *anomalies.* Return to first principles, challenge basic assumptions. The same crime, but different perpetrators. Cage could feel his mind restoring, back to the real world in all its indifference, a world that turned and would keep turning, the actions of a jealous, unloved little boy the smallest of its stories.

'Two counts, you said? Kenward has been charged with two murders.'

Cross looked at him finally, a flicker of unease in his eyes. Cage realised what he was about to say just as the detective opened his mouth. 'Emma Kenward is dead.'

Cage stared back. The light in the room had the dust motes dancing between them: a thin veil, but a million particles that lay between that sentence and the fist that thumped in his chest.

'A few nights ago, a local constable was summoned by the maid of the house, and arrived to find Kenward beating his wife in a rage. It took another man, who happened to be passing by, to help the constable restrain him. He was wild, shouting "*I'll kill you, and then I'll kill him.*" Mrs Kenward was taken to hospital, but it was too late. She died of her injuries.'

More silence.

Then Cross said awkwardly, 'I'm sorry.'

A world full of sorry. 'He found out about us.'

I'll kill you and then I'll kill him. Had Justin simply guessed what had been under his nose for so long, or had he stumbled on her plot to frame Cage and questioned her motives? Emma was dead, at rest beside the shadow of the woman he had loved. He wasn't sure what he felt. Nothing. Everything.

'There's something else I have to tell you.'

Cage looked up.

'Your mother was there.'

Cage could feel his face stiffening in anticipation, as if skin alone could protect him from the detective's words.

'She was hurt. By Kenward. Quite badly. But she will recover, I am told. Eventually.'

Cage stood up. 'Where is she?'

Cross rose to his feet, his hands placating. 'She is safe, at Charing Cross—'

'Let me go.'

'There is paperwork first, your things—'

'Now, Jack!' The energy he had left at the door of Newgate Prison came flooding back, dynamic and vicious.

Cross must have seen it in his face. He nodded at the guard

but Cage had already reached for the door. They ran behind him as he made it to the desk where he had first been processed. Two guards came towards him, hands outstretched. This was not how it was done.

Cross shouted behind him: 'Get it done, lads. Quick as you can.'

Maybe it happened quickly, Cage couldn't tell. Each second, each minute, dragged cruelly. He thought of the giant clock in the CID office of Scotland Yard, could hear in his head the reluctant clunk of each moment that passed, like a heartbeat. Was his mother's heart beating with such an unwilling defiance? One more, just one more. *Stay alive.*

There was a form to sign, then his travel bag appeared. One of the guards ticked the items within off a list: Moses's notebook, the Rubens. Then came the money. There was so much of it. Chubby fingers began to count, numbers announced in a lingering monotone. Cage reached forwards and grabbed the piles towards him, tipping the lot into the green bag.

Cage planted himself before the main door that led through to the Old Bailey, four inches from freedom. An arm reached around and a key was thrust into the lock, the bolts withdrawn.

Cage ran forwards into the busy corridors of the court, the shock of seeing his old life again no more than a faint flicker. Familiar faces parted before him, pressed against the walls in open-mouthed stares as he flew past it all, into the main hall now, the great doors to the bail dock beyond.

But still he ran. The street beyond was thriving: carriages, pedestrians, life. He halted at the curb. He stepped into the street and a cab ground to a halt, the horse rearing to avoid him. The driver shouted his curses but Cage ignored them and leapt inside, yelling, 'Charing Cross Hospital!'

CHAPTER FORTY-FOUR

He couldn't see her at first. There were only ten beds in the ward, all of them occupied by shapeless lumps, covers pulled high like shrouds. The smell of carbolic assaulted his nostrils, masking something else: the tang of death.

She was in the last bed on the right, her slim form lying on her back, barely disturbing the sheets that covered her. He didn't recognise her at first. A bandage covered her head and half of her face. The other half was bruised like a peach. One arm lay outside the sheets, encased in a thick grey smock that almost covered her hand. He could just see the tips of her fingers, frail and tiny, like a child's.

The nurse brought a chair. He pulled it up beside the bed and reached for his mother's hand, expecting it to be cold. But her fingers were warm, pulsing with life. He kissed her fingers and massaged her knuckles, the skin rippling across them like the sea.

The one eyelid he could see began to flutter. There was a film across her eyelashes, gluing her eye closed. Eventually, the seal was broken and her eye opened, just a fraction, blinking rapidly.

'Mother. It's me. I'm here.'

Her fingers gripped his, surprisingly strong, although her eye had yet to focus on him.

'What did you do? The Kenwards, why were you there?'

Her voice was a rasp, her chest heaving with each effort. 'To make them confess. To make the world see them for what they are, for what they had done to you.'

'You told Justin about Emma and me.'

She tried to nod, but he could see the pain of the movement on her face. Talking was easier, but not by much. 'Dramatica, the ancient theories. Deus ex machina, an act of God will spin the story to another place, see where it falls. I played God once before.'

He thought he had seen every performance, but he hadn't, had he? He hadn't seen the half of it.

'Emma is dead.'

She blinked once but said nothing.

He kissed her hand again. 'I am so sorry. For Charlie. For all of it.'

'As am I.'

'You have nothing to be sorry for.'

'You are everything.' Her lips puckered as she willed the tears away, but the words fought free of her, escaping one at a time. 'You always were.'

He rested his head against her hand. What lies he had told himself once. Whitechapel had been no place for a gentle mother's love. Her love had been fierce, the love of a lioness.

He looked up at her, but her eye had closed. He thought she was asleep, then her lips moved once more. 'Searching for the truth can make you blind.'

He watched her for a while longer, until her breathing changed and he knew she was asleep. After a few moments, he realised someone was standing behind him. He turned to see Granger holding his hat in his hands, a livid scratch along his cheek.

Cage let go of Honor and stood up. 'You were the passer-by. The man who helped.'

Granger held his arms wide, his face the picture of agony. 'I was too damned late. She made me promise I would stay outside until she signalled. But the signal never came. I heard shouting, but I assumed everything was going to plan.'

'And the maid?'

'She must have left the back way. Next thing I knew, she was hurrying along the street with a constable in tow.'

Cage patted his arm. 'It's all right, Granger. It was her show. You did what you could.'

'I don't think I shall ever forgive myself.'

Cage looked back at his mother, barely recognisable. 'What do they say?'

Granger's hand went to his mouth and Cage placed an arm around his shoulder. 'She's lost an eye, and her leg is broken. He beat her with a poker, Cage. A poker!'

'But she'll live.'

Granger nodded. Sort of. It would be a different life. Honor Dossett would never work again. This had been the last act of her final play, and it had a title: *The Sacrifice.*

CHAPTER FORTY-FIVE

After a conversation with a harassed surgeon, they left the hospital. Cage said goodbye to Granger on the pavement outside, insisting he was happy to be alone.

Memories of the day he had tried to escape came flooding back. He could go now if he wished, return to that platform at Liverpool Street and take the train to nowhere. But he would not leave her now, not yet, at least.

But he was free now, wasn't he? Free of everything except Pincott and Baxter's ghost. Tomorrow he would go to see Jack Cross, see what could be done to track the boy's killer. He would not forget the promise he had made. Pincott, on the other hand, could not wait.

He made his way back home, walking part of the way. It felt strange to be moving in a straight line, as if his feet had been trained now to walk in circles only. The tailor was astonished at the sight of him, and took some convincing to return his front door key, left there weeks before after the police searched his house.

He ignored the mess and fired up the stove in his apartment. He hauled the bath into the middle of the floor and patiently filled it with pan after pan of heated water. Over an hour later, he finally stepped in, the grime lifting from his skin as he scrubbed himself clean, washed his hair and shaved his jaw. Afterwards, he had no choice but to dress in the spare set of clothes that had been laundered at the prison: grey and stiff, but clean nonetheless.

His stomach rumbled – he had not eaten since breakfast, his last meal at Newgate. Was it really only that morning that he had woken in that cell, almost content to be there? He grabbed his coat and searched the tweed bag for his gloves, but they weren't there. Instead his hands found Pickering's journal. He'd take it with him to peruse again over supper, before he gave it to Jack Cross the following morning.

But first, there was something else he had to do.

The bell clanged overhead as he entered the Pestle and Mortar. Merriwether was on a ladder, arranging dusty jars on the shelves.

'Bloody hell!' Merriwether climbed down, all the expected questions tumbling from his lips. Cage gave him the bare bones of it, eager now to see Pincott and know how his story would end.

'The password?'

Cage didn't even know what day it was. He reeled them all off, one code for each day of the week, until Merriwether shushed him to silence and pointed him towards the yard. Cage skirted the counter and walked through the back of the shop. He paused, his fingers on the handle of the secret door. This was it. He thought of what Honor had done for him. Now it was time to do something for himself.

He pushed out into the yard. The light hit him right in the eyes, and he held up his hand to block out the dying sun. Now the snows were gone, the yard had returned to its usual flurry. Two huge carts were being unloaded by a group of youths, barrels of liquid sloshing on the ground.

The driver shouted, 'Careful, you little bastards!'

Cage recognised in their number the young lad he'd procured bail for weeks earlier. On closer inspection, he saw the lad was still wearing the gloves Cage had given him on the courthouse steps.

He approached Pincott's quarters on the far side of the yard. The door stood open, and he could hear voices within but he knocked nonetheless.

'Come!'

Cage stepped into the room.

Clifford Chester stopped talking at the sight of him, and Pincott's gaze turned towards the door.

'Hello, Obediah.'

Pincott stood by the fireplace, his delicate fingers wrapped around a yellowing tusk. A crate of similar artefacts stood open on a table before him. Cage held his placid gaze. Did nothing ever surprise this man? Only his silence betrayed even the slightest sense of amazement that Cage should be there.

A sudden flick of the head scattered his minions into the warren of rooms beyond: only Chester remained, still openmouthed. Pincott continued to examine the fragment of dead animal he held, turning it over in his hands. 'Mammoth ivory. The rarest kind,' he shared, a certain awe tingeing his customary monotone.

'Will you sell it or keep it?' Cage asked.

'Both.'

That had always been the game. Sell it, steal it back, sell it again.

'So, it is always yours.'

Pincott shrugged. 'Tell me, are you an escaped convict or a free man?'

'Something in between.'

Pincott stepped forward. 'Why are you here, Cage Lackmann?'

'I'm done, Obediah.'

His words hung in the air. Chester took a sharp intake of breath, but there was no Dub to beat Cage to the floor this time. Maybe Pincott would do it himself: take the knife from his belt that Cage knew lurked beneath his greatcoat and open his throat with one clean swipe. He was ready for it, if it came: his last words the only obituary required. *I am done.*

Chester recovered himself. 'So, you have spent every day in your cell writing it all down. Dates, cases, people. If you die, the hidden will not be hidden any more.'

He should've thought of that. That's what a plan would have looked like. He could lie, of course. Instead, he shook his head and looked at Pincott.

'No.'

Pincott stared back, unblinking, his glassy forehead lined by the vaguest of creases. There it was, Cage thought. I've surprised him at last. What would the man do? The silence between them grew: Cage could still hear the driver shouting in the yard outside. He thought of the boy still wearing his gloves. It was as good a legacy as any.

'Go.'

Said so quietly, Cage wasn't even sure he had heard him correctly. Chester too was staring at Pincott: could his own bonds be broken so easily? His eyes revealed hope, but without any belief.

Cage looked back at Pincott and wondered if he should say thank you, but the words wouldn't come.

'Goodbye, Obediah.'

He walked back across the yard, avoiding a barrel that leaked something fermented across the ground. He could feel the last of the sun on his back, expecting to feel something else at any moment: hands, a dagger, Dub's rancid breath. But no one came for him, just the sun, reminding him he was there, and he was free. Perhaps he had become the only thing Obediah Pincott admired: a rare beast, fighting its own extinction on the streets of Whitechapel.

An honest man.

CHAPTER FORTY-SIX

He stopped at a chop house on the corner of his street. It was quiet, and the food barely improved on the Newgate fare he had become used to. The wine wasn't bad, but he found his taste for it had mellowed after a few weeks of sobriety.

A shadow fell across the table. Cage looked up to see Detective Jack Cross looming above him.

'A neighbour saw you come in here. May I?'

Cage assented and the man sat down, placing his hat and a brown envelope on the table between them.

'How is your mother?'

'As you said. She'll live.'

Cross's fingers played with the brim of his hat: black, as was his suit.

'You've been to a funeral?'

Cross nodded. Emma Kenward had been buried quickly and quietly, south of the river in Mortlake. Apparently, weeks earlier, as Cage languished in Newgate, the couple had also buried Moses Pickering there: Pickering, who had trusted Emma and Justin always. Maybe they had hoped to bury their guilt with Moses, but it was not to be. Cage promised himself he would go and visit their graves – say goodbye to Moses, say goodbye to the woman he had loved but never known. Not today. But some time.

'Why have you come here, Jack?'

Cross opened the envelope and took something out. He looked at it for a few moments, then slid it across the table towards Cage.

It was the photograph he had given to Cross, the one marked murderer, the face of Baxter Spring in front of him once more. Cage looked at those butterfly lashes, the ruby mouth: the dead boy poet of Whitechapel.

Cross said, 'It's not one of ours.'

Cage looked up. 'What are you saying?'

'Whoever killed our boy stopped to take a photograph.'

Cage stared at the detective, his brain churning.

Cross jabbed a finger onto the image once more. 'Take another look. What do you see?'

Cage cast his eyes down and described what he saw. 'A boy in a blond wig, his face made up, white sheets, a bedside table, a vase—'

'Exactly!' There was a gleam in the detective's eye.

'Exactly what, Jack?'

'The vase is intact. When we arrived at the scene, it was in pieces.'

'Meaning?'

'The boy wasn't dead, Lackmann. This image was taken before.'

Cage looked with fresh eyes at the living face of Baxter Spring. The image was as clear as ever, the pores of his skin, a dusting of stubble like pinpricks.

It wasn't true, then – that the camera always told the truth.

How could it, when the lens could not distinguish between life and death?

Something was beginning to take hold: a thought pushing up through a loam of facts and lies. Pickering's notebook was in the pocket of his coat. He needed to look at the drawings again, but not under the detective's watchful eyes.

He threw some coins on the table. 'I have to go. I need to think about this, but I'm tired. Maybe tomorrow we can talk.'

Jack Cross barely hid his disappointment, but he let Cage walk away. Once outside, Cage turned in the direction of St Thomas, stopping once he had gone a hundred yards.

He opened the notebook, fumbling to find the drawings for Baxter's poem. He saw the cypress and the yew, and the never-ending hills. But all those weeks ago, he'd seen something else, hadn't he? Standing on that platform at Liverpool Street, the moment before those hands had reached for him. He had watched the train pull in, the crowd around him on the platform lining up to the carriage door. And a single man, shadowed against the light, waiting at the window to open that door.

Cage turned the page to find the drawing of the white chapel against a black sky. He stared. There it was.

A smudge of charcoal only, what could simply be a tiny error committed in the rush to capture an idea, but it was there. It all made sense now. His mother was right. Searching for the truth had made him blind, but Moses had seen it.

Cage looked up, his eyes searching out the spire of St Thomas. He kept his eyes on the tower as he walked steadily towards it, resisting the urge to run: judgement weighed him down, each footfall landing like lead upon the pavement.

Minutes later he turned into Archie's street, but the rectory was dark. He walked on towards the church, where a light shone from within, the door held ajar by a pile of prayer books as the cypress trees stood sentinel to either side.

Cage stepped into the church. Archie was at the altar, his back turned, his shadow stretching down the aisle, reaching out with flickering fingers. Cage moved towards him, his worn-out boots soft on the flagstones. At the last moment, Archie turned.

'What the hell!' He grasped his chest with one hand.

'You look like you've seen a ghost.'

Archie caught his breath. 'My God, Cage. They've let you go? How? What's happened?'

Cage kept moving forward, climbing the stone steps to the altar. 'Kenward killed his wife. Then he confessed to everything.'

Archie stepped towards him. 'Good Lord! Emma Kenward is dead?'

Cage nodded.

Archie grabbed his arms, his grip strong. 'I am sorry for it. But I am not sorry to see you free. When did they let you go?'

'This morning.'

Archie hugged him then. Cage allowed himself to reciprocate, his arms reaching around his friend.

They broke free of each other. 'Please! Come for supper. Elizabeth will be returned any moment. We're preparing the church for the Mothering Sunday service. Amy and the children are arranging flowers in the parish room, but we will be done shortly.'

Cage couldn't think of anything nicer. Supper with the Westons. Wine and laughter, clever conversation, the warmth of a household loved truly by God. But God did not exist, not here, not in Whitechapel.

'The camera never lies, you said.'

Archie looked at him quizzically. 'You must be tired.'

'I saw it that very first time, I think. When you showed me her photograph. The photograph of Baxter's mother. I saw it, but I had no name for it. Was it love, perhaps? Or maybe obsession? Did you capture her many times, or just that once?'

Archie's eyes had grown wide.

'All those books. Such a yearning for romance. How did it happen, Archie? Who seduced whom? Or did you just take what you wanted?'

Archie stepped back, his arm flailing wildly as it reached behind him to grab the altar cloth. 'You cannot think that! Of course it was love. I didn't mean for it to happen. I prayed, I—'

'When did it start?'

'What?'

'Answer the question!' Cage shouted, as if the gallery at the Old Bailey could hear.

Archie stuttered, 'A year perhaps, before she died. We tried to ignore our feelings, but they were strong, Cage, so strong. I couldn't fight it any more, I couldn't.'

Emma: her head bent towards his, the desire so intense he couldn't breathe.

Cage advanced towards him. 'When did Baxter find out?'

'What?'

'You heard me!'

'Oh God!' Archie closed his eyes and swallowed. 'When she became ill. It was so quick, so wretched. I came to her, to say goodbye. Baxter heard us.' Archie's eyes opened and immediately read the look on Cage's face. 'Surely, you cannot think—'

'Oh, but I do think, Archie, that is exactly what I think!'

'No!'

Archie leaned back across the altar as Cage towered over him. 'It was in the poem, Archie, all along. *A chapel in white, its doors clamped shut. To lock me out or else to keep him in.* I thought he meant God. But he didn't, did he? He meant you. To keep you away from her, that is what he meant. Moses saw it too. A shadow at the window of the chapel: that is what he drew.'

Archie whispered, 'Baxter was wrong. She loved me.'

'Did she? Servitude can look a lot like love if you're fool enough to believe it.' Cage thought of his time with Agnes, and the illusion that was all his. 'Did Baxter threaten to expose you?'

'No! We never spoke of it. Then I read the poem, and wondered. I tried to broach it with him, but he was not keen to discuss—'

'Poor Moses. The moment he arrived at your door you saw the opportunity, didn't you? Stop the truth from ever coming out, stop the boy from writing any more poems, shut him up for ever, protect your precious reputation and make sure Pickering shouldered the blame. Cross saw it all along. Nathaniel Crewler's death was an accident, but Baxter's wasn't. A copycat killing. How clever.'

Archie pleaded. 'I didn't do it. I didn't kill him, Cage!'

Cage's hands snapped around his throat. 'Is this what it felt like? Silencing his voice for ever?' Archie's hands grabbed at his wrists, to no avail. 'But it will never go away, will it? You'll hear his words in your head until the day you die, accusing you! The death of hope. The death of joy. All at the door of men like you!' *And men like me.*

'Stop!' A woman's voice echoed off the stone walls.

Cage froze. There was something cold and sharp at the base of his skull.

He released Archie, whose hands flew to his throat, rubbing at his skin as he coughed several times.

'Amy!' Archie rasped. His voice was raw, but there was no real damage done. Cage would have let go eventually, wouldn't he?

So the woman at his back was Archie's sister-in-law, a ship he had passed in the night but never met. Cage turned slowly, encountering first the large pair of shears she wielded in his direction. And then he encountered something else: that face.

It was her.

'Hazel Smythson,' he said.

'My name is Amy Ormond.'

Ormond. The name was familiar. But from where?

'Amy!' Archie Weston had recovered himself and was moving towards her.

Cage turned to Archie. 'She is your wife's sister?'

'Yes,' he spluttered, his hands still pulling at his neck.

Hazel Smythson had been under his nose the whole time, staying with the Westons, stepping slowly along the street with her sister rather than get too close. He should have seen it: should have shown more interest in the mysterious sister-in-law.

Cage stared at Archie. 'She is your accomplice, then?'

Archie continued to look dumbfounded. 'I have no idea what you are talking about, Cage. Please!'

And he didn't, did he? Hazel Smythson, or rather Amy Ormond, was not the accomplice at all. She was the perpetrator.

He turned to face her. 'Does Elizabeth know what you did?'

She shook her head.

'Know what, Cage?' Archie's hand reached out, but her grip on the scissors was unwavering.

'She killed Baxter.'

'What?'

'This woman is Hazel Smythson.'

She said nothing, but Archie stared at her. 'Amy?'

Her eyes were fixed on Cage as she spoke. 'Go away, Archie. I will finish this.'

Cage began to back away towards the altar, but she followed him, the weapon mere inches from his throat.

'She did it for you, Archie, to protect you and Elizabeth.'

'Not him! Just her, just my sister. And for my husband, too.'

'Your husband?' Keep her talking – it was his only strategy until his hands could find something to defend himself.

'Oh, you wouldn't remember him. He meant nothing to you. Francis Ormond, the manager of a ship's merchants in Wapping, murdered by the thug you chose to defend.'

Connor MacGregor. That was why her face had always been familiar: the grieving widow who sat in the gallery day after day as Cage had spun the lies that would see his client exonerated of murder. That is why she had shown herself at Connor's hearing a few weeks ago. He looked at her face again: another woman brutalised by what the world had ripped away from her, himself included.

Cage turned to Archie. '*You've been pointed out to me on the street.* That's what you said.'

'I . . .' Archie's eyes flickered between them. 'I wanted to spare your feelings. When you came to me, you were broken. How could I tell you of this connection? Of Amy's animosity towards you? It wasn't relevant to Baxter's death, or so I thought . . .'

But if only he had said something, Cage might have put the pieces together and realised where he had seen Hazel

Smythson before. Then Pickering might still be alive, and so would Emma.

'Why, Amy? Tell me why?' Archie pleaded.

She shrugged his words away. 'I knew what you'd done. I saw you with that whore years ago, saw the way you looked at her, touching her hand when you thought no one would see. When I read that poem I knew the boy had seen something too: he knew, didn't he? Maybe when he was a child he was willing to keep your dirty secret. But that poem, those oh-so-subtle hints, he was learning to say the unsayable out loud, finding his voice at last. It was only a matter of time. I know you're weak, Archie, but a weak husband is better than none. There was only one way that story would end. One whiff of scandal and you wouldn't have been able to live with yourself. I would not have my sister widowed as I had been.'

Archie was her interrogator now. 'You killed a child, Amy.'

Her eyes were defiant. 'When Pickering came that day, it was like a gift from God, telling me what I should do. Telling me how to protect her. It was easier than it should have been. You'd been teaching us all to use that camera of yours. I told the boy I was making a collage to surprise you for your birthday and I needed him to dress up. He looked like her, didn't he? I took the picture, then I took another. We were laughing so much, it was hard for him to stay still.' She broke into a smile at the memory. 'Then I did it. He was still grinning at me, and I thought I might not be strong enough, but I was. His neck snapped like a bird's. The light went out so quickly.'

'My God!' Archie's voice was choked with horror.

The smile fell from her face. 'It took my husband days to die. Almost a week. The blood wouldn't stop, inside, leaking into his belly until his veins were all but empty.'

Cage had reached the altar now. He had nowhere further to go. The point of the scissors pressed into his neck.

'I am sorry, for your husband, and that justice was not done.'

'Justice?' She held her weapon with both hands now, arms straight as arrows. 'This is justice.'

'Amy, please!' cried Archie.

Cage was leaning backwards over the altar. Was this how it would end for him? He held her stare, not daring to break the connection. 'Why the photograph? Why did you come to me the next day and leave it there?'

She pursed her lips. 'It wasn't the plan to develop the pictures. But when I met you at the courtroom that day, you didn't know me. That was good. Only it wasn't.' The pain revealed itself – her features alive with her suffering. 'I realised I wanted you to know who I was, to see me, *really* see me, but you didn't. You never saw me. All those days, in that courtroom, and you never saw me! I needed to make you suffer: what better than the promise of a rich, foolish client with money to burn, ripped away by the sins of your past. Sticking the knife in.'

The sharp point dug deeper and Cage felt his skin puncture. 'The photograph, Amy? Why the photograph? Why that word?'

A single tear rolled down her face. 'So you would know who you are! And that actions have consequences. Why is it only the innocent who die?' Her voice broke on her words.

'Like Francis?' he asked.

She nodded, not trusting herself to speak as the tears fell freely.

'Like Baxter,' he whispered.

He felt the tiniest release in the pressure on his throat.

'Auntie Amy?' A child's voice shouted from the door to their left.

The woman glanced away just briefly, but it was enough. Archie Weston lunged forward, his arms tight around her waist as they flew backwards down the stone steps and into the aisle. Cage heard the crack, the sound of bone yielding to rock.

The child was screaming. Cage ran forward to where the two bodies lay entwined: Archie Weston on top, the face of Amy Ormond staring past his shoulder, a crown of blood seeping around her head.

Cage bent down and pulled Archie up like a rag doll. 'Your child!' he whispered in the man's ear. 'Go to her.'

He pushed Archie away.

Cage knelt down at the woman's side. Her eyes still glistened, as if there was life in her yet. He picked up one hand and felt for a pulse in her wrist, but there was nothing. Amy Ormond was dead, and Hazel Smythson was gone, the woman whose existence had tormented him: a murderer, partly his own creation. He would own the truth of it too – Baxter's blood on the hands of the many, not the few.

He heard feet running towards him. Elizabeth Weston dashed to her sister's side. 'Dear God, no!' Her hands flapped about her dead sister's body, wanting to touch her, to hold her.

'It was an accident. She fell.'

Was that the kind thing to do? And what of the right thing? He was no judge of such matters. He had birthed the lie at least, but this time it would be someone else's choice to let it thrive. Baxter's great secret was no longer his to uncover, or to bury.

CHAPTER FORTY-SEVEN

After the confrontation in the church, the truth came out immediately.

Archie told his wife of his affair with Alexandra Spring, and of what Amy had done to prevent Baxter sharing his knowledge, beyond the opaque words of his poem. Elizabeth Weston heard it all, hands folded in her lap as her husband laid himself bare before her. She said nothing until her polite request to Cage to fetch the authorities. Only when her sister's dead body was shuffled onto the coroner's cart did he see a break in her graceful demeanour. The look that flashed across her face as she stared at her husband's back was gone again in seconds. A brief flick of Moses's pen or the click of Archie's camera could not have captured the absolute revulsion he saw.

Most women break. Men break them. But a few survive to deliver their vengeance.

Later that night, Jack Cross came to the rectory. Cage sat beside Archie as they told their story together. When Cage showed Moses's journal to Cross, he stared hard at the drawings.

'I cannot see it.'

Cage looked again. The cloud of ink was there: a shadow at the window of that white chapel on the hill. Or was it simply a smudge on a sketch made in haste? Maybe he had seen what Moses could not.

He left the rectory with Cross, walking back down the steps and through the wakeful streets of Whitechapel, both apparently going in the same direction.

'What will you do?' Cage asked.

'Nothing. Amy Ormond is dead. Justin Kenward is in prison. There is no guilty party left to charge.'

'I'm not sure that is true. Archie Weston. Me. We're guilty of much in this.'

Cross smirked unkindly. 'You're a bloody poet, all right. My advice is don't ever get them confused.'

'What?'

The detective stopped and turned to him. 'Felonies and transgressions. Different things, Lackmann. Different punishments.'

Then he turned and walked away.

Cage invited Cross to Baxter's funeral ten days later, but he didn't come. It was just himself and the Westons: Archie leading the service of internment as the rain poured down on Elizabeth's stony face.

They buried him in Honor's plot at Highgate, next to Charlie. She had offered it up herself, although she was too unwell to attend the pitiful ceremony. When the time came, she would lie alone, she said. Freddie Southgate had not once come to the hospital. Cage only knew this from Granger, for his mother had said nothing.

Now it was May, and as Cage and Honor turned on to the familiar path, the sun broke free and warmed his skin. The cemetery was a symphony of colour and sound: the leaves had returned to the great sycamore trees and the wrens and blackbirds scurried between them, picking lichen and moss from the tombstones to make their nests.

The path was uneven, making the chair difficult to steer. He waited for Honor to suggest that she walk the final length with the aid of her stick, which she was very well capable of doing. But she seemed to enjoy being hurled from one side to the other as they rode over the stones. She wore red today, cutting a dash in her invalid's chair. The only black she wore was her eye patch, made from the best silk, her hair arranged to show it off to the world as it wrapped about her graceful head.

They reached their destination, and Honor rose from her chair. Charlie's headstone had weathered the winter well, speaking its words to the world in a clear voice. Next to it lay the fresher grave: the reason they were here.

Honor placed her hand atop Baxter's headstone. 'Read the poem.'

Cage unfurled the paper from his pocket. He thought he knew it off by heart by now but wanted to be sure. He read Baxter's words aloud as a rare clouded yellow butterfly swooped and dived in the hedgerow beyond.

When he finished the poem, Honor's fingers gripped the headstone in silent communication with a boy she had never met. Neither had Cage, yet here he was. We all make our transgressions, he thought, and maybe the victims of others can forgive us more easily.

Honor turned away and stepped towards him, the limp barely there any more. He settled her back into the chair and made a meal of turning it around to face the right way, in a hurry to return. He had received a postcard that morning from Weston-Super-Mare, although there had been no message.

A few days by the sea would be nice, he thought: watch the ships, talk about haberdashery.

As they returned to the main path, he looked back once more at Baxter's grave. He had agonised over the inscription, from Keats to Browning, even Baxter's own poem. In the end, he decided the words should be Charlie's. It was the only thing that made any sense to him.

That was how it started, and that was how it should end.

Baxter Spring
The Poet of Whitechapel
1867–1882
I let you go

ACKNOWLEDGEMENTS

This book would not have been written without the stalwart support and encouragement of my agent, Jonny Geller. His enthusiasm kept me going from the beginning, and his belief in me has been a beacon of light on the darkest days. Ed Wood, my editor at Sphere, is an amazing storyteller, and to collaborate with him continues to be a delightful education, carving out the story together and finding the emotional truth of it. Making Ed cry will always be one of my proudest achievements.

On the research front, I have many people to thank. Alison Gilby, whose work at the National Archives originally inspired the idea for this story. Cat Renton, for her deep dive into the English court system at the end of the nineteenth century. Amy Chappelhow for her timely introduction to Jarlath Killeen, Lecturer in Victorian Literature at Trinity College, Dublin, who in turn helped me navigate the painful waters of late Victorian poetry. My attempts are my own, and I apologise to both if I let them down. Thanks to Nick Thorogood also, who was on hand to help me tread the fine line between a historically legitimate portrayal of homosexuality in 1880s Britain and our more enlightened sensibilities.

The editorial support team at Sphere had the hard task of correcting my manuscript. Thanks to Thalia Proctor and Charlotte Chapman for their attention to detail and historical accuracy. I can only apologise that the correct use of the semi-colon continues to elude me. I'm hoping in vain that you and Ed find it charming.

Finally, I want to thank the long list of friends and family who continue to support my mad life of attempting to do two jobs at once. To my Two Brothers family, and Harry and Jack in particular, thank you for making it even possible to try. My bezzies – particularly Sarah and Sonia – for coping with all the trauma I stir up. And of course to the men in my life – my partner, Karlos, my dad, Howard, and my brother, David. You are the rocks around which I splash and splutter. I love you all.